AMY WINTERS-VOSS

Rise

The Liminal Chronicles

Shy Red Fox Publishing

First published by Shy Red Fox Publishing 2021

This novel is a work of fiction. Any references to historical events, real people, or real places are used fictitiously. Other names, characters, places, and events are products of the author's imagination, and any resemblance to actual events, places, or persons, living or dead, is entirely coincidental.

ISBN (Paperback): 978-1-7366720-1-3

ISBN (Hardcover): 978-1-7366720-4-4

Library of Congress Control Number: 2021907905
Shy Red Fox Publishing - Sioux Falls, SD

First edition

Editing by Sarah Buhrman
Cover art by Odette.A.Bach

This book was professionally typeset on Reedsy.
Find out more at reedsy.com

Contents

Author Notes

I've used aspects and events in Japanese culture and history as the basis to write this tale, but the universe in the book series is a Japan-based fantasy world. Please note that any people, places, and beliefs in the Liminal Chronicles are used fictitiously and I have done my best to treat them with respect.

I wrote out of an excuse to dig deeper after my trip to Japan in the fall of 2017 and to deal with the growing desire to return. Though I am not Japanese, I love Japan and only wish to do my best to portray the 'Japan' in Rise as truthfully and close to the real one as I am able. While Japan is not a perfect country (there isn't such a thing!), it has an incredible and unique culture. I feel even in researching and asking my Japanese friends—that I can only touch the surface of each topic's depths.

My hope is that this humble tribute to a land, society, and mythology I adore, brings enjoyment and expanded interest in the country to all who read it. Many aspects this book shares are lessons I've learned after meeting amazing, patient, and kind people from Japan.

This writing journey began on December 1, 2018. I was on the plane trying to fend off the JLPT N5 test jitters, listening to ONE OK ROCK's song 'Stand Out Fit In'. I remember all too well what it was like to be on the outside when I was younger. To be different. So, the story bubbled up from inside. I hope this tale will inspire my readers to take a stand and support others. Everyone, from every faith, can do this.

Be the difference.

Culture Notes

Just a few quick notes for you.

Names

In Japan (and many Asian countries) the family name is presented first. This ties in with the idea that the group is more important than the individual. People are referred to by their family names until a certain level of familiarity is reached. Then they'll use personal names.

Respect is king. A suffix is almost always used to show respect and levels of familiarity. Lack of a suffix is either rude or the speakers are on such a familiar basis that both sides agree the lack of a suffix is acceptable.

The vowel sounds are similar to Spanish, where 'a' is 'ah'-as in father, 'e' is 'eh' as in elk, 'i' is 'ee' as in 'eel', 'o' is 'oh' as in boat, and 'u' is 'oo' as in 'moon'. So the name Date is 'Dah teh'. It doesn't sound like 'date' the fruit.

Locations

Only the large cities such as Kyoto and Tokyo are real locations in this book. All others are fictional, modeled after the area.

Words

I have done my best to describe and give hints for words that aren't native to English. Sometimes a loan word from Japanese that made its way into English doesn't mean quite the same thing to a Japanese person as it does to a Westerner.

You'll find this with words like 'futon' which is a stuffed mattress that is put on the floor to sleep on in Japan, but in America is a folding frame and mattress that can be used as a couch or bed. Same for the idea of the bath—American baths and Japanese ones differ greatly. In Japan, one washes and rinses off outside the tub, before getting in to soak. I just wanted to give you a heads up.

The Cast of Characters and Glossary are in the back of the book to help you with names and unfamiliar words.

Acknowledgments

To my family: Mike, Audrey, and Ethan - for your patience, love, support, encouragement, and putting up with my babbling about characters that existed only in my brain for the longest time.

To Kyoko-san, Makoto-san, Rihoko-san, and Chiaki-san - for sharing your culture, your insights, tips, and tours to visit Japan, extreme patience for my questions, and your friendship.

To Johanna, Mark, Corwin, and Rune - for your happy, excited queries about this book's progress. You drew me out of my shyness to speak about my writing.

To my critique partner: Liz - for pushing me to improve my work with your detailed thoughts and challenges. You have been such an encouragement!

To my betas: Angela, Eric, Lengna, Victoria, Laura, Niklas, and Jimmy - for your bravery in reading a raw book and giving me honest, open feedback. You can't know how valuable that is!

To Rhonda - for the critique of my first three chapters. You gave me the kick I greatly needed to cut fluff.

To my editor: Sarah - for your patience and being willing to deal with a new author.

To my sensitivity readers: Kyoko-san and Cat - for helping me keep the details about Japan spot on and avoid mistakes that could offend.

To my cover designer: Odette - for working with me and making the cover even better than I had imagined.

To my readers - for taking a chance on an unknown writer. Without all of you, this novel would not exist.

Thank you very much. どうもありがとうございます

1

CHAPTER 1: HIDING IN PLAIN SIGHT

Mid-November

Kneeling to stock the low shelves at TaniMart makes my knees ache. Though I'm not gonna risk complaining. I'm lucky to have this job, even if it's mind-numbing. Someday, I'll have my own business. Right now? I have to save up since the feds took every yen of my savings when they threw me in the slammer.

Pain shoots through my forearm as something bounces off. Crash! Years of ready-to-fight reflex have me jumping to a defensive stance. *What the...*

Shattered glass and pickled plums litter the polished floor. Reflections of the overhead lights glare at me in the puddles of brine. Then the green, spicy scent of shiso hits my nose. *Breathe, Umeji. It wasn't an attack.*

"Sorry, Mister!" A boy and his mom stare wide-eyed at my hands after giving a bow.

"Please, finish your shopping. I'll take care of this." When I reach to pick up the glass pieces, my heart sinks as the distinctive blue-black wave and red maple leaf designs of my irezumi tattoo sleeve show through the transparent wet fabric of my shirt. Despite the deafening silence, the hint of the ink that marks my past wails like a siren, warning all in my vicinity. *Why the hell does our uniform have to include a white shirt?*

1

The woman hunches, tensed as if ready to run. Backing away, she wrenches her son along in a white-knuckled grip.

My hand crushes the shards in my palm as my head hangs.

When I report the injury to Satou, my volunteer parole officer and boss, he shakes his head and grabs his jacket. "Let's get you to the doctor. Tell me what happened on the way."

I stare out the window. The buildings blur by as the scene replays in my head.

"Out with it," Satou's low voice prods. He made me promise not to lie to him when he took me on as a parolee.

So I regurgitate the wretched event. "I knew my past wouldn't stay buried forever. But I didn't expect it to be revealed this soon, so I squeezed the glass in my palm. It was that or punch somethin'."

His hands tighten on the steering wheel as we pull up to the clinic. "Why didn't you wear something with long sleeves under the uniform?"

The price for my mistake? Five stitches in my palm.

It was bad enough I didn't quite have the cash needed to buy the black long-sleeve shirt he told me to pick up, and he had to help me buy it. Satou shouldn't have to waste any more time or money on me. So I opt for the hour walk home to the room I'm renting from him. He said I could stay until one opens up in town.

So much for blending in. My attempts to ditch the Tokyo accent are probably worthless now. Satou said there are fewer than 1,300 people in Nonogawa, so everyone in town will know by tomorrow. Letting the old swagger back into my step lacks the feeling of control it used to give as I walk past neighborhoods of traditional and modern housing.

My insides continue to twist as I wait for my boss to return home. Tomorrow's gonna suck. Might as well get in a good soak to relax, instead of pacing. So, I start the fire to heat the water for the bath. I'd place good money down that Satou picked this old house based on the big wooden tub. When I can afford my own place, a good bath will be a priority for me, too.

It's been years since I had daily access to the most relaxing activity of everyday life. First, because of my jail sentence. Second, most public bathhouses ban gangsters. They say our ink threatens. The previous generations won't forget the yakuza heydays, when only mobsters sported ink.

Naked and settling onto the low wooden stool beside the tub, I scrub and fill the bucket at my feet to rinse off. I could use a shave. *Should I ditch the mustache to fit in better?* It covers the knife fight scar. *So either way, I don't fit the norm. Shit.*

With a slam, I flip the small hanging mirror over. Don't want to see the reflection that stared back. Before everyone knew I had been a mobster, could they tell I was just trying not to stick out?

Splashing water on my face rinses away the questions. Despite the chill of the tile floor on my feet, I revel in not having to hurry as I scrub and rinse. Damn, it's good to not have the prison guards timing me anymore. My chin-length hair needs some attention, but I don't have the cash for a trim and don't want to bother Satou any more than I already have. I was lucky the prison didn't make me get a buzz cut. Most do.

Finally, I slide into the tub. A hiss escapes my mouth as the fire-heated water contacts my chilled skin. The tattooed kitsune in their traditional designs on my shoulders seem to enjoy the warmth, too. Soon the heat seeps into stiff muscles, and I lean on the edge, soaking it in.

Satou said the community is hard to break into. So, I've got to avoid sticking out any more than I already do. In a small town, once you're known for something, it's never forgotten. With a determination to focus on one day at a time, I sink deeper into the water.

* * *

On my next shift, whispers and side glances greet me. The yakuza taint broadcasts its presence stronger than the stench of diarrhea. Everyone gives me a wide berth. Not even a week in town and I'm an outcast again. The only way out is hard work and humility. *I will endure.*

The mom returns just before my shift ends. She avoids the aisle I'm stocking, but her little boy points, announcing, "Mama! There's the guy with the tattoos!"

Her shushing causes him to insist all the louder. *Focus on the task at hand, Umeji.* I force myself to look away as she lugs him out of the building.

That's the moment Satou's elderly aunt gives me the stink eye. Shuffling up, she waggles a crooked, accusing finger right in front of my nose, causing me to back into the shelves and knock several plastic tubes of mayo on the floor.

"Get your head out of the sand, boy. You saw that mother's reaction. I advised my nephew not to take in a stray like you. To make things worse, yesterday I heard you're covered in irezumi tattoos. Nonogawa may be in the sticks, but we all know what that means here."

I blink. *Why are little old ladies so rude?*

"Well? Are you?" she presses.

While I deserve the disdain, I don't want my boss to take heat for me. "Ma'am, the community respects Satou-san. I'll do my best for his sake."

She draws out the syllables. "You dodged." As she crosses her arms, her sharp eyes shift to a predatory glint. "If you won't answer, roll up your sleeve. I know yakuza ink when I see it."

My head swivels. *Satou, where are you? Make your vicious aunt heel.* She's really causing my hackles to raise, but I don't want to do anything stupid. "Ma'am?"

In the Hiragi clan, I was good at remembering names, because the alternative could be costly. *What did Satou say her name was? Oh yeah— Nakamura Hisako, the town's beloved matriarch.* When I was yakuza, I would have never let a little old lady corner me. But I'm caught flat-footed because I can't use any of the in-your-face phrases that bubble up to get her to lay off. *I haven't done a damned thing to her. What gives?*

So, I take a deep breath. *No attitude.* "Nakamura-sama, it's becoming more common in the cities. People keep 'em out of sight to avoid the stigma."

As if I'll tell this biddy the full truth. Later, I can scream rebellion in gokudou drawl all I want. But her outburst is the proverbial piano hanging overhead, threatening to crash down on the little hope I have in this town.

At twenty-four, I should have a high school diploma and a college degree or employment experience. This is my only chance. *Suck it up, Umeji.* So, I bow deep. "I apologize that my tattoos offend. If I could turn back time, I'd not have done it. How may I help you?"

Harrumphing, she turns on her heel with the grace of a ballerina, leaving me with some serious heartburn. Hiro, my big brother in the Hiragi clan, had taught me to ferret out everything that seemed out of place. *How does an old lady move that fast?*

When I finish stocking, I grab my baseball-style jacket with its embroidered fox on black and gold silk and beeline it to Satou. Just my luck, his aunt beats me there.

I wait behind her and examine my shoes. Faint reflections of fluorescent lights show on the tile floor.

"That tattooed punk is bad for business." She points, doubtless aware of how rude she's being. "He dares to flaunt his past wearing that rebel jacket, instead of considering this store's reputation. I've heard all manner of rumors. Mark my words, Kazuo, people will stop shopping here." Full-to-the-brim grocery bags strain her arthritic knuckles.

While Nakamura's concern is understandable, does she care that this 'rebel jacket' is the only one I own? I was fortunate someone dropped it by the penitentiary after emptying my apartment. My fists clench, pulling on the stitches from yesterday's wound. *Why does this town love her, anyway?*

Satou clears his throat and tilts his nose toward me. "Aunt, tattoos or not, he's being much more polite than you. I've never seen you in such a state."

Give it your all. My voice almost cuts out as I ask, "Nakamura-sama, may I carry your groceries?"

She grumbles, lumbering off. My cheeks burn, but Hiro's hard-learned lessons on observation kick in. *Where's the grace she had?*

"Aunt Hisako is opinionated and protective of our community. But she's almost always reasonable. Wish I knew what got her undies in a bundle." With a raised eyebrow, Satou says, "You rendered her speechless. That's quite the feat."

Shoving my arms into the sleeves ruthlessly, I shrug on my coat.

"It'll be ok, Umeji-san. FYI, I need to stay late, but you can wait in the break room."

Most days I remain beyond my assigned hours to assist with the day's tasks. Every dutiful employee does. But I mumble, "I'll walk."

"Suit yourself."

In the parking lot, a shitzu puppy breaks loose from its owner's grasp. The mutt charges for Nakamura as it barks its head off. Nakamura, calm as a windless day, lifts her index finger toward the potential attacker, halting it in its tracks.

The owner scoops up the stiff, silent pet and bobs. "I'm so sorry, Nakamura-san! I can't imagine what little Taro-chan was thinking."

"Thank you for catching him. I think he intended to bite my leg off. Didn't you, pup?" Satou's aunt flashes a wry smile that must have created most of the lines in her wrinkled face. The other woman's eyes widen in horror. She bows again, scurrying off.

Unperturbed, Nakamura sets her groceries in her red Nissan sedan. But a can drops and rolls, causing her to mutter under her breath.

Here we go again! Scooping it up before it's flattened under a moving van and jogging over, I hold it out in my hands—a peace offering. Her lips purse and she snatches the item as if my touch might poison the food inside.

Fine. If this is a war of attrition, I'll fight it to show regret for what I've done.

Mid-afternoon, I'm almost to the house. Strolling through the forested farmland, sunshine and the warm, late fall day breathes life into me again. The dense, fiery landscape of reds, oranges, and yellows set off by the evergreens of bamboo, cedar and cypress has me grabbing for my cellphone. I'd seen parks like this, but not horizon to horizon beauty. Then my shoulders sag. The damn feds took my cell, too.

Compared to the compacted cityscape I'd grown up with, the open farmland leaves me exposed. Tall buildings always surrounded and protected me before I came here. A weight fills my chest. Despite being in the middle of nowhere for a week, I keep half expecting to see some tall structure around the next bend. Out of habit, I shove my hands in my jacket pockets to fiddle with the dog-eared collection of Japanese myths. My breathing slows upon contact with the book from my father. The one connection I have left with him.

A glint of vermilion in the trees stands out even in the bright foliage beyond the rice field, so I squint against the sun to get a better look. Beckoning me, a path leads through the paddies and over the river to a torii gate.

Sori Okunugi, the Hiragi clan leader, insisted every member pray at public shrines, though I only ran through the motions to appease him. My clan brothers didn't give it a second thought. But I always felt unworthy when we'd go. My parents used to tend a shrine across the street from our apartment. They would comment as they watched out the window, waiting for the couple of yakuza, who often visited, to leave. Those words haunted me every time I visited. So I shoved the feelings into a mental shoebox, one that got pretty damned full.

My stride turns to a jog as I'm greeted by the fox statues with red bibs at the top of the stairs. Pausing for a brief bow at the gate, I bound up, skipping every other step. I shouldn't run because I'm entering a sacred area. But a tug on my heart invites me to peek at what I've avoided so long.

Memories flood in as I climb. When I was a child, my dad would read to me. My favorite stories were of the kitsune. Whether they were the messengers of Inari or the shape-shifting trickster spirits, they fascinated me. Mom also fed my obsession with the mythical animals by buying me a fox mask and taking me to the Ouji Inari shrine to be in the Kitsune Parade when I was ten. After that, I drew foxes on everything and devoured every myth I could find.

When my clan brothers went to get inked, dragging me along, I hoped the artist would agree to my plan. Traditional tattoo artists are picky and may refuse an idea. On top of that, they charge a fortune.

I'd printed a picture of a Meiji era photograph with a man showing off his tats—a nine-tailed fox on each shoulder with them chasing each other, one red with a flame above it and the other white with a scroll in its mouth.

My brethren teased me because kitsune aren't the typical symbols gangsters pick. They quit when the tattooer was so intrigued he did the initial outlines of the ancient design for free.

At the summit, I follow the dirt path through the foliage to find a squat shrine building that probably never had a lick of paint. Moss covers sections of the tiled roof and footings. Yet, the steps and floor are spotless. A bell and a few crisp white paper ornaments, hanging from the rope that demarcates the spiritual space, decorate the simple place of worship.

That jam-packed shoebox of shame threatens to burst open. My fingers shake. *The things I've done.* The offering coffer makes me look away. I won't get paid for a while. Nothing to offer. I've got to be the only one in the entire country that doesn't even have a one-yen coin to throw. *Pathetic. Coming here was a mistake.*

As my fists slide into my coat pockets, there's a crinkle—the salmon riceball that was supposed to be my lunch. My stomach growls. I've gone without meals before. *This time it's my choice.*

With reverence, I place it beside the other offerings. Then, after a deep bow, two claps, and ringing the bell, I pray. My throat constricts as I dare to voice my request to the kami. "Help me stay on this new path and assist others as Satou-san has me."

Heading back down the trail, my tally of all the things that could go wrong tomorrow is interrupted by prickles forming on the back of my neck. Then a rustle comes from behind. I whip around. A quick scan of the area doesn't reveal anyone, but years of keyed-up-instinct say someone was there.

After passing under the torii, a rustle makes me check my surroundings again. The tail of a gray fox disappears into the dense foliage. I'd not seen a wild one before. *That was so cool! Did it enjoy my meal?* My love for the creatures drives me to follow it, but I stop after my first step past the gate. *Idiot.* The animal is long gone and knows this area. *Maybe I'll see it again.*

2

CHAPTER 2: ARASHI (STORM)

December

A few days after Nakamura's outburst in the store, a conversation carries out of the break room. "Mie-san, do you think he joined the mob because he had no other choice?" Ohno's soft, bright voice contrasts harshly with their topic.

"Why are you obsessing? You're smarter than getting involved with the likes of him."

"I'm not obsessing. It just seems wrong that everyone avoids him if he's starting over. And there's a string—"

"You keep asking about him. So, I did my homework. Umeji's yakuza, no doubt about it. Rumor says he had a lot of charges against him, and that he was a pimp and a drug ringleader."

"You're serious?"

"I don't care how handsome or how lonely you imagine he is. I'm telling you this as a friend. Stay away from him. His type will only take advantage of your kindness."

I take a stabilizing breath. *Zip in and grab dinner. Get out.*

"I still want to know if he had no other choice."

The concern in Ohno's voice gives me pause. *Maybe one of them won't cut*

9

me down?

"Nah, he probably thought it was cool."

"Maybe it was for the money?"

"Or the girls." Venom drips from Mie's voice.

"I just thought there was more to him. Though, I was missing two-thousand yen from my drawer yesterday."

That makes my teeth grind. *She's out to get me fired?* Everyone says Ohno is cute and sweet, but she's just shown her true colors.

When I barge in with tough-guy mode in full force, Mie dares to glare at me and slips her brand-new phone into her pocket. "Let's go." She tugs on her friend's arm.

Before I can rein in my tongue, the words spew out. "I wasn't near you or your damned till."

Ohno gasps and her freckled cheeks flush.

I swagger over to Mie, the more confident of the two. "You two enjoy talkin' 'bout me? Right now, we set the record straight. It was the mob or go hungry!" To stress the point, I slap the wall by her head. She flinches. "A rich chit like you always showing off what she has wouldn't know how it feels to miss a single meal!"

Striding past them, I snatch my dinner and out of spite plant myself at the far table. I won't back down for the likes of them.

The girls leave me to eat in solitude, scurrying away faster than frightened mice.

Then my puffed-up chest deflates. I took pleasure from their fear, didn't I? A monster like that isn't who I want to be. Society needs to see remorse for what I've done.

Resembling the sweetest little grandma, Nakamura greets all the employees, except me. Every single day. When she sees me, her expression turns to a scowl. Today, she runs over my foot with her full cart, giving no apology and no look back. Since one doesn't accuse a customer, I suck it up and limp the rest of the shift.

Got my first paycheck and cashed it after work. I couldn't deposit it, since the law says I can't have a bank account for five years. That way the government can ensure I severed my yakuza connections.

Payday should be happy, right? But the crap from earlier still gives me heartburn. *Be a mercenary. Do the work, get paid, and save up for your own business—in another town.*

At home, Satou and I go over the day and my parole report. He doesn't have to show me the paperwork. However, it fits with his expectation of honesty between us.

"The altercation with the cashiers had to be included. But I mentioned it calmed down. By the way, Ohno-san found the money missing from her till. Anything to add?" Satou asks.

Did she? Or did my boss cover it to stop the rumor mill? "I've got an idea of how to handle it better. 'Cause the incident won't be a onetime thing."

"True. Well, let's clean the outbuilding for a dojo. Then there'll be somewhere for us both to blow off steam."

Is he taking more flack for me than I've seen?

We get the floor cleared, scrubbed, and polished. Making progress toward a goal helps. But the words from the gossips still swirl in my head, leaving me on the crabby side.

After chores, I grab a flashlight and my grocery bag to sprint over to the shrine. Hitting the first step makes my tightly coiled insides unwind. No one else seems to come, except to tend it. Even the fallen leaves on the path remain undisturbed.

Today, the wind blew the fabric into the face of one of the fox statues. *How can it guard the shrine like that?* So I flip the bib down on the way by.

Upon reaching the top, my head tips back and my eyes close. I take in the icy breeze blowing through the trees and my heart lifts. This quiet, out of the way location is the one place I look forward to visiting. It's odd because I feel at ease without the population density of the big city. *People can't judge me here.*

Each offering I leave disappears by the next visit. Today's is a tray of inarizushi—small rice cakes wrapped in fried tofu. A supposed favorite of kitsune and Inari. *Is that local fox the recipient?*

After ringing the bell, bowing, and clapping, I offer a silent prayer. *Kami-*

sama, thanks for the paycheck. I almost got into a fight again. Help me control my temper because I don't know if I can keep this up. How did my boss fit in again?

When I step back, there's no apparent difference. *Can I just stay here tonight? Idiot, you'd freeze.* But staying for a little while to take in the view won't hurt.

Looking through the trees, over the night scene with its few house lights in the distance, the moon, and a smattering of honest-to-god stars peeking through the clouds makes me gawk. Is that stripe from the horizon the Milky Way? I saw so few stars in the big city that I can't be sure. But this would be a great hill for an observatory.

Satou said this western mountainous region contains quite a few valleys where squalls can sneak up from behind the hills. As the wind strengthens, goosebumps form on my skin. Lightning eerily illuminates the shrine and trees.

Better get home. When I book it down the stairs, the first snowflakes hit my face. *Since when does it snow in a thunderstorm?* This never happened in Tokyo.

Shouting from up the hill reverberates in the valley, kicking my old instincts into gear. When I spin around, a green flash forces me to shield my vision. Then more shouting pierces the air. "...you'll pay!" is all I can make out. More strange glows and flashes create an unnatural show.

Can't afford to be in a fight! So, I book it in the opposite direction. Another voice echoes, "...won't harm anyone ever again!"

As I pass the torii, something whooshes overhead with a paper-like rustle then banks back up the hill. I can't make the thing out before it's beyond my flashlight's range. It's not a glider—the wings move.

What the hell kind of bird could be big enough to carry a canine? That poor dog will probably be a meal. *Please, don't be the fox I saw last time.*

Staring into the oncoming snow, I glance at where the shrine should be. Lightning hits a cypress which falls next to the building.

Then an unearthly shriek pierces the air, followed by a desperate, whimpering howl. In this storm, that animal might not survive without shelter, and the fight seems to have stopped. Maybe I can help.

Even a flashlight can be a weapon. So I grip mine tight and dash back up the stairs. The beam defines the scraped side of the shrine.

Another yelp brings my attention to a silver fox struggling to bite a glowing orb in the grass and accumulating flakes. As my breath catches, "K-kitsune," escapes my mouth.

I stumble backward before my heel catches. Flailing, I fight to keep a hold of my flashlight as I land hard on my rear. *Am I dreaming? Nope.* The sharp pain in my backside means I'm gonna have a bruise or two.

Pathetic cries continue as the beast stretches for a glowing blue sphere just out of reach. The mythical creature needs its hoshi no tama—the ball that holds its magic. Upon seeing me, it tries hard to wriggle out from under the log. But its cries pitch higher and more pathetic.

My heart twinges. It doesn't matter how dangerous the creature is, I'm its best hope. Keeping the beam of light out of the fox's face, I crouch, holding out my shaking hands in a placating gesture.

"Let me push your tama closer, then I'll attempt to free you. Understand?"

I'd forgotten to give it a signal—like one yip for yes, two for no. But it utters a labored, scratchy, "I understand. Though, why should I trust you, yakuza? You'll take my tama and force me to promise you a favor."

That's how it often went in the legends. *Not this time.* "I-I have a lot to atone for. This is a start."

Crouching, I use my light to push the sphere toward the fox's mouth. The patterned surface of the ball gives way, kind of like a sticky rice dessert cake. With a snap, the kitsune clenches the tama in its jaws.

Now that the creature can't bite me, my task is the fallen tree. Though I'm not a weakling by any means, an attempt to lift it shows my city boy ignorance. A muffled, "Idiot," comes from the animal.

What the... While I don't need thanks, the kitsune sure is being a jerk. I shoot back, "More than griping at the person helping you?"

Silence.

Another lightning strike gives me a glimpse of a broken branch. Now we need a fulcrum. The cement bricks!

"Kami-sama, I'll repair the damage as soon as I can!" While I prepare the lever, I direct, "When this lifts, you crawl out."

Wary eyes watch me as the magical being nods.

I grunt, "Yoisho!" as the bark cuts into my chilled palms.

The tree raises enough for the kitsune to paw its way forward. With its injured hip, the pathetic thing can't run away.

Damn. I slip off my jacket. "I'll carry you to the house, so we can shelter in warmth." The cold penetrates my thin shirt, biting my skin with every gust of wind.

Laying my coat on the snowy ground, I slide the nine-tailed fox onto it, making a sling from the snaps and sleeves. The creature's musk assaults my nose. But I know better than to say anything.

"When we're safe, maybe you'll tell me how you gained your tails. There should be a story behind each—some deed or miracle."

No answer. Though, the move doesn't seem to cause more damage. Cradling the kitsune in my arms, I zip home. Furious white sheets fly horizontally, only to blind us as we flee. Snow accumulates, then melts on my side facing into the wind. Cold exposure on top of everything else tonight? *I can't feel my toes.*

Unable to make out any lights across the fields, I tread with care to avoid falling into the rice paddy's frigid water. The animal growls whenever my body gives a big shiver.

Looking down into the salt and pepper furred face and yellow-orange eyes, I see it wince. "Sorry! I know it hurts." The distraction makes me trip and I get a sharp nip on the shoulder. "Don't be stupid Kitsune-san, I might drop you!"

By the time we arrive at the house, my shaking is violent and my steps clumsy. Under normal circumstances, I'd take care to remove my only pair of shoes. Tonight? They're sloughed off before I hobble to the squat kotatsu warming table to set down my guest.

The heater's not on. Satou must not be back yet. Trembling hands numbly fumble with the switch before it starts.

Gotta get these icy clothes off! I tromp upstairs for dry ones. My room is colder than the main area. So, back downstairs I go.

"Giving an old lady a show, boy?" she taunts.

Even after years of seeing the worst of humanity, her comment stops me mid-way through removing my shirt. Why is the creature watching me? *Creepy.*

"Who was tucked into my coat, while I froze?" My wet button-up and undershirt get tossed to the floor. Hearing a gasp behind me, I rush to slip on a dry tee. It ends up backward. So, I duck around the corner to finish changing.

When I return with blankets, the silver fox faces away. "Why did it have to be you?"

"Everyone else had sense enough to stay home tonight. Why were you there?"

No answer. So, I try a different tactic as I scoot under the warm kotatsu. "Kitsune-sama, do you have a name?"

Still silence. *She's in pain.* "I don't think I should give you human medication. We'll get you to a vet in the morning."

Extracting the poor animal from my muddy coat without hurting her takes time. Then, I drag her next to me under the blankets. Despite the kitsune's occasional whimper, the warmth calms our shaking and lulls us both.

The light above flicks to life. "Umeji! Why the hell are you sleeping with my aunt?" Satou's thunderous voice booms.

3

CHAPTER 3: OMISSIONS

Dark eyes blink awake in the harsh brightness. An old woman's muffled, "Yuki?" has such a tender tone. My heart stops. The heated table and blankets fly across the room as I scramble away.

Waking up next to a strange woman and someone yelling at me means awful things—death, arrest, or cutting off the knuckle of a finger. *Where's the fox?*

"Who's Yuki?" Satou demands.

Nakamura's face falls. "Not him. It's only the yakuza." When she tries to sit up, her unearthly howl carries echoes of the previous evening.

Frozen against the wall, I gulp in air while checking to see if my heart started beating again.

Satou tries to aid his aunt. But she protests in a wail, "Careful, Kazuo!"

His eye twitches, and the words turn hard. "Why didn't either of you call for medical help? Now the only place that is open is in Shimosaki."

Grimacing, she pants. "I insisted on waiting for you to take me to the hospital."

Concern replaces the fury on his face. "What happened? How long have you been here?"

Not taking my eyes off her as I try to piece this puzzle together, I set the worse-for-wear kotatsu upright again. So Nakamura, the old biddy that has nothing but nasty words for me and runs over my toes with a cart, is a shape-shifting kitsune?

She perseveres with only an occasional wince. "I was cleaning the shrine, as I always do when that storm popped out of nowhere. It wasn't in the forecast. He rescued me from under a fallen tree and carried me through the snow. I still don't approve of you bringing in a yakuza. So, it pains me to admit he was a gentleman. We were both soaked-to-the-bone freezing. Lying here kept us warm and saved my life, nephew! We owe that young man."

Nothing about being a fox. The tingle at the base of my neck says I've just got to know. "So, it was you who always took my offerings?"

"Darn right. Can't you do better than that?"

Wiping my hand over my face, I try a double entendre. "Nakamura-san, you're something else." It earns me a thump on the head.

"I'll wallop you again if you don't watch it!"

"Understood, Ma'am." *So, Satou doesn't know. And Nakamura could ruin me. No good deed goes unpunished.*

Despite his aunt's protests, my boss insists on calling an ambulance. Her lips purse as she watches Satou dial. Then, squeezing my wrist with a strength an old woman shouldn't possess, she commands in the barest whisper, "Not a peep from you, boy."

I can't even jerk away, and my teeth grind in our tug of war until I comply. Then a minute flash of light and a prick of static electricity strike where she releases me from her death grip. My stomach tightens. In the legends, kitsune fled after being discovered. *Is that why she forced me into a promise? So she doesn't have to leave Nonogawa?*

The ambulance whisks Nakamura to the closest hospital, twenty minutes away on a winding road to Shimosaki, just south of Nonogawa. As we follow in my boss's car, we drive out of the freshly fallen snow. Silhouetted trees loom over us on each side of the highway. Still not slowing, my heart pounds roughly in my chest.

"Thanks for helping Aunt Hisako. She can be difficult," Satou says.

"Sure." The chill of the leather seat goes straight through my pants, winding up my muscles and nerves further.

"Why was she lying beside you?" Satou's flat, controlled tone sends prickles through me.

"When the tree crashed, I heard the scream, then ran back and helped her crawl out. Neither of us had cell phones, and I couldn't leave her alone. So, I carried her. We fell asleep in the warmth as we waited. Just as she said."

"She gripped your arm when I called the paramedics. You didn't mention that." When he pulls over, his penetrating stare pins me in place. He hisses, "Listen Umeji, I was the top club host in Osaka before I moved here to remake my reputation. Spent years telling people what they wanted to hear. I know damned well when someone isn't speaking the whole truth. You knew she was there. Why'd you abandon her in the storm?"

That's why he speaks a little differently, he's not from here either. Though his accent is closer than my Tokyo one. My hands fly up in defense. "I didn't know she was there until I saw her. I swear!"

The garlic on his breath overwhelms me as he leans in. "And she trusts a convict that she doesn't like one iota to sleep beside him in his arms? You didn't threaten or dig up information on her, did you?"

To appear more at ease, I lean back. "No, Sir. Sure, she's had it out for me. This evening, she insulted me as I helped, and asked why it had to be me. I don't understand it! We had to thaw out or risk hypothermia. We were so cold. Even giving her my coat on the way home didn't help much. I would've dumped her, clothes and all, into the bath. But in her condition, we couldn't do that. So the kotatsu was the next best option."

With narrowed eyes, he states in a voice sharper than a knife's edge, "I thought we were alike, in wanting to change and leave our past behind. If I find just one tiny white lie, Umeji, I'll drop-kick your ass directly into jail. Is that understood?"

"Yes, Sir!" That host shit is messed up. If he was so keen on bringing you halfway across Japan, was it from the goodness of his heart? *Don't bet on it.* Everyone has something to hide around here.

His nod is curt as he pulls onto the road. I force my breathing to slow and peel my fingers from the door handle, but a shiver runs down my spine. It's not from the low temperature.

Satou fiddles on his phone as we sit in the empty, vanilla-bland, dim waiting room with its vinyl chairs. Whatever the industrial cleaner is in the emergency room stings my nose as it wafts from the check-in and exam rooms. The incessant typing of the receptionist nurse grates on my nerves. My fingers tap hard on the arm of the chair.

Might as well ask. "Sir, it had to be hard to leave. Quite a few of the clubs are yakuza-owned, and they're possessive of their best. How'd you leave?"

In a thicker than usual accent, his words spit out and his look hardens. "Umeji, if you want to know that, be completely honest. Secrets are how you repay me? Get to the bottom of it, or we're done."

My throat tightens and the old uncomfortable coldness settles back in my chest, returning like a clingy ex-girlfriend. "Sir, I can't tell you. I promised. I'll share anything that involves only me."

"You know the outcome. I'll contact the police in the morning with my report." Tilting his face and hissing a breath between his teeth, he delivers the crowning blow. "Is whoever it is worth it?"

My eyes sting as I clench my fists. "I believe so," *Doesn't make it easy.* If only I could tell him, but I promised one of the mythical creatures I idolized as a kid. I know better than to piss off a yokai, a supernatural being. In the myths, that always goes bad—much worse than jail.

He doesn't let up. "Is it someone from your past?"

"No, Sir." The pregnant pause hurts. As I dare to glance up, his expression says another question is imminent. The roughness in my words comes from trying to quell the roar inside. "Satou-san, I have the utmost gratitude toward you. Please, no more questions about anyone else."

To see him lean back resigned is a stab in the chest, the final nail in my coffin. Will the old bat understand or care about what I've sacrificed? With dragging steps, I grab a tea from the vending machine around the corner. One of my last acts as a free man. While my head rests on the wall, the unopened warm bottle dangles in my grip. *Idiot.* I should have known better than to hope.

4

CHAPTER 4: TRUST EXTENDED

Four and a half hours after admission, Nakamura is awake, and we're allowed to visit. The doctor intercepts us as we pass the privacy curtain, explaining that her femur had multiple fractures. Because of her age, he had to do a total hip replacement. He's prescribing physical therapy and a walker.

A huff escapes my mouth, despite the looming threat of my return to the slammer. The proud old kitsune will be a handful for anyone watching over her. How will Satou manage?

"Do you have any family near to assist with her recovery?" the doctor asks.

His head hangs.

So, my hand raises. If I say what I know, I could stay to help. Sure, she'll probably insult me every day just like she did before, but it would take pressure off my boss. Then my arm falls and my heart aches. I break a promise to either Satou or Nakamura no matter what. He wouldn't believe me, anyway.

His gaze flicks to me, then resolutely to the doctor. If I won't share the whole truth, then I'm not worth his time.

Finally, we're able to see her. She's paler than the hospital gown as she squints against the harsh fluorescent lights. Instead of the old biddy who could get even me to back down, she looks more like a child in the gigantic bed. On top of that, the IV poking from her skin adds to the sense of fragility.

As Satou pulls up a chair, he takes her hand, just as mine reaches out to do the same, then falls. I have no connection with her that would warrant such intimacy.

His voice drops low. "How are they treating you, Auntie?"

"Terrible! They tried to tell me I'll have to use one of those stupid walkers!" she sputters.

Coughing, I smother the snort and spasms of laughter at her fiery spirit only to get a glare from my VPO.

"Yakuza, the irony of being wrapped in the very coat I cussed you out over isn't lost on me. Did I hear your name was Umeji?" She pats the bed for me to move closer.

"Yes, Ma'am. I'm here to let you know you got your wish. I'll leave Nonogawa soon." My chest tightens at having to verbalize the impending doom.

As her brow wrinkles, she grabs my coat sleeve. Her grip isn't as strong this time, but I stiffen. She asks, "What do you mean?"

"He'll be returning to where he came from." Satou scowls.

"Where might that be, Nephew? Tell me this instant!"

We're drawing too much attention. Running my free hand through my hair, I stare at the floor and whisper. "Prison, Ma'am."

"There's no reason for that! Too busy with work, visiting the shrine, and cleaning that dojo. No time for friends, trouble, or a girl." She ticks the items off on her fingers.

I wince. Sure, I didn't have much of a life. But it's still preferable to the slammer. How does she know all of this? My parole officer wouldn't share that kind of info.

Satou's eye twitches and he takes a few seconds to answer. "Aunt, he and I made a deal. I'd be his volunteer parole officer as long as he was frank with me. I can handle all manner of things, but not deception."

Squeezing the wrist she hadn't released yet, she bites her lip. "And you'll go to prison for a secret this old lady asked you to keep?"

My voice fails, so I swallow. My boss observes our interchange like a hawk.

"Unacceptable!" Her outburst startles both of us men and has the nurse running to fetch help. "I finally find a replacement shrine keeper and YOU, Nephew, are punishing him for a favor. I won't stand for it!"

The pitch stresses of his Osaka accent deepen. "Aunt, what the hell is going on? What secret is he keeping for you? Now you want to keep 'the yakuza' around?"

"Satou Kazuo, do not take that tone with me! No amount of bullying will compel me to divulge a confidence I've kept from all but my husband!" Her finger, with its bent knuckles, waggles at him like a snake warning before it strikes.

"But you shared it with my parolee instead of me, your family?"

In response, her lips purse and her eyes narrow in the same glare she used to give me at the store.

"Aunt..." A solid wall of frustration is contained in that single familial moniker.

The standoff halts when the hospital staff ushers us out and urges quiet for the sake of the other patients. Needing the last word, she hollers. "You will not send him back. You hear me, Kazuo!?!"

My head whips around in her direction as I'm pushed from the room. *She just commanded him? To keep me here?*

In the waiting area, my boss paces around the formation of chairs. He's not shown so much vulnerability before. Me? I press my fingers into my pockets so hard that they rip through the seams.

Satou's circles stop abruptly in front of me. "Is there anything you can share? What really happened? Why are you so loyal to her?"

He's only concerned about her safety. How about being vague? "I witnessed something. Walked in on it after the tree fell, and I heard a scream—an event I have a hard time understanding. Maybe from the spirit world. Beyond being pinned with a broken hip, I think she was ok. That's all I dare say, Satou-san."

Non-plussed, he lets his stare bore into me. "You're suggesting the supernatural?"

"Something I had a hard time believing, Sir."

A patient's buzzer goes off at the nurse's station and we hear a calm answer to the request for aid. With hands covering his mouth, he lets out a few deep breaths. "Any details?"

"Sorry."

My answer makes him kick the floor, and he does another round of pacing muttering about 'paranormal bullshit on his watch' and 'why him'. When he swings back around, he says, "I can't put a finger on what there is between the two of you."

"Not sure I understand it either. I expected her to be ecstatic I'll be gone."

"Can you tell me about replacing her as shrine keeper?"

"No clue, Sir. She's the one that tends the little shrine across the field, right?" My hands leave the safety of my ruptured pockets to spread in helplessness.

"She is." After closing his eyes for a few seconds, the spasm above his cheek stops. "I'll inform Aunt Hisako you can't do this again. Your loyalty almost cost you. Because it's to my relative, that's the only reason I'll renege today. And only this once. NO MORE SECRETS. Do you understand?"

I nod several times, giving a belated, respectful bow. "I'm most obliged, Satou-san." Inadequate, but the proper words don't exist. With a curt bob, he chooses a seat.

Reprieve granted. Holy shit. My knees go weak and I flop into a nearby chair. Tremors cause any attempts at sipping my tea to dribble down my chin. The only hope is to recap it until the adrenaline withdrawal stops.

Under his breath, he mutters, "What is so damned important that she's got to hide it from family? I'm not her favorite. Still, she's never spoken to me that way before."

* * *

Nudging my shoulder, the boss says he's ready to go home. It's past 6 AM, and the bags under his eyes make him look dead tired. The green-tinted fluorescent lights only give a sickly cast to his complexion.

Groggily, I yawn and uncurl from the uncomfortable waiting room chair that made my muscles stiff. "How is Nakamura-san?"

"Sleeping. I'll come back late afternoon to check on her." Satou stretches before striding off.

"Mind if I join you?"

"Neither of us will be fit for work today. I'll let Matsuo-kun know you won't be in."

Oh yeah. I'm supposed to be at the store in an hour. Sure, I've done harder, more unpleasant tasks on less sleep, but the chance to catch up on rest is a good thing.

* * *

The sun tips under the rim of the hills into the valley when we return.

In the sterile, harsh-lit hallway, we wait for admittance to Nakamura's room. My boss holds a vase of cheerful pink and yellow blooms, while I lean on the opposite wall with a small tray of white strawberries.

My boss said she won't buy the fruit for herself—too expensive. But she loves them. So maybe she won't return to cussing me out if she sees the attention-grabbing fruit.

When they allow us entry, Doctor Uehara greets us. "I'd like to discuss the length of Nakamura-san's hospitalization and post-surgery treatment."

Tilting his chin toward his aunt, he follows the surgeon. The mention of three weeks makes me shake my head. *Is the doctor going to sit on her?*

Nakamura's color is improved, but she still looks fragile. Bowing, I offer the berries with both hands. Her face lights up at the sight of the fruit. "You shouldn't have."

"Please, enjoy them." After they're pushed toward her once more, she snatches them with the eagerness of a child. To ensure she doesn't just set them aside for show, I add, "Don't wait. The clerk said they were ripe."

Nakamura breaks into the package and holds a berry out for me. Despite her gnarled hands, the gesture has grace. "Eat one, so this old woman doesn't feel foolish."

Since I'm here I'll keep watch. Taking a seat on the far side of the room ensures a good view of the door.

With closed eyes, she savors the pale berry as if it was the nectar of the gods. How many people see her child-like side? Then, her countenance darkens as she sets the rest of the berries on the bedside tray. "Thank you for keeping me company while they talk about me as if I'm a deaf invalid. It's not like I can't hear them."

The weight on me lifts. Her sauciness is an excellent sign, but I try to steer away from the topic. "How are you doing? Did the surgery cause problems?"

"With the transformation? No more than clothing does. I'll be fine. Since they're occupied, we can discuss a few matters."

I lean in.

"Would you keep the shrine maintained while I heal?" She knows I can't say no to an elder without being rude. But it's not what I expected. An earnest nod from me lets her segue. "Next. A few nights ago, a dream revealed the symbolic tattoo that a man I loved many years before had. Imagine my surprise when I saw his ink design across your shoulders. You also willingly kept my secret. My spell didn't have to be enacted."

Wait. I got the design from a hundred-year-old photo!

"Now you know what I meant by 'why did it have to be you'. You can see it wasn't a coincidence."

"But..." Then, that comment wasn't about the rescue. Her stare is palpable, so I focus on the floor out of respect. "What does that mean? And what spell did you put on me?"

"Fate meant us to meet. The ward would have warned me if you broke that agreement and I would have taken actions to avoid being revealed. Nothing harmful mind you. So, just let that brow of yours settle back down before it flies clear off into space."

Scrunching my eyes shut, I can't help but laugh, deep and loud. She's already stuffed another strawberry in her mouth by the time I look again, and her expression dares me to say something. When I don't, she chews slowly, and her stare turns intense. "You're humble for a yakuza."

That makes me flinch. "I have to show remorse for what I've done, Ma'am. No room for pride."

She nods to herself. "That settles it then. I pay my debts and have a picture of your character after this latest debacle. You could be so much more than a mobster. So I'll train you for a different destiny—if you're willing—to earn a proper place in society again."

"Come again, Nakamura-san?" Is tempting me to hope her devilish alternative to cussing me out? As if I could be more. My family is as common as they come. I'm just a city slicker who made terrible choices that I'll pay for with my dying breath. The yakuza label is permanent, just like my ink.

"I'm sure you're aware of my tendency to be a busybody. So I researched you as a potential threat to my town. What I found is that you dropped out of school when you joined the yakuza, but you were also one of two survivors from your clan. My hunch says that was no accident. Too many coincidences lining up."

"N-not an accident? Same design?" Lightheadedness kicks in. Before I can get an answer, the door cracks open.

Her whisper carries an intensity that sends chills through me. "Everyone has a choice, boy. Will you leave behind your past, to become someone others hold in high regard?"

Is she serious? Swallowing, I lean on the chair until the dizziness fades, then gesture to the seat for my boss. Satou's voice echoes too loud after the hushed conversation. "How are you feeling, Auntie?"

"Better, now that Tatsuya will manage the shrine in my absence."

Double take. Talk of strange things, then using my personal name without a suffix. Was that a jab, or does she feel we know each other that well already?

* * *

Over the next several days, tending the shrine, visiting Nakamura, and judo training to let off steam at Satou's dojo keep me busy and give me something to look forward to.

At work, when I walk in on Ohno asking Mie if I had rescued Satou's aunt, Mie brushes it off as she twirls the end of her ponytail. "It was a ruse to make others think better of him."

Ohno doesn't respond. So, Mie presses the attack. "Why does Nakamura-san accept him? It doesn't do her reputation any good. You know, rumors are going around that she's covering something interesting for him. Why in the world did Satou-san take him in? People might shop in the next town over."

My body stiffens mid-step. There's no reason to bother with excuses or pleasantries. This latest gossip is unfounded, and it involves more than just me. Lights flicker above, only adding to my irritation.

Strutting in, I lay on the mobster drawl. "Yeah, I'm a no-good ex-yakuza. I deserve what I get. But don't go draggin' Nakamura-san or the boss into the rumors, capisce? Few people have visited her. You'd think a respected customer who came in every single day would have at least a few visits from goody two shoes employees like you two. Then you might learn the facts about what happened." Hitting my stride, my mouth curls in disgust as I get in Mie's face. "That's not what you're interested in, though, is it? The real story's not as juicy. Pathetic."

Storming out of the break room, Mie won't even cast a glower my way. *The truth hurts. Doesn't it, stupid chit?*

When Ohno's lip trembles and her head drops in shame before she follows Mie, it knocks the stuffing out of me. I was the monster. Again. My arms drop to my sides as I deflate. Ohno's the one asking the questions, it's Mie who's the first to jump to conclusions and accusations. Here and now, I have one opportunity to fix it. "Ohno-san..."

With her back to me, she stops.

Shifting my tone into neutral to make it respectful, I say, "I went too far. Sorry." She can't see my bow, but I give it anyway.

"Me, too," is her soft response as she beelines it for the ladies' room.

I'm gonna need that workout in the dojo tonight.

5

CHAPTER 5: HEALING

We haven't had more snow or ice since that freak storm, so the doctor lets Nakamura exercise outside each day. Strolling on the path, we take in the hills on each side of the valley that cradles our town. The deciduous trees are bare, but the evergreen of the cedar, pine, cypress, and bamboo sustain color on the steep hillsides and the breeze wafts the fresh earthy scents our way. Stark light-colored paths to the tops stick out like scars that don't diminish the raw beauty.

In the chill air, Nakamura's breath creates dissipating fog puffs. At least she's not winded from the walk. "Tatsuya, is there something on your mind?"

"Nah," I dodge, not wanting to worry her about the argument that still plagues me with Ohno and Mie. "But you seem to get a kick out of calling me by my personal name. Not that I'm complaining."

Her chin lifts, and her mouth purses in a smug smile. "A small price for a first friendship here, I'd say."

"True." Who would have thought I'd rush from my job each day to spend time with an old lady?

To have someone who might believe in me has done wonders for my confidence over the last week. I still doubt myself often, wondering when things will turn on me again. But it's not my every waking thought now. A new confidence has entered my stride, a natural, relaxed one as opposed to my old, forced yakuza swagger.

For lack of a better topic, I bring up another change. "Nakamura-san, I think I'm getting used to it here. The open countryside isn't uncomfortable anymore, and I'm not constantly expecting to see tall buildings."

Her nose wrinkles in delight. "Ha! You won't be able to go back to the metropolis without feeling claustrophobic now."

"Probably. So, may I ask about your people?"

"Sure."

"In the legends, the fact that kitsune couldn't say the syllable 'shi' gave them away. How do you avoid it?"

"You'll know when you see it." She winks. Her walker hits an uneven section of the cement, and she shoves it forward with a viciousness one wouldn't expect from an elderly person. "If only they'd let me get rid of this stupid contraption! It makes me feel old. But I'll convince them to release me early."

Looking down, I try to hide the grin I can't dispel. "You'll use your kitsune wiles on them?"

"If need be. The doctors won't know what hit 'em. Young man, wipe that smirk off your face right now."

"Yes, Ma'am." Only by biting the inside of my cheek do I manage it.

"Next subject. Your education concerns me. I was hoping to start the training I promised immediately. But you dropped out of school to join the yakuza when you were quite young, so you can't read or write many kanji and are missing knowledge of a few other important subjects. Kazuo told me about your troubles with labels on products. And education in history will help you understand the background of what we'll cover later."

Nakamura has me start that day, even asking Satou to arrange my work schedule so I have time for her lessons after our walks. She has me drill kanji characters and words made with them in her private hospital room. The way she teaches with imagery and connections to previous symbols, and, of course, a ton of repetition, makes it easier to learn than when I was in school.

If my cramping fingers let my handwriting get sloppy, she taps my knuckles with her pencil. "People will need to read what you write. You can rest when you fill the paper."

So I splay my hands to stretch them out and keep going. The overhead fluorescents could stand to be brighter for practicing the detailed kanji. This one for 'heal' has eight tiny strokes, and it's one of the symbols in my family name. To make up for the lack of lights, I hunch over my work. I've been working close enough to the paper I don't notice the pattern until I lean back to stretch. Pointing to several in a row, I ask, "Sensei, are these from a specific set?"

Rubbing her palms together, she grins. "You'll see."

"Chinese medicine?"

"Nope."

My eyebrows waggle as I press her buttons. "Love potions?"

She swats the top of my head playfully, then taps my paper. "Enough procrastinating. Write."

"Yes, Ma'am." While practice isn't exciting, the ability to read more words is. Yesterday, I helped a customer find a special shampoo for dyed hair. Literacy is so underrated!

During the second half of today's lesson, she brings out Satou's iPad and thrusts it at me. "Kazuo lent me this so we could listen to a history podcast that a neighbor suggested. But I can't navigate the thing. Figure it out for me."

Adding her own take after almost every episode, she makes it easy to remember the events. Dates not so much, but that doesn't matter as long as I recite them in the correct order and century.

"Sensei, will you tell me about the man with the same tattoo?"

Her look turns dreamy. "Tsuchimikado Yukitada. He was a young samurai."

Pulling out one of her history journals, she turns to a dog-eared page with an old photo dated 1856. My jaw drops. The man's cheeks are a little fuller and he has bushier eyebrows, but dang, he resembles me. So, that's why she called me Yuki when we woke up after the snowstorm.

"He was the samurai you loved in 1856? How is that possible, Sensei?"

A soft knock at the open door causes her to close the journal. "Next time, Tatsuya."

Argh. Just when I was hooked! Looking over my shoulder, I'm surprised to see Ohno waiting alone, holding a bouquet of pale blue flowers in both hands. The apron peeking out from her coat reveals she came straight from work. With bangs swept over her brow, the angled bob accentuates her sweet round face as my coworker gives a meek smile.

She listened! Does she understand how much that means as I bob my grateful acknowledgment? Turning back to Sensei, I offer, "I'll go so you can have time with your other visitor."

When I bow to Ohno and pass by, she asks, "She calls you by your personal name already?" The amused twinkle in her eye causes my cheeks to warm.

This is a side I've not seen of her before. I'll take it over the gossip with Mie any day. "About that..." Shoving my hands into my pockets, I say. "Sensei and I have been through a lot."

"Now I'm curious." With a hand going to her mouth, she's even more entertained.

"Gotta go." I scoot out of there on the double, though her stare bores a hole through the back of my jacket. Thankfully, I don't hear her laugh as she greets Nakamura.

Will Ohno ask what happened? Man, I hope not!

6

CHAPTER 6: MEETING

Visiting Nakamura the next day, I give my greetings, shove off my jacket, and drape it over my lap as I pull a chair up beside her. She's finishing up her snack. Her chewing slows.

Gah! She's doin' this on purpose! "The suspense is killing me, Sensei! You've got to tell me how it's possible you knew What's-his-name Samurai-san over a hundred fifty years ago."

Her brow furrows as she moves the tray to the bedside table. "Good day to you, Tatsuya. Tsu-chi-mi-ka-do. Memorize that name. He was a humble warrior, but his choices made impacts far and wide."

Crap. I earned that. "Understood. Tsuchimikado-san. Now, will you share?" Her raised eyebrow makes me add. "Please."

Opening her worn leather journal to the page, she runs a finger over his photo—like she's smoothing the wisp falling out of his topknot. I lean in. How unusual for a samurai to permit a picture with even a hair out of place. They were sticklers about appearance.

Nakamura begins, "I was born in the first year of the Kanpo era, in a bamboo grove on Mt. Atago northwest of Kyoto. That would translate to 1741 in western-style dates."

In the myths, kitsune had long lives. But to be talking to a being who's over two-and-a-half centuries old? *Whoa.* My open-mouthed gape receives a harrumph, but Sensei presses on. "I first saw Yuki in 1854, a few years

32

before this photo. I remember it so clearly…"

March 28, 1854, Forest Hills on the outskirts of Kyoto:

Dew on the grass and fallen leaves from the previous year dampened my paws but muffled my movement. Birds sang their gratitude for surviving the harsh winter. Though, they quieted with my approach. Scents of pine, bamboo, cedar, and new blooms filled my nose.

Slinking into a lope as I tracked a rabbit, I watched keen-eyed as it stopped to graze on a patch of grass. The rodent's ears twitched at the silent warning from its feathered friends. This was my chance to catch supper.

Leaning on my haunches, I sprang, snapping the creature's neck. When I lifted my kill, an arrow pierced my shoulder—where the hare had been not a second before. My prize fell from my jaws and I sank to the ground with the momentum of the projectile. Alternating between keening and rasping, I laid there helpless, in more pain than I'd imagined possible.

A young warrior, dressed in modest blues and grays, sprinted to kneel beside me. He was dignified despite his clothes not being new. This didn't fit my expectation of samurai pride, and the air of humility about him soothed me enough not to growl.

Seeing my two tails and what was then my red coat, his posture stiffened. "Kitsune… So the stories are true. What have I done?"

When I coughed, blood dribbled down my chin. The shaft embedded in me made it nigh impossible to breathe since the tip hadn't pierced the other side.

His expression went slack, and his words monotone. "You're too small to remove the crescent arrowhead without killing you. I don't want to end a mythical being such as your esteemed self, but you shouldn't have to suffer. Please know, it is with great regret that I do this."

The ringing of his sword drawing from its scabbard sent a shiver through me. I had to act fast. My family would hunt him the rest of his days if he carried through.

Between panting breaths, I rasped, "I beg you! Let me change forms so you can remove the arrow." My chances slimmed every moment as my ki waned.

Sighing, he slid his sword into its sheath. I would be forever grateful to him for listening.

Acting as a human had never been something I fancied. So I'd only practiced the transformation once, despite being over a hundred years old. It took three tries to assume the form, but my tails remained and I'd not managed clothes. Who considers fashion when at death's door? I was fortunate to have accomplished what I did.

His eyes bulged. Removing his quilted vest, he covered my nakedness. Though the fabric leant little warmth as I lay on the cold ground, I was grateful.

His words caught before he took a deep breath. "This will be painful." Pressing a hand to my collarbone, he grasped the shaft where it met my skin and yanked.

My shriek of agony would have scared off a ghost. But the arrow remained embedded. Tears ran down my cheeks, and my voice was ragged from hitched breaths as the muscles tightened around the wound. "Try once more. Please."

Trembling, he straddled my form and put a piece of leather in my mouth. With his tanto dagger, he sliced open the edges of the wound to allow the crescent-shaped arrowhead space, so it didn't rip my flesh even more. As he did, my teeth bit through the hide.

For more leverage, he rested a knee on my arm. Gripping the arrow with both hands, he asked, "Are you ready?"

I nodded, and he pulled with his full strength. All the city below must have heard the scream that emanated from my mouth.

When I'd caught my breath, he slowly hoisted me up onto his gentle bay mare, who reached around with ears perked to sniff me. Her whinny announced her concern.

Panting my reply, I gripped the pommel's ridge with my good arm. "Thank you for bearing me, good horse."

On foot, the samurai lead us through the darkening forest to a tiny house. There he pressed a cloth to my wound, wrapped me in a gray kimono, and tucked me into his bed before heading into the night to fetch a doctor. The futon mattress was so thin I could feel the uneven floor beneath me.

There wasn't enough ki left in me for a spell. I was only vaguely conscious of someone treating my wound and forcing me to down a bitter liquid.

* * *

When I woke, light shone through the latticed shoji doors. Taking in my surroundings, I spotted a central, sunken cooking hearth. A pot, bowl, and utensils rested on a lacquered trunk nearby. The tokonoma display alcove had a worn suit of armor.

From the opposite side of the fire, the warrior sat on a cushion at a low writing desk. With his chin on his knee, he watched me. That gaze was an incoming storm—intense and unyielding.

Trying to sit up sent a wave of pain through me. I was expecting constant agony, not one that came and went. My ki remained low. When I collapsed on the bed with a whimper, a slip of parchment falling to the floor caught my attention.

As the man scrambled to me, concern filled his face. His repentant, kneeling bow spoke his sincerity. He'd already apologized. This time his voice cracked as he expressed his regret again. "Please forgive me for injuring you, Great One."

When he raised his head, he didn't dare to meet my gaze. "Can you eat?" Helping me sit and placing a bowl of rice on a tray, he filled me in. "Your esteemed self has been unconscious for over a day. I'd feared you might not wake up."

Unfamiliar with chopsticks, I fumbled—dropping several bites. My lack of coordination tempted me to shove my face into the dish. He plucked the utensils from my grasp and offered the warm white grains with enviable grace. I vowed with every bite I would learn to use those infernal chopsticks if it was the last thing I did.

To distract myself from the negative feelings, I examined my surroundings. Spotting the ofuda charm, I noted the handwriting was exquisite, and it balanced well with the choice of paper. I doubted the practitioner could be human since magical aura crackled from it.

He brought a towel, a tad more comfortable around me now. "Here. To wipe your mouth."

Opening the shoji enabled a warm, gentle wind to refresh the air in the small home. It provided a pleasant view of the road, forest, and the lone cherry tree in full bloom.

As he stepped off the veranda to wash the dishes by the pump, I saw he had no servant or woman to do it, and this was only a one-room hut. So he was a lower-class samurai.

"I'll fetch the physician to redo your bandages now, Kitsune-sama," he said, bowed, and turned on his heel.

Kitsune-sama, I rather liked the sound of that. "Wait. Please," I held up the charm made of fine paper. "I'm sure you had to pay a handsome sum for a healing spell this powerful and written in such a beautiful hand. Would you bring this onmyouji so I can express my thanks?"

Someone had to train a magic user to manifest such powerful spells, but this exceeded my expectation of human capability. I'd never been subtle, worried about what others think, or held my emotions in check. Father often scolded me, saying I'd not do well in society until I could. The bluntness prickled my conscience, but I reasoned my predicament was this man's fault. So, he owed me.

I'll never forget the twinkle in his gaze as he looked over his shoulder. "Sorry, Kitsune-sama, he's busy today." Then he continued on his way with a swagger.

Of all the nerve! First, he shot me, then he wouldn't let me meet the one human that might be of interest? My family members were also onmyouji practitioners. This slip of paper hinted at true talent! Thus, it was my duty to tell my family who else had in-depth knowledge of such a difficult subject! So many practitioners were frauds!

When the warrior and the doctor returned, the lingering pain had agitated me enough that I'd worked myself into outright indignation over being denied my request. "Took you long enough."

The chill breeze blew into the room. Stopping in his tracks, the samurai furrowed his brows.

The doctor's eyes twinkled with mirth. "Tsuchimikado-san, you have a bona fide princess on your hands." Switching his attention to me, he directed, "Come now, Lady, allow me to change those bandages. We weren't sure you'd survive. When he came to my house, he was in an absolute panic."

The doctor wasn't aware of what I was. But deterring me was impossible. "Tsuchimikado-san won't introduce me to the onmyouji that, along with you, provided such help." That sounded disrespectful, even to me. So I backtracked. "It's an honor to meet you, Sensei, and I'm grateful to you for your services. Thank you." I gave a respectful nod. "But there are two who have attended me, and I am denied thanking the other half."

With an eyebrow raised at my rudeness, the samurai kneeled beside me. "Hime-sama, I'm sorry to have displeased you. Let us focus on one thing at a time. I will tell you of him after Doctor Inoue re-binds your wound. I used his services in addition to the doctor's because I heard onmyoudo can speed healing. Is that agreeable?"

He was dodging, but why? The quickness of the samurai's redirection showed he knew how to deal with difficult people. Very well. I would play along and dipped my head.

Since I'd given him a modicum of quarter, he moved to the porch with his back to me, offering privacy. I needed to keep my mind off the pain of the physician investigating the wound and the embarrassment of exposure for fresh bandages.

So, I continued sparring. "Will you tell me why he cannot visit?"

The sliver of his profile showed his eyes crinkling. Again, his volley was quick. "Hime-sama, he is also busy taking care of a guest. He wishes to do his best by her, so not to risk her ire."

"A multitude of haughty ladies in the area?"

"As you say." His shoulders moved in rhythm, matching his feet's boyish swinging from the porch. He was pleased with himself.

I would see about that. My kind brought down the proud. Next, to test how well he knew this mysterious person. "And he is a good friend of yours?"

"You could say that." He leaned back on his hands. The grin on his face as he gazed at the sky only confirmed my suspicions.

I reneged every thought I'd had about him being the least bit humble. This onmyouji must wield quite the influence if Tsuchimikado was that smug about their relationship. But I knew I could trump this samurai.

So, I upped the ante. "And what if I said I would marry him out of gratitude? If he's not already taken." Father had tried to find me a husband for decades. A magic user would be preferable. If I was lucky, I might have a say in who I married. This was my chance.

Doctor Inoue stopped mid-wrap. Tsuchimikado's head swiveled so fast I worried it would spin right off his shoulders. Thankfully, the doctor had already covered my chest with bandages, so I was spared further embarrassment. The samurai's slack-jawed gape verified I held the advantage.

While Inoue-sensei finished his work, I pressed, "Will you give him the message?"

The warrior's posture stiffened, so I beamed a wicked smile. With crimson cheeks, he stammered, "I-I think he'd be most pleased."

A light breeze picked up again, sending a swirl of petals from the cherry tree behind him. He fought to keep his tone neutral. "That is, if Hime-sama is not teasing. Who could expect someone as high as yourself to commit after a frivolous remark?"

Instead of saying he'd relay the offer, he provided a way out. *Why would he do that? Oh.* Suddenly, the blood drained from my face.

"Are you all right? You went very pale. Rest now." Inoue-sensei placed his hand on mine.

I didn't resist as he guided me to recline on the futon. Here I was in the bed of the man to which I, a wily kitsune, lost a battle of wits. All because of a defective character trait I thought had been only his. But, no. It was mine. All mine. The irony couldn't have shocked me more, nor the warrior to which I'd flippantly proposed.

I had to give the healer credit. He kept his tongue in check as Tsuchimikado walked him down the hill and paid for his services.

Taking his time, the samurai plodded up to his hut. He must have needed to compose himself. I did, too. My hands fidgeted and my throat went dry. Hesitating to enter the house, he stood outside on the veranda, mute and unable to tear his gaze from me.

So, I dipped a toe into the pool of conversation again as my heart pounded in my chest. "Tsuchimikado-san is the one I wanted to meet?"

His leery look stung, but he bowed. "Please call me Tsuchimikado Yukitada. I am most honored to make your acquaintance and am at your service, Kitsune-sama."

Gritting my teeth, I forced myself to sit. He moved to assist, but I held out a hand. "I am Nakamura Hisako. The pleasure and honor are all mine." I bent as much as I could, recognizing the winner of our game. Rising, I took him in, refusing to look away. Still being too forward, I yearned to witness his next reaction. "I would be most honored if you would allow me to know this brilliant onmyouji who outfoxed me."

It meant the world to me that he didn't hide his beautiful smile as he shook his head before bowing once more. "As you wish, Nakamura-sama. But it was I who was the first to lose composure."

Nakamura's Hospital Room, December 14:

Shutting the journal with the treasured photo after her retelling, she closes her eyes and smiles wistfully.

"Whoa, Tsuchimikado-san was a magic user?" I get up to pace, trying to put the pieces together. "And humans can do that kind of stuff?"

She opens one eye, and her pleasant look turns mischievous. "It's difficult, but not impossible."

"I have so many questions. But it's late, so I'll leave you to reminisce."

"Now you see the unsettling similarity in how you both gained my trust. We all made choices that lead to where we are, but I believe destiny allowed our paths to cross."

7

CHAPTER 7: LOOKING BACK

Mid-month allows a celebration for my second paycheck. After setting aside most of the money for my own place, I pick up a few beers to share with Satou, a new journal and pen, and ingredients to make salmon onigiri rice balls for lunches.

To leave another offering later that evening, I zip over to the shrine. This time my offering comprises a bit of cash plus some of my homemade onigiri.

* * *

The next day, the oddity that the rice ball is still there, frozen to the spot I left it, proves I'm the only one at the out of the way shrine. It leaves me a little off kilter that the place of worship is in my care. I'm not anybody special. This should be the duty of someone noble like a priest.

Is the responsibility for this place what's turning me into something more than a yakuza? I shake my head to get back to my task. No slacking. Sensei will have my head if even a speck of dirt remains.

* * *

At the store, Ohno is the only other employee on lunch break. She's eating and thumbing through something on her phone.

Since I have a connection with her through my teacher, I shove aside the butterflies. "Mind if I sit here?" I hold my bento above the table, ready to place it in the spot I'll claim. Looking up, she tugs a bud from her ears. So, I take back my request. "You look busy."

"Go ahead. I was only studying but can't stand to look through my flashcards one more time."

My words gush out. "Thanks. And thank you for visiting Nakamura-sensei in the hospital yesterday. It's just been the boss and me stopping by. She chattered on about you when I visited this morning. Totally made her day."

"You were right." Taking a bite, she shrugs and says around a full mouth, "Sorry, my break is almost over. Anyway, Mie-chan wouldn't come because you might be there. So I told her that was stupid. Just because you have a past doesn't mean you can't be spot on sometimes."

"Ohno-san, you're the one person here who acknowledges me, besides the boss. Why?"

"I've been on the outside."

What's she mean? Instead of pushing, I ask, "What are you studying?"

"Massage therapy. Tests are coming up."

"So you have plans for the future?"

"Yep. I'll start my own massage practice."

"Cool." *Not ready to share my dreams.*

* * *

Two days later, after our stroll on the hospital grounds, Nakamura says. "Today I coaxed Doctor Uehara to release me. He still insists on this stupid contraption."

"So you used magic on him?"

"Darn right. I know I'm healed. He just insisted on trying to stick to his preconceived timetable because that's how he's always done things. The stubborn goat took a ridiculous amount of convincing." Her hands hover above the walker as it moves without her touching it. Sucking in my lip, I smother my grin. But she must have seen because she harrumphs.

41

When the staff has her sign the release papers, Satou swings by to pick her up. A nurse puts the walker in front of the wheelchair she used to bring Nakamura out. Using my arm for supposed support instead of 'the contraption', Sensei grins sweetly, waving farewell as I guide her around the device to the car.

The physician motions to the nurse. "Ensure Nakamura-san takes the walker."

We pick up a few groceries en route to her house. At the checkout, we spot a man in a hoodie and allergy mask charging for the door. Matsuo's in hot pursuit, shouting, "Stop! Thief!"

Sensei shoves me. "What are you waiting for?"

As I exit the store, Matsuo grabs the guy's jacket, allowing me to catch up. Swinging to face my coworker, the guy pulls a knife, wielding the weapon like a cornered animal. *Shit.*

Matsuo releases him.

Time slows. Adrenaline pumps through my veins. Blocking and grabbing the blade arm with one hand, I pull him off balance. While he falls forward, I strike at the elbow, pushing the weapon to his shoulder. Matsuo removes the knife from his grip, and together, we force him to the ground. His head hits the cement with a thud.

As the thief struggles under restraint, a spark of recognition lights in his size-mismatched pupils. He snarls, "What's a Hiragi clan member doing out here? Hiding 'cause your boss got mowed down? Oh, you wanna make connections with the lady, too, don't ya."

I rip the mask down. Nope, I don't recognize the thief with his square jaw, high hairline, and bushy eyebrows. So, my voice drops in a staccato declaration, "I'm. Done. With. That. Life."

His sneer follows a familiar saying that hits me to the core. "Once in the mob, always in the mob."

Blood rushes in my ears. *This two-bit loser threatens my co-worker, then has the gall to think he understands me?* There's no hesitation as I pull back for a punch.

Matsuo's voice breaks through. "Stop! The cops are here!" Sirens of the squad cruisers wail as they drive up.

Letting the officers cuff the crook, I double over, panting to cover the shame of my past and inability to control my temper. If it weren't for Matsuo, I would have been in a fight and that would put Satou in a tough position. It could have landed me right back in jail.

Throbbing in my hand suggests the angry red of my knuckles will be all kinds of Technicolor by tomorrow. I must have hit it on the cement as we brought the shoplifter down.

The thief's words slur. "Done? Could've fooled me." He motions toward me with his chin. "Officers, why were you bothering with a small fry like me when you got yourself a real yakuza over there? He almost decked me."

Shaken, my head whips up to see him leering and an officer approaching. *They'll never see me as anything more than a gangster.* With eyes squeezed shut, I try to silence the voices.

Matsuo meets the officer in the middle. "Um, Sir... I-I haven't heard Umeji-kun's entire past, but he works with me. Taking down the shoplifter required both of us."

Satou's even voice behind me brings support I couldn't have anticipated. "I'm Umeji's boss and volunteer parole officer. He protected his coworker when that idiot drew a knife. The thief deserves what he got."

After the officers shut their car doors, Satou tilts his head toward the store. "Come on you two."

Cold fills my insides. The retreating cruiser transfixes me as the wind blows hair into my face. *What's gonna happen now?*

Society needs to see I'm not a violent criminal anymore, but the whole store saw me ready to hit that guy. Only when the car is out of sight, do I join the others as the chill turns to a rock in my stomach.

Sensei is the first to greet me inside. "Tatsuya, your hand! Sit." Next, she directs Ohno, "Don't stand there gawking, girl! Get ice!"

In a daze, I plop onto the sturdy bench.

"The hero that disarmed a knife-wielding villain!" Matsuo's slap on the back jolts me to the present. Oblivious to my startled jump, he continues, "Hey man, thanks. I was in trouble 'till you stepped in. How'd you do that?

I've not seen anyone move so fast!"

I shrug, unable to focus on him. "Judo. But I couldn't have done it without you." *Or your warning.*

"Will you show me?" His sentence flows out in practically one word. At my agreement, his puppy grin turns infectious. If Matsuo had a tail, his wag would knock those around him down in his exuberance.

The crowd closes in, with brows furrowed and a barrage of questions. Nothing good comes of being in the spotlight, and I spy a few glares in the sea of faces. *Gotta get outta here.*

Shuffling to a stop, Ohno holds a moldable ice pack and an open jar of a yellow-orange ointment. As I reach for the cold compress before I leave, she sets down the items to grab my fingers, moving them about. "Any breaks?"

Her intense gaze as she inspects my bruised knuckles makes my heart speed up. She's not model perfect, rather a pretty that won't fade over the years. The kind you wouldn't mind seeing with or without makeup.

Several locks of hair have fallen into her face, obscuring her freckles and dark half-moon eyes, but it doesn't faze her. As she turns my hand for a better look, her glossed pink lips purse.

Movement causes my treacherous eyes to focus on what's beyond her gaping collar as she leans over to verify the diagnosis. I'd banished any thoughts about her before because we'd clashed. But the woman sure doesn't have to hide those curves. When I turn away, the heat in her fingers scorches mine.

Her current boldness hints she might deal with injuries often. Can she feel me trembling as the adrenaline rush recedes?

"Nuh-uh," I finally answer. It hurts, but not like a break.

"Good. We don't have to drag you to the clinic." Slathering my hand with the pine and sage-scented balm, she wraps the ice pack on top. "That should help with the bruising." Shoving the jar my way, she urges, "Please, put this on your bruises daily."

"Thanks," I mumble. Why couldn't I say something more intelligent?

Now that the excitement has died down, Satou shoos everyone to work. "Let me get my aunt settled at home. Umeji, you carry the groceries."

Walking to the Mitsubishi, Nakamura leans on my boss. "Ohno-chan couldn't tear her eyes from you as we left, Tatsuya. She's cute, isn't she?"

My head swivels to lock gazes with Ohno through the store's window. That's when my wobbly legs collide with the Mitsubishi, and Sensei ducks inside as she snickers. My coworker walks away, covering her mouth.

The chill wind stings my cheeks. At least I didn't smash anything. Satou glares at my lack of grace before taking the bags.

In the car, Nakamura prattles about when Ohno visited her. Only half listening in the backseat, I stare out the window. Who wants the grandma-type-figure in their life to be gabbing on and on about an attractive girl who might like them?

"You know, she blushed when I shared how it felt to be in your embrace."

That makes me bolt up. Staring wide-eyed at his aunt, Satou realizes his Mitsubishi drifted into the next lane. The quick correction jostles us all.

My mouth opens and closes a few times before the ability to form words returns. "Sensei, please, tell me you didn't do that."

"Why? Every lady wants to know if a man is kind and gentle."

I slam my head against the seat. Did Satou ever have to endure this particular misery, or is it a kitsune game?

Click. It's how Nakamura treats family. The side of kin I didn't get to experience in my teens. Though the realization does nothing to remedy my mortification.

8

CHAPTER 8: TRAINING

Nakamura's tile-roofed house welcomes us with its pair of pine trees standing like butlers ushering visitors down the flower-bordered sidewalk. Separated from the main living space, the kitchen with its ancient wood-burning stove and dining area are much larger than my boss's home and more comfortable.

Once we put the groceries away, Nakamura abandons her walker, starts the kettle, and arranges her tea service. Rubbing my palms together to warm them up, I offer to help.

"Carry this." She holds out the wooden tray with a blue and black wabi-sabi style teapot, cooling bowl, high-quality gyokuro tea, measuring spoon, and three cups on saucers. The irregularly shaped tea-ware stressing the beauty in imperfection must have been expensive. "Join Kazuo. Let me serve you both."

When the kettle whistles, she totters over, pouring water into our cups and the bowl. While the vessels preheat and the water cools enough to avoid a bitter taste, she measures the green tea leaves. Not wasting one drop, she replaces the water in the pot.

Her hand's fluid movements must come from plenty of repetition. How many years has she served from this very set?

In less than a minute, she pours small amounts of the pale green tea, rotating between the cups until they're almost full. With grace, she slides the saucers—first to Satou and me, before serving herself.

My heart swells at being invited to share this with her and Satou. We give a slight bow and say, "Itadakimasu," expressing our gratitude. Taking up our cups in one hand, supporting the bottom with our other, we sip the aromatic, earthy brew. The drink warms my insides as well as my soul.

Sitting at the low table strengthens the familial bond of the ride here as we share some of the best tea I've ever tasted. It's the perfect temperature, refreshing but not sweet or bitter, with the use of high-quality leaves from a brand I can't afford. No words needed. Doing this together is what's important—a bond, a unity.

Replacing the teacup on the saucer with care, I give my thanks.

"Thank you both for helping me today and during my hospitalization." She gives a humble smile.

When my VPO hints we should leave, Sensei says, "Tatsuya, you're ready. Stay for your first lesson."

After seeing Satou out, she pulls a tattered tome from the bookshelf, and we return to the well-lit kitchen table. I strain to get a better look, but she points to a cushion. Then she sets the book down with the care one would place a holy text before sitting next to me.

"Yuki's treatise on Ofuda. The ravages of time destroyed most onmyoudo texts. This volume survived the Ansei Purge, the separation of Shintoism and Buddhism that caused the fall of onmyoudo, the great Kanto Earthquake, multiple wars..." Sheepishly ducking, she adds, "And a fire in my kitchen."

Maybe I can ask another day. For now, my expression remains a pasted on neutral, respectful one. It's not worth the risk of offending her.

Deflating a little, she barrels on. "Starting today, you study magic. After you break through, we'll see where your strengths are. Then I will know if you'll be my replacement here in Nonogawa."

What does she mean? Clamping my mouth shut, I resist asking. Masters are to be listened to and observed. They reveal answers in their own time.

"A technique like this is taught to so few anymore, though many can learn. Teachers must be particular about who they instruct. Know this doesn't make you 'the chosen one' or any such nonsense. Every time you work a spell, you choose what to do with it, good or evil, and who to serve with it, yourself or others. Thus, I charge you with the responsibility to use it well and pass it on to new generations with care."

She opens the cover and guides the pages to lay flat with the reverence one would give a religious relic. "You won't be able to read all of it yet. So, I'll say it aloud. The kanji for the ofuda charms and talismans, though, you've mastered."

Pages have yellowed, but the ink still looks fresh. Touching the vertical lines in the middle of the sheet, she reads his fluid calligraphy style with ease. "Kotodama—The spirit of the word affects all around it with tremendous power to nurture harmony or war, create or destroy, and bring light or darkness. Speak or write each with utmost care and consideration."

Absorbed in her memory, she explains, "Words gain a life of their own after being loosed—often in a different shape than we intended. Seeing that effect, Yuki became a man of few words, but each was important when he spoke.

"Kotodama is the base for all magic, for those of us with natural ability or those like you who have to push through to learn it. As a human, you'll be more limited. It'll cost you more ki—more life energy, as I'm sure you've heard it called. Ki flows through all things, but those able to harness it have a collection point. For you, the space inside has to be opened.

"Ofuda is the easiest style to break through because it utilizes a conduit and less energy overall. In this case, paper and ink. Understand that it's limited to a single use and disappears afterward."

Flipping the page, I see descriptions and diagrams of vertical boxes. She points out a few characters. "He wrote the spells, marring each so we could keep them for future generations. Before that, they handed teachings on talismans down by word of mouth. Otherwise, a diverse collection such as this would cause chaos for kilometers around."

A particular box gains her interest. "Yes, this healing spell. The one Yuki used on me when we met. Considering your injury, it's a good place to start. And it should be easy for you, since it's part of your family name and you know it well."

How can she think I'm ready for that? I'd only practiced basic elementary printing style, not calligraphy.

"Trace the characters with your finger. I'll fetch the ink, brush, and paper."

Hesitantly, I do as told. Running my fingers over the symbols, I recall the strokes. But what I see is frickin' illegible! The marks don't match up with what I'm trying to write, and the kanji become harder to draw, let alone push through for the motion.

Prickling my skin, harsh, scratchy static from the parchment annoys me. Tension gathers under my ribs like something is threatening to tear. When I attempt a quick test, the characters are easier when not on the old tome. To trace on the book's surface is harder again, and it's a struggle to even move my finger across it.

Sensei puts ink and a brush in front of me, before fetching her knitting. With needles clicking away, she watches, allowing me to muddle my way through this. By the end of our session, the supplies still sit there, waiting. I'm not sure I want to see those two symbols again. My hand aches from drawing the strokes repeatedly, and my abdomen swears I've done a thousand sit-ups.

"It can take time to feel the full meaning of a word—to exceed the barrier." As she ushers me to the door, I wish I didn't have to leave her house. Something about it draws me in. Perhaps because it's the first home I was welcomed besides where I live. But a niggle persists in the back of my mind like there's something I'm missing.

"Tatsuya, I won't expect you to keep your study of magic a secret. Though, please only share that you are practicing it with those you trust, and do not share that I'm a kitsune. I've seen very mixed reactions to my kind over the centuries."

Handing me a photocopy of the spell as homework, she adds, "Practice your martial arts each day, too. It'll do more than help burn off the frustration. Because the two disciplines are related, it should assist with the focus to break through."

The martial arts will be easy to do. But the kanji?

* * *

Over the next few days, we read the book's opening phrase, then work on the same word. No improvement. Those calligraphy supplies taunt me. My fingers twitch from the unpleasant paper texture, mini electric shocks of resistance, and sharp twinges in my gut. Yet, Nakamura offers no suggestions.

At the dojo, during my sword drills, I imagine striking those blasted kanji characters.

* * *

Over lunch, I keep practicing.

"Hey, Umeji-kun. Mind if I join you?" Matsuo asks, not giving me a choice as he flops into a seat at the round laminate table.

I'd chosen as usual to sit facing the exit, not for physical safety anymore. Nobody walks in sharing yakuza rumors if they see my face.

Tugging a handful of hair in frustration, I stare unfocused at the page and mumble a noncommittal, "Sure." My hands spasm at the thought of trying again.

Sitting across from me, he inquires, "What's up? I was gonna ask you about that judo takedown, but if this isn't a good time..."

"Nakamura-sensei's assignment, I don't get it. A break would be great."

"Calligraphy?" he prompts.

"Kind of. Edo Era kotodama stuff she made me cram to catch up in kanji for. It's supposed to be a healing talisman. But I have trouble seeing the strokes in it, let alone getting any effect out of writing the characters."

He slides the paper over. With knuckles to his mouth, he considers. "An unusual script, for sure. Do you believe in this stuff?"

"Sensei does. It'd be easier to accept if I could get it. Though studying keeps me out of trouble."

Peeking over my shoulder, Ohno asks. "What's this?" Her cheerful voice grates on my nerves, despite a hope she'll join us.

"Homework," I grumble. Sitting at our table, she examines the writing as I explain.

She's quick to comment. "You sound almost defeated. After the other day's excitement, I'm surprised to see this attitude. The two of you took down that shoplifter. There was no doubt in your actions. You aren't going about this half-hearted, are you?"

"Women's intuition is scary sometimes," Matsuo mutters.

My glare causes Ohno to push away from the table. So I backpedal. "Sorry. Don't go. I'm just so fed up with trying the same thing and getting nowhere."

Tilting her head, she opens her bento box. "You said you know judo, right?" At my agreement, she clarifies, "How many times did you have to practice the move you did yesterday to be effective at it?"

"A lot. But that came naturally."

"So? Learning is about the journey. There aren't shortcuts. Accept the discipline—the whole of it. You'll get this."

I rub the kink out of my neck from hunching over the last two days. Maybe I can wheedle Sensei for more info. "Understood." To change the subject, I display the reverse side of my palm. "That ointment you gave me did wonders. It's almost healed. Will you share the recipe?"

Pleased, but embarrassed by the attention, she stares at her food. "Glad it helped. Family secret, sorry."

Matsuo leans forward. "Ohno-san, you could make a fortune on that salve!"

"I couldn't! Mom wasn't happy that I shared that jar."

Pulling the container from my pocket, I shove it her way. "Don't want to get you in trouble. Here."

She gives a soft head shake. "Please, keep it. Just don't tell anyone."

"Ohno-san, what gives? Why the secret, when it works so well?"

Surveying the room, she ensures we're alone. "Promise not to tell anyone else?"

We agree. Who could resist?

Furiously, she types on her phone, holding up the message. 'My family practices old spells. The potion kind plus a few others.' Then she erases it.

Pantomiming the question, I point to my hand.

She mouths, "Magic." Louder she says, "Arnica." At our blank looks, Ohno adds, "It's a medicinal herb. Great for curing bruises and reducing pain. Just don't eat it, 'cause ingested, it's poisonous."

Not that I'd lick the salve. But why didn't she say something about that before giving it to me?

Matsuo holds up my writing. "How's that different from this?"

Frowning, she jabs at the device again. 'Onmyoudo, that's an accepted use, well documented in history. The balm is not, because of modern medical science. They might think I'm... Never mind. You two were already discussing that kind of thing, so I figured it was safe. My family had trouble in the last place we lived.'

Mie flounces in. Her demeanor changes as Ohno erases the message and hides her phone. Rounding on her, Mie blasts, "What? Now, you're best friends with the yakuza and talking about me?"

Stricken, Ohno falters, "Mie-chan..."

What can I do? She's not wrong about me. But she hurt Ohno, who doesn't trust her with the secret.

Standing as he grits his teeth, Matsuo leans on the table, "You've gone too far, Mie-san! You weren't here when Umeji-kun helped me deal with the armed shoplifter. He did this amazing takedown!"

"So? He probably learned that in the mob." Marking her defiance, her fists jab into her hips.

"You're always putting people down, Mie-san—" Matsuo fires at her.

They can't get caught up in the burden of my past. Cutting off Matsuo's retort, my hand slices through the air to reinforce my clipped word, "Enough!"

Hopefully, pinching the bridge of my nose will fend off the oncoming stress headache. "Matsuo-kun, thanks, man, for standing up for me. You can't know what a rare experience that is."

Next, I address my accuser. "I'm the problem here, so I'll leave. But Ohno-chan was showing us how my knuckles should look today. The pictures were graphic with lots of bruising. I'd bet she didn't want to ruin your meal. Lay off."

With fingers going to her lips, Ohno whispers the friendly suffix I'd used. Sensei says it so much that it slipped from my mouth. I'll apologize later.

When I sneak behind the store, I try to cool down. It's only an alley. But it's quiet. So, I lean against the brick wall and splay my fingers in my hair. Refreshing frosty air rushes into my lungs, reviving after the stifling disagreement.

Can I shut out the world for a few moments? *Idiot.* Why should their friendliness last? They know what I am.

The door squeaks as Ohno peeks around the frame. "Umeji-kun?" Her soft voice makes it impossible to stay irritated.

"Hmm?" My hands tuck into my pockets out of habit.

"Oh, sorry! Am I bothering you?"

"It's ok if it's you."

Perking up, she shoves the folded photocopy toward me. "You forgot this."

"Uh, thanks."

"You stuck up for me earlier." Her words rush out and the tiny grin she tries to hide could disarm even the most callous man.

"It was the least I could do. Sorry for using such a familiar suffix with your name. Sensei calls you that, and it slipped out."

"I don't mind." Clasping her hands in front, she sways then disappears into the building.

9

CHAPTER 9: THE BREAK

Later, Matsuo catches me. "Hey Umeji-kun, I got distracted earlier by the magic stuff. You said you'd show me how you disarmed the thief."

Practice should help my core muscles, sore from yesterday's onmyoudo training. "I did. I'm off at 2 pm. After that?"

"Perfect. I'll swing by about 4:30."

My coworker shows up carrying a padded bo—a wooden staff. I'd probably have to sit on him to get him to stop bouncing. "I've been looking forward to this since I saw you do that move."

Something in his happy, open manner keeps loosening the locked-down shell I'd built over the last decade to protect the real me. "Not obvious at all."

He gives me a shove.

With a grin, I lead him to the dojo. The polished wood floor gleams from the lights overhead. A calligraphy scroll and photo of Satou's father—who taught him karate—are the sole decorations in the simple plaster walled room.

After we bow in, he says, "Wow, I wasn't sure what to expect when the boss said it was a redone outbuilding. You two really spruced this place up!"

"This and the little shrine I help maintain have been a refuge."

"Look Umeji, I'm s—"

I wave the apology off. He only did what was expected after finding out my

54

past. In his place, I'd have backed off, too. But he gave me a second chance. "It's fine. Really."

Pulling a wooden tanto dagger from the weapons rack and giving my respects, I walk him through the steps to disarm before he attempts it with resistance. Then we try it real time.

I advance with the knife like the thief did. Matsuo is lightning fast as he blocks and grabs my arm, hurtling me forward and forcing my elbow to bend with the dagger pointing at my shoulder.

When he shoves me down, I freeze up. *Breathe. He's not handcuffing you.*

Matsuo must sense the tension. He doesn't pry the wooden weapon from my grasp. True to his friendly puppy nature, he offers me a hand up then stretches. "Oh man, I missed sparring! Since Genta moved, I haven't had anyone to practice with. Wanna keep going?"

Until today, training was always deadly serious. I nod, not wanting the camaraderie of the moment to end. So, we scurry to don our kendo gear. Mine is borrowed and we had to replace the cords, but it was kind of Satou to ask about a set for me to use.

I tie the tenugui towel over my head as a sweatband and slip on my helmet. "I'd been wanting to practice more than by myself! Kendo's not Satou-san's gig. But he hopes to have the space be a public dojo someday and stocked the place. Says the kids need an outlet as much as we do." The shinai, a slatted bamboo training sword, balances well in my hands.

"I won't hold back," Matsuo twirls his bo, halting it as the weapon tucks under his shoulder. Giving a mischievous wink, he motions, then drops into a solid stance with one hand on the end of the staff and the other in the middle.

I start with a standard sword strike to the head. Blocking, he makes three quick ones to disable my return blows. The typhoon force kiai shouted with his strikes rings in my ears. Shifting out of the way, I drop my shinai over my shoulder to shield my upper body.

"Gonna have to do better than that, Umeji-kun!"

My happy-go-lucky friend can be fierce, too. Excellent. He seems to favor the right side. I attack from the other at his midsection. So he jumps away and jabs toward my ribs then deflects my next assault from underneath.

In a flash, Matsuo wraps the bo around my wrist, spinning me as if I'm only a leaf in the wind. *How the heck did he do that?* Despite attacking many times, only once do I land a strike.

Thwack, thwack! His second hit sends a sharp spike of pain just above my elbow where only the padded gi sleeve covers. If this wasn't practice my arm would be useless now. As it is, I'll be slowed.

"Jeez, Matsuo-kun. You're fast." I circle, looking for an opening.

"You weren't toying with me?"

"Nuh-uh. I'm best at hand to hand. Though, practicing with you will push me to improve my sword work." My elbow smarts and cramps up. I try to shake it out.

"Let's rest to ice your arm."

"Want a drink?"

Inside, we find our boss at the blanketed warming table writing up my weekly parole report. "Enjoying yourselves?"

"Yeah, despite Matsuo-kun kicking my butt!" I share while pouring a couple of waters.

"He humored me. We started with my favorite, so next is his." His eyebrows raise as he adds. "If you're up for it."

"I will be."

After offering him a glass, I dash upstairs, skipping every other step to fetch Ohno's jar, slather on the ointment, tromp down again in double time, and gulp down my drink to give a satisfied sigh. "Ready!"

Leaning on the legless chair, Satou lets his normally dour expression warm. "Glad you two get along well. I'll cook gyuudon tonight. There'll be plenty to share."

"Awesome! Mom hardly ever makes beef." Matsuo's wide grin could rival a Cheshire cat.

Most days, it's me who has to do the domestic work. I bow deep but quick. "Thanks, Boss!"

Going head-to-head, Matsuo's broader circular movements aren't as effective if I move in to grab his clothing. That way, I can grapple or trip him to the ground.

He throws me several times in a row when he puts more distance between us. Though, not as often as I force him to the floor. He's not had to fight for his life like I did.

For once, the vicious animal inside me doesn't have to kill or win. Every thud of one of us hitting the mat gives me more enthusiasm. I'm gonna sleep so well tonight.

Satou walks in to see me recover from a throw and pin Matsuo, before calling us for dinner. *Man, is it time already?* My stomach growls on cue.

Our boss tilts his head toward the house. "You two are a good match, able to teach each other your strengths."

Wafting from the kitchen, the smells of onion, beef, and rice make my stomach rumble even more. Steaming bowls of gyuudon piled high wait for us on the table. I've not eaten this well since my dad died, even when living the yakuza high life.

"Matsuo, I'd like you to teach me the bo," I request, before scarfing down a piece of meat. The workout made me so hungry that I might ask for thirds.

"You mean you want me to give you more bruises?" He winks.

"Not too many, 'cause I learn fast! Had to." No need to go into detail about those times. Awkwardness hangs in the room, so I cover by shoving in another bite.

Rescuing me, Satou asks, "So you're experiencing a late taste of boyhood?"

"Yeah."

Together, Matsuo and I hold our bowls up for seconds.

Later, Satou drops me off so I can make it to Sensei's on time. The sun set an hour and a half ago, so Sensei brings an oil lamp to our working space and her needles click away, eating up the yarn from the ball. A warm glow adds to the peace in the room.

After sitting at the low table and reciting the opening phrase in the tome, I attack those kanji with renewed vigor. Sensei looks up from her knitting, though her hands still work.

Then doubt ghosts whisper again. *I'll never be as talented as the man who wrote this. Why even try? Isn't this only an old superstition, anyway?* My finger punctuates each line against the book's resistance as pain stabs me in the solar plexus where Sensei says my ki pool should reside.

Beside me, she tsks. "Tatsuya! You have no quarrel with the book or spell. Stop poking at it, or you'll damage the manuscript. Internal griping doesn't help. Words you allow your mind to focus on are what you end up saying about yourself. Instead, concentrate on the task at hand."

My fists ball up and my fingernails dig into my palms. "Sorry. What is it I don't understand, Sensei?"

Her mouth shoves sideways before she says, "Passing the mental barrier is hard for humans, who aren't magical by nature. Granted, I've not trained anyone in a long time, and I forget human limitations. My Yukitada sometimes had to remind me of the difficulties he had learning. So, I'll show you what you're aiming for."

Holding out her palm as she chants, blue kitsune fire flares into existence above it and the air shimmers. "Mind, spirit, and body must be in sync. Concentrate on each word and character. Think about it stroke by stroke. Say the phrase out loud as you draw it. What does it mean? What do you want from it? Be relentless."

Reading the inscription aloud, she has me repeat it. She traces the characters as if it requires no effort as she guides my hand. Blurring then taking on more familiar shapes, the figures become legible. To extinguish the fire, her palm closes—as if nothing out of the ordinary just happened. But the shivers won't stop running up and down my spine.

Glancing to her, to the book, and back, I draw out the words, "What was that?"

"You saw through my eyes. But I couldn't show you the feel of the will, because that comes from inside you. It's similar to the shout in martial arts." She pokes below my rib cage for emphasis. "It adds the power of the word. Now, try again."

Fixated, not on the resistance but the kanji themselves, I trace the symbols in their alien calligraphy. With air that comes from my sore diaphragm, I bark the phrase as a command.

My arm moves as if through still water. Taking my breath away, something expands sharply under my ribs. In a shimmer, the strokes shift, solidifying into my personal writing form.

Whoa! I lean closer to verify what happened. Then, with gleeful ease, I retrace the characters.

My teacher's arm sweeps, indicating the calligraphy supplies. "You broke through, didn't you? That's the level of concentration you'll need for all your work. Write it for real this time."

The crisp, clean bamboo-based paper is cool to the touch as I use a hand to keep it in place. Picking up the brush, I dip it into the black ink, refusing to rush creating the characters.

Bristles mark the dots and check for 'water,' the angled elbow for 'self,' and the squared open 'mouth' for 'peace'. The straight and curlicue strokes for the verb ending complete 'heal.'

Sunshine warmth runs up my arm through the handle, and I gasp when the symbols sizzle with sparks. Running my fingers over the warm paper, all I can do is stare slack jawed.

"Impressive for your first talisman, if I say so myself. You can increase the effect as your skills improve, depending on how much ki you're willing to expend. Though we can only use each ofuda on one part of the body. Be aware that the power behind the spells must come from you or use energy freely given to you, otherwise things can go very wrong. But we will talk more about this another time. Now, to determine how you did. Thanks to Ohno-chan's magic, your bruises healed. So, we need a different test."

"You know about Ohno-chan?" *She wanted that kept secret.*

"Of course. I sense it. Her kindness paired with her natural talent and astonishing ki capacity are another reason I think well of Ohno-chan. She'd be good for you. Rare women like her, require a dependable partner or things go badly for them and those around them."

Shuffling over to the kitchen, Sensei pulls something from the drawer. I'm about to redirect the conversation but freeze at the glinting edge of Sensei's blade.

"Bring the ofuda here." The dead calm in her voice raises the hair on the nape of my neck.

A decade of honed instinct causes me to retreat a step. So, I hold out the paper from a distance. My scars are witness to the reinforced lesson never to trust people who carry knives.

Instead of attacking me, she slices her palm to the bone, hissing at the pain. Moving it over the sink, she keeps the spreading mess off the floor.

Hand wounds are nasty. *Why the hell'd she pick that?* At least, she didn't turn on the overhead light for the gore to be on full display. Plenty of brightness from the other room illuminates the blood streaming into the sink, causing my stomach to lurch.

"The ofuda, please." She requests in halted words, setting down the blade.

"Oh." The adrenaline rush halts, making my knees wobble.

Draping the charm on her palm, I'm careful to cover the whole wound as sparks flow into the gash. But she has to hold the paper in place. So, I pat my pockets for my handkerchief and tie the talisman over her cut. Then blackness threatens to close in, and I have to sit down.

"We'll know by tomorrow how effective it is," she says matter-of-factly. Changing topics so fast it makes me blink, she returns to the one she enjoys torturing me with. "Well then, has Ohno-chan confessed her feelings to you yet?"

"Uhhh."

She scowls and thunks my head with her uninjured fist. "Tatsuya, you're not broken, are you?"

Did that just happen? My "No, she didn't," comes out all too lame.

"Darn. I thought she would."

Time to change the subject. "Will you tell me more about Tsuchimikado-san? You said his choices were important."

"Yes. Before that, let's give you a bit of protection. Now that you're unlocked for onmyoudo—we can't leave you open to the dangers out there. A new magic user makes an easy target."

She leans down to tap my sternum twice, muttering a few words, before the distinctive blue glow encompasses me. "These are dangerous times. More is going on than you're aware of, so I put two layers of magic in place. Do not assume other yokai will care for your wellbeing, even other kitsune.

Since you know of our existence and have magic ability, you should be able to discern facades. This protection will not make you invulnerable. It will wink out when it's spent. Remember that."

"Yes, Sensei." Then a light bulb turns on. "Speaking of being able to see through disguises, is it ki use that lets you get around not saying 'shi'?"

"Figured that out, did you? I'll count for you to see it. Ichi, ni, san..." As if via ventriloquist, the 'shi' comes from off-center.

"If I didn't know, I wouldn't guess it's not you."

Her nose wrinkles at the compliment, but she waves it off. "I've had a few centuries to perfect it. Scoot to the table. Make yourself comfortable for the story. Today, you'll see why you can't trust all of my kind. My journal and the letters will help me recall the dates and details better."

10

CHAPTER 10: JOYS AND TROUBLES

Nakamura, March 30, 1854, Kyoto:

Wards, to misdirect any curious passersby, hid my family's den, nestled into the hillside. I had to reassure Tsuchimikado, as he led the horse I rode, that the impulse to leave the area was part of the projection and there was indeed a door if we continued straight up to the cliff face.

His lips pressed into a fine line before he helped me dismount. The wound still made movement stiff and uncomfortable. But I wasn't in danger from it any longer. Did the samurai think I was leading him into a trap as revenge for shooting me?

"I am trusting you, Tsuchimikado-san. My family does not admit strangers."

His face only relaxed a tad. "Why can't I detect the magic?"

Before taking a big breath, I shrugged and placed my hand on the stone slab. A haze cleared to reveal a wall of spring green plaster above dark wood paneling. The natural linen noren entry curtain with my family's crest of a circle enclosing three heart-shaped petals over a rounded triangle waved in the gentle breeze. When the samurai rubbed his eyes, unable to comprehend the powerful magic outside his specialty, the chilly ride here was worth it.

At the entrance, doubts crept in. Was exposing the location of my family's den the right thing? My mouth went dry as I slid open the shoji door. We removed our footwear in the wood paneled entry.

My sister was the first to greet us, nuzzling my leg with her black nose. Then spotting the man behind me, she yipped. "I'll fetch Father." With a nudge before leaving, she spoke in our fox language, "So this handsome one explains your absence?"

I looked away, leading my guest to our stone walled, spacious tatami floored front room. He gulped as he gazed around the open dwelling, extravagant compared to his own. Light filtered in from the shoji windows to highlight the well-executed art scroll and flower arrangement in the carved-out display alcove.

Kneeling on a cushion, the samurai set his swords by his right side to show his good intentions, then gripped the knees of his hakama. Was it fear from what he'd done or that my father would not listen? His case of nerves only twisted my insides.

The rest of my family greeted the warrior in their human form. Mother beckoned me to her side. I would have rather sat beside Tsuchimikado, but I did as told. Between my clan and the samurai was a small brazier with a set that mother served tea from as we shared the incident.

Father was the first to respond. "Hisako, our numbers dwindle every year. Yet, you have the gall to give reckless, whim-based promises to a mere human. Consider your duty to your kind and kin! Don't make me end this human for you to understand our plight."

He was more upset with me than the man who'd shot his daughter? My mouth gaped wide enough for a gnat to buzz inside. But I didn't choke on the insect. Instead, it was Father's scathing words—ones that caused me to dig in my heels. Only on the outside could I humble myself, kneeling and bowing my head.

My spirit raged red hot. "Father, please do not make such an unjust ultimatum. This man more than compensated, by healing me. For that, I defend him."

"So, he earned your admiration by ruining your reputation? Child, I know the rumors."

Jumping up, Tsuchimikado had his sword in hand. "I'd paid that doctor well enough to keep his mouth shut. Nakamura-sama, I swear the only physical attention your daughter received from me was medical. I walked, leading the horse she rode. I slept outside while she dozed and stayed warm inside my hut. I did everything in consideration of her higher standing. I can't expect her to uphold the marriage offer. But that braggart will pay for his insolence and the harm done to your daughter's reputation!"

The warrior was indignant not over the threat to his life, but the one to my position in society. His selfless defense made my heart swell. Oh, I prayed I could follow through on the proposal, even if I'd spoken it recklessly.

"I verified this before you two arrived. It was the doctor's gossiping wife. Tsuchimikado-san, I see from your reaction the rumors were unfounded. Thank you for returning my daughter. You may take your leave." Father crossed his arms, ending the discussion.

He let me accompany the disappointed samurai to the edge of our property.

* * *

Even weeks later, my family limited my range to sight distance from our den, beyond that I had to be chaperoned. While it was irksome, fighting it would only make my parents restrict me more.

It was important to encourage Tsuchimikado, so he wouldn't give up on me. Not just because I liked him, but I wanted some say in whom I married. This thoughtful, humble man was my best bet, despite many potential suitors from other kitsune clans.

Males are rare among our species. Those that visited were spoiled rotten or didn't want an independent wife. Exposing their vanity was easy. Not long after they announced being interested in the beautiful daughter of Nakamura, I sent each packing. Father worried over the plight of our kind because the entire generation seemed to consist of self-important idiots.

It took several days to befriend a crow to carry my magical messages to the one-room house I remembered so fondly. My heart leaped for joy each time a shikigami puppet spirit delivered a reply to my messages in the middle of the night. Each paper servant had a poem written on it and carried a sprig of whatever the warrior found in bloom.

After I released the attached spirit, I tucked every note into my journals. One, in particular, was my favorite:

Days spent in darkness

No spark without word from you

Then blaze in your light

* * *

After a month and a half, Father calmed. Mother invited the samurai's parents to meet at an inn. The two groups felt it would be best for my reputation, and that of both houses, if Tsuchimikado and I married. Even my parents could see the reasoning, despite their desire for me to wed within my species and rank.

Families normally arranged upper-class marriages to improve each side's level in society. It would enhance the Tsuchimikado family's standing. So, I counted myself fortunate to have my pick of a husband and to fulfill my promise to the kind onmyouji who healed me. My clan was known in human form and spoke well of my fiancé, so it didn't take long to receive permission to marry from our daimyo, the feudal lord of our region.

* * *

In April, I completed my training to learn how to be a proper wife, and we were married. On his side, it was a simple affair, and we kept the ceremony to his immediate kin. On mine, it was a significant event! Such a gathering of foxes had not been seen since the marriage of Abe no Seimei's father to his kitsune bride in the tenth century.

All who attended wanted to meet the warrior who quietly practiced onmyoudo and had the good fortune to marry for love. The procession trail of kitsune bi—fox fire—ranged kilometers, carrying me and a generous dowry to my fiancé.

Greeting me before the ceremony at the shrine my family managed, he whispered in my ear. "I will always regret that my aim was true the day we met. But I cannot regret meeting you, my Hime."

I may not have been an actual princess, but he made me feel I was. What did it matter that his ancestors fought on the wrong side of the Battle of Sekigahara? He was from a long line of onmyouji, and he cared for me. We would continue that lineage, bringing joy to both families.

Yes, I learned to use chopsticks. So, after we drank sake together to seal the bond between our houses, I put on the beautiful red and gold kosode robe—his wedding present to me. Then I ate using the utensils for the feast. His warm smile, when he saw me showing off the new skill, filled me with a radiant glow.

My Yuki and I were happy. We moved to a larger home than his old one-room dwelling. My dowry helped us provide for his aging parents, and we found a scribe position for his brother.

* * *

A month later, we received news of Yuki's childhood companion and his interactions with the Shogunate controlled government, the Bakufu, that set the course for our lives.

> My dear friend, forgive my not writing sooner, but I have only yesterday been given access to paper, ink, and brush. Obviously, I had to write to my father first. Do not be alarmed, I am alive and healthy.
>
> From our last visit, you are aware of my feelings. The Shogunate has lost legitimacy through forsaking its most important duty—to

the Emperor. This you may not yet know, and it only solidifies my case. The Shogunate committed our country to a disadvantageous treaty without the consent of our glorious Emperor.

We cannot allow Japan to become a mere colony! We are the Divine Land and shall never be conquered nor looked down upon. But we must modernize to remain so, while not giving up the spirit that makes us truly unique as a people.

Do you recall how I wished to study Western technology? Going abroad should not be an offense! Kaneko-san and I snuck aboard Admiral Perry's ship, requesting passage. It was unfortunate he had just negotiated the alliance with the Shogunate. My request would have violated it. So, I was outraged not only at being denied asylum but that the refuser was the very one who forced the high-handed agreement!

Despite it all, we did the honorable thing and turned ourselves in. We were arrested and stuck in a cramped cell where it is hard to sleep or eat. Kaneko-san and I have reason to suspect the Admiral inquired after so callously sending us to our fate since we did not receive the death sentence for our disobedience.

At least my good brother brings us books to study, so our minds won't grow dim.

If you would respond, I'd be grateful.

The tenth day of the fourth month, Ansei 1 (May 6, 1854)
    At Demmacho Prison in Edo, Yoshida Shoin
    To Tsuchimikado Yukitada, Kyoto

The news distressed my Yuki so much he didn't eat or sleep for two days. Writing to all our connections, he pleaded for help for his friend. Worn out and unable to think, he withdrew into himself.

Concern nagged at me as I paced. When I could take no more, I intervened. "What if we go to Edo? There we'd be better able to assess the situation and offer assistance."

"Yes. Though you'll stay. In this turbulent political climate, it could be dangerous in Edo." My husband felt a wife's input was not required.

Now Yuki knew he'd married a strong-willed, opinionated fox. He wasn't foolish enough to assume my guise would make me like a demure human woman. Wanting to protect me so much that his fierceness reared its head, he was a force to be reckoned with. And I was his match.

After our first real argument, I emerged the winner—in name only. He allowed me to accompany him. But the cost? Broken heirlooms and wounded hearts.

Since we had a solid plan, he allowed himself sustenance. I reconciled in the tenderest of ways for every unkind word I'd said. With our bodies entwined, I stroked his long hair, and he slept.

* * *

We settled in Edo a year later, after receiving the proper permission. The trip was hard because of my pregnancy and I gave birth in June 1855 to our son, Kinya.

"Hisako, will our child have your magical abilities?" Yuki asked.

My eyes closed as I replied, hoping that the truth wouldn't disappoint him. "No, he's human. Natural magic only passes on to full-blooded kitsune. He'll have a talent for learning ki usage, like his father."

Patting his son's head, he said, "The boy will be a powerful practitioner if he wishes."

After Kinya slept more through the night, Yuki began recording his knowledge of onmyoudo. There was less call for its use by members of the government as we transitioned to modern ways, and he didn't want to let the learning slip away.

To bring manuscripts and missives, we visited Yoshida-san almost every day. He studied them with his fellow prisoners and even his jailers. If his mind was busy, he was content. Seeing our son grow pleased him.

On the way to the market one day, I encountered a woman whose magical guise I could see through. Since she was my junior in the fox sphere, she only had two tails compared to my three. Her clothes indicated that, in human terms, she was far above my station and her feminine form would stop the heart of any man she wished.

I wasn't jealous, but she put me ill at ease for reasons I couldn't pinpoint. After acknowledging me, she continued on her way.

* * *

November brought the Great Ansei Earthquake. My animal instincts for flight in the face of natural disasters saved us. Our entire house fell as we reached the street. Fires spread from inside hearths.

After ensconcing Kinya and I on the outskirts of town, Yuki returned to check on Yoshida-san. We had nightmares of death and devastation.

* * *

At the turn of the year, we visited a photographer for the novelty of having our photo taken. Because it was cold, we bundled up. Yuki's hair was a little wild after we removed our heavy winter gear. Why didn't we fix it?

The government transferred Yoshida-san to house arrest back in Hagi, far to the West. In encouragement, Yuki reminded him of the importance of the word and its power. If our friend had to remain in his room, then perhaps he could still influence the world.

* * *

Spring brought a surprise visitor arriving in a palanquin who turned out to be the other kitsune. Chills ran down my spine, not only because we're a territorial race but something seemed off.

What could she need from my family and me? Only out of respect for her position and her polite request to speak with me, did I invite her in for tea.

Sitting primly on a cushion, she held her fan as if sharing a secret. "You may call me Date. And I'm eager to confide in a fellow shapeshifter. Are you aware that Chief Minister Ii has taken me as his mistress?"

Nodding, I poured our best hojicha tea. Did she think the bragging would impress anyone? We kitsune are a sensual race, but that doesn't mean that selling oneself for a high position is looked well upon.

Still, I figured I should be polite. "My name is Nakamura. A pleasure to make your acquaintance."

As we drank, she adjusted her kimono. "Are you happy in your current position as the wife of a low-ranked sword for hire? I wonder. You weren't forced into marriage, were you? Because I can't understand your choice."

I gave a clipped retort. "Unlike many, mine is a love match."

"Forgive my intrusion." Fanning herself, she shrugged—an indifferent gesture, contrary to her words. Her attitude caused my teeth to grind, but she ignored my response. "So, did your husband talk Yoshida-san into working his influence despite captivity?"

My cup stopped halfway to my lips. Yet, she persisted, "Ii-sama has an extensive spy network. It would be wise if you both kept your distance from Yoshida-san."

Niceties be damned! Whores who sold themselves for lofty positions have no say in this house. Standing and pointing to the door, I raised my voice, "You exhausted your welcome." No way would I give her the satisfaction of what I knew.

Stomping out, she had to have the last word. "Don't say I didn't warn you."

Following that experience, Yuki and I warded our home.

* * *

When news reached us that Yuki's mother was ill, we moved back to the capital. Arriving just in time, we said our goodbyes. She was the best of in-laws. So kind, so accepting. Not all would allow a fox into their clan.

* * *

We received another letter from Yoshida-san.

> Thank you for continuing to write to me after you returned to Kyoto. It's good to receive news of the outside—in any form. So young Kinya is walking now? How fast he grows!
>
> I spend my days teaching any who will visit my uncle's school at whatever time they come. You were right, I can reach the youth of our nation. This brings me contentment.
>
> We study what interests them. Some say they want to learn to read. But I've said it repeatedly: Learning for the sake of knowledge is of no use. It should lead to action. We should be the 'twenty-one times audacious samurai,' not blind followers of the foolish Bakufu that abandoned its true purpose—to serve the Divine Emperor.
>
> The students are my everything. So I've chosen to teach them as a friend and learn alongside them, instead of a teacher over pupils. Uncle has honored me with the headmaster's position.
>
> It will amuse you that sometimes we all fall asleep in class, because we stayed up all night, so engrossed in our studies were we.
>
> Is there anyone else nearby that isn't ashamed of me? If so, please pass my letter on to them.
>
> The fifth day of the fourth month, Ansei 3 (May 8, 1856)
> At my uncle's house in Higa, Yoshida Shoin
> To Tsuchimikado Yukitada, Kyoto

We shared the letter with our family.

Yuki finished compiling and reorganizing his tome on ofuda and kotodama. Excellent timing, because his lord transferred my husband to be the captain of our local police station. It was a demotion, and he didn't enjoy the job. Though, we were grateful for the income. We believe the nobleman was in a great deal of debt but tried to provide for those he couldn't afford to keep employed.

Our daughter, Kanoko, was born. She was much louder than her older brother. When Yuki said she'd be like me, I poked him in the ribs.

* * *

Two years later, I asked what sin had I committed that the gods would do such a terrible thing to us.

Unable to face my husband, I secluded myself in the forest for weeks after the miscarriage on June 4.

When Yuki found me, I was almost feral in my misery and grief, snapping and growling. Undaunted, he picked up my muddy, unkempt fox form and tucked me into his kimono against his bare chest.

"Your sister divined your location. If you're ready to speak, I'll listen." Holding me there, he waited for what may have been hours as I struggled to pull myself together enough for words.

"Why would the kami end a late pregnancy? Take our second son from us?" I sobbed.

Crushing me to his chest, he carried me home, refraining from saying more.

* * *

Near the end of summer the next year, news reached us. Chief Minister Ii Naosuke had signed the Harris Treaty with the West.

Yoshida-san wrote regarding his displeasure of the current political climate and how unpopular the agreement was. Our comrade's pro-Emperor views to unite the country became increasingly radical. Yuki worried for him every day.

Adding to those fears, Ii and cohorts rounded up the opposition. Several were Yoshida-san's students. Our friend's political activism brought him into the Bakufu's sights.

Not long later, I heard a terrible keening. Yuki had collapsed on the ground, with a pair of letters in his hand.

My dear friend, they have moved me to Edo again. I stand accused of attempting to assassinate one of Ii's servants, who was bringing a request to the Emperor for support of the West's terrible agreement. But I could not, and still cannot remain silent while the Bakufu destroys the Imperial government. Holding my head high, I declared the truth at my hearing and am prepared for my execution.

Thank you for all the encouragement you've given me through the years.

The twenty-ninth day of the ninth month, Ansei 6 (October 24, 1859)

At Sakurada in Edo, Yoshida Shoin

To Tsuchimikado Yukitada, Kyoto

It is with a heavy heart that I write. But we felt you should know, the Shogunate beheaded Yoshida-san three days ago. He faced the end, calm and dignified.

Our brilliant teacher was another victim in the Ansei Purge. He believed that his beheading would inspire future revolutionaries. And it will.

Until we are ready to act, I must remain anonymous. Please forgive my cowardice.

The fifth day of the tenth month, Ansei 6 (October 30, 1859)

A student of Yoshida-sensei

To Tsuchimikado Yukitada, Kyoto

* * *

My Yuki uttered not a sound for a week after Yoshida-san's death. Guilt haunted him, causing him to regret encouraging his companion to voice his beliefs and influence our country's youth. The power of the word truly was a double-edged sword.

Yuki still felt that it was essential to bring change, but losing Yoshida-san shook him to the core. Gone were the simple hopes of speaking for reform.

From that day forward, Yuki used his words with extreme care. I missed the playful banter we used to engage in, so I cursed Ii and Date for taking our innocence.

Another message arrived. This time from the vixen witch, gloating over Yoshida's death. In a rage, I burned it before Yuki saw it, asking the gods to let her tails wither and fall off. Those hateful letters of hers would not reap more havoc.

That night, Kinya repeated my vicious words about the message in front of his father. So, I confessed to my husband what I'd done. He needed to know Date remained a threat in order for us to act together for the protection of our household.

(Present Day) December

"Date is still around." The room feels unnaturally cold as my teacher closes her journal.

11

CHAPTER 11: POWER'S BURDEN

On my next shift's lunch break, I share last night's experiences with Matsuo. Of course, he wants a demonstration. "Do you think it'll work with plain old paper?"

My shoulders rise and fall to say, 'no clue'.

After rummaging through the break room cupboards and drawers, my co-worker scoots a pen and napkin my way, then folds his hands.

For the zillionth time, I write the kanji for healing and emulate the concentration needed. Those characters are so burned into my brain it's automatic.

The paper gives resistance, making it harder to move the pen. Sparks scorch the napkin and spread as if the magic knows it's not the perfect medium for the spell.

"No, no, no!" To stop the sharp smoke smell from spreading, I stuff it under my lunch box.

"Cool! Do it again, so I can be sure I just saw that!" Matsuo says as he examines the napkin.

"Don't need the fire alarm going off."

He grabs a bottled water from the vending machine, opens it, and sets it down on the table. "There."

"Well, here goes."

As he holds the paper up and babbles his excitement, Ohno walks in, halting

75

and sniffs.

Matsuo points to the napkin's inscription. "Check this out! I wouldn't have believed it if I hadn't seen it myself!"

Her attention darts to me with the stoniest frown, then away before tramping past us. Fetching her lunch, she leaves without a word.

"What gives with Ohno-san?" Matsuo asks.

"Dunno," I stare, fixed on the spot she left, reeling in the heavy weight of her judgment.

"The glare wasn't at me, so she's mad at YOU for something."

The sour taste in my mouth prompts me to act. "Better find out why."

So, I tuck the papers into my pants pocket and follow. My lope speeds up when she's not around the corner. Checking everywhere in the store doesn't yield her location.

But Mie is out back. She pounces. "Stay away from her! Whatever you said or did upset her badly! She won't talk about it even with me, and I've known her since she moved to Nonogawa! She deserves better than a shitty criminal like you. You got that YA-KU-ZA?"

Her biting response causes my head to ache and my voice to turn cold. "Mie."

"I'm not afraid of you!" She steps forward in challenge.

Is it defiance or stupidity? In the blink of an eye, I could have her down on the cement begging for mercy. A grab of the wrist, a sweep of the feet, and an arm behind her shoulder. Show her she should give me respect. My body tenses. On auto pilot, my arm darts forward.

Her eyes narrow and her mouth turns up in an I-told-you-so smirk, as if she could read my mind.

The blood drains from my face. *Idiot!* Only a monster would assault Ohno's friend. She was pushing buttons so she could call the cops and be rid of me, wasn't she?

Spinning around with my back to her, I kick the ground. "What the fuck?!" My head droops, and my fists clench. "Yeah, Ohno-san deserves better. I know what I am, 'cause I gotta live with the memories every single stinkin' day. Right now, I just gotta apologize."

"She's at the park. If you don't—"

To skip her oncoming threat, I beeline it in an all-out sprint through the parking lot, down the road, and across it. A black Lexus sedan lays on its horn as if shouting 'Watch where you're going!' Swerving, it screeches at an angle far into the crosswalk. *Sunday driver!*

My eyes lock on Ohno, as the car knocks me astern with an intense blue flash and a loud cracking sound. Not wanting to lose my momentum as my foot hits solid ground, I shout a word of 'kiai' to push me forward again. Another flash appears as I vault over the hood.

The commotion catches Ohno's attention. Her hands cover her mouth as my feet hit the sidewalk. But my stride isn't interrupted as I cut through the frosted brown grass and sand, past the playground equipment and barren trees. Skidding to a halt less than a meter from her, I'm panting.

"Are you ok?" she exclaims, bolting from the bench as the sedan's driver shouts the same thing.

"I'm fine!" I holler, sucking in a few more breaths. Then a lump forms in my throat as I bow, "Mie-san told me where you were. Whatever I did, I'm sorry. Really, truly sorry."

"Mie-chan actually spoke to you?" Her face screws up.

I nod as I lean on my knees to catch my breath and try not to cough from the frosty air in my lungs.

"Surprising. She lost her brother a few years ago when he wouldn't pay a protection payment. Doesn't talk much about it. I don't even know where that was."

"I see." Mie makes so much more sense now.

Giving me a visual once-over, Ohno makes sure nothing's broken. "Did the car hit you? There was that strange blue light."

"No." Suddenly exhausted, my knees turn to rubber. I slump onto the bench she'd been sitting on. "I think what you saw was Sensei's protection ward."

"I'll call an ambulance!" the driver offers as he jogs over, retrieving his cell from his suit pocket. Concern etches his features.

I need to be more careful. "Really, I'm fine."

Jerkily, he retrieves his case and thrusts his business card toward me with both hands. "My employer says to contact us if there are any issues. Any at all."

The Rolex and Italian suit speak volumes about the company, if they can afford such things for a driver.

Ways to take advantage of the situation run through my head. *You're not that kind of person anymore.* I nod. Accepting and scanning the card, I have to focus on the Romanized version of 'TekMagi' and the driver's name because I can't read a few of the kanji. Does that company name mean what I think it does?

"Thank you for checking on me, Takeuchi-san" Glancing between Ohno and me, the driver hesitates as if he's about to speak, but gives a formal bow before departing.

When he's out of hearing range, I ask my coworker, "What did I do to upset you? How can I make it right?"

She sighs before sitting beside me. "You were showing off in the break room, weren't you? Didn't Nakamura-san teach you better than that? Don't make light of such skills!"

Guilty as charged. I drop my gaze and regurgitate the lesson from the opening page of Tsuchimikado's book. "The spirit of the word affects all around it with tremendous power to bring harmony or war, create or destroy, and bring light or darkness. Speak or write each with utmost care and consideration."

Letting that sink in, she waits before adding, "And as you jumped over that car—that was magic, too, wasn't it?" My head whips up. Seeing my gape, she reasons, "It had to be with that light flash."

I had said a kiai. "Maybe?"

"Umeji-kun, you've been given an immense amount of power. I grew up with magic and understand how to treat it with respect. Tell me, did you learn to shoot in the mob?"

My hackles raise and I force my expression into neutral. *Why is she asking?*

Her lips purse, but she continues, "What I was trying to explain, is that I've heard you have to respect a weapon. Yakuza don't brandish guns or swords all the time, right?"

Birds chatter sweetly back and forth in the trees above in contradiction to the conversation. With hesitation, I admit, "Not unless we intended to use them." She gulps. *Why'd I say that?*

But she persists. "So, you understand?"

"Heard you loud and clear." Running a hand through my hair, I can't meet her gaze after the freshly learned lesson. At least the breeze cools my burning cheeks.

Her expression brightens now that she's hammered the point through my thick skull. "Then, I forgive you."

"Thanks." All the tension inside unwinds. That pardon from her is worth the earlier insanity with Mie and the near collision.

A gust picks up again bringing the thick air of oncoming rain, penetrating my shirt. Why didn't I remember a jacket?

"You're shivering," she says, bundled up in her parka.

"I'm fine." Though, my chattering teeth betray me.

"Come on, dummy. Break's over. The supermarket's warmth beckons."

Hunched over to ward off the coming evening's chill, I jog to catch up.

Inside, Matsuo catches me after Ohno returns to her register. "Forgot your coat, didn't ya'? Mie-san said you took off like a shot. So, you got it bad for Ohno-san."

At my death-glare, he playfully punches my arm. "No worries, man. I won't tell."

* * *

That night I show the card to Nakamura, who tosses it in the wood-burning kitchen stove. "Yes, it's a company that likely uses magic. Stay away from them, until I can verify who they are. I have a bad feeling about it."

"Sensei, my background is ideal for this kind of investigation work."

"We'll see. First, let's redo that protection ward."

* * *

Stocking is stupidly repetitive on my next shift. I keep stealing glances at Ohno as she checks groceries for customers. Stifling a yawn, I look at the clock at the back of the store. Half an hour to closing.

Ten, eleven, twelve... Is Matsuo right? Am I crazy about Ohno? Focus! I'm not being paid to watch her. *Where was I? Ten? Aww, crap.* Better count again.

"There he is!" The gruff exclamation catches my attention. A stocky man points from the far side of the coffee and tea aisle. Peeking out from under the cuff of his sleeve, his tattoos verify my suspicions.

My gut clenches as I verify exits. Another thug, packing heat under his coat, covers the other end of the aisle. I gulp. *Can I make it over the top of the shelves?*

Satou intercepts. "Is there an issue with one of my employees?"

From behind the end cap, a slender woman in a red power suit steps out, towering over everyone in her stiletto heels. Her skirt is on the short side to accentuate her long legs.

When she scans me, her angelic face framed in cascading gentle curls lights with recognition. Graceful fingers with manicured nails grasp the cover of her digital tablet as the scent of jasmine wafts toward me.

People gather to watch. Mie, Ohno, and Matsuo are among them. *Idiot.* Why'd my eyes pop out of my head? Sure, the businesswoman is attractive and isn't afraid to show it off. Even Matsuo is staring. But Ohno-chan shouldn't have to see me act that way.

The new lady zeroes in. "You were the one that made my driver hit the brakes so hard it slammed me into the front seat?"

"Sorry, Ma'am. Are you ok?" An apology spurts out, accompanied by a low bow.

Noting I look anywhere but at her, she simpers. "After coming that close to death, you apologize? It should be my driver making amends to you. But the skill you showed as you dodged my vehicle, that's a rare one. Your raw talent could use refinement."

She moves birdlike, side to side, to get a look at me. "And you have an uncanny resemblance to someone I knew." Fixing on my name tag, she retrieves her card from the iPad cover. The device glows a sickly green—

pulsing an irregular beat. "Umeji-san is it? This number will put you through to my secretary, who can arrange an interview for a better-paying position."

More money and a better chance to start over would be great.

Quickly, she slides her card into my hand. "Know that I specialize in helping those making their way into society again. My company would use your abilities for a noble cause—cleaning out the very organization that enslaved you and so many others, allowing a path for those who need somewhere to go. When are you available to chat in person?"

The idea of helping people avoid the yakuza path I took—it has me salivating over the job prospect. *How does she know about my past?*

My hand reaches for the card. I freeze as I pronounce the Romanized version of her name. "Dah-teh... Date? The Date Sari?" She grins at the recognition. This is the kitsune that Sensei had to ward her house from over a hundred-fifty years ago. "Uhm. Thank you, but I have a respectable job already."

"Stubborn like him, too. Think before refusing, Umeji-san. I do my research well, and there's much more happening here in Nonogawa than you can see."

With a prick at the base of my neck, words appear in my mind almost as if they were my own. *Know that there are things I cannot speak of here. Nakamura, the old bat, is hiding secrets from you.*

What the...? My jaw shoves forward. "I said, no thank you."

Date's chin lowers as if accepting a challenge. A goon steps behind me and the hairs raise on the nape of my neck. Tapping my nose, she presses on. "Talent such as yours cannot be wasted when there's so much good that could be done."

The choicest words get tamped down to avoid losing my job. *You heard my answer, vixen.*

She flinches.

The kitsune put thoughts into my head. Does that mean she heard what I thought of her? *I know what you are.* Behind me, the goon's hand squeezes my shoulder enough to make me wince.

Satou interjects, sweeping his hand toward the double doors, "Date-san,

Umeji should return to work. If you would see yourself out, I won't have to inform the authorities of your intimidation attempt."

With her nose in the air, she barks, "Let's go, boys."

The goon from behind me releases my shoulder to catch up, allowing me to spot a ring with that same pulsating green on his dead pale hand. Date sweeps out with minions in her wake, leaving behind more of a chill than the breeze that rolls in from outside. My knees feel wobbly. I just stood up to a powerful spirit being. *Shit.*

When she's out the door, everyone converges. Satou charges over. "Umeji, what the hell was that about? And hand over that card."

Still caught up in the confrontation, I surrender the contact info. Words tumble out of my mouth as I recall the image of a canine form being hauled off by a giant flying something or other. "Date, you're the one who attacked Nakamura-sensei that night..."

"Attacked? My aunt?" Satou shakes my shoulders to get a direct answer.

"Yes, Sir."

"This is about the secret you almost went to jail over?"

Nodding, I deflate. *Why'd he have to bring that up?* "May I see if Sensei's ok?"

"Yes. I want my old contacts to check on this Date-san. I'll be right behind you."

"I can drive!" Ohno offers. Our boss approves, putting Matsuo and Mie in charge for the few moments until the store closes.

The need to be there for Sensei eats at my gut. As soon as I slide into the passenger seat of the CR-V, Ohno careens the vehicle out of the parking lot. A pickup honks as it dodges, and my heart pounds in my chest from the near miss.

Who'd have thought shy little Ohno-chan would drive like this? That's saying something after being in mob car chases. Better belt up.

12

CHAPTER 12: REVELATIONS

Revolving red lights illuminate broken windows and the front door off its hinges. My pulse races. Before Ohno's car comes to a complete stop, I bail out.

"Sensei!" All eyes light on me as I spot four policemen wearing allergy masks in my teacher's home. *They're not after you.* "Sensei!"

A typhoon tore through here. Papers lay scattered, furniture cut and overturned, cupboards rifled through, plant pots shattered, and books swept off the bookshelf onto the floor. A rotten egg stench hangs in the air. I try to breathe through my mouth, but that's nasty, too.

When the officers part, allowing her past, relief floods through me. Skidding to a stop, I join my teacher. "Are you ok?"

On the outside, she's the paragon of serenity despite moving closer. "I'm fine. It happened during the Orchid Club meeting. My neighbor, Goro-san, called the police after the coast was clear."

"Nakamura-san, call if you notice anything else amiss." The officer proffers his card before taking his leave. Another officer finishes taking pictures, so we wait until he's gone.

Seeing the mess in the kitchen, my brain replays the gory scene from the night before. "How's your cut?"

She holds out her palm to expose the red scar, but there's no bandage on it. "Good for your first healing. I'll finish it later."

Poking her head in, Ohno-chan gasps before blurting, "Eww! What's that smell?"

Sensei finally gives in and wrings her hands. "How did you know to come? Where's Kazuo?"

"Date showed up at the store, after almost running me over yesterday." Rubbing the nape of my neck, I confess, "Unfortunately, I must have used my new skills to avoid an accident. So she saw what I'm capable of. When she left, we wanted to check on you. Satou-san will be here after he inquires about Date and her company, TekMagi."

"So that's why I felt the protection ward on you go out. Well, well, it was her company. Kazuo will encounter surprises when investigating that witch. I'm sure she's behind it. But, without proof, we can't do a blasted thing. And your resemblance to my Yuki doesn't help you one bit."

Redirecting to Ohno, she asks, "May I borrow a phone? The intruders ripped mine off the wall."

Ohno offers her cell. "Who would do this?"

"Goro-san described two burly red guys with glowing rings. So, they were oni. Evil ones, I'd say, because they wrecked my home. It would also explain the stench."

I swallow. My co-worker's eyes flit to me as she points out, "Those rings sound familiar, don't they?"

As Nakamura dials, my boss races in, plugging his nose. His phone chimes. "Aunt Hisako!"

She waves the phone before handing it back to Ohno. My coworker doesn't place it back in her purse. Instead, she grips the device tightly.

Satou's brows furrow deeper and deeper as he surveys the disaster. "Aunt, stay with me until we get your house repaired." Sensing her reluctance, he begs—something I've not seen him do before. "Please, I'm worried about you."

Returning her kotatsu to standing doesn't help the room much. *We won't get this done tonight.* So I suggest, "Let's clean up tomorrow. Is there anything you need to gather?"

"They didn't find what they were after—me and the works. Let's move them for safekeeping." She points to her small library. "Over there."

My boss and I blow out a breath in concert. Navigating through the scattered books, I grab Sensei's elbow to keep her from tripping.

Her palms come together as if in prayer. Commanding, "Open," she pushes them apart with an effort that shakes her arms. A blue glow emanates from her bookshelf, revealing a hidden compartment.

Pulling out her journals, scrolls, and Tsuchimikado's manuscript, she shoves the pile my way. Then she hands her brushes and ink to my boss. "Carry these."

Damn, this stack is heavy. How was she able to lift it? In the stunned silence, we could hear a pin drop if not for Nakamura and me heading outside.

Finally, Satou growls, "What was that, Aunt?"

She doesn't respond, only continues out the door.

"Aunt!"

Another secret. Satou's gonna freak when he finds out.

Peeking back inside, she pleads, "Kazuo, please. I need to move these out of the danger zone, then I'll explain."

That's when Mie and Matsuo join us. The girls can handle Sensei's needs better than a guy like me. "Would you get a change of clothes and her toiletries?"

Ohno eagerly nods. *I owe her.*

Mie adds, "Nakamura-san where's your coat and purse? I'll fetch those."

In the meantime, Matsuo volunteers to help finish inspecting the damage for the insurance company.

Satou directs Ohno and me, "Take her to my place and prepare your room for her. If push comes to shove, I'll vouch for whatever is necessary to protect her. We'll follow soon."

Thankfully, Ohno's not driving like a speed demon this time, because the reek at the house was nauseating. Unlocking the front door, I give a sweeping gesture.

"Let's take her things upstairs to my room. I'll sleep down here."

Nakamura scowls. "You'll do no such thing!"

Satou would never let her sleep on the floor or couch. Neither will I. "Sensei,

I'll be on guard tonight." *That should let her save face.*

She gives me the stink eye, but no further argument. Then Mie provides cover by starting up a conversation, allowing me to lead Ohno upstairs. It'd be just my luck to have a pile of underwear out.

Ohno won't meet my gaze as we reach the end of the short hall. She's embarrassed to be in the bedroom with me?

"I'll finish up if you wanna go downstairs with the others." Blocking the view from the doorway, I double-check that I'd put away my laundry.

Instead, she squares her shoulders and traipses in. "Where should these go?"

Setting down the box, I direct her to the curtained closet. Then I work on changing the bedding for our guest.

Ohno places Sensei's clothing and calligraphy supplies on the shelves. "Nice space, but you don't have any belongings out. Is staying at this house still temporary, even after a month?"

Looking down, I freeze at the jab. Why did she point out I have so little? Or hint I could return to prison?

She waves frantically. "I'm sorry! I didn't mean to infer... What I mean is... This is your home. You should make this room your own space."

Nice recovery. "I don't need much. What would make it homier?"

"Well, what do you enjoy?"

"Judo, mythology, history, foxes, and food. It might be nice to catch up with music."

"Then how about items that remind you of those things? A picture? Some CDs? Even borrowing books from the library might make it more individualized—when it's yours again." Helping me wrestle the duvet into its protective sheet, she adds another thought. "Do you have a way to listen to music?"

Having seen the space, she has to know the answer. But it's nice she didn't make a point of it. "Nope."

"Wanna borrow my old iPod until you can buy your own?"

"Uh, sure."

"What type of music do you listen to? I'll add it if I've got it." She leans in, quirking an eyebrow. "Because you don't look like a K-pop kind of guy."

Looking away, I cough to cover my laugh. *She's flirting?* Gads, it's been so long since I joked around with people that I can't even tell. "I'd try most anything. The boss listens to classical which is fine. But something with a little more..."

"Hard rock then?"

"That'd be great. So you're a K-pop girl?"

Lifting her hand in mock solemnity, she giggles. "Guilty as charged." Her antics unwind the tension inside me enough to grin genuinely in return. She adds, "I'm glad you come out of your shell sometimes. So we're both shy in a group?"

Ohno's being so considerate. Maybe that warrants a bit of vulnerability. "I was more easy-going like Matsuo when I was younger. But, in the mob, I learned not to stick out. Keep my head down, stay outta trouble."

"But Matsuo-san, Nakamura-san, and I are safe?"

Hearing the front door creak and people talking in the living room brings me back to focus. *Idiot. Sensei's the priority right now.* "The boss is here."

Ohno nods, then fluffs a pillow—the last touch.

"I'll grab my things for tonight. Meet you downstairs." When I'm about to follow, my eyes return to the bed we made together. The one that used to be mine.

As I tromp downstairs, I hear someone hiss between their teeth. "Aunt, is that necessary?"

Arriving in the middle of the disagreement, I deposit my stuff out of the way and sit at the kotatsu with the others. "Sir, they're protection wards. They'll warn us if someone attacks."

Giving me a pained glare, he asks, "And you would know this, how?"

"He's correct, Nephew. We can't let our guard down. My home's wards were too old. Look where that got me!" Sensei crosses her arms to force a stalemate that everyone knows she'll win.

Sashaying in, Mie carries a tray of tea, setting it on the table and pouring for the five of us.

Nakamura's voice turns syrupy. "Thank you. I couldn't remember where he keeps it."

How did Mie find it? Neither the boss nor I ever could. And the boss swore he had a set.

Then Satou rounds on us. "Aunt. Umeji. Explanations, now."

"Tatsuya, are your friends superstitious?" she asks. They shake their heads. "If you stay, you are bound to keep this secret. You may speak of it among yourselves, but not to others."

She meets the gaze of each, raising her palm so it's open. We all agree except Satou, who drums his fingers on the table. The faintest flash smothers when she closes her hand.

"Very well, impatient nephew of mine. I know you will keep this secret, because of the one you hide. I just haven't volunteered to share this with anyone in a very long time. While I tell the group, Tatsuya, finish the wards. One for each outside wall, the top ceilings, and the outer doors."

She put the same spell on my friends. I never asked the details of the consequences for betraying that promise. Sure, she has to keep a low profile, but my stomach twinges a bit at her using the ward on my friends. She did say that whatever she did wouldn't be harmful, and either I trust her or I don't. *So be it.*

So I scoot the brush and ink over and select a sheet of paper from the stack on the table. Though, how she expects me to focus, I'll never know.

With a murmur, the air shimmers around her. Her form blurs, shrinks, and transforms to reveal her silver coat. Leaping and landing with claws clicking on the low table, she fans her nine tails in a graceful arc. I can't breathe for a moment and shivers form on my scalp. She's much more majestic than the night I first learned her secret.

Satou's words come out in a rasp. His hand slaps the table as he rises and his head juts toward her. "What the hell? A kitsune possessed my Aunt? What did she do to you? Free her this instant!"

So he accepts kitsune exist? But he doesn't trust them and isn't afraid. Not what I expected.

My friends don't fare much better. Ohno's fingers splay on her chest. Mie's eyes bug out of her head. Scrambling backward and hitting the wall, Matsuo causes our heads to swivel in his direction as he pales. "K-kumiho-s-san?"

The Korean word for fox? The creatures that hunt and eat people? I shake my head and smile so he knows Sensei won't harm us. Sensei's eyes close and her chin dips. Is his reaction what she'd feared?

"Be at peace, Nephew, Matsuo-kun, everyone." One of her tails flicks, casting a glow over us that fills me with a warmth like my mom holding me when I was little. "I am kitsune. Kumiho are a terrible lot. Had to kill one to protect my husband when we visited Korea. Though the people there were kind to us."

Directing her gaze to Satou, her look softens even more. "I am the aunt you grew up with, Kazuo. The one who first held you after your mother birthed you. I loved your uncle and the children I bore him. I also know what you did when you were ten to get suspended from school, if you still have any doubts."

My boss returns to his seat, but his eyes narrow.

Nakamura's muzzle motions down her length. "This is my true self. My race blended in to survive since humans overran our territory centuries ago. Rarity of males, hunting, and intermarrying with people are the reasons few kitsune remain. Only a full-blooded pair give birth to another of my species. So, as I'm sure you've concluded, this is the form Tatsuya saw at the shrine. And why he couldn't tell you what happened that fateful night. Would you have believed him, if he'd told you?"

"So you used a spell to force him into secrecy?" Satou's voice drops to a growl.

He believes in magic, too? What the heck?

Nakamura shakes her head. "I told him not to tell and placed a ward on him to warn me if he broke his word. Just like I did with the group here. But Tatsuya's loyalty surprised me."

"So why are you revealing yourself now?" His tone lightens considerably. The rapidity in which my boss changes emotions—is that a leftover of his host club days?

"You need to know. More is afoot with Date on the loose. I may not be able to handle it on my own. I always had help before. Tatsuya's friends need to know, too, because they'll all need to support and protect each other because of their association with me." The hint hovers over us like a specter in the room.

My VPO shakes his head, mumbling, "…department…gonna throw a fit." Then he dares to voice what we all want to know. "Aunt, please explain."

"Of course."

Before I have time to ask what my boss meant, he ducks his head a bit as he stretches out a hand. "May I, Aunt? Then I'll know it's not a dream."

Studying the ceiling as if it might contain the answers she seeks, she mutters. "Why is it only Tatsuya and my Yuki didn't have that reaction? Be quick about it."

I venture, "Because we had to hold you to save your life?"

"Perhaps. You humans are an odd lot, needing touch to comprehend."

"Yuki? There isn't anyone by that name in our family and you've mentioned it before," Satou points out.

"My first husband." Seeing her nephew about to ask for details, she holds up a paw. "Kazuo, it will take a while to answer the rest of your questions because most of them come from well before you were born. Let me catch you up."

13

CHAPTER 13: STAGE FOR WAR

Nakamura, April 20, 1862:

A group of Isshin-Shishi, the 'men of high purpose' revolutionaries, assassinated Chief Minister Ii on March 24. The man who had signed the disastrous treaty for Japan and changed Yoshida's sentence from exile to execution could no longer hurt my country or my family and friends.

Ii's supporters reported he had the best intentions for Japan. But I could not see that in his actions. Yoshida's prediction proved correct; his death was stirring revolt, though I could not predict what the revolution would lead to.

We kept the ward spells refreshed on our happy little three-room, tile-roofed home, with its white plaster and dark stained wood panels, situated on the corner of our block. I loved the location with its grass expanse nestled up against the forested ridgeline, because it allowed me to escape when I needed a break from hectic city life to be a fox again, even for a short while.

That night, we were tucking our kids into bed, when Kinya asked. "Will you tell us a story?"

"Which one would you like to hear?" Yuki always spoiled our little ones.

"How you and momma met!" Kanoko's eyes sparkled with hope.

Yuki glanced to me. At my nod, the tykes bounced on the thin family futon.

"We shouldn't deny them knowledge of their heritage."

No matter how many times my husband told the tale the children listened with rapt attention. Yuki would revert to his lively self for a few hours which allowed us to banter as we did the day we met.

Interrupting the night's retelling, the first ward on our house extinguished with a thunderous crack. A cheer from outside and the scent of smoke made my hackles raise. Pale green flames ate at our wood and plaster walls. Then the low booming laughter started.

My mouth went dry, and what came out was a bare squeak. "Oni! Grab your ofuda! I'll buy us a few moments."

With a grim mask, my husband nodded, running to scoop up the talismans, writing supplies, and his swords. The oni raced to claw through the walls and strip away the protective tiles. Their stench wafted into the room, causing my stomach to protest. As the second ward gave out, it blew a harsh warning screech.

My trembling made it difficult to concentrate. Centering my ki, I held my daughter while Kinya clung to my kimono. I scribed a circle into the air, revealing a glowing, blue-edged portal to the forested hill behind our house.

As Yuki dodged falling timbers, banshee screeches congealed into an off-kilter rhythm. My blood ran cold. That was not natural magic.

The final ward failed while we bailed through the shimmering hole to the safety of the tree line. I felt the opening tighten on my leg and jerked my foot away to avoid it severing from my body. Rolling to our feet, we witnessed our home cave-in with a crash.

Yuki worked, while I gaped at the loss. As I snapped back to our plight, he'd created a shikigami paper spirit to protect our children. His ability to remain calm made me adore him all the more.

"No bodies!" The grating voices shouted. "They've escaped!"

"FIND THEM! Burn all of Kyoto if you have to!" a shrill female voice demanded. Bolts of electricity pounded the remains of our dwelling. As the wind picked up, it spread the flames to the close-packed houses.

A shiver ran through me. I knew that voice. "Date must be here to complete Ii's work eliminating the rebels."

We had to get our tykes to safety. Not caring how much ki it took, I opened a portal to my mother's den from behind a bunch of cedars. Shoving the children through with the spirit protector, I couldn't bear to look, or I'd have accompanied them.

My duty was to my husband. I would not forsake him, no matter what. Panting from the exertion of that long distance spell, I dropped the human guise to conserve energy.

Yuki wrote banishment and protection ofuda as fast as he could in the flickering firelight. An ember from the burning trees landed on his talisman. To finish the kanji strokes he brushed it aside, his serenity undiminished.

Nudging him with affection, I shared, "Kinya and Kanoko are safe. We can't run from this battle, but I dread having to kill my kind."

"I know. So few of you remain." He touched his nose to mine and applied a ward to each of us. "She won't leave us in peace after the death of her lover. I fear she thinks we were involved in it." The only warmth was his skin against my muzzle, grounding me.

"They're in the trees!" From the clearing between us and the house, the man's armored silhouette had an ominous green aura that competed with the fire behind him. The ugly light intensified then subsided.

With bone-cracking movements, his helmet fell off to reveal the horns and wild hair of an oni. A deeper, unearthly voice cackled, "Can't leave the killing fun to a pathetic human!"

With his jaw set, Yuki rose—an ofuda in his first two fingers. He threw the talisman from our cover in the forest. I gritted my teeth and gave a flick of my tail to cast a spell on the burly ogre—slowing its perception.

Sailing through the winds, the ofuda avoided the oni's delayed swipe. Slap! It landed on the forehead of the terrifying red face. With hideous crackling, the form he inhabited disintegrated to ash.

Neighbors poured out of burning houses only to be questioned or struck down by the puppeteered soldiers and oni. My heart ached. But I could do nothing for them while three of Date's samurai in demon-infused armor charged down on us and an arrow whizzed by my ear from the shelter of trees to the north.

Splaying my tails in threat and barking from my core, I formed a shield for us. Yuki drew his katana, and we pressed toward the center of the open grass. Maintaining a barrier only he could cut through took tremendous energy.

I'd never seen my spouse use his samurai prowess. Thanks to my spell, he could skip blocking and make strikes in rapid succession. The deadly grace in each swing put me in awe, despite the ringing and squelching of his sword slicing through the soldiers' armor and flesh.

Yuki's kotodama enhanced strokes were so powerful and fast each enemy barely quivered before they fell to the ground in pieces. Within seconds, he'd taken three attackers out.

I dropped the shield so it wouldn't drain me and resolved to trust my husband's skill. My task was to stalk the archer tucked in the shelter of the pines to the north.

Twirling a tail, I snarled the time dilation command. Everything slowed. My lope accelerated to an all-out sprint with my claws dispersing clods of turf in my wake. His bowstring, drawn taut, released to send a shaft slow-motion toward me.

Rolling in a leap over it, then dodging lightning strikes and burning wreckage, I raced. Paws pounded, pulling in succession, ever harder against the grass extracting more and more speed. My lungs protested, but I couldn't stop. He dropped his bow to wrench his wakizashi from its sheath. But he was sluggish.

Fangs bared, I leaped to bite down on the helmet knot under his chin. The momentum pushed him off balance. Flailing, he fell. The impact knocked the wind out of him, and his wakizashi clattered to the ground.

Trying in vain to pull me off, he struggled for breath. But I tore off the neck guard. My canine teeth ripped out his throat as bile rose and burned inside. Date would pay for all these lives.

As the archer gurgled, my ears twitched at lumbering footsteps behind me in the clearing. Another red horned oni swung a spiked club. The stench that preceded him threatened to dislodge the contents of my dinner.

I'd have to expend more spells to take down this giant. *Damn.* Some ki had to be rationed to deal with the vixen witch.

Wind swirled around my enemy and me, making us struggle to stand. Lightning struck and my talisman sputtered out of existence.

As I prepared a spell, a stream of ofuda came out of nowhere. The oni couldn't dodge them all, and several stuck to his face. A roar followed a puff of smoke.

My Yuki's left arm and cheek were bleeding, but not badly. Cantering over to his cover in the trees, I nuzzled him in thanks, while he slapped new charms on us.

Two pairs of oni and samurai stood on alert in the courtyard. The remnant of nearby townsfolk must have fled the battle and spreading fire. Smoke filled the air, so we crouched low and Yuki sliced the sleeves off his kimono to provide us masks.

Date emerged from behind her minions. The glowing collar she wore drew attention as it pulsed. It was bad enough that she attacked us. But how could she consider mixing her pure magic with that of evil? Ours was of the natural and spirit worlds. This type of oni only corrupted what they touched.

Reverting to her fox form, she gave a glare that spoke her hatred. "Tsuchimikado, you and your bitch convinced Yoshida's followers to murder Ii-sama! Now that I've tapped into a source of power that makes me unstoppable, your judgment is nigh!"

"Minister Ii changed Yoshida-san's sentence from exile to death! But we ordered no such thing!" I shook as I shouted back.

"She's forcing an oni connected to the collar to take the energy drain," Yuki murmured with his trademark detachment.

I could see his fist tightening on the hilt of his blade and smelled the tang of his fear. As his free hand reached into the front of his kimono, he removed the last few ofuda.

But when his eyes met mine, I saw resolve and intensity. "Hisako, I've not said it before because we know the power of words. But I may never have another chance." He reached down to caress my muzzle with the same tenderness as he showed our wedding day. All too soon, he withdrew that hand to clutch his wakizashi. "I love you with all my heart."

Before I could respond, he dashed from the cover of the trees toward the oni in the clearing, bellowing a shiver-inducing war cry.

Bounding after him, I had to choke down my feelings. What was he thinking saying something so intimate that it's only spoken on one's deathbed?

My gait faltered. Yuki didn't see a win in this situation. Our ki was waning along with our stamina. The enemy still outnumbered us, so this was a suicide charge. *Yuki!*

When Date lifted her tails the collar's glow intensified, she shuddered as the atmosphere sizzled with the coming electricity. Bolts rained down as we wove and dodged. Why hadn't the witch hit us? With that many strikes, she should have. *Our talismans? No! Her struggle for control!*

Casting again, I burst forward with extra speed as I passed Yuki in his charge. If I could eliminate Date, the oni would be less of a threat. In my next steps, I crouched, vaulted upward, and glided over the beast in my path.

Intense pain racked me. The oni's meaty three-fingered fist latched on to one of my tails, pulling me from flight. My ward snapped from existence, saving my spine from being ripped out. But I smacked to the ground—wheezing. There was only a slight chance to stop him from pummeling my life out with that spiked club.

Gritting my teeth, I lifted the tail that carried my hoshi no tama, the ball that contained a reserve of my spirit and magic. Dragging my paws together, I panted the single word I could think of—'naginata'.

As the oni raised his cudgel, a blue glow engulfed me then compressed into a tight beam with a razor edge. The weapon surged forward, piercing and returning him to the realm he came from. No trace left.

With great hesitation, I used a tad of my dwindling ki to get on my feet again. Yuki had eliminated his oni. He sucked in air. Two soldiers remained. With cracking, grunting, and lurching, one was transforming. The other warrior saw his fate and slashed at the silk bindings of his armor with his tanto.

A screaming furor overtook Date. Was it because she couldn't control him anymore? Conjuring two paper servants, she flung one at him and another toward my husband.

That was my cue to creep behind the cover of a building. Yuki could deal with the two remaining opponents. So I lunged for Date, forcing her to the dirt and bit deep into the shoulder muscle of her foreleg.

Her blood mingled with that of the archer in my mouth. His tasted natural. But there was something off about the fox's. Was the oni magic tainting her very essence?

Out of the corner of my eye, I saw the shikigami doll grow until it towered over the mercenary. It lifted its arm as the grim-faced warrior readied his weapon. They swung in sync—the man through the center of the paper spirit. The puppet's razor-edged arm sliced the man's head clean off, toppling both.

Date rolled, ripping her shoulder open to free herself from my jaws. Flattening, she sprang from her three good paws. I barked for a shield. Though it exhausted my ki.

As she bounded over the barrier, I jumped, catching the collar under her chin with my teeth, then twisted hoping to break it or choke the witch. We slammed to the earth and my protection winked out, but I whipped my head to shred that collar. Her fangs sunk into my skull. I bit down harder in desperation, severing the leather.

Concentration broken, Date's jaws opened enough for me to jerk out of her vice and fling the cursed controller. I heard her mutter followed by a popping sound and stench. She'd summoned another oni.

I had to stop her. So I seized her shoulder. The next thing I knew, the oni lifted me by the scruff of the neck. Without qualms about his master's safety, he ripped the fox from my teeth and tossed her aside.

"NO!" Yuki was leaning over a pool of blood and paper in the clearing, scribbling a smear of ashy mud on a white scrap and clutching a second. After throwing his final two talismans, a spike from the heavens hit with a boom that echoed around us. Electricity radiated from his limbs. He slumped, causing my heart to tear from my chest.

One of Yuki's ofuda reached me. Upon contact it glowed, infusing magic into my body—my love's remaining ki. The other charm slapped onto the oni's forehead, causing the ogre to disintegrate, and I crashed to the grass with a thump.

Loathing's sharp burn filled me, allowing me to push aside the throbbing pain in my head and spine. I advanced to avenge my Yuki and end Date with no thought spared for the rarity of our species.

She was a pathetic sight with her tails fluffed and blood matting her fur. Crippled, she flopped down, exposing her underside. The pulse of the magic that followed her heartbeat was negligible. I had her!

Flames of hatred gleamed in her eyes as she whispered, using up the last of her ki. When it popped into existence, a paper dragon snatched up her limp body, and in rustling serpentine coils it lifted off, stealing my victory when I was an instant away.

In a last desperate spring, I struck her throat. My bite only grazed the delicate skin, leaving me to plummet toward my fate. Using the remaining energy from Yuki, I created a fire arrow which pierce the dragon's wing. The puppet spiraled off, trailing smoke. I knew not in which direction.

Dirt and ashes flew from my impact, coinciding with sickening crunches. I could feel the trickle and smell the blood seep from my wounds. Every movement was excruciating. Coughing caused red to spatter the cobbles from who knew how many broken ribs. I was alive, but for how long?

Dragging myself to my mate's prone form spent the rest of my will. There wasn't even energy to cry. I crumpled with my muzzle on his chest to breathe the phrase I'd wanted to say before he charged, "I love you, too."

That's when a brilliance blotted out all else and a white fox appeared above. Was I dreaming? What was it saying? But the apparition touched my head and that of Yuki, transferring us to the safety of my parents' home.

* * *

I awoke to candlelight and the familiar earthy scents of my family's den tucked into the side of Mt. Atago. The fragrance of the tatami mat's reeds and a freshly picked arrangement of wisteria stirred me. I found Yuki's arms wrapped about me as we lay in my old stone-walled room.

Startled by a twinge in my chest and shoulder, my mind replayed the memories of our last battle. So, I snuggled in closer to my husband to sob in the warmth and surety of the covers of our futon. Needing to be sure he was real, I shifted forms to return his embrace and allow us skin to skin intimacy. That contact was a godsend.

He opened his eyes, flashing his breathtaking smile as his trembling palm cupped my cheek. "I feared you might not wake."

"And I thought you were dead!" My hand slipped under his to entwine our fingers. Trailing kisses down his arm, I stopped midway, frozen at the sight.

"Hisako?" He froze.

Gingerly, I traced the tree-like red lines radiating down his spine and limbs. "How did we survive?"

"Don't know." He whispered. My chin tucked into his neck and he stroked my hair. "Your mother said a sun-like illumination surrounded us as a white messenger fox brought us to the den."

"I think I saw that light after saying I loved you, too." Running a finger over his collarbone, I explored the fresh scars. Were they still painful? Would there be repercussions from his injuries?

"You did?"

"My eyes were closed, but it was so bright."

He chuckled. "No, wife. Your words." After pulling me into a kiss that left me wanting more, he pressed his forehead to mine. "I'd wondered if you only accepted me because of the obligation to your challenge those years ago. I'd feared you'd leave someday when you'd had enough. You always had me, heart and soul. But I didn't want to burden you."

Wrapping myself around him, I murmured those words into his ear over and over again as our bodies moved together.

* * *

Exhausted and famished, we clothed ourselves and emerged from the solitude of my room. Neither of us had fully healed, so my husband intercepted the children in their happy dash across the wood floor of the living area. He wasn't successful in hiding his wince. As I hugged Kinya and Kanoko, I hoped our earlier activities hadn't aggravated Yuki's wounds.

My parents padded up to greet us with friendly nuzzles and wags, then sent our son and daughter to serve breakfast. The low table with steaming bowls of fish and rice beckoned. As we devoured our meal, Father explained what happened after the battle.

"I'm afraid your neighbors won't allow you to return. The attack from that bitch was enough. Your sister and I even returned in human form to help clean up. But they refused, wanting nothing to do with our kind. Stupid humans!" Though, he ducked in apology to Yuki and our children.

"I agree." My samurai shrugged it off. Stuffing the last bite of fish into his mouth, he held up his bowl for more.

As Mother filled it, Father gave us more news. "Soujoubou-sama's Tengu clan sent word that Date was fleeing west. And I've written to her family."

* * *

Thanks to my family's magic, we fully healed in only a few days. We also received notice from Date's clan.

> Thank you for the news that my daughter survived the encounter. It brings us hope.
>
> Though, I apologize for the brief letter. We find ourselves on opposite sides of a coming war—one that will engulf our country.
>
> The fourth day of the fourth month, Mannen 1 (April 29, 1860)
> Date Hongyou, Mt. Inari, Kyoto
> To Nakamura Nobu, Mt. Atago, Kyoto

The witch would be back. Yuki and I needed more training. "Father, please teach us both further use of kotodama and divination."

Considering my request overnight, he replied, "Kitsune do not share such coveted secrets with humans. But I agree with your assessment."

* * *

The lightning scars bothered my Yuki. Each occasion he'd see it, he felt the helplessness of being unable to do more to protect me. Even my gratitude for his help and sacrifice couldn't change his mind on the matter.

After much thought, he covered it with a tattoo that commemorated the day we spoke our love. Me as the red fox on his left shoulder, and the white one that provided the miracle on the other. Thus my head always laid over his heart.

14

CHAPTER 14: UPHEAVAL

The clock says it's 2 AM. Sitting around Satou's kotatsu, we avoid making eye contact in the light of the hurricane lamp Sensei insists on using to lower Satou's electricity bill.

I'm not innocent by any stretch of the imagination. But Matsuo's and Ohno's expressions... Who shares that intimate of a story? I can't resist taking one more peek at Ohno's wide-eyed blush. *Girl, you're killing me.*

My boss clears his throat. Sensei soldiers ahead. "The takeaway from the story is my Yuki believed in the power of words."

After a moment, Satou asks, "So, your brashness is because you're a two-century-old kitsune?"

"In part." She winks. "Even Father got after me for being so blunt. The dowager aunt guise gives me an excuse to be more outspoken. But it doesn't explain your directness, Kazuo, because I married into your side of the family."

Satou rolls his eyes. "Daybreak is only a few hours away."

"Tatsuya, are all the wards placed?" Nakamura asks.

"I have a few for upstairs. Didn't want to miss the parts I hadn't heard yet."

"Aunt, we'll be fine," Satou states.

Pursed lips signal her mood. "Don't brush me off, Kazuo. I'm aware you place little faith in the paper charms. But did you hear anything I read to you? That was over a century ago. Date's only grown in power! We must not lower our guard!"

Raising her hand as if in class, Ohno waits for a lull. Sensei motions for her to proceed. "Uhm, so the glowing tablet and rings the thugs wore are oni powered?"

"Correct, dear. Date's primary weapon is oni-infused technology and magic. It allows her to use more powerful spells, such as controlling multiple people."

Matsuo mutters under his breath, "The day keeps getting weirder and weirder." I nod in agreement.

Putting protection wards on us, Sensei adds, "Matsuo-kun, this is only the beginning."

My boss's eyes narrow. His aunt ignores the dirty look and reverts to human form, busying herself by giving each person a stack of ofuda, then folds her hands in expectation. But nobody reaches for their pile on the low table. The silence taunts us all.

Satou is the one to give in. "Would you care to explain?"

"Has Tatsuya heard your past?" As he huffs, she holds up a warning finger. "All of it?"

"What are you getting at?"

Kneeling beside him, Sensei's voice softens. "Don't play daft, Kazuo. You brought Tatsuya here for a reason—one beyond atoning for your sins. I know him. He won't take that kind of surprise well. Since you insist on truth, it's time for you to be forthcoming. The sooner, the better."

His ten-ton glare shows what he thinks of being ratted out. Taking the cue from the disagreement and late hour, my friends leave. It'd be nice to go with them to escape the storm between my boss and my teacher, but I have to ward the house. The few unintelligible staccato whispers, cause tension to creep up the back of my neck.

By the time I finish, I have a full-blown headache. Sensei calls me over to the kitchen after I take some ibuprofen.

"Tatsuya, I wanted to wait until we were in private for the next topic—your likeness to Yuki. Are you ready to hear this?"

It's got to be better than being stuck around their fight, so I nod. Satou's footsteps startle me from behind. Wasn't he upstairs? His gaze pierces as he retrieves a beer from the fridge, and my throat goes dry.

"Let me guess. Umeji's your grandson." Those sarcastic words fall so flat they sound wickedly out of tune.

"Alas, I had hoped that would be the case, once I realized he wasn't Date's minion." The trace of sadness in Sensei's eyes leaks into her voice. "My research revealed no such connection. Yukitada was faithful to me. Unlike many of that time, he didn't see his wife as only the means to produce heirs. And I ensured he didn't need to seek affection in the pleasure quarters. His brother never married. After the war, he sought solace from the world as a monk. Tatsuya, they say everyone has a look-alike. I think that's the situation for you. Though, I'm curious how you came by that particular ink design."

The news is a kick to the gut. Random genetics. Random timing on the hill when I rescued Nakamura. Random chance of having the same tattoo as her husband. *I'm nothin' special. Never have been. Never will be.*

Glumly, I mumble, "I found it in historical photos. It spoke to me from my childhood kitsune obsession. I wanted one that reminded me who I was."

"Fate meant us to meet. Now that you're on the right path, you're doing my Yuki proud." Nakamura leans down to make me look into her eyes for a moment before retiring. Still disinclined to share whatever his aunt hinted at, my boss sips on his beer and follows her upstairs.

The lingering pain washes logic away. My eyelids droop. Can I just crash for the night in my clothes? I have so few, so I plod through to curl up on the sofa with the blanket and pillow left for me.

Memories replay of last week's events—looking back at Ohno after she took care of my hand, breaking through with magic, Ohno's disappointment when I showed off, the relief at seeing my teacher was ok after the ransacking of her house, and Ohno's disarming openness as we prepared my room for Sensei. If only I'd thought to trade blankets—to have a small connection with Ohno-chan. To stop the churning, I pull out my trusty copy of Japanese myths, thumbing to the one about Abe no Seimei's kitsune mother, Kuzunoha.

15

CHAPTER 15: CLEAN UP

The aroma of toast and eggs greets me, making my mouth water. Why am I sleeping on a couch? Is this a safe house or a girlfriend's flat?

Rays of sun illuminate the newspaper Satou reads at the kitchen table. "Mornin'. Aunt Hisako cooked. Come eat, while she dresses."

Oh yeah. Still at my VPO's place.

My boss shares the plan while I wolf down my food. "We'll clean up at my aunt's house. I'll pay you for the work, so her life returns to normal ASAP. I want people with her 24/7 until she's safe. So, I'll watch over her. Think you'll manage here?"

"You can count on me. Though she's a tough woman. I suspect she could have handled those thugs with her magic." *Wait, he's got bigger responsibilities.* "Sir, would it make more sense for me to stay with her? If she's comfortable with the suggestion, that is. I go over daily for lessons. You have the store to run. And this could be a start to how I repay all you've done for me."

"Maybe."

"One more thought, Sir. You know the secret I kept for your aunt, now. I wouldn't have brought it up, but Sensei asked about it last night because she thinks it's important. Does it affect protecting her?"

Slowly finishing a bite of egg, he frowns before responding. "You weren't the person to tell me. And she should mind her own damn business."

"Wasn't my story, Sir. What would you have done?"

Mid-sip, he stops. "Are you reliable enough to share that info with yet?"

My chopsticks return to their rest and I stare at my lap. *Ouch.* My yakuza days showed that people who don't trust have something to hide, and it's never beneficial to me.

"You and my aunt get along well. Considering you kept her secret and she's training you in this magical whatever it is, I'll run your suggestion by her. The problem is I'm having troubles accepting that she hid this my entire life."

Fair enough. Maybe another tidbit will smooth things over. "For what it's worth, I wasn't aware the fox I rescued was Nakamura-san until you yelled. She hadn't shown her human form at the shrine. Though, I should have bought a clue when she sounded exactly like your aunt."

His mouth quirks before he gives in to a stilted laugh, dispersing the tension in the room. "So, that's why you reacted as if she was a poisonous snake."

"Yeah. Last thing I'd expected."

"Well, the two of you keep challenging my perception. I'll consider it."

"Thank you, Sir."

While I work on the dishes, he brings up another topic. "My contacts confirmed that Date's been collecting former mobsters. Her security firm must be a cover—using those desperate to return to society as guinea pigs for her corrupted magic tech."

Interesting contacts. "I'm glad you and Nakamura-san found me before she did. 'Cause her offer would have tempted me."

* * *

The gold light of the morning sun allows us to witness the full devastation at Sensei's house. The thugs were thorough in their search—every piece of furniture slashed, books torn, dishes shattered.

Sensei scowls at the disaster. Pointing out the areas, she assigns tasks. "Tatsuya, you start with wards, then work in the kitchen. A home doesn't function without that space. Kazuo, you help me with the bedrooms. If one of you is staying here, we'll need places to sleep."

"Aunt, you're ok with it?"

"When will you stop underestimating me?" Her fingers snap. A cyan glow blurs our view before another woman appears.

Decked out in a blue kimono with a unique calligraphy print, she has her hair up in an elegant traditional style. A young, flawless woman with the ideal in beauty, confidence and dignity exude from her comport. She's Date's match in looks, and more refined.

Satou's mouth gapes. I whistle. "Whoa, Sensei. No wonder Tsuchimikado-sama fell for you on sight."

Like a snake about to strike, she advances on my boss causing him to step away. "Nephew, it's time we get something straight, now that you keep my secret. I don't have to resemble a defenseless little old lady. I can appear any age, just within the confines of one human identity. The guise was a convenient way to remain with family."

His hands fly up. "Got it, Aunt. Not helpless."

Click. "I should have seen it sooner! The broken hip... You didn't have to wait for it to heal. Was it to maintain the disguise?"

Satou's head whips to me, then to Nakamura. Primly, she acknowledges the deduction. "In part. Date used dark magic, blocking access to my ki pool, so she could steal my tama and end me once and for all. With little access to spells, I was helpless. All I could manage was my human disguise. I suspect Date paid dearly for that spell, and she knows I'll be watching for that trick. When another magic user removed the block, I helped the healing along.

"Another reason was to see if you were worthy of being my apprentice. My nephew won't bother sharing his intentions. But when asked, at least I'll share that."

"Sensei, he's considering it. We talked again this morning."

Her brows furrow.

With a skeptical glance, Satou says, "Should it be Umeji-san staying with you?"

Rolling her eyes, she pshaws.

"I'm serious!"

"He reminds me too much of my Yuki. That kind of relationship wouldn't be right for either of us. So, I've encouraged him to pursue Ohno-chan, who's well suited for his personality." Snapping her fingers again, she reverts to her sweet elderly form and winks. "He's safe from my wiles."

"You know darn well, I'm more worried about things the other way around."

Thanks for throwing me under the bus. Not! "Sir, with all due respect, Sensei, she's a grandmother figure to me. And I like..." My mouth goes dry. I'd not admitted it until now. "Someone else."

"I knew it!" Sensei's sly smile shouldn't be on the face of a grandma.

"Fine." With clipped words, he turns. It's gotta be hard for the man so used to being in control.

Softening, she puts a hand on his arm to stop him. He bristles but relents as she speaks. "Nephew, that aside. Thank you. For assisting and always being here when I need you. Whether that be to preserve my cover, true help, or putting up with me when I'm difficult."

We finish most of the assigned rooms before the gang filters in. Mie and Matsuo arrive first. They're assigned the bath and washroom.

My next assignment is the toilet, an add-on room to the original building. Access is outside via the veranda. When the home was built, it probably had an outhouse. Exiting with my cleaning bucket and trash bag is when Ohno calls my name, running smack dab into me.

"Oh!" She backs up, her freckled cheeks color, and she covers her face giving only a hint of the silver object in her grasp. "Sorry! I didn't know you were indisposed."

My chin dips as I hold up the cleaning supplies. She goes a deeper shade of red. Setting down the bucket, my fists shove into the safety of my pockets. I want to take her hands from her mouth. But I just cleaned the toilet. Despite washing, it still feels gross because I have the supplies. And it would probably scare her off.

"It's fine. You wanted to talk?"

"Oh! Yes!" She beams, offering the metal item and a small packet. "The iPod, as promised. Songs organized by year for the last five years, because I wasn't sure how long you were... uhm, gone. The lists with notes about each song are in the envelope. Also, I tucked in new headphones. My old pair was a little..." Dark circles underline her eyes.

Say something, idiot! "Uh, thanks. I hope you weren't up all night working on it." At least I didn't mention how tired she looks.

Rocking on her heels, she relaxes. "I couldn't sleep, and it was a fun project."

Matsuo returns to work after lunch break is over. Mie and Ohno opt to finish the second-floor rooms, while Sensei and I clean the living room. Putting plastic on the windows and door is my boss's task. We're almost done for the day. When Sensei asks me to retrieve her slippers from upstairs, the girls are deep in conversation.

"But you and Satou-san were dating, weren't you?" Ohno asks.

"Yeah, but he cut off the relationship when I asked about his past. Shh! Someone's coming up the stairs."

Well, well. The boss dated an employee. To each his own. And his trust issues aren't only with me.

"Do you two know where Nakamura-sensei's slippers are?" I holler to announce my presence.

* * *

The number of tasks left boggles the mind—the front door and windows, several cupboards, the phone line repaired and new phone installed, books have to be rebound, pictures and dishes replaced, and the list goes on.

Sensei agrees to stay at Satou's until the minimum of security repairs are complete. He also insists that she buy a simple cell. While we're at the store, Satou helps me pick up a pay as you go variety—the kind that doesn't require a bank account.

None of us want to cook, let alone clean anymore. So, we swing by for takeout. I'm stupid tired. My back aches from cleaning. Before the others head upstairs, I flop on the couch, stick the headphones in my ears, and absorb Ohno's letter.

She put detailed notes for each song and what it meant to the nation, to her, to her friends, what was happening when each big hit came out, and also a K-pop playlist. Since she said it's her favorite, that's where I begin.

This window into her thoughts is like she's here with me. She even wrote about the tunes that got her through the time her family moved from Hokkaido after the residents discovered their ability. The small town was split over the spells their clan practices and the pets Ohno keeps. Her feelings, in part, mirror my own about leaving the mob.

Poke. Nakamura looming nearby startles me so badly that I fall off the sofa. How did I not notice her approach?

"Love note?" She waggles her eyebrows, showing no remorse for scaring me.

"Nah. Playlists. Music to catch me up for the past several years. She put so much effort into it, that she must have stayed up all night."

"Hmm. You seem glued to it. It's only lists of songs?"

"And her thoughts on the music."

"Ha! You can't fool me. Any love songs?"

How would Sensei react if I stuck my tongue out at her? Maybe if I ignore the statement, she'll drop it.

"Anyway, my nephew says you'll be staying with me until this blows over. Puts the secretive, magic-using troublemakers in one place. He's able to keep an eye on us both or some such nonsense. Are you ready for more intensive training?" She's so spry now that she doesn't have to hide behind the old lady facade.

"If you say I am, then yes."

16

CHAPTER 16: ALL THE POSSIBILITIES

Matsuo offers a staff lesson over lunch, while Satou takes Sensei shopping to replace her damaged things. With the acceptance from Sensei, Ohno-chan, and Matsuo, maybe someday I'll fit in to Nonogawa.

This afternoon, the wood floor in the unheated dojo quickly chills my bare feet. Matsuo has me drill an advancing step strike while we chat.

"Umeji-kun, I saw you and Ohno-chan on the veranda yesterday. Are you gonna ask her out? It is Christmas Eve after all. Supposedly, the most romantic night of the year."

Was that thirty-four or thirty-five? "I can't count with you asking questions." My sternest glower is just short of murderous. Even to mister 'bright side of life', it should be more than obvious how bad an idea that would be.

His arms cross as he cracks a grin. "An opponent won't wait. So?"

"A former yakuza wouldn't make good boyfriend material." That's what I keep telling myself.

"Aww. She'll be hurt. You're starting your life over. Why not?"

Putting the staff aside, my hand swings out to point in a challenge. "If I take you to the mat, I don't have to answer."

"Deal. Prepare for defeat!" He motions for me to come at him.

The need to not have to explain spurs me to swoop in fast like a hawk. As he tries to dodge, a grasp on his sleeve combined with a sweep of my foot behind his has him trying to twist out of my hold. A rough shove trips him and his shoulders hit the floor with an ungraceful thud.

Ruefully he grins, holding out his hand for help up. "Dang! You really didn't want to tell me!"

"Dunno if I could have. It's not that simple."

"How so?"

It's so black and white for him. "Matsuo-kun, you know that I've only been on parole for a month. So, I'm still trying to figure life out. I feel so... how do I explain it? F—ed up inside? As if two of me exist—the person I started out as, and the one that ended up on the wrong side of the law. But hanging out with friends like you allows the old me to emerge."

"Got it. I'll lay off. Though I'm glad the real you is resurfacing. You're mellowing and it's good." He offers his fist, so I tap my knuckles to his.

This solidarity—does he understand what that means? Not even my Yakuza big brother realized it, and the mob was all about that.

* * *

After I rouse the next morning, Sensei greets me as she knits on her socks at the table. We won't work on her house today, since the carpenters are there. Instead, she wants to clean the shrine and to train me. This will be our first visit together.

When we head out, the air is brisk but has that humid, heavy smell like it might snow. She picks a brisk pace for an elderly lady.

"Sensei, how much of what we see is cover and how much is real? I mean, you're stronger than you seem. But I felt I should steady you when the police were at your house."

She slips a knobby hand on my arm for support, going up the stone steps. "I am as I appear, in the body of an old woman. I ache when I get up every day. But after two hundred years, I've learned how to exceed the limits on me by using magic—something you, too, must do. Only, we lack the luxury of time. You and your friends are on Date's radar."

"So are you."

"I'm fully trained, unlike you. I may be powerful, but I know my bounds.

So, I have contacts in case of an emergency. Don't you fret."

After we're hidden by the trees, she shifts into her natural state. Stretching, she yips, scampering ahead, and her tails trail behind in her happy lope.

"Oh, it feels good to be a fox again!"

My first order of business is cleaning—sweeping the floors and steps, changing the paper ornaments, and wiping down the windows. Next is my offering.

This morning, I'd picked out the luckiest coins, the ones with the holes in them. So, I toss them into the coffer. Then Sensei directs me on how to place my twin bottles of sake with her gift of rice and salt.

"Going all out today?" she asks.

"I have a big request."

"Oh?"

Zipping my lips, I defer the answer.

"It's a shame my nephew won't keep a home shrine. Then you could do this there."

"But we wouldn't have met."

"True enough." Her eyes crinkle in response.

Will she ever know how much meeting her changed my life? We give our respects side by side, and I linger a tad longer with my request. *Make me worthy. Please.*

"Ready?" She leads me to a grassy clearing surrounded by towering bamboo and cedar.

The rush of the wind through the trees has my head whipping at every clack and creak of the multiple-story tall, grey-green bamboo tops colliding around us. Every loud crack makes me twitch as if there's a fight going on. Though, I like the fresh green, woodsy smell.

Snapping me to attention, Sensei asks, "Isn't it peaceful?"

"Not really." Shoving my hands into my pockets doesn't relieve the twitching. "How could we hear if someone is approaching with this racket?"

She chuckles. "I suppose you didn't grow up in a forest like I did. Anyway, do you remember when I said mortals are limited in magic use? With Date in the picture, we have to push your potential to its maximum ASAP. Starting today, we do the impossible. What you are about to learn my family hasn't taught to a human since Yuki studied under my father. But you need to prepare for anything since the odds are stacked against you."

"Me?"

Halting and harrumphing, she causes me to stumble as I avoid walking over her. "Is there anyone else here?" Her next question comes with a softer tone. "Do you trust me?"

That's never followed by anything good. "Yeah. Why are you asking?"

"Because when we started, I thought I had the luxury of time. I'll make your body a puppet to show the possibilities. It will speed up your training significantly. I won't subdue you. If I do, you won't experience what's needed. And I hate possessing people. But, if you fight it right away, there's a risk of hurting you as I teach you to use your ability."

"Okaaaay..." The hairs on my arms raise. It's not from the breeze.

"We start now. While you showed ability dodging the car, you didn't have mastery over that skill. Learning control is the priority." Three tails whip in the air, knocking my legs out from under me.

With limbs flailing, I pitch forward and my breath hitches. The thick foliage is inches from my face as she slows me to a feather-soft descent. Instinctively I push away, but there's no need. It's as if I'm hovering. Upon touching down, her influence leaves. *What just happened?*

"Now, clear your mind, Tatsuya."

Frost forms from my breath on the nearby grass blades as Sensei's voice permeates my thoughts. 'I've established the connection. If someone else attempts this, they'll be subtle and silent about it. But you know what to look for.' A push on my conscience compels me to stand.

"Again. When I knock you down, use kotodama with the effect you want. Like when you write the paper talismans, but for humans this requires your voice and uses much more ki. Expect exhaustion. Part of the goal is to increase your energy pool."

Three more times I freeze up, unable to say a blasted thing, as she whips me to the ground. I'll have bruises, and my pants and satin jacket won't be the same.

Watch for it. My fists tense. I could swear she's drawing this out to torture me. When I look up, the pressure builds. I shout from my core and brace for the impact. A light blue haze fills my vision as sunshine warmth expands from the inside. I still land with an 'oof' but it's less harsh. *Oh yeah, that sapped energy.*

"Come on! Fall down seven times, stand up eight!"

Hiro used to yell that same proverb. Panting, I haul my sorry butt to standing again.

"Higher," she commands.

A shudder runs through me at the thought of a longer drop. Finally, there's the prick to my consciousness. Before she lifts me, I belt out the kotodama so her grasp lightens.

The warmth turns to a flame inside. My surroundings turn a brighter blue, and I hit at a speed that's possible to roll out of. But I collapse, spent.

"Sensei, are you training me to fight the control or did I slow actions?"

"Both. Notice the manipulation so you react at the start. It's Date's forte, but it's possible to resist. Know this well, the witch won't hesitate to dominate you—forcing you to do things you wouldn't dream of doing."

I'm too sapped to comment. Nudging with her nose, she curls beside me. "Also note, for this part of time dilation, only you change speed. Everything around you is irrelevant. Let's take a break before your friends arrive. You don't need another walking into a car moment because you're distracted by Ohno-chan."

That brings a chuckle. "Thanks."

"Don't thank me. There'll be plenty of distraction."

Sensei wouldn't ask Ohno to do anything risqué, would she?

The fox continues, "While we rest, I'll tell you about the limits you'll have and what to be aware of. First is the view of yourself, from your perspective and from others. While it's good to be humble, it's impossible to please everyone. Decide who you will be when all hell breaks loose.

"Also, humans, as you've seen, can only use spoken and written kotodama. Expressing what you want to happen as an effect for an action already in motion. You can't create with the word. Ofuda use also has limits. We yokai, as mythical beings, can fashion magical objects and illusions. So you'll be at another disadvantage compared to us. But we have weaknesses."

To see her expression, my head lifts. "Tell me you're not saying we might have to end Date."

"Possibly."

Deflated, I let my skull thud back to the grass. "And if we don't? 'Cause, I'm not sure I can deal with any more deaths on my conscience."

"She keeps returning. Chop one of her hydra heads off, two more grow in its place."

"Isn't there a different way?"

"I haven't found it yet."

My past is why she picked me. My voice cracks as my heart shrinks in on itself. "So I'm just gonna be a more efficient killer. Shit."

"Tatsuya! I wouldn't be training you if I thought you'd be eager to spill blood. You and I both value life, after having had to take it. And she's proven her ability to escape death. Though, I hope we find an alternative, if only because my people are dwindling."

After the uncomfortable moment passes, she says, "Now, the most important point. When something seems effortless, that's a warning sign— such as an easy source of ki or an extreme amount of power. Energy that doesn't manifest in your ki well or isn't given to you, cannot be used. That's forbidden magic and, if relied upon, leads to death for the user and others around. Do you understand?"

"I think so." Though my insides still wind up over the thought of taking a life again.

"Then rest before your friends arrive."

A cold nose pokes my cheek. "Wake up, Tatsuya," Sensei says.

Rubbing my eyes, I find my coworkers staring. Matsuo helps me up. I spy the bo tucked behind his shoulder.

He says dryly, "Sleep training? I expected to see something more... spectacular."

"Hardly. Sensei was rough on me."

Ohno's already holding out a jar of that awesome balm. She's an angel.

Mie, in contrast, stands as dour as ever with her bow and quiver, twirling her ponytail. Her usually perfect mouth is pinched as if she sucked on a lemon.

"Matsuo-kun, you're up. Will you let me control your movement to maximize Tatsuya's training?" At his deep furrowed brow, Sensei clarifies, "After a few times, you'll see the gist. Then I'd like you to fight the control, so you learn to avoid domination by fox magic."

"I... can agree to that." He still sounds hesitant to me, though.

"Good. Tatsuya will learn anticipation from you." With a swish of her tail, Sensei provides a shield and adds a spell to his staff.

Matsuo gives a maniacal grin, then squares off with me. *What kind of beating am I about to get?* My jacket will provide little padding for his strikes.

Giving a tug to keep my stocking cap from falling off, I nod my readiness. Then his face goes blank, and with a mighty shout, he attacks headlong.

Is he hesitating because we aren't wearing kendo gear? Belting out the word to slow him, I dodge to let him run by. *Easy peasy.*

Smugly, I look to Ohno. When her impressed look changes to her hands covering her mouth, I turn. The staff slams into my gut. I'm thrown, winded by more force than he should have had.

He's already coming at me again. No time to choose. I roll, coughing the spell for healing. Warmth and a little new ki flow in as I stand to voice a command to speed my moves.

A flick of my wrist allows me to grasp the bo and tug hard to bring him within reach. But his staff circles to the outside, twisting my wrist off it. So I have to dodge his jab and try again. This time, he tries to retreat, but I trip him. One point for me.

Assisting him sends him flying, and he yelps. So, I hang on to add stability.

"Stop dancing, you two!" Sensei hollers.

We go at it once more. The point where he resists Sensei's control is when his expression switches to the playful-puppy one I know well. *Good boy, Matsuo.*

As if scolding me for taking my eyes off the threat, he lands a hit on my shoulder that hurts like the dickens and a flash obscures my vision. Though nothing's broken that I can tell. Venting the hot energy from the pain as I kick, my voice echoes in the clearing and it knocks Matsuo ten meters away flat on his butt.

Wide eyes accompany his exclamation. "Cool! Do that again!"

Stopping for a quick break, Nakamura asks Ohno to apply the salve.

Sensei, come on. Don't put me on display. Pulling my hat over my face won't hide the tats. But the injury is keeping me from moving effectively. *Gotta do this.*

As I peel my shoulder out of the top layers, I wince. The exposed ink makes me more naked and vulnerable than the day I was born. People often ostracize Yakuza over their ink. Should we have gone to a private place for this?

Undaunted, Matsuo moves closer, wanting a better look. "Whoa. Those kitsune are amazing!"

Mie rolls her eyes at Matsuo and turns around. A feathery-light touch on the knotting muscle in my shoulder lifts. As I twist, Ohno draws away. *She's afraid.*

Thrusting out my hand, I speak fast to get this over with. "Gimme the jar, I'll do it. It's damn cold out here."

"Dear, please ogle him later," Sensei snickers.

My eyes narrow in a nasty glare at my teacher. *Don't embarrass her, Sensei.*

"I'll apply it." Now, Ohno probes with more surety. "Tell me where it hurts. It's hard to know the extent of the injury under all that ink."

"That was part of the purpose."

Her "Oh," falls flat. When I hiss, Ohno slathers the ointment then applies a bandage to keep my shirt clean. "Glad I investigated. The wound goes beyond the initial welt."

If I weren't freezing and on public display, the attention would be great.

She persists. "What about the hit to your stomach? You seemed to recover fast. Was that a healing spell?"

"Yep."

Then Sensei adds her magic to speed the recovery. "It's less taxing when it's not all from your own spell. The effect is exponential with multiple casters."

Mie's up next. Sensei runs a tail over each of the bird-blunt arrows and her bow. "These shafts will fly faster. So adjust your aim."

As I snag my shinai, Mie mutters so only I hear, "I dunno why we're bothering to make a so-called former yakuza more powerful. Hurt Ohno, and it won't be blunts. Got it?"

Putting my arms up in surrender, I'm tempted to shout so everyone can hear out of spite.

Instead, I whisper, "You're the one spewing mobster threats. She's outta my league. Truce?" What was Sensei thinking when she invited Mie today?

"Keep that attitude, buckwheat."

As she tromps off about fifty meters, my pulse speeds up. *She didn't believe me.*

Hitting the arrows aside goes pretty well, but only because I'm practicing time dilation. At normal speed, there's no way I could do this. Though Mie keeps changing her timing by coming closer.

When I catch an arrow mid-flight at short range, she swears and stomps her foot. Turning away is the only way to cover my grin. But Matsuo spots it, just nodding his approval.

The next task is learning to run up the bamboo, like I saw in Wuxia movies as a kid. Going up is great. Going down, not so much. I'm running low on ki, and Sensei got distracted by a discussion.

Upon seeing my ungraceful shimmying, she rushes over. "Sorry, Tatsuya! Let me help."

Mie smirks.

After that, Sensei races me. While I lose, for a biped I do well, arriving a few steps behind her.

Despite ki boosts, I'm winded. A nap sounds fantastic. But it's Ohno's turn. Sensei saved her talents to push my determination. It'll be the toughest, most dangerous test with no extra ki to lean on.

My opponent drops a bag, standing there sucking in her bottom lip as if unsure she should attack me. So I give her a push. "Ohno-chan, pretend I'm one of those who chased your family from your home."

That worked. She tosses a pair of dark canisters that crash in the grass to my side. Whatever the black things are, they move fast and merge. Kotodama based dodging isn't enough.

When the thing grows tentacle arms to grab me, I swear. The more I struggle, the faster it takes more purchase and the faster the coldness inside grows.

"Reach Ohno-chan to be free," Sensei commands.

Fine. Only about three and a half meters. Moving my foot turns out to be harder than lifting a cement slab. I get about twenty centimeters.

Another stride. And another. Each one becomes more difficult. My strength wanes. I glance up at Ohno. Through her pained look, she continues to mutter. She trembles as she conducts the black whatever it is.

Gritting my teeth and murmuring, "Yoisho," I manage one more step.

Eighty centimeters down. A little over two meters left. When I stop to breathe, the ooze crawls farther up.

A kiai despite the lack of power gains me a step. *One meter down.* My thighs shake as I wipe the sweat from my forehead. *So tired.* The cold in my core creeps outward.

Ohno's fists ball up tightly and raise above her head. *Is she holding back?*

The slime hits mid-thigh. It's not connected to the ground now and squeezes the blood out of my calves. My muscles burn as I push. Ohno's face pales. There's a time limit before I pass out and areas I don't want it to reach.

Kick your rear in gear. Just two more steps. But my energy is tapped, and dizziness sets in. *Idiot. There's got to be an option.*

Her clear voice cuts through the din, and she reaches toward me. "Come on Umeji-kun!"

The point the blob grabs my fingers is when the panic kicks in. I need those to reach the goal!

Growling and thrashing don't help. Swear words slosh through my thoughts. Iciness burns in my chest. *This damned thing is keeping me from Ohno.*

Then a flicker appears in my mind—a flame lighting up a dark cavern. One final smidgen. Snarling the word for strength gives me enough to make those three steps. Sensei never said I had to walk the whole way.

When the ooze pins my arms to my sides, it fills in toward the center. Blackness and cold threaten to overtake me.

Meeting Ohno's eyes, I mouth, "I trust you," as I hurl myself forward in one momentous effort, sinking into her embrace.

Matsuo rushes to help as Ohno grunts against the force of the impact. Everything around me spins. It takes both friends to ease me to the ground.

When they have my limp body settled, Ohno drapes her jacket over me and a warm glow grows as she places her hands on my chest.

"So, you're healing him?" Matsuo asks, voice tinged with wonder.

"Helping him survive." All too soon, she steps away, and I hear her coax the damned blob thing into a container.

My legs tingle and the fog clears. That must mean the blood is flowing again. When I can see straight and the ooze's jar is closed, I ask, "What was that thing?"

"A semi-sapient slime named Chou. She picked her name, by the way."

"I thought it was gonna eat me."

That earns a chuckle. "Nah, we fed her last week. Since you gave us quite the challenge, Chou-chan likes you."

"The feeling isn't mutual." *If I never see that thing again, it'll still be too soon.*

Ohno's voice goes quieter. "But I was scared. I didn't fight Nakamura-san's control, because I'd have saved instead of pushing you. Chou drains ki, and you had to use the very last of yours to reach me. It's deadly unless the victim is immediately infused with some. Nakamura-san allowed me to give you enough to survive. She's drained, too."

Every muscle hurts, but I have to get somewhere warm to stop the shivering coming from my core. When I lift my head, it swims, and Matsuo helps me sit up.

"So I passed?"

"Did you learn anything?" Nakamura prompts.

"I think how to resist mind manipulation and find the last bit of energy inside me."

"Beyond that."

"Dunno. I wouldn't have dreamed I could do what I did today—not without everyone's help."

"If you learned that you're capable of so much more than you thought—yes, you passed. It doesn't make you the chosen one or any such nonsense. But you've got potential. What will you do with it? Think on that."

Sensei's too wobbly to walk. So, Ohno scoops her up.

Instead of complying, Sensei says, "Give me to Mie-chan. I need a word with her. Then go assist Tatsuya."

"Should I share more ki?"

"We'll be fine after we rest. Hand me off, please dear."

Matsuo pulls me up to standing. He and Ohno slip an arm around me as we work our way down the hill to their vehicles, and the sky spits snow at us.

This isn't my proudest moment, but we gotta get home. "Thanks, guys."

Ohno whines, "Why did Nakamura-san say I can't share more energy?"

"Maybe they shouldn't depend on that? What if it's addictive or there's a long-term price?" Matsuo gives a thoughtful look.

"Sensei warned me about taking shortcuts," I add.

Ohno shifts under my weight. "There is the aspect of building your reserve. I've used magic all my life, so I've built up a lot."

Click. My feet halt, causing my friends to lurch. They give me worried looks, so I share my thought. "Then Date might not be as strong as she should be, because she's used an oni shortcut for over a century."

"That could be true." Matsuo considers when we resume.

As we hobble past the shrine, my gaze lands on the now-empty sake bottles. *When did Sensei have time to drink them?* Hope she enjoyed it. Those were expensive.

Once I'm dumped into Ohno's Honda, Matsuo zips over to let Mie and Sensei into his vehicle. So it'll be just Ohno and me on the return trip. *Sensei needs to stop playing matchmaker.*

My fingers shake so badly that they fumble with the seatbelt. Without a word, Ohno gets out, opens my door, and leans my seat back. Taking my trembling hand off the buckle, she tugs on the belt.

So, I'm not allowed an ounce of pride today. *Fine.* Though, her face is ridiculously close. I could kiss her. Last minute, I stop myself. *She could do so much better.* If I care for her, I'll let her go.

Even if my words are inadequate, she deserves the courtesy. "Thanks for your help today and for lending me the iPod. I'm enjoying the music."

Starting up the car, she pulls out. "No prob. What did you listen to first?"

"The K-pop list," I state matter-of-factly, not going into the reason.

"Is that so?" Her eyes sparkle with a mirth that makes everything alright.

17

CHAPTER 17: SKY FALL

When I wake facing the couch, darkness fills the room. My head hurts so bad it threatens to turn inside out. Every muscle aches.

As I turn over and mutter a few choice words, I find Ohno at the kotatsu. She looks up from her book and tiny light and emerges from the blanket cover to kneel beside me. It must be before dawn. *Why is she here?*

Rubbing my eyes, I ask, "What time is it?"

"Eight."

That can't be right. My brows furrow as I point to the window, "Why's it dark?"

Putting a wrist to my forehead and an index finger to her lips, she whispers, "Eight PM. You slept for twenty-eight hours. Satou-san asked me to take turns with him watching over you and Nakamura-san. We worried about you both. Though, Nakamura-san warned us you two would be out for a long time." She points to the silver fox, snoring softly, curled up in a blanket by the couch. "You hungry?"

"Starving."

"Meet me at the table, I'll grab soup. If you can handle more than that, we'll investigate what Satou-san left for us."

So, I hobble off to find ibuprofen. The aroma of the soup in the microwave entices me to hurry. Unable to talk much to avoid waking Nakamura, we eat in the comfortable silence of an 'electricity is out, but we're safe' kind of vibe.

After dinner, she pats the heated table. "Should we listen to the iPod together?"

I nod, then retrieve it and the letter. She points to each song with its explanation to emphasize her feelings about it. Pulling a pen from her purse and writing a few more notes in the margins, she asks what I think.

So, I point out the songs that resonate with me. "Especially the one that talks about wanting to be somebody."

She writes, "Why? You already are."

An urgent rap at the entryway saves me from having to reply. *That better not be the NHK guy.* The last thing I need is someone trying to collect the TV contract fee right now because I don't have the cash and those guys are so damned annoying.

The persistent knocking continues even as I open the door. When familiar ferret eyes light on me with pleased recognition, every muscle in my body tenses and my free hand clenches.

"Hiro." Memories of my clan's betrayal, my arrest, abandonment, and every time he slapped me upside the head slam into me, and my throat tightens.

On instinct, my fist connects with his jaw. His head pops back. Recovering, he cracks his neck, dropping into a fighting stance. I'm able to block his first two punches.

His third jab catches me under the ribs, knocking the wind out of me and causing me to slump against the open door. From my limited ki supply, I gasp a healing spell.

"Nice to see you, too, Tatsuya," he mutters darkly as he wipes the blood off his lip.

Bile rises in my throat when I spy the glowing green ring.

Ohno runs up behind me. "Umeji-kun!?"

Taking off his overcoat and hat, he places them with familiarity on the hook. His left hand lacks a pinky knuckle, and he doesn't hide it. I remember all too well the nausea as I witnessed him make the gruesome offering to our leader.

Then my eyes flit to his suit jacket. A holster strap hints at the Sig Sauer he always carries. On the inside of his right boot that he just took off, I spot the pocket for his tanto dagger. It's empty. He's armed to the teeth. *Shit.*

Retrieving a device from his pocket, he sets it below the entrance step, then switches it on. The high-pitched, bug-ish buzz it emits pierces my skull, increasing the headache.

Removing his ring, he drops it into the well in the device's top. "Now we can talk." A black line remains on his hand where the band was.

"No greeting for your aniki? Ah well, where's Satou-san? He said to meet him here."

His sharp-tapered face, close-cropped hair, penetrating stare, and quiet, self-assured air haven't changed a single bit. *Same old guy, yakuza to the core.* Striding into the living room doesn't cover his limp. *That's new.*

"Why is he saying he's your older brother? Umeji-kun, who is he?" Ohno's voice rises as she flips on the light.

To keep her a safe distance, I move between them holding out my arms. "My mob sponsor, Otsuka Hiro. The mob is family."

"Who's the arm candy?" Hiro looks her over. At least, he had the decency to avoid leering. He always preferred the innocent ones like Ohno-chan.

"Leave her out of this!" I prep another spell.

He tsks. "I won't harm your girl, little brother. Skip the attitude."

My insides twist at the repeated reference to our bond. The promise he broke. Taking a step forward, my words come in a burst. "I haven't been your 'brother' since you sold out the Hiragi Clan and left me to rot in jail. Gimme your message for my boss, then get the fuck out."

Nakamura, still in fox form, appears by my side with tails bristled and growling at my old mentor. If need be, the two of us should be able to handle Hiro.

His expression hardens. With bird-like movements, he gets in my face. "It was Kuji who betrayed us all! And your lifelong oath included taking the fall for me. Or did you forget? I hardly call bargaining for your sentence to be cut from twelve years to six with parole halfway through selling out. Your sorry ass was up for racketeering, possession and use of firearms, and four counts of second-degree murder. There were a lot of strings to pull for a reduction. Can't ya' show some gratitude, boy?"

I back down, unable to argue. Though, it burns that he's able to force his way yet again and I'm still nothing more than the punk he took in ten years ago.

"Murder?" Hearing the horror in Ohno's voice snatches my feet out from under me.

Truth's riptide might as well carry me out to sea for good. "I was yakuza, Ohno-chan. I did as ordered. It's the code. The oath." This loosed reality won't be stuffed in the corner so neatly again.

When the door clicks and creaks, Satou announces, "I'm home," then blanches at the face-off with my former mentor. "Hiro, you're early."

My boss knows him well enough to leave off the suffix. *So this was all a ruse?*

"Kazuo, you didn't speak with Tatsuya. Did you?" Sensei rounds on her nephew. There's fire in her eyes.

Hiro smirks. "You have a kitsune here? Satou, you sly dog, I thought you said you weren't into the supernatural. You've changed."

What the hell? My glance flicks from Nakamura to Satou and back to Hiro.

Sensei changes to her older human form to hold the energy she prepared for a spell in one hand and with the other shake a finger in Hiro's direction. "Watch your tongue, yakuza. He's my nephew."

Other than eyeing the glowing flames in her hand, Hiro's only reaction is a slight bow. "My apologies, kitsune-sama. I have no quarrel with you."

She sniffs but extinguishes the fire.

"I found out three days ago she's a yokai. The news that's she's a powerful spirit being won't go over well, will it?" Satou runs a hand through his hair, only to give a weak grin.

In the pause, Hiro shakes his head as Sensei clears her throat.

"Aunt, I'm still determining if Umeji is trustworthy. Tell me, how did you bewitch him into loyalty to you? I know you used a spell, but there's something more to this story that I haven't heard."

Nakamura turns her back on him adding to the chill in the room. To me she directs, "Tatsuya, stay if you wish. Or, if you need space from this mess, I'm calling a taxi."

When Satou gestures for the gangster to take the spot of honor near the tokonoma display alcove, my chest tightens. As Hiro sits, he says to my VPO, "I made Umeji be the best for a reason. You know that."

He never said that to me. Nothing I ever did was enough for Hiro.

"I'll give you a ride home. I was leaving anyway," Ohno volunteers, without enthusiasm. She won't look at me.

The normality that I'd been working so hard toward crumples. *Time to cut my losses.* Same as when Mom wouldn't respond to my letter and when my aniki sold me out. *Good doesn't last for my kind.*

Hiro leans toward me. "Tatsuya, unpleasant things lurk in the shadows. It's not safe out there, so ensure they get home."

I hate him. But my former mentor won't warn without reason. "Let's go, Sensei."

"He can't force you to return, can he?" Ohno asks as she unlocks her Honda.

My shoulders droop. "I can't go back to that life."

Her glare says my lack of direct answer didn't fool her. But my mind races for a way to avoid that fate. Will I be capable of severing a knuckle from my hand to escape?

Silence hangs sticky and bitter in the air on the drive. I'm relegated to the cold rear seat. But there's a chasm between Ohno and me, and I have no way to fix it.

It's for the best. So why's it make me want to hit something? *As if she would have ever been mine.* The damned stigma will follow me all my days.

When I exit the car at her house, the cold tang in the air bites through my unzipped jacket. I leave the iPod on the dash. Ohno's gaze focuses straight ahead, tears rolling down her cheeks. Worse, she won't acknowledge me as I offer thanks for the ride.

After Ohno is inside, Sensei and I walk the few remaining blocks from the modern neighborhood to the older, traditional one across the river. Letting the chill of the night air fill my lungs doesn't ease the alternating deadening and boiling in my veins.

Kicking a light post and bellowing streams of profanity does nothing to soothe, either. Though, it lets out pent-up energy. Neighbors peek out their windows. If I keep this up, it won't be long until the cops come.

Sensei murmurs a word of kotodama. "Let it out, Tatsuya. You're in a muffling spell."

At least this way I can vent over a girl I offended by simply having been in the mob. Raging, I scream at the top of my lungs about the unfairness as we reach Sensei's street. "No matter what I do, nothing goes right for long. Satou is a fucking hypocrite. Hiro's ass should be in jail. It's so damned wrong that he's out and doing well while life shits on me. And I didn't want to hurt her. I didn't wanna ever hurt her."

Slumping to my knees on the living room's tatami, I've spent my words. Ohno was out of my league from the start. But why couldn't I keep from falling for her? Why did the kitsune push us together? Didn't she know this would happen?

Instead of leaving me alone, Sensei pours me a cup of sake, keeping me company in silence. She keeps the cup filled. But the alcohol doesn't stop the internal voices. Before I get too drunk, I slow the consumption. The last thing Sensei needs is a drunk ex-yakuza.

I'm trapped here. Things were fine until Hiro showed up. Matsuo will probably ditch me, too. How can people see I left the mob behind with a yakuza connection around? Will I be ever able to save up for my own place, let alone start a business? I have no idea what that would be yet. But it would be nice to have some control over my life.

* * *

We finish cleaning Sensei's house the following day. She asks if I want to tend the shrine with her and practice afterward. I decline all but the stroll. I'm too dirty to tag along. I sit on the bottom stair to read. But my tattered mythology book brings no comfort.

When she returns, I ask, "Sensei, how can I make something of myself when I only react to the shit that happens?"

"Your question is a good start. What will you do when you see Otsuka-san again?"

"No idea. I just can't go back."

"Another step in the right direction. You need to decide your response or be forced to react next time. That predictability would allow him to manipulate you."

* * *

Back to work again. Satou says the situation has settled down. Like it or not, he's my boss and VPO, even if I'm not able to trust him. How the hell did he become my parole officer when he's got mob ties?

To his credit, he gave Ohno the day off. That lets me ease into the swing again.

Matsuo works late, and my teacher has appointments. Too bad there's nothing to look forward to. Numbness settles inside. I turn into a machine as I stock the shelves.

"Mama, there he is!" shouts the boy who's obsessed with my tattoos.

Please. Not now.

The mother tries to shush him from making shooting sounds and forces down his pistol-shaped hand. He'll be the next generation taken in by the lies. Is it rude to jump in where I'm not welcome so I can tell him what he idolizes is not cool?

The truth upset Ohno. It's better to keep the past buried, but not saying something could cost this boy.

Sucking in a deep breath, I approach them. "Ma'am, I know it's not my business. Though, I might be able to help. May I have a word with your son?"

Her small eyes narrow. Grabbing the boy's hand, she drags him away.

"But he's a yakuza! He wouldn't let anyone beat him up in school!" the child howls. A yellowing bruise on his round cheek causes my heart to stop for a second. His mom gives an apologetic bob for the ruckus.

Shoving my hands into my pockets and lowering my head, I confess, "Yeah,

I was in the mob. But it won't solve your problems. It'll make things worse."

Warily, she releases him. He books it over, skidding to a stop right at my toes to look up into my face. "But you're tough! You could kill anybody who bullies you, right?"

He's probably only in elementary school. Why's he asking this? "What's your name, kid?"

"Suzuki Sojirou. What's yours?" His lifted chin defies my treating him as a child.

So, I point to my employee badge. "Umeji."

Taking a moment to gather my thoughts, I plow forward despite my stomach being tied in knots. "It's not what you see on TV, Suzuki-san. Once you take a life, there's no undo. You don't feel better afterward. You feel awful. Most nights, I have nightmares from the things I've seen and done."

Ticking off items on my fingers, I count the costs. "My mom won't speak to me. I've lost so much—people I cared about, my freedom, all the money I earned, my reputation, any possibility for college, and the list could go on for hours.

"In a gunfight, I wasn't able to stop my clan brother from dying. No matter how hard I tried, he bled out. I couldn't even attend his funeral, 'cause I was in the slammer. So, every day for the rest of my life, I'll be trying to atone for what I've done. Even now, my past hurts people. Last night, a friend cried when she found out why I went to jail. She was one of the few who would talk to me. I don't know if she will anymore."

Shoved up sleeves on his 'I love dinosaurs' t-shirt expose more bruises and scrapes, along with some tattoo imitations drawn in pen. "So, nothing will stop the bullies at school? The teachers get mad at me for fighting, and they don't do anything!"

The woman's hands cover her mouth as she nods.

Waving, I catch the assistant manager's attention. "Hey Matsuo-san, would you be willing to teach young Suzuki-san here how to defend himself?"

"Sure." He smiles in encouragement.

The boy's shoulders droop. "Why not you?"

"This guy will be a better teacher because he's never been a gangster. Also, Aikido is for defense, so you'll be less apt to get in trouble at school." Then I stage-whisper. "He's thrown me to the mat more times than I can count."

Suzuki's eyes widen before his look turns skeptical. "But he's shorter than you!"

I shrug. "Matsuo-kun knows how to use my momentum against me."

Once the mother is sure my co-worker is reputable, she approaches him to arrange lessons and introduces herself as Suzuki Chiyo. Matsuo's expression says I just did him the biggest favor.

The boy looks uncertain. So, I offer him a fist bump, and I'm surprised when he's allowed to return it. "Go help your Mom. Ok?"

Suzuki nods, scampering off with his mom and Matsuo. A lightness fills my chest, unlike any I've known before.

"I wish Ohno-chan could have heard that." Mie's voice from behind causes me to jump.

Ready for a fight, I whirl around. Editing out the swear words slows my answer. "Where'd you come from?"

"That was a compliment, buckwheat. Considering Ohno-chan was so distressed when she called me she didn't sound like herself, that's a big concession." Mie crosses her arms and leans on the shelves behind her.

What did Sensei say to Mie after the training session? "I can't blame her. She didn't understand the truth of what I used to be 'till that moment."

"If you meant that bit about atoning for what you've done, I won't be at your throat. I thought you were here to recruit for the yakuza clans. It brought back too many bad memories for me. Since you're not, I'll relay what you said. It should allow her to reconcile what we see today and what you were. Though, don't think I'm gonna help you date my friend." Then she startles, glancing over my shoulder and dumping the responsibility on me before escaping. "Someone needs help."

"Excuse me. Where's the red miso paste?"

I count to five, to avoid decking the owner of that voice again. I hadn't planned how to deal with him yet. *Aren't there other employees he could bother?*

"Hiro, is this cover, or do you actually need miso?" If only I could wipe that smirk right off his face.

"So skeptical, Tatsuya. Help me find the stuff, and I'll share a piece of advice."

"Dunno if I'll take it." None-the-less, we head to the cooler section with the bean paste.

"You always were hard-headed," my old mentor says with the surety of knowing me for a decade.

Pointing to different varieties, I wait for him to select one. His voice hushes. "How do I put this? I recommended Satou-san be your VPO. Ask him."

"Why? I want nothing to do with that life anymore, and you know it."

"There were things I wanted to share before that attack. I'd planned to talk with you about it the next day. Fate threw a fucked-up curveball with Kuji squealing. It wasn't supposed to go down that way. For that, I'm sorry. And for messing up the relationship with your girl. Parolees need to be around those who have an investment in them. So, believe me when I say that I won't force you back into that life, but I still hope to offer you an option."

Apologies aren't Hiro's gig. I only heard him apologize when he had to cut off the end of his pinky finger. On top of that, yakuza don't let their subordinates go free. *Something's off.* "I can't trust a man who wears Date's ring. So I'll have to decline."

"You can't be sure if you can trust me, or of what you're turning down until you ask Satou-san. Anyway, thanks for assisting with the miso. See you around." He nods, limping off and pushing his cart toward the vegetables before I can turn him down again.

Sometimes ya' just don't wanna know. At least I stood my ground this time.

18

CHAPTER 18: CONFESSIONS

When I enter the break room on my next shift, Mie's voice carries from the boss's office. "Why are you always being so secretive? I know you have a past, but you don't have to keep it from me."

Abort! No wonder the break room is empty.

After buying a cheap egg bento, I walk to the park. Scenes from last night keep replaying relentlessly through my head. Sand from the play pit sprays in a high arc when I give a good kick because no one's around. Such satisfying childishness calls to me after the crap from the last few days.

The impulse overtakes me again before I settle into a swing. A chill from the seat seeps through my pants. So, I scarf down my lunch as clouds rush in to hide the lone peep of happy sunshine from earlier and the sky spits a few snowflakes directly at me. Just my luck.

To spite the weather I stroll, weaving through the maple and ginkgo to find the occasional fallen leaf until the end of my break. At least, the brisk air helps clear my thoughts.

Sensei often hints about Satou's plan. What if I ask her about it?

Returning from break, I spot Ohno in the parking lot. Some guy intercepts. But she shakes her head and walks away.

When he grabs her arm, I break into a run, calling her name. That gets his attention. As he turns and those ferret eyes light on me, my brain inserts every bit of profanity at once.

Using kotodama for a speed boost, I pour my all into the sprint and scream at the top of my lungs, "Hiro! Leave her alone!"

"Please, hear me out." My aniki's mild request of Ohno raises my hackles.

I don't give a damn if it's hypocritical. The mobster can't be trusted farther than I could throw him. My voice drops deep to threat level and I step in front of Ohno. "I told you to leave her alone."

"Tatsuya, you idiot. I want to repair what I broke the other night. Then I'll leave. It's the least I can do," he grumbles through gritted teeth.

He won't force her to listen. "Drop it." My arms cross and spread in finality.

"Hello! I'm right here. Let me hear what Hiro-san has to say!" Ohno's tone has the 'You're in trouble' vibe.

"You'd listen to an active yakuza member?" My voice squeaks, but I keep my gaze locked on my old mentor. He was the one who taught me to never take my eyes off the threat.

"If it gets me into work. I'm late." She's tapping her foot and crossing her arms, so I keep my gob shut.

Hiro jumps at the chance. "Ohno-san, what I didn't say a few nights ago was this. First, I won't coerce Tatsuya into being yakuza again. He doesn't believe me, but I have my reasons. Second, he saved lives that fateful day. Returning too late to save our boss from the sneak attack by another clan, we walked in on a bloodbath. Tatsuya applied first-aid as I fired off rounds to keep the attackers at bay. In the end, he saved me and a rival clan member. Tried for four, but two were too far gone. I was hit moments before the swat team arrived.

"That's why I bargained hard for a reduced sentence. You think ill of me, but I wanted to do the honorable thing by offering the other side of the story. Thank you for listening." He gives a respectful bob and departs.

I'm frozen in place with my eyes glued to his back. That's not what the cops said—he sold our clan out. *Why aren't two and two making four?*

"Earth to Umeji-kun?" Ohno taps my forehead, startling me. "Walk me inside?"

"Uh. Sure." Stuffing my fists in my pockets, I tuck my face into my coat to ward off the cold. Fog from my breath escapes in streams.

"I was saying, it was good we listened." She gives a meek upturn of her lips. "Though I'm glad you were there. He made me nervous."

"No problem." After the incident two nights ago, she shouldn't talk to me again. Maybe I'm a little higher on the ladder than dirt.

Looking up at the 'TaniMart' sign, she clasps her hands. "Mie-chan told me what you said to Suzuki-kun and how you helped by setting up lessons with Matsuo-san. Pretty brave, considering my reaction."

She rummages in her purse, pulling out the iPod. "So, let me give this back. I'm having trouble reconciling your past. But I want to listen to your story if you're willing to share it. You up for udon tonight?"

My throat goes dry. Spilling my guts is a damned if I do, damned if I don't situation. I'll probably lose her either way.

Wait. Did she just ask me on a date? Accepting the device, I point to myself in the unvoiced question as we reach the break room.

She clarifies, "As work friends, buster."

Friends! Not dirt. Breathe. "Sensei and I are training until five. After that?"

"Meet you at Nakamura-san's at seven." She clocks in, waves, and jogs to her till at the front.

How in the world am I gonna tell her? The remaining few minutes of break allow me to soak up her favorite song and re-read her notes. 'I like this one because it describes how caring for others can make a difference.' My heart thaws with the renewal of our friendship. Though, my stomach knots tighter every time I think of sharing my tangled past.

* * *

Nakamura notices the iPod when I set it on the table beside me as I prep for the lesson. "So things improved? We should have a New Year's gathering. Invite your friends. I usually have visitors over on the first, but young people these days seem to celebrate like the Westerners."

"You wouldn't mind? It'd be great to thank them for the second chance."

"It would also be a way to mend with Kazuo and keep those important to us safe in one place."

How Satou and I will ever see eye to eye is a mystery. I blow out a breath. Sensei's right, though. With Date on the prowl, this is the safest spot for the group to be on a party night. "I'll try. What can I do to help?"

"Practice." She taps the paper in front of me. "Then let's talk."

"At least let me pay for the preparations."

"Deal. We'll shop tonight. Now, write."

Running a hand through my hair, I paste on a grin. "Uhm. Sorry. Ohno-chan and I are going out for udon at seven. Tomorrow?"

As she leans in to ask for details, I hold my hands out forestalling her hope. "Work friends, Sensei. She wants me to share my story after what happened at Satou-san's. Think I'll pass the test?"

Putting a hand on my shoulder, she says, "Just be yourself."

She has no idea how scary that is.

Today's task is learning to make a portal. This spell is hard because it's not an ability-boosting one. It modifies reality, thus it's only possible using ofuda and going to a place I've been. The farther it is, the more ki required.

Trying one to the next room, I hang the talisman with the symbol for 'gate' on the wall. But the opening it creates is glitchy, sputtering sparks.

"Don't go through." Nakamura gives me a raised eyebrow as she holds up her hand.

So we toss a paper airplane at it. The portal collapses as soon as the plane hits, leaving the paper stuck in the plaster as I shudder to think that could have been me.

On my second attempt, she smacks my skull. "Work friends, he says. Ha! Ohno-chan has your brain all addled!" Pointing to the book and to my writing, she scolds, "You've written it wrong. You need the hook on the gate kanji's right side, and you wrote the strokes out of order. Will alone won't be enough to power an ofuda spell! Do it right this time to get that paper plane out of my living room. It's tacky."

My scalp doesn't hurt, but I rub where she hit, anyway. "Sensei, how did you feel when you hid from your husband after the miscarriage?"

"I see. Not only butterflies you're dealing with?" Kneeling beside me, she offers the support of her presence.

"Dread."

"You think she can't handle the truth?"

I growl, "That's not it!"

"Isn't it? There's more to that girl than you give her credit for. But you must be honest with her."

"What if she doesn't want to be friends anymore?" *Or anything else. Ever.* "I mean. She'll be the first normal person to know the full measure of what I was."

Nakamura gives my arm a decisive pat. "It's more than just telling her. It's facing yourself, isn't it?"

Ouch.

"I've raised three sets of children and a grandchild, Tatsuya. I know how guilt poisons the mind and that we all have to face our demons at some point."

"What if—"

"Keep showing the world who you are, like you did with me. The 'what ifs' will do you no good. Now, concentrate on the task at hand."

On the second attempt, I retrieve the plane. Next is creating a new portal to the shrine that allows passage both ways, along with an extra talisman before I'm tapped. Closing portals is much easier than manifesting them.

Attempting to avoid bugging my boss, I ask, "So what is it you want Satousan to tell me?"

"That's his story to tell. Be careful tonight."

Having to divulge my past is getting closer by the minute. My stomach roils and my fingers feel so cold. "Sensei, it's udon. The worst that'll happen is it's too hot, or I spill the bowl. She's not gonna bite or anything."

"I'd love to see your face if she did."

Her comment steals my voice.

"Can't beat the old fox yet, can you boy?" Rocking on her heels, her head bobble shows just how content she is with herself.

Then changing gears, she tucks a portal ofuda into my pocket. "All teasing aside. Last night, a friend sighted an oni in the park, possibly Date's minion. Get out of there if that's the case. Understand?"

"Roger that."

* * *

When I greet Ohno at the door, rain dumps from the sky outside. She's holding a small umbrella. Sensei, noticing my quandary, loans hers.

I'm shaking so bad it's hard to buckle up in Ohno's car. She says, "I hoped to walk, but our shoes wouldn't dry out before tomorrow."

As she drives, my grip on the car door is tight enough that my fingers cramp. The longer I postpone this, the harder it will get. "Ohno-san, you ready to listen?"

"Shouldn't we wait until after dinner?" She pulls onto a side street, just in case.

"No." My curt answer turns monotone. How am I gonna manage? "Won't be able to eat if I don't get this over."

"I'm sorry, Umeji-kun. You don't have to do this. I just want to hear sometime. Ok?"

"Dunno if I'll have the nerve later. Let's get this done."

"Glad I drove, so we don't freeze." She cranks up the heater and finds a spot to park.

Leaning back against the seat and closing my eyes, I gulp in the chilled air before I confess what I'd never dared to share. "My mom was sick for so long. Her doctor sent her to America for a new treatment. Dad worked his butt off to pay the bills and ensure he provided for me. They both had jobs so we could make ends meet. When she couldn't go back to work, I was so worried about her. My grades fell, and I dropped out of school. My teachers checked on me. And social services stopped by, encouraging me to return to class. But they quit after a while.

"When Dad died, I had no options. Mom was still overseas. She said my uncle would pick me up, but the asshole never showed. At fourteen, I was too young to hold a job, and I hadn't had a decent meal in weeks. So I did what I had to in order to survive, I joined the Hiragi clan. Shit, that sounds like a sob story."

Ohno chimes in softly, "I know that's not what you mean, and I'm still listening."

"They paired me with Otsuka Hiro. He tried hard to talk me out of it because he didn't want anyone slowing him down, especially not a snot-nosed little punk. When he realized I had nowhere else to go, we made our oaths. That means they expected me to lay down my life for him and our leader, Sori-san, in return for them showing me the ropes.

"Hiro was ruthless in everything he did. He taught me how to defend myself—unarmed or with a sword, dagger, or pistol. One of the few kindnesses from him was that he asked me what design I wanted when he took me to get my tats. Knowing it's maddening when they keep poking you, he distracted me with stories of his early days.

"From him, I learned how to blackmail companies into allowing us to purchase large amounts of stock at obscenely discounted prices. This allowed our clan a controlling interest in the firms. They weren't only in Japan. We also had connections in China and the US. While we paid tribute to those higher in the chain, we still made more money than I'll ever see outside the mob. And every single stinkin' yen of it is gone."

Ohno crosses her arms, but she's not turned away from me. Yet. "Do I want to know how many businesses?"

I shrug. "I lost track. Our clan had other rackets—prostitution, drugs, gambling, host clubs, you name it. But Hiro and I stuck to the financial side—extortion and protection. It was the best approach to stay out of the drugs. Though the things we saw were rough. When a clan brother dragged his former girlfriend to the brothel or when we watched a member cut off his pinky, we drank to forget."

"Oh my god. I can't imagine seeing that kind of thing." Her hands cover her mouth, so I share a different aspect of the story.

"Our specialty made us popular with girls. I'm not saying this to brag, it's just part of what happened. Ok?" At her nod, I continue. "They felt we weren't as likely to be abusive. Though, it was never much of a relationship. Quick, get me to sleep with them so I'd be hooked and keep 'em off the streets.

"Soon, I was nothing more than a meal ticket for them. I hated being used because I tried hard not to let it be that way on my end. Depression would set in over the fact that being with a yakuza marked them or that they were in a rough place in life. It'd drive 'em to drugs or club hosts where they'd rack up a bill and end up in prostitution to pay it off.

"I'd break up with them then. I hated it but couldn't let myself go down those paths. Only Chisa went back to her family. I have no idea what happened to her after that. Though, she was the one I missed most. Hiro roughed me over and worked me extra hard so I wouldn't drink myself into a stupor."

Ohno's lip sucks in. "Hiro mentioned you faced four murder counts. So, your clan was part of the street fighting that was in the news?"

Aw, fuck. Now for the worst part. I heave in a ragged breath. "Sure, we fought some on the streets. But the government crackdowns forced clans to leave their areas, which caused brutal and bloody territory clashes. I think the police wanted us mobsters to eliminate each other.

"Hiro and I got caught in a few of the battles. That's when I first gunned down a man. It was awful. Gore spattered everywhere, and I was sick to my stomach. Hiro kept me moving. Dunno the exact number of people I killed in those battles. Don't wanna.

"While the yakuza consider death in battle honorable, I hope it's what they wanted. I've been shot and have scars from knife fights, including the one under my mustache. Remember when I told you that part of the reason for the tats was to cover injuries?"

She nods as she rubs her forehead. "So, what about the part that Hiro brought up? That was the day you were arrested, right?"

"Yeah, it was the most brutal of those clashes. Only Hiro and I survived from our clan of twenty-five. We refused to swear loyalty to another group, 'cause you start at the bottom. Totally sucks.

"By then, I'd gained a little brother of my own. His name was Arata Kentaro, and he gave his life protecting us. Everything went to hell. I tried to save him and another member named Jun from bleeding out, but I couldn't."

I have to choke back a sob as the memories rush back, clear as day, or I won't be able to finish. "After that, I remember picking up Hiro's Sig Sauer in a rage and blowing away a couple of goons. Things went silent.

"So, I tended an unconscious man I didn't recognize. When the special assault team arrived, the fighting started again. Hiro was hit. The other guys opted to go out in a blaze of glory. Instead, I put pressure on Hiro's wound while trying to keep us alive. Somehow, we survived.

"When they arrested us, the bastards shoved me to the ground in Ken's blood as they handcuffed me. The police said Hiro squealed on me in exchange for a lighter sentence of his own."

Ohno's brow furrows. "But he said he bargained for a better sentence. I believe you, but it doesn't make sense."

"I'm still trying to figure that out. But I spent three years in that hellhole prison and have nightmares of my days in the mob. Then I came here with Satou-san to make a fresh start. And you know the rest." Numbness mixed with a heavy weight settles in my chest.

She's not responding. I must've stunned her speechless. Letting my face drop to my hands, I focus on breathing and croak through the tears that stream down my cheeks.

There's still no reaction from her. So, I'll save her the trouble of having to say she's done with me. "I'll walk home. Thanks for hearing me out."

When the handle clicks, she grabs my sleeve. "Wait."

I freeze.

"Aren't you hungry?" she asks, handing me a few tissues.

"I'm so wrung out, dunno if I can eat. Besides, since you know, you won't want me around. So, I'll go."

"Umeji-kun, stop it right now!"

Flinching as if she slapped me, I grab the handle again—flight mechanisms engaging. She sighs. Her voice softens. "Please don't put words in my mouth. Yes, I'm having trouble taking in your story. But I asked for it so there wouldn't be any more nasty surprises in our friendship. I had to find out because, well..."

She hesitates. "Remember when I attempted to learn more about you after you arrived? And that my family practices old magic?"

Robotically, I nod.

"I saw a sign. One that says we were destined to meet." She looks down at her hands and one of her fingers twitches, then her gaze moves to my hand on the door latch.

I'll only drag her down. "But..." Tightening my grip on the handle, I tug it.

"Please, don't look at me that way! There's a reason we found each other. I'm unsure what it is, but I want to know. What about you?"

I press my point, hearing the click of the latch. "But I killed people. You shouldn't be around a guy like that. The gossips will go wild."

"I heard you the first time. I'm also aware of the gamut of rumors. Some in town have bets on how long you'll last. It wasn't at the store, so it's not anyone in your social circle. The point is, I've seen how hard you're trying. I believe you are starting over, and I'll be here to cheer you on."

Her response is so far from what I expected. I flop into the seat, letting the lightness fill me.

They say we can't fly. But at this moment, I'm one of those helium balloons mom used to get when I was a kid. "Thank you. I want to be a better man."

"I know. But I'm also starving. Ready?"

"Yeah. But let me step out for a sec." Blowing my nose is gonna sound like an angry goose, and I don't want to subject her to the brunt of that.

She releases my sleeve to let me salvage a sliver of dignity before driving the few remaining blocks. We park by the shop on the old-style street with wooden buildings and tile roofs.

Lit to attract customers at night, the shopfront with a noren curtain welcomes us, casting a warm glow. The word 'udon' shines in a neat hiragana script so even those of us not fully literate can sound it out. A lucky cat statue's arm waves, beckoning customers inside.

Splashing like kids in the puddles, we run holding our umbrellas. I let her in, wanting to be the gentleman. After placing our wet rain gear in the stand, we're welcomed and offered a spot in the rear. The lighting is cozy, the table is worn but clean, and the warmth is pleasant.

I must be quite the sight. Before we get the menu, I sneak off to wash my face and hands.

While we peruse the udon varieties, she says, "We were lucky to find a restaurant today. Most shops close over the New Year holidays."

"I wouldn't have thought of it. I guess something is always open in the big city. By the way. Please, let me pay tonight."

"But I made you come out in the rain and share things you weren't comfortable with."

I lean in. "You listened. To thank you for that, allow me."

"You're serious?"

"Absolutely."

While we eat our pork soup with the thick wheat noodles, she brings up another topic. "You stopped calling me Ohno-chan."

"Didn't think you'd want me to continue using such a familiar suffix."

"I miss it."

19

CHAPTER 19: CHOICES

Torrential rain morphs into a howling, angry thunderstorm. Ohno turns on the radio for the forecast as the Honda's wipers swish full bore, unable to fend off the driving deluge. Since the narrow side streets are flooding, Ohno sticks to the main roads.

Only a block beyond the park to the bridge and then to Sensei's house. We should be able to get across the river—the town built the embankments high. I don't want my friend to drive the rest of the way home until the storm passes.

The sky lights up to shock our eyes, followed by a sonic boom that hurts my ears. Crack! A tree falls and branches scrape the Honda's hatch. In the intermittent flashes, Ohno's face tightens as she speeds up.

My phone buzzes for a text, though I can only feel the vibration. The storm drowns out all other noise. It's a message from Satou. 'Hiro's in trouble at Hotaru Park. Can you get there before me? He's worth saving.'

Passing that very area, we see electricity pounding the ground at a single point, silhouetting the surrounding trees. A poor schmuck collapses at the center. My insides try to lodge themselves in my throat. *Hiro!*

"Stop the car!" I shout at the top of my lungs. Eerily, the wind, rain, even the storm, vanish.

"Are you kidding me?" Ohno screams over a sudden lack of sounds, only to slam on the brakes.

When I brace to collide with the dash, the wipers squeak with the remnants of water. Just clouds above and a haze of steam rising from the grass are visible. The hair on the nape of my neck stands on end. As I roll down the window to get a better look, I hold up the phone for Ohno to read the text.

After being struck by lightning that many times, the person out there will assuredly be dead. I don't want to witness Hiro's charred body. *Wait. How is that person still moving?*

Then we spot the sickly green glow of a portal by a band shelter at the far end of the park. The stench of something that hasn't bathed for days mixes with the humidity, causing me to cover my nose.

Is this the oni appearance that Sensei warned about? I know she said to go back to her place. But I don't want to be the guy who wishes he would have done something, especially for one I vowed to protect. Satou is right. Hiro can start again, too.

"Be back in a few." I bolt out, using kotodama to speed me there. Gotta ration ki use since I've not recovered from training.

"Wait!" Ohno hisses and another door slams. She must be right behind me because I hear her mumbling about a lack of plan.

The fog thickens. Slowing upon reaching the sand of the playground, I spot Date trailed by her goons in their soaked suits, and a red muscle-bound oni with its caveman style pelt clinging to its legs. She's wearing a glowing bracelet and carrying her iPad. One of her minions holds an umbrella for her.

A string of swear words escapes my mouth. On top of the ominous hoard being just over yonder, the prone figure they abandoned curls into a fetal position, groaning and shuddering. Gotta get him help.

None too quiet, my footfalls lurch to a halt beside the fallen man. Terror fills those ferret-like eyes and I gulp. Struggling for control of his spasming body, Hiro reaches for the dagger in his boot. My heart sinks, but my fighting instincts kick in as I shift my weight and murmur 'speed'.

"Tatsuya, don't let her get this. No matter what." He forces the words out in a gurgle then throws the blade, sheath and all, instead of attacking.

Date advances with her minions in tow.

Spell heightened reflexes allow me to snatch the weapon from the air, and

I unsheathe it. It's not Hiro's old tanto. The handle's too long with aged, worn braiding. Besides, there's nothing to cut with. That is, until I hold its hilt like a sword to inspect it.

The ghostly image of a blade extends to katana length. My hands fumble, almost dropping it. I know you're supposed to let a blade fall, but I can't stop myself from trying to catch it. The blade extinguishes until my palms come into proper contact with the handle again.

Regaining my breath, I pant, "What the fuck is this?"

"Later," he croaks. "The vixen is a cruel mistress. Found out I was on to her."

Mist tendrils flow off, then dissipate. Despite the cutting edge being nigh invisible, the katana is well balanced. Cautiously, I place my finger on the back—the iciness stings. "Deal. Let's get you to the hospital."

Date's voice cuts across the park. "The traitor's wingman shows up to witness his transformation to an oni? Delightful. If you join me, I'll spare him, Grandson."

Traitor? Aniki's words replay. 'It wasn't supposed to go down like that.' *Does that mean he's...?*

Then Date's other statement slams into me like a kick to the gut. *Grandson?*

The vixen taunts, "Did the old fraud fail to mention you carry the Tsuchimikado genes? Join me to learn about the power your kitsune heritage gives you."

What? No way! Sensei would have said something. I'm as common as they come. A huffed laugh shows just how much stock I put in her words. "Lies!"

Date pounces on my disbelief. "Don't trust everything that witch says. I can prove she had Ii-sama murdered. She didn't tell you that either, did she? Or that she plans to leave you stuck in this pathetic godforsaken town to free herself? You could be so much more."

Flight mechanisms threaten to engage. But I can't leave Hiro unguarded, so it gets shoved aside. An eerie emptiness I know all too well replaces it as I edge my words with steel. "Hiro should have told you what our gig was. Your manipulation is useless."

"Oh, dear boy. It's no lie. Nakamura knows the reason you look like a duplicate of that despicable husband of hers. Ask her. And ask her why his apprentices met their demise. Then tell me who's manipulative."

My blood boils. Pressure in my head grows, giving me a wicked headache. Tsuchimikado's students died? Sensei kept a secret from me about my ancestry? *Too many damned secrets in this town!*

Behind me, I hear the reassuring sound of my friend's bag of potions clinking on the ground. "Umeji-kun, can't you feel the pressure of her magic?"

I should have seen it. Was I running on emotion and too busy fighting off the headache to recognize the subtle presence?

Taking a deep breath, I growl, "Tsuchimikado-san was faithful to his wife!" Burning a bit of ki shoves the kitsune possession spell from my head.

Date spawns a toothy grin that sends a shiver through me. "You doubt I birthed a Tsuchimikado bastard?"

More lies.

Hiro's gurgling and thrashing intensifies, pulling on my attention. The pressure returns. So, I cast to pierce the illusions. Only then do I spot her hands manipulating silver tethers in the lamplight. They connect to everyone here, except Ohno and me. No wonder Sensei asked permission when she trained me.

Gotta stop Date. My heart pounds as my hand clenches the sword. "Enough of your lies!"

"I can't make you believe the truth." She tsks and motions forward the horned oni that towers over her. It hurtles toward me, flailing its nail-spiked club.

One of her men steps up beside her in that invisible servant style. "My lady, shall we go? Since he's a magic user, it may be best to get you to safety."

"Thank you, Kenji. No, I wish to evaluate his abilities. We've divided his attention. Will he underestimate the women around him, the same as his great, great grandfather did?"

Shifting my stance, I raise the weapon. Every muscle turns twitchy as I wait for the right timing. It would have been nice to have more sword training before I faced Date and an oni. Will I be able to protect Ohno and Hiro at the same time?

"See, he thinks the little hussy of his can't defend herself or he'd charge by now. He's got to watch them both," Date says with a knowing chuckle.

A jar crashes in front of me freeing the black blob which adheres to my old mentor's side, as Ohno sends a warm rush of ki into me. Shoving me forward, she shouts, "I've got Hiro-san! Rin will help you! Go!"

I trusted her with my past. *Trust her again.*

With each pounding step, the oni's footfalls shake the ground and leave eddies in the mist. A vine, springing from behind me, digs its thorns into the ogre's arm and club. One of Ohno's pets? *Yikes.*

Howling, the oni tries to pull the plant off. The vine only digs in deeper. Muscle and skin rip free as the beast yanks. Black ooze spurts from the wound to release a gut-wrenching stench.

Pouring magic into my running leap, I bark a kiai that sends sparks of energy through me and I sail through the air. The katana swings toward the oni's stringy-haired head. But the ogre twists.

My blade still contacts flesh, wrenching my wrists as I whiz past. In the nick of time, I belt out a word of kotodama. The oni's one-handed follow-through strike muffles as it smacks me toward the ground. With a thundering crack, my protection spell extinguishes.

The impact knocks the wind out of me. I hate blowing through ki this fast, but I need to breathe. So, I use up another spell. I should have seen that dodge coming.

My strike almost severed its arm, though it wasn't enough damage to banish it. Howling through its tusked teeth, it bites at the dangling appendage to tear itself free from the attack plant and its useless limb, spitting them both aside.

The oni raises its spiked club in its remaining arm. But I roll to the side, hearing a whoosh as the weapon sails past my head to bludgeon a crater in the ground.

The razor vine leaps again to grab the ogre's bare foot. As the oni flails, I come in on its wounded side and fill my stroke with the power of kotodama. Upon impact, the sword crunches through the neck to sever the monster's skull. Steam rolls off as it crackles, dissolving into ash. How did the blade cut through that much mass?

Three more of Date's minions charge in a group. Cold washes over me. Is it possible to avoid killing people? As it is, I'll have more fuel for my nightmares.

"Otsuka dies today for his treachery." Date snaps her fingers, which flash with a disquieting glow.

"Umeji-kun!"

That's Ohno's scream! So I glance back. Hiro's left forearm twitches and bubbles.

She clarifies in a high, staccato pitch, "He's turning, despite Chou doing her best to suck all the energy from his ring!"

Chou burps. Ohno chants, creating a blue glow that envelopes Hiro as he reaches for her. *Shit. Ohno's having trouble.*

Time slows as I burn ki for each action—a u-turn and sprint for Hiro, plus assurance to hit my next target. Then a shikigami figure falls in my retreating path, expanding to human size.

"My grandson made his choice, thinking the girl can't handle the situation. Too predictable. Boys, we leave now!"

Could Ohno have managed it? Either way, coming to the aid of a friend will always be the priority. The paper man swings at me. In two strokes, it's down—a soggy mess in a puddle, and I'm running again, sword at the ready.

Hiro worms a hand around Ohno's throat. If I don't do something, he'll hurt one of the few friends I have. My heart sinks as I raise the weapon, preparing to take out my former mentor. *Why did it have to be Aniki?* Sure, I hate him, but he didn't betray us.

Ohno directs Chou to pull away Hiro's hand from the chokehold, freeing her. She coughs but gives a thumbs up.

A few strides away, I skitter to a stop to grimace at the growing transformation of Hiro's arm. Stepping between her and him, I point the sword at my old mentor as he quivers.

The words stick in my throat. *I can't kill him.* He was being controlled! Whispering a spell to see the link again, I swipe to cut the revealed puppet thread.

Sirens fill the air, getting louder as they approach. Hiro pants as his mouth froths, but his eyes are clear as he struggles to speak. "Sever my arm. That's an order!"

My chin juts back and my stomach churns. Date's portal closes in my peripheral vision. *This isn't over, vixen.*

"His ki and will are spent! Do it NOW or he turns!" Ohno screams, leaning in to shield Hiro's head.

It's one thing to kill someone who's gonna hurt people. But this? My eyes scrunch shut at the thought of maiming a father-figure I've known for so long. He's the one who mentored me and gave me a home—the man who just asked me to do something excruciating.

Whispering 'clean cut', I clench my jaw and swing before losing the nerve. The strike cleaves with a squelching thunk, meeting resistance on the way through. Vibration from the crunching of human bone causes me to lose my dinner. Blood spatters our trio, Hiro's scream pierces our ears, and I collapse to my knees—letting the katana clatter and extinguish.

"Hands up! We saw you injure that man!" The police's footfalls squelch in the mud as they surround us.

Will they get Hiro to the emergency room before he dies? An ambulance could take too long. Where the hell is Satou?

Oh, yeah. Sensei tucked a talisman in my pocket. I slap the paper into the air. "Hospital!" Stabbing pain from a police baton smacks my shoulder, and I crumple.

"Fancy pants magic ain't gonna help you escape. We've seen too much of that kind of trouble the last few months," the officer states in a grating manner. *Not a chance in hell they'd believe me.*

A blue glow from the ofuda grows, opening up to the emergency room in Shimosaki where Satou and I took Sensei. Then, a knee pins me—digging into where they struck only a moment ago and rendering me helpless.

An officer wrestles my hands to my back, while I plead, "Get him to the hospital! He'll bleed out!"

All gawking, a crowd gathers at a safe distance from the opening. I hear the murmuring, but they stare frozen. Too many people on the emergency scene and everyone figures someone else will deal with the problem.

I strain to glimpse Ohno cuffed, too, pleading with her monster pets to heel instead of attacking the officers.

Hiro lies limp, while a cop nudges him and pokes at Chou who's distorted from swallowing the entire demonic appendage. The officer's "What is that? Is it gonna try to eat us?" is clear as day.

"Get him medical help! Please!" I wail.

"That man was hurt by your actions." The officer shoves my face to the wet ground as I struggle.

A nurse gingerly sticks a pen through the shimmering door. "Is this safe to go through so we can get the injured man over there?"

"Yes," I grunt and wriggle enough so my eyes can meet hers. Seeing the pleading in my look, she calls for a stretcher, takes a breath to steel herself, and steps through.

Fighting the hand trying to cover my mouth as the police wrap me burrito-like in a blanket, I shout, "Portal won't last much longer! My magic is spent!"

How can the officers be this calm while surrounded by magic and chaos? Do they see that much action?

The nurse motions for the policeman at Hiro's side to help her get the patient through the strange gate. When my big brother is out of sight, I stop resisting, allowing the portal to close and the police to finish securing the straps for carrying me.

I've broken the law by using a weapon, mortally wounded my pledge brother, and dragged Ohno down with me. Yet again, I'm headed to the slammer. Worse, my friend will have a record—a stain not only on her coat but her life. *A curse. That's what I am.*

Rocks dig into my cheek, but it doesn't matter. Numbness fills me. Like when they arrested me three years ago. At least the smell of the grass now is better than the tang of Ken's blood back then.

The twang and hiss of the blade hitting something solid echoes through the valley. "Whoa! What kind of sword is this?" A few more childish swipes tempt them before they log it as evidence. "What the hell do I categorize it as? A damned lightsaber?"

"Beats me. Let the experts figure it out. That's why they're paid the big bucks," his partner says.

Still encouraging her monsters to do as the police say, Ohno is the first shoved into a squad car. The officers use their batons to herd the creatures into a second vehicle, then radio the bomb squad to grab her bag of glass jarred mysteries.

Finally, they hustle me to the hard back seat. As I stare from my prone position out the window, I take in my last glimpses of the outside. The familiar storefronts and lights whiz by the few blocks to the station. *Why'd it have to end like this?*

20

CHAPTER 20: HELPING OUT

"What happened? I couldn't get there before they hauled you off." Satou runs a hand through his hair.

"It's complicated." I shrug. The cell is cold and the other occupants reek of alcohol. *Not like he's gonna believe me.* Too bad, 'cause the stench here could curl toes.

"Tell me, or there's not a chance in hell I can get you out. Ohno's family picked her up just after midnight. The police say you attacked undercover officer Lieutenant Otsuka."

Hiro was a hardcore mobster. The irony of him ever being on the right side of the law causes me to snort. When my VPO grabs my collar, my laughter cuts off. "You're serious?"

Satou flashes Hiro's badge before letting me go. "He planned to recruit you. Back to last night. In the arresting officer's words, 'The kid chopped his arm clean off at the shoulder with some kind of energy weapon.' Spill it."

Several of the other prisoners scoot to the far edges of the cell.

Recruiting. That's what Hiro was talking about when he said he wanted better. Things would have been so different if he could have brought me in on the operation three years ago. I would have accepted in a heartbeat. Now?

Satou growls and hits the cell bars, making me jump. "So explain what the hell happened. When Otsuka is out of surgery, we'll confirm it."

So, I share the events of the entire insane evening. The harsh fluorescent light does nothing for the bags under my VPO's eyes, as he pinches the bridge of his nose. "So I'm to understand that Date discovered him, and you 'saved' him by cutting off his arm?"

"He was gonna turn into an oni! Ohno-chan's ooze thing—whatever it's called—must have it." Mutterings of my cellmates confirm my words are the ramblings of a madman.

"Explain."

The second attempt sounds just as ridiculous.

"Fine. To confirm, Otsuka-san gave you the sword. Then he ordered you to cut his arm off so he could avoid turning into an oni?"

My single nod is decisive. He exhales. "Considering the craziness he told me before last night, I'll offer the benefit of the doubt. But there's no chance of convincing them to release you until the Lieutenant wakes up to give his testimony. Be patient."

Not like I'm going anywhere. There's nothing to write a portal talisman with.

Miracle of all miracles, Satou retrieves me at 6:30 AM, and I suck in deep breaths of the crisp air outside the station.

He says, "You and Ohno-san have the day off for saving my partner's life. Hiro's sleeping now. Telling his side of the story wore him out."

If I had any energy, I'd ask about the mention of 'partner'.

Since the boss is too tired to drive home on a narrow curvy road, we crash at his aunt's house. She was up cleaning for the new year when Satou heard of my predicament and said he'd get me out. To deal with the stress, she persisted with the task until the wee hours. But she rose early to greet us with tea and breakfast.

After putting some of Ohno's arnica ointment on the baton welt and sleeping a few more hours, I grab my cell. *Ugh.* I forgot to ask for Ohno's contact info. I'll walk over once I'm ready for the day.

Toweling off after a hot bath makes me feel human again. My phone chirps. The message reads, 'Ohno here. Matsuo-kun gave me your Line ID. You home yet? You ok?'

'Got back about 6:30 this morning. I'm fine. You? Sorry I got you messed up in this.'

'Glad you're ok. I'm all right, though I don't see why they had to release me to my parents. I'm an adult! Chou and the others are still being held. Don't you forget I chose my involvement!'

When Sensei tries rising to her tiptoes for a peek at my messages, I lean back on the sofa, pulling the screen to my chest. With a knowing waggle of her eyebrows, she mouths the word 'party'. *Oh yeah.* So, I convey the details.

Nakamura already invited my boss, and the gang replies they'll come tomorrow. Ever curious, Matsuo asks for more information on the news reports and gossip.

Later, Nakamura and I venture out to do our shopping for the festivities. As Sensei shows me a text from Satou, she asks, "Tatsuya, how do I send a message to my nephew?"

'Where are you? Stopped by on my way to work. No one home. Considering the insanity, you better be with Umeji or me if you leave the house. Will stop by after work.'

"He hasn't seen us, has he?" I verify.

That adorable mischievous twinkle appears in the old woman's eye, letting her inner kitsune show. "He's right over there. Quick, step behind the vegetables. Teach me how to do one of those selfie pictures."

"Ok."

Nakamura puts carrots up behind my head to resemble horns. Helping her with the phone, I snap a picture of us together in the produce section and show how to send it. She'll never grow up, will she?

Sending myself a copy of the photo, I forward it to Ohno. It should give her a laugh. My first selfie here and it's with a goofy old lady.

Satou's response? An eye roll emoji accompanies a text. 'Need to chat with Umeji. Don't leave yet.'

Catching us at the checkout with our huge stash of New Year's food, Satou asks, "Umeji, do you want to tag along when I visit Otsuka this afternoon?"

"Yeah."

"I'll pick you up at four."

* * *

While I wait, my teacher and I complete the New Year's cleaning.

Why didn't Sensei tell me about the things Date said? Did the witch speak the truth about Tsuchimikado being unfaithful? My enemy would enjoy the doubts too much. Time to deal with this.

The first question about me being Date and Tsuchimikado's descendant catches Nakamura off guard. As she pales, her cleaning rag and bucket drop, sloshing the contents on the wood floor. "Impossible…"

"Sensei?" With concern tinging my voice, I scramble over, guide her to the couch, then clean up the spilled bleach water.

"My Yuki was faithful to me."

She's trying to console herself with a truth she thought she knew all along.

With conviction, I concur. "He was." Then kneeling in front of her, I ask, "So how? Did his brother resemble him?"

A tear rolls down her cheek. "His identical twin—Kinya. We named our son after him. His encounter with the vixen must be why he became a monk when the war was over."

Click. "After the Restoration?"

"Yes. She must have seduced him. He announced his wish to withdraw from the world the year after. Had we only known!" Covering her face, she sobs.

I'm from Date's line. An abomination. No wonder I turned out as I did. *Wait!* My heart lifts. That also means I'm the many times great-nephew of Tsuchimikado and… "Sensei, it's not your fault. Kinya-san and Date made their choices."

A very unladylike half snort, half laugh emerges. Then pulling me into a hug, she tucks her head into my shoulder. "Welcome to the family, great-nephew."

She's as vulnerable as when I first held her in fox form. Sensei may not be thinking straight in this weak moment. "Are you sure you should claim me? What if people judge you for my past?"

"Tatsuya, don't be stupid. We both hoped we were related. Don't you deny it."

My muscles thaw to return the embrace as my heart beats loudly in my chest. "Maybe I am dumb sometimes, 'cause I wanna know how many greats I'm gonna have to use. You're not just my great, great aunt. Would a hundred and fifty years make that seven or eight?"

"We'll find out just how great you need to tell me I am." Releasing me and pinching my cheek, her head bobbles in triumph at besting me yet again.

Moving to the bedrooms in our cleaning, she tackles the question about responsibility for Ii's murder. "A partial truth that I had to come to terms with. After Yoshida-san's death, Yuki and I were distraught. We said things that may have been taken out of context as a possible suggestion, perhaps even an order to one of Yoshida-san's students. We never found out because they killed him during the assassination mission. Date always blamed me. Her anguish drove her down a dark path."

"What about leaving me stuck in Nonogawa?"

"Not stuck. You will have the choice to watch over this area or not. If you say yes to replacing me, then you simply look for another apprentice when you are ready to retire. Finding an apprentice in these modern times can be challenging. But they do turn up."

My mind reels. "Watch over? Replace you? What are you talking about Sensei?"

"I have to receive approval before I can share more. Hopefully soon."

I give a huff but accept. "And the last accusation? What happened to the other apprentices?"

She turns to the second-floor window, remaining quiet for several moments. When she speaks, her voice cracks. "Please, give me time to answer that."

"Ok," I respond with a respectful calm.

Because my aunt did most of the work the night before, we finish the cleaning quickly. Next, we put out the decorations of bamboo, pine, and plum before we work on New Year's cards. I haven't written these for ages. It's much more fun when Mom's not making me do it.

* * *

Silence hangs stale in the air while my boss drives to the hospital. I've already thanked him for the ride. What else is there to talk about that isn't awkward territory?

"I was surprised when Sensei didn't protest at having one of your contacts act as a bodyguard while we're gone."

"Same." Keeping his eyes on the road, his meek demeanor reminds me of a scolded schoolboy. "You and Matsuo-kun haven't sparred at the dojo for a while."

"Didn't want to bother you, Sir."

"You're both welcome. Matsuo-kun can even teach young Suzuki-kun there if he likes. I've scheduled him opposite hours from me to keep things covered at the store, so I didn't bring it up. Will you tell him for me?"

"Sure. Thanks, Boss."

"My Aunt enjoys your company. I know because she hasn't thrown a New Year's party in years."

"I wouldn't have believed she and I would get along so well."

That causes him to chuckle. "I remember how she treated you in the beginning. So what makes you so loyal to her?"

Is he bothered that I'm more devoted to Nakamura than to him? "She was the first to believe in me. Ironic, isn't it?" Fiddling with the book and pencil I brought, I force my gaze out the window.

"Otsuka insists we should have brought you in on the job right off the bat. Now that it's blown to hell, I guess it doesn't matter anymore. I'm not sure where we go from here." He pulls into a parking spot. "Despite that, I'm glad you were there."

As we enter, the nurses insist we not stay long. My old mentor raises the Sudoku puzzle book in thanks. "You even put bookmarks in it."

Radiating tree-shaped scars cover what crackled skin shows from under the bandages. It looks wickedly painful. And how does he stand being in such a vulnerable spot? The curtain blocks the view of people coming in.

"Talismans. They won't do you any good in the book. This one's a protection ward and the other's for healing." Pulling the slips of paper out, I place them on his shoulder and chest. What I don't tell him is that there are a few extra spells placed on them, just in case.

As his eyes widen, he pats the glowing figures. "So I wasn't hallucinating that you made the portal last night."

"Nope, Sensei taught me earlier that day. Maybe she had some premonition. Anyway, how are you feeling?"

"I'll remember to thank her. Doing better than I expected, considering a demon would have possessed me and I had no control over myself around Date. Learning to manage with just one arm will be a challenge. But I'll live, thanks to you and... Ohno-chan. That's your girlfriend's name, right?"

My chin dips. "Not my girl. An amazing friend."

"A pity. You two work well together. She'll probably piece everything together now. I take it you trust her?"

"Yeah." Everybody's trying to hook me up with her. We only just renewed our friendship last night. *Can't they just let us be?* Seating myself on his 'good side' in the stiff-backed chair, I broach the elephant in the room. "So, you were an agent all along." *How did he reach the rank of kyoudai, just under the head of the clan, if he was a spy?*

Satou pulls up a seat as my aniki answers. "Yes, little brother. Know that I intended to bring you in on the job back then. It took them forever to grant permission. We were a day late to save you from a jail sentence. And now, you're wondering if you really knew me."

My chest tightens. At my minute nod, he looks toward the ceiling.

"There were days I wondered myself. Becoming what I pretended to be, the real me faded to the point I wasn't sure that the original remained. The important thing is that I kept my oath to you.

"It killed me to have them prosecute my little brother for what we'd done together, knowing I wouldn't serve a single day. Your trial took so long because I was arguing hard for a reduced sentence. That's what blew my cover. A compromised officer reported it to Date. She's got ties everywhere."

Rubbing my forehead to fend off the headache, the new knowledge swirls in among my memories. Hiro couldn't say a peep.

"So, Satou," Hiro says, "Are you willing to share your past with Tatsuya or not?"

Sighing, my VPO concedes. It turns out Satou's job as a club host was cover. Sometimes his clandestine work ended up being information warfare. Others, it was an exchange.

"With charm and drink, I could convince girls, heck, even the occasional guy, to talk about almost anything. The things I learned. If I used the intel, I could ruin lives, corporations, and clans, even cause major ripples in our government. There were weeks I couldn't sleep because of what I knew. When Otsuka and I started working together eleven years ago, it provided a point of sanity to share the secrets. Always leading people on ruined lasting relationships for me."

Holding up a finger, he narrows his eyes. "Don't you say a blasted thing about trust issues. And yes, many of the days I said I was working late, were for my undercover job—meetings, investigations, and whatnot. You know how capable Matsuo-kun is. I'm barely needed at the store."

No wonder he went ballistic when I couldn't tell him about Nakamura being a kitsune. *Wait a damned minute!* "So I was only a recruit again?"

His soft, "Not exactly," doesn't make it any easier to hear.

Pain pounds the inside of my skull. Instead of giving me a fresh start, Satou planned on dumping me in that mess again? And he gave me garbage about the full truth—threatening to return me to the slammer if I didn't spill Sensei's secret. Was he grooming me the whole time? The roar of a glacier breaking off and settling inside my gut fills my ears.

Hiro—he was on assignment. But my VPO doesn't have that excuse. Satou acted like he brought me here to leave behind a life where every breath is a compromise. Going back, even undercover, would destroy the small start I've built here.

Shooting up from my seat shoves my chair so hard it slams into the wall. To halt my shaking requires burning ki for a spell.

After several moments of my glare, Satou clears his throat. "If it makes any difference, it would be an offer."

They still want my help? My knees threaten to buckle, but I won't give him the satisfaction of seeing any weakness. *Not that I wanted the mob life. But I owe Satou for being my VPO, getting me a job, and giving me a place to stay. So, I'm damned if I do go undercover. Damned if I don't.* My dry ice words hiss as they hit the tepid air. "One that I can't refuse, I see."

"Tatsuya," Hiro interrupts. "Date was the bitch responsible for the devastating attack on the Hiragi clan. The snitch sold us out to her. The kitsune's modus operandi is to cause a fight and absorb any survivors.

"Since last year, she's been moving in on surrounding towns. Kazuo thinks it may have to do with bad blood between his aunt and her. Because I'm out of commission and we're all targets, we hoped you might help protect Nakamura-san and Ohno-san. Then we can regroup and plan our next moves to go after her.

"You won't be able to infiltrate her group, now. But we'd like you to be on the investigation team. You're good at ferreting out important details."

When my arms cross, I lean up against the wall, with my head jutting forward. So, I'm just supposed to believe that they'll sweep my past under the rug and things will go better than three years ago? *As if.*

My tone shifts to a dead neutral. "I'd need guarantees. Not sure you can give those."

Hiro shakes his head. "See, Kazuo? I told you he'd revert to his controlled mobster mode pretty damn quick. Yes, we can, but those are still being ironed out. You were supposed to report directly to me. Everything changed now that I'm out of commission for a while. Satou is working to be the one you report to, though there are concerns since he's already your VPO and boss for his cover work. We'll be asking Nakamura-san to work with us, too, now that we know her secret."

Called on the carpet. And it was all instinct. "Tch. It's not like this discussion is giving me warm fuzzies." My hands jam into my pockets as I scowl. "I know I can watch over Sensei and Ohno-chan. That's not a problem. Though, both women are powerful in their own right."

My aniki reaches behind his pillow, then shoves the weathered blade with its short scabbard toward me. "There'll be more confrontations with Date. Take this. I'll cover any heat you get for it while protecting the ladies."

Carrying a weapon is illegal. He preached, 'A sword is a tool to kill. Only draw it in defense, and if you're prepared for the consequences. Do not make the first strike, so you leave a way for peace.' My hands fly up in refusal. "I don't wanna take a life ever again."

Flashing a glance at Satou, Hiro smirks. They must have had a bet going.

My old mentor says, "I know. That's why I trust you. It's not safe to keep this here. Your actions last night proved your intentions. But your magic isn't enough to protect against the oni that Date's minions turn into. Remember what I taught you about using all tools available?"

"Yes, Aniki." Words I never thought I'd speak again. As I accept the strange katana with trembling hands, I could swear it feels heavier than last night, now that it's my responsibility. "What is it? How'd you come by it?"

"It's the sharpest blade in existence and its ID is concealed to all but those who have been given permission—"

"Incoming," Satou hisses.

Tucking the magical blade in the back of my pants, I cover my movements by adjusting my coat as the nurse walks in.

"You aren't the only guys with mysterious connections. But that secret and its name are a story for another day." He winks as the woman evicts us from the room. *It has a name?*

Satou gives me time to process the encounter as he pulls out of the parking lot. The renewed peace between the trio of us isn't perfect, but I'll take it. "Hey, Satou-san."

"Hmm?"

"It's impossible to be with both ladies at every moment. I'd like Ohno-chan's pets returned for protection."

"Not possible. The police won't let the bizarre creatures go until the blob surrenders the evidence. It attacks the officers each time they try to retrieve the objects."

"Can we stop by the station? At least one beast is intelligent. It might be worth a try to reason with it. Though, Ohno-chan will have the best chance of doing that."

"Sure, after that I have a quick meeting to discuss the guarantees Hiro mentioned."

* * *

We spot Ohno sitting on a bench. She's furiously typing, and my phone buzzes when she hits the enter key with a flourish. 'They won't give my pets back!!! Any ideas??!??'

I knew it. Gotta pity those who get in her way.

Kneeling in front of her as she glares at the desk attendant, I whisper, "Boo."

She jumps, then her lips purse. But the lightheartedness as she pokes me repeatedly loosens something wound tight inside. Her last prod comes with a mock warning. "Buster, you're in so much trouble for scaring me!"

I'll have a slight bruise on my arm tomorrow, but who cares? Her feistiness could warm even the sun.

As my head tilts toward the attendant, I offer, "The boss has some pull. Let's see what we can do."

After he talks them into allowing us into the stark, utilitarian evidence room with its set of pushed-together tables, Ohno zips over to Chou and the vine.

The sheer number of tagged items in the dim, chair-less space is staggering. Should there be this many issues in a small town? They don't seem separated by case. Just massed all together. *Why?*

"That black thing ate the arm and ring we needed!" Indignant, Sergeant Kimura points at Chou, who turns around on her table to reveal a sloppily written tag sticking out of her. The plant must take offense for its ooze companion, feinting a stab at the officer, causing him to shrink away.

Ohno scoops up and cradles the shiny blob. The very idea sends shivers through me after what it did a few days ago.

Speaking to it as a small child, she says, "Chou, I know you're not happy. Please give the policeman what he needs. Then we'll go home."

The ooze raises a portion of itself only to shake the head-like section in a toddler 'no' fashion.

164

My friend eyes the officer with suspicion. "Did you do something to her? She's never this obstinate."

Sputtering, Sergeant Kimura points a finger, "What? That thing tried to eat us!"

"She's an energy drainer, not a carnivore!" Ohno holds her pet closer, aghast at the accusation.

Satou, clearing his throat, tries to hurry things along. "Perhaps if the sergeant would apologize."

It takes a cough to cover my reaction at Chou's nods of enthusiasm. Kimura protests, but seeing the strange creatures will have to stay otherwise, he ends up giving a darn good apology.

Squelching, the slime sloshes to the desk and with wet hacking, spits out ash and the ring. Then she leaps to Ohno again. A lump rises in my throat. Looking away doesn't help. That sight can't be unseen.

Gingerly using his handkerchief, Satou picks up the band—that lacks its previous evil aura. "I can't believe I'm asking a gelatinous mass." He has to swallow before continuing. "Chou-san, did you do anything to this? It used to glow."

She extends a tentacle-like appendage and pokes at it, then says 'no.'

"And the arm?"

The ooze points to the soot, repeatedly.

"Did you do that?"

Another 'no.'

I jump in to clarify. "The host turns to ash when the oni vanishes, Sir."

Rubbing his temples, my boss asks, "Officer Kimura, are we good?"

The policeman makes a sharp shooing motion. "Remove those things from the premises ASAP!"

"Umeji-kun, will you carry Chou, while I get the bag? She trusts you." Ohno flashes a pleading look.

No way! "Shouldn't I bring the duffle instead after my last encounter with Chou-chan?"

The slime's already reaching for me with two 'arms'. Ohno hands her off with a smirk and her voice turns a little too sing-songish. "Sorry, can't be helped." The appendages encircle my neck as if hanging on to a parent.

To avoid touching the monstrous pets, Satou zips over to the tote. "I'll bring this, as long as nothing escapes."

"Come on, Rin." Ohno giggles. When she extends her hand, the vine retracts its thorns to spiral her arm, and she gives it a tender pat. "Good boy."

As we leave the building, everyone gives us a wide berth. Their reactions to the creatures range from a shudder to plastering themselves against the wall.

So, another reason the town up north had driven her family out could be that small communities won't welcome dangerous pets. On top of her family's magical abilities, it might be difficult for ordinary folk to cope with. But Ohno, with her heart of gold, sees good in me and I wouldn't trade her acceptance for the world.

Then there's a slurping on my hand, causing my voice to hike an octave, "Uhm, Ohno-chan…"

"Yes?"

The slime belches as my arm pulls away. "Chou's eating my ki again."

Ohno sucks in her bottom lip. She's trying not to laugh. *Come on!* My friend quips, "She likes how you taste."

Stopping in my tracks, even single-syllable words evade me.

Ohno tsks, "Behave yourself. You embarrassed him enough he's speech-less."

The ooze takes the scolding seriously because she doubles in on herself, and my heart stops for a moment as I almost drop her. The thing really has feelings. "So, what is Chou-chan?"

"We suspect she's a batch of agar left in a cupboard over a hundred years ago. Remember in the legends how old items such as umbrellas and whatnot came alive? Chou's proof. Though there are other ways to make oozes, too."

No way am I gonna ask about the other goodies in her duffel.

Satou thrusts the bag at her. "Ohno-san, can Umeji catch a ride back with you? I have somewhere to be…" He hisses as he looks at his watch. "Five minutes ago."

"No prob!"

He dashes off.

The wind tosses a bit of hair into her face, and she tries to blow it away as she opens her Honda's door. If Chou didn't require both my arms for carrying, I'd tuck that lock behind Ohno's ear. Not that it's my place. The potential job from Hiro puts her further beyond my grasp.

After I buckle in, my hands shove into my coat pockets only to find my comforting mythology book isn't there. Did the police forget to return it? Oh yeah—I left it by my pillow.

When I stop patting my pockets and let out the breath I'd been holding, Ohno asks, "Everything Ok?"

I take a minute to answer as she waits patiently to start the car. If anyone would understand, it's her. "I just remembered where I put my book. But I wanted to talk with you."

"You know I'll listen." Wariness replaces her bright tone.

Sensei showed me how to make a privacy bubble talisman, so I pull one out of my pocket, applying it to the door. An azure ripple spreads inside the cab of the CR-V, then flashes to signal completion before disappearing.

At Ohno's raised eyebrow, I say, "No one will overhear us. Well, I have a hard choice to make."

"Okay..."

"You're the one who knows the most about me and my time with Hiro. So, I'm sure you've put a few puzzle pieces together. Today I found out things weren't what I thought. Hiro had legit plans for me."

"Isn't that good?" Now, there's less of an edge in her voice as she prompts.

"Three years ago, I would have jumped on the chance. It would have turned my life around. When Hiro said a version of those plans still exists, I didn't take it well. Yet, I don't think I can turn the offer down."

"What's the worst that could happen?"

"It might ruin the trust I've worked so hard for here in Nonogawa. And people could get hurt."

As she turns in her seat, her brows furrow and her hands fidget with the cuffs of her sleeves. *I've made her upset. Shit.* "Never mind."

"Hiro hasn't asked you to go back to the mob, has he?"

My big brother knows Ohno has my confidence or I couldn't have this conversation. "I said it's legit. It might look like I went back, though. They want me to help with the investigation on Date." Having to go back under the radar makes my stomach churn.

"Then..." When her fingers point and cross, the light turns on. "Hiro-san was undercover! That's why Date had it out for him! And Hiro is recruiting you."

"Bingo."

"So why are you telling me?"

"You were there last night. We knew you'd figure it out. It also makes you a target. If I do this job, I might have to distance from you for your protection."

She rolls her eyes. "If I was a target for being there, distancing won't change that. Anyone that Hiro and you knew or talked with will be in danger—Satou-san, Matsuo-kun, Mie-chan, Nakamura-san..."

"But it'll protect you from the rumors of me going back."

Jamming the keys in the ignition, she gives the key a rough turn as the engine comes to life. "Have you considered that cutting and running will also raise suspicions, only adding to those rumors? Matsuo-kun and I deal with some of that garbage already."

"Sorry." My friends sucked it up for me. How did I not know? "If I was still in the mob, I would have just cut ties. But now..."

Whipping out, her hand clutches my coat cuff. "Stay. Promise me you won't give the gossips reason to think they were right about you."

Why is it so important to her I stay?

"Promise me." Her grip tightens on my sleeve. "Because if you disappear, you won't be able to come back to Nonogawa."

I swallow, caught between a rock and a hard place. Though she's right. I'll have to find a way to keep my obligation from destroying the little I've built. "Promise."

Only then does she pull away from the police station.

21

CHAPTER 21: BEGINNINGS

New Year's Eve:

Catching Satou turns out to be tricky. He finally rolls in at my first break, slipping into the office. The way he stalks in says I should wait to talk to him. But he peeks out into the break room.

His accent is thick as he asks, "Umeji, have a minute?"

"Sure, Boss." I trot over, abandoning my bento. Tension creeps up the back of my neck.

"Shut the door." When the door clicks behind me, he folds his hands on his desk.

I haven't done anything wrong that I can tell. Nevertheless, my hands shove into my pants pockets. "Sir?"

"Relax. It's about the guarantee you wanted."

This has to go right, so I summon the outward confidence I used while in the mob, straightening to a military-like stance, refusing to clench my fists. "I have a list, Sir."

That makes his eyebrow raise. "You should have said what you wanted yesterday. Let's hope our lists match."

"Lack of a good plan makes for sloppy results, Boss. What I need is this. The job can't resemble yakuza work. It has to be all above board because I don't want to cut ties. I also require immunity from prosecution for past offenses. And the agreement for all of this in written form so I have proof."

"Hiro and I predicted your needs. I won't tell you how many strings we had to pull to help you avoid severing ties here. My aunt would throw a fit if you left. Done. They're still debating on who will be in charge of you on assignment."

Not so fast. I lean in. "Plus, these for the investigation job—a laptop, high-speed wi-fi, VPN access, and contractor level pay—half upfront."

The bravado makes him flash a rare one-sided grin. "We'll see. Planning to start your own business?"

"Possibly. Wanna talk about what was wrong earlier?"

"Nah. It's just how they're treating Hiro, now that he's out of action. Nothing you can do about it."

* * *

The gang all works until the early holiday closing at six. But Satou bows out of the event, due to a prior commitment. So much for Sensei's plan to get the two of us to reconcile. Though, after the talk over lunch, we're on the right path.

During break, Mie mopes, only picking at her bento.

"You ok?" Ohno asks.

Mie flops in her chair. "He's avoiding me."

Oblivious to the conversation, Matsuo zips over. "Want a quick sparring session?" Holding up my index finger to him, I join the ladies for a moment. "Mie-san, is it the boss?" She glares.

Bingo. "Offer to tag along when he visits Lieutenant Otsuka in the hospital. Later." Giving a salute, I follow Matsuo to his car.

I could use all the practice I can get. If this mysterious sword will be in my care, I need to improve my technique before I face Date again. "Mind if we work with shinai today?"

* * *

I wasn't able to write ofuda for everyone before the party. So as the group chats and watches the NHK Red and White Song Battle, I work at the low table.

Sensei and Ohno ensure I take breaks to sample the party foods and sake. Chestnuts are Ohno's favorite, so I give her mine. Mie shows up late with a spring in her step and a warmer attitude. Did she heed my advice?

When the gang is all here, my aunt says we should serve the soba. When we eat the buckwheat noodles, we cut off the old year and start fresh in the new.

At midnight, booms of the fireworks and clangs of the temple bell catch our attention. At least everyone finished their soba before it started—eating the dish when the clock strikes twelve is bad luck.

Sensei points to the window. "We can view the show at the river from the road."

It probably won't be much of a display since it's only little Nonogawa. But, as one the gang rushes out to the street to join everyone in the neighborhood.

Flashes draw our eyes to the star-speckled sky as rockets streak straight up to create new explosions centered inside the falling cascade of sparks. Each firework is perfectly timed. There's not even a pause between volleys.

Out of nowhere, Mie nudges me with her can of Yebisu ale. "Not bad for a backwater town, eh?"

"It's impressive."

"My cousin spends all year planning the display. Every business in town donates. Even though the town is shrinking, the funding hasn't since it's one of the big tourist draws."

As I take a swig of my beer, I'm the only one whose gaze isn't glued to the sky. Ohno's wide-eyed smile as she watches captivates me. She turns and points to a fiery bloom that lingers. "Did you see that one?"

After the show finishes, we've all drunk more than is safe to drive home. So, we haul out blankets. Sensei's plan to keep us all together worked.

A few hours later, I have a set of ofuda left to do for Hiro. But my eyelids refuse to stay open, let alone allow me to write another protection talisman. The warmth of the kotatsu insists on summoning dreamland. I've caught my chin falling to my chest several times already.

If I rest for just a few minutes, I can finish them later. So, I slump to the heated surface. A clink and movement, then the comforting weight of a blanket on my shoulders registers in my mind.

In the Hiragi clan headquarters, I try to block out the vacant expression of the fallen and the moans of pain from the dying on both sides. But my gaze keeps being drawn back. Worse, the slick red stains on my palms and clothes make me sick as I tie off wounds, hoping to save my little brother and a man I don't recognize. The guys bleed out, leaving me to usher them to the afterlife.

Firing shots to keep the attackers at bay, Hiro goes down. Then shouts and heavy boots echo in the halls as the special assault team enters the building.

They wanted us all to kill each other off. My heart sinks as I raise my hands in surrender.

Jumping centimeters off the floor from pressure on my shoulder, I grab the wrist on instinct. Looking before allowing my defense mechanisms to kick in, keeps me from twisting Ohno's arm to throw her. When her wide eyes come into focus as I squeeze the arm that's tight with tension, the situation snaps into place.

I scared her. How could she know that if I'd reacted with the years of keyed up instinct, that gesture could have gotten her painfully pinned to the tatami, or worse, until I had my wits about me again?

"Sorry!" I fumble before letting go.

Casing the surroundings ensures we're safe and the entire gang's asleep in Sensei's living room, except for Ohno and me. My aunt must have retired to bed.

Concern shadows Ohno's expression. "Nightmare?"

Nodding, I struggle to control my breathing and get my pulse to shift out of overdrive.

"Wanna talk about it?" she asks, still stubbornly maintaining contact with my shoulder.

Whispering a vehement 'no' while wiping a palm over my face, I spot the black ink smudge from the ofuda I'd slept on. *Smooth move.*

Pointing to the smear, I cringe. "How bad is it?"

Instead of answering, she covers her mouth. Shrugging out of her blanket, she shuffles off. "Be right back."

Still cussing myself out over my stupidity, I stroke that spot of former connection between us. Water runs in the kitchen, and there's rummaging in the closet before she returns with paper towels and rubbing alcohol.

Expecting her to offer me the supplies, I reach up. Instead, she pulls off my covers, then drapes a towel to protect my collar.

Prickles form on my skin, not from the rush of brisk air but the unintentional graze of her fingertips on my neck. It's more provocative than whispering in my ear. While she helps me salvage a bit of pride, I'm riveted in place. None of my former girlfriends were ever this kind.

"Thank you." Is the scent of cherry blossoms her perfume, or her shampoo?

When she lifts my chin, her lips curve as she dabs the cold rag to the smudge. "I wonder if the magic works on skin. If it weren't reversed, I'd suggest you leave that protection ward. But backward, it won't do you any good, will it?"

I could listen to her quiet rambling all day, it's that soothing. "Not advisable. The word and item disappear after the spell absorbs the ki, part of the balance."

"Oh my!" With the next application, she renews the disarming bedside-manner conversation. "I have a hard time believing you could have been yakuza during innocent moments like this. It can't be what you were meant to be. Almost done. Then we'll get you under the heater."

Leaning in, she purses her lips and scrubs my cheekbone. "That spot was stubborn. Hope I didn't hurt you."

"Nuh-uh."

"Now your palm." She takes my hand to wash off the black smear with a touch so light it tingles, then traces the spots as she inspects her work.

I flinch. That's not what I wanted to do, but she used such an intimate gesture.

Startled, she shrinks away. "Sorry. We got it all."

"Don't be." Wrong thing to say, because she perks up. Everything in me screams to pull her close. To ask her to be mine. But the stain of my past is permanent, not easily cleaned off like the ink. *Let her down easy.* "Ohno-chan, you can do so much better. Being your friend is more than I deserve."

When her brows furrow, something must click. "But that means you're trying to protect me, aren't you?"

It might be better to remain in vague territory. So, I shrug.

"You like me, don't you."

It's not a question. *Shit. Get it over with.* "I mean it! I'm bad news."

She blinks before dabbing at tears with her sleeve. "Such a contradiction. Acting as if you care about me, instead, you shove me away. I never confessed, you know."

True, she didn't say so. But it couldn't be more obvious. "Sorry."

"I can't reconcile your past with the guy who smears ink on his face when he falls asleep because he worked late, bumps into a car when he glances back at me, and then has the gall to tell me I should date someone better than himself. How does that sound to you?"

I gulp. What do I do now? Sensei wanted us to all stay together tonight for safety. Otherwise, I'd beat it to the exit.

"I see your struggles. Those wouldn't be there if you were bad at the core. You wouldn't care about others. The choices I've watched you make since you arrived have been good—to save an old lady who hated you, to look after her, to help stop a thief, to spare the life of the man you thought betrayed you, to use your knowledge for good, to set the record straight when Mie-chan and I couldn't figure you out, to not blow your cool when I miscounted and... and accused..."

None of those is out of the ordinary. *Wait.* "You remember that?"

Her bottom lip sucks in as she nods, with regret in her eyes.

Sheesh, that look. "Knowing my past, I could see why you thought I might have taken the money. But when we became friends, it didn't cross my mind."

Her skepticism is plain as day.

"Truth."

So, she adds to the tally. "More proof."

Mie's words resurface. 'Hurt Ohno-chan, and it won't be blunts.' Forget the intimidation attempt, she was thinking of her friend. Will candor dissuade Ohno? "What happens when I break your heart?"

Her reply accompanies a defiant raise of her chin. "And pushing me away isn't?"

Damn.

No longer the timid mouse, she leans in. "Listen. I like you. So there's your confession. And I think you feel the same. What's so hard about that?"

"I just—"

"Doubt yourself? It's past time we tell you to knock it off. We've just all been too polite."

Keep your guard up, Umeji!

She takes a shaky breath before continuing. "Being a quiet girl, I've spent my life watching people. But thinking I'm not willing to fight for what I want is a mistake."

"You know the awful things I did. Former mobsters don't deserve happy endings. We spend our lives atoning for the wrongs—"

To hush my protest, she puts up a hand. "Everyone carries scars from the past—a reminder of how we healed. In kintsugi, they mend a broken vessel with gold and lacquer. It's more beautiful for having been shattered. Don't you think people are that way, too?"

Letting me process, she adds, "Yes or no, Umeji-kun. It doesn't have to be immediate, and I won't pressure you either way. I only want an answer at some point."

We've all got scars? Kintsugi? Despite knowing my history, she sees the best in me? My throat tightens as I catch her trembling hand, encompassing it in my own. I can't voice the word she wants at this moment. So maybe actions will suffice. *Don't let me be too late.*

Closing my eyes, I kiss her fingers curled around mine, lingering, unwilling to release these hands that have shown me such kindness. When she caresses my cheek, I lean into it as if her touch sustains life itself.

"That was cheating, I'll have you know." This time, the tear that escapes her eye isn't the sad variety.

"Maybe I'm not so predictable?" As a warmth I'd not felt before fills my chest I refuse to remove my lips from her skin, causing her chin to dip with the shy grin that first caught my attention.

"I can deal with that kind of surprise. Though, could we get under the kotatsu again? I'm freezing!"

Scooting to lie under it, I lean back and hold the blanket open in invitation.

"Oh!" She stops in the middle of wrapping herself in a duvet of her own, only intending to put her feet under the table's cover. "Um. Matsuo-kun and Mie-chan are just over there."

My hand rubs the back of my neck. Ohno cares about what others think, unlike my past girlfriends. "After all that bravado, and you're worried about them now?"

Shrinking, she meekly says, "I spent it all at once. Didn't have a plan after that."

Adorable. Who else would barrel into a situation with no thought of what happens next? "Mind if we just lay next to each other?" Cautiously, she snuggles into my side, while I wrangle the covers over us.

"This goes on record as the girl getting the guy, I'll have you know. One of the few times, I got what I wanted. And my family's magic proved right yet again. Guess I need a different New Year's resolution."

The sakura scent fits her—optimistic and making a lasting impression for the fleeting moment she's here. "Me? And your family's magic?"

"No, silly. Asking you. Regarding the magic, you can imagine the surprise and excitement when I first saw a red string between us. Nakamura-san saw it, too."

That's why Sensei kept pushing me. "Like in all the super sappy love stories where two people are destined to become lovers?"

She pokes my chest. "I happen to like those stories, buster."

It draws a smile out of me. "Noted. So when you found out my past, it had to be a shock."

"Oh yeah. I was super confused for a while. So, do you have any resolutions?"

Will she think my prayer is corny? I reveal my often-uttered phrase, "To be worthy." When she rests her palm over my heart, it tries to jump out of my ribcage.

"You're off to an excellent start."

Brushing a lock of hair out of her face, I broach a tough topic. "Have you dated before?"

"There was a guy in High School, but he broke up because Chou scared him. A whopping two weeks. Then we left Hokkaido after a brat ate a potion of mine and almost died. Why?"

There's a vast gulf between my experiences and hers. "The ooze is scary. But the point is... Well, the girls I've been with before haven't been the kind you take home to meet your mom."

She clenches my shirt.

Letting out a breath, I lift her curled fingers from my button up to gently smooth them out and place them back on my chest, resting my hand over hers. "What I meant is this kind of relationship is new for me, too."

When she relaxes, my pulse slows. We remain in time-oblivious bliss, allowing the shared warmth to lull us. Being here with her feels so right, so peaceful—as if nothing could go wrong.

I'd like more, but I don't want to scare her off by going too fast. This isn't America where I heard they kiss on the first date. And there's no telling how long this will last. *Remember this for the rough days.*

* * *

Light filters through the rice paper windows. Ohno remains beside me, her pinky finger locked around mine in an unspoken promise. Her dreaming twitches prove it's real. But my neck is killing me, and I'm sore from lying on the hard floor mats.

"Whoa, Mie-chan. Did Ohno-chan hit him over the head?"

Thanks a lot, Matsuo.

"You didn't hear them? Ugh! So stinkin' sappy. It was tough to pretend I was still sleeping."

Opening an eye to give the look from hell, I grumble, "I hear you two."

Ohno stretches and sits up. "WE can hear you."

"Fill me in later." Matsuo winks at his co-conspirator, causing me to groan.

Snitching a sheet of paper and wadding it up, Ohno primly hands it to me. My lazy aim is off, so Matsuo doesn't even have to dodge as he spits out, "I'm happy for you both. Really! And I won't tell anybody what Mie-san says!"

Ohno wads another page and tosses it. When a ball comes out of nowhere to hit my head, I whip around only for Sensei to hit me with another.

Whistling, she hides another behind her back. "I should fuss about wasting supplies. But you all were having so much fun."

Ohno seizes the opportunity. "On the count of three, get Umeji-kun!"

"Hey!" Aghast, I duck, protesting as I'm pelted. "Isn't my girlfriend supposed to be on my side!?"

When the coast is clear, I catch the sparkle in my aunt's eyes.

* * *

Sensei makes sure everyone has breakfast before they return home—simple eggs, toast, and coffee. She puts her heart into cooking for those she cares for. So, I'm glad she didn't go to more trouble. We were all up super late. Even Satou stops by to eat with us. Ohno pokes me under the table as Mie moves to sit by him and twirls her hair.

"How about we all visit the temple today?" he offers.

"Sorry, Boss. Ohno-chan and I have plans."

With arms crossed, Mie gives him the stink eye. To witness the former smooth-talking club host, squirming is one for the record books. "I-I meant Mie-chan. I will be happy to take you later. My apologies. I've been so focused on Hiro and ensuring my aunt is safe."

As our guests head out, I hand each their stack of ofuda. Ohno's the last to leave. So I rack my brain to delay her departure. Perhaps one of our favorite topics will work. "The K-pop's growing on me."

Giving me a playful shove, she steps outside. "Liar."

The brisk breeze goes right through my shirt, but I'll endure any amount of cold for a moment more with her. So I shut the door behind me to keep the heat inside.

As we slip apart, I hook my fingers with hers to delay the goodbye. "Am not! I wouldn't have ever listened to it, if not for you."

Stepping toe to toe with me, she pokes my chest. "Watch it, Umeji-kun, or I'll make you wear matching band t-shirts!"

"Call me Tatsu, and I'll put on anything you want."

"You really would... Tatsu-kun?" A cautious hope pairs with reverence as she speaks the nickname.

Nodding, I squeeze her hand. My heart is so full it could burst. "Not pink. But the way you're looking at me, I wouldn't be able to hold out on even that very long."

Impishly, she taps my nose. "Challenge accepted." She's so close. The urge to cup her face in my hand overtakes me before I can stop myself. Her freckled cheeks warm. But she doesn't pull away. Instead, she adds. "And I'm Su-chan to you. See you tomorrow, Tatsu-kun."

We break contact. I've never felt so alive as I watch her drive out of sight. *Not even Mie calls her Su-chan.*

22

CHAPTER 22: DISTRUST

Sensei and I take turns bathing at night. Yesterday, that didn't work out with the party and clean up. I was going to only wash off, but Sensei insisted I take time for a proper soak this morning.

Reminder to self, don't let her prepare your bath ever again! She turned me into a walking pheromone. I tromp down the stairs into the sunlit kitchen, and she leans in to sniff my collar. When I try to dodge, she walks off to sweep with a dreamy look plastered on her face.

"Sensei—"

Her broom halts. "Call me Aunt now. We're family."

"Okaaaay, Aunt. By chance, did Tsuchimikado-san wear the same cologne?" I mumble through the ponytail holder in my mouth while pulling my hair back. *Man, I need a haircut.*

Making a tsking sound, she crosses her arms. "I wouldn't do that to you. Just had to make sure the mix is right."

"So, I'm not charming enough on my own? Tell me you didn't put some love potion in my bath."

"Really, Nephew?"

A raised eyebrow speaks of my experiences with Sensei's wiles.

"No, I did not. You wearing that scent shows you care enough to know Ohno-chan's preferences. It's yuzu and sandalwood, remember that. Someday you may have to buy candied yuzu peel to apologize to her."

180

"How'd you find that out? You aren't stalking her online, are you?" That gains me a flick behind the ear. "Ow!"

Her lips purse. "We talked about essential oils when she visited me in the hospital."

"Oh."

I'm about to leave, so Sensei wraps my neck in a scarf and puts a few ofuda into my coat pocket. "Don't want you to catch a cold. You have the sword on you, right? It never hurts to be careful."

"Aunt. I'm a grown man. No need for a mom substitute."

Her look turns steely as she adjusts the muffler around my neck. "Your mother's a fool."

Harsh.

"I invited your mother for New Year's and asked for a copy of your family tree to have proof of what we know. I'll spare you the reply."

When I gain my composure again, I squeeze Sensei's arm. "Thank you for trying, and for believing in me."

Pshawing, she shoves me out the door. "Hurry now. Don't keep Ohno-chan waiting! And invite her for lunch today."

Jogging from the bus stop, through the path in the dusting of snow, and up steep stairs to the walled-in temple doesn't allow me to beat Su-chan there. Sure, I could have used an ofuda for a portal. But that wouldn't be using the magic wisely.

It's my first time at the temple, despite living in Nonogawa for a month and a half now. The columned entrance comprising a bell-curved roof and a weathered wooden gate has imposing doors wide open for visitors. A peek through the entry hints at the ancient inner buildings and large upswept roofs.

My panting creates cloud puffs in the brisk cedar and pine-laden air. As I bow with an apology, Su-chan thrusts out a black t-shirt and her bottom lip sucks in. "Tatsu-kun, you said you would."

Does she expect me to refuse? Accepting, I laugh at the pink and white English letters gleaming in the sunlight. I have to squint to make out her favorite K-pop band's name—the glitter's shine in the sunlight assaults my eyes. "I did."

"Hold this for me." Unwinding my scarf, I put it around her neck before slipping out of the rest of my winter gear. A hint of her sakura perfume speaks again of the hope and fresh starts that come with spring.

"But! It's cold out!" she protests, snuggling into the scarf and inhaling deeply.

Score one for Sensei's meddling. Throwing the shirt on over my button-up, I whip my coat and hat on to avoid the brisk air seeping too far under my shirts. "I'll warm up. So, we match?"

"Uh-huh." She beams as she unwinds the muffler. "Should we shop together tonight to show them off?"

"Sounds fun." She didn't bring a neck warmer today. So, I re-wrap it. "Shall we?"

Her fingers weave with mine, and her face tucks down into the fabric. "Mmmm. Thought there was a whiff of my favorite scents when you arrived. You might not get this back. Nakamura-san told you?"

Squeezing her hand, I admit, "My great aunt plotted and even sniffed me to see if you'd approve. Talk about awkward!"

Her laugh rings in the valley before she blinks. "You're related? But Date? They hate each other!" She bobs and weaves as she attempts to find a resemblance.

Before we bow to pass under the gate, I share about Tsuchimikado's twin. "How wouldn't he have known to keep his distance from the vixen? Families talk."

"Umeji-san!" Little Suzuki skids to a stop, sending snow flying in front of us.

His mother trots to catch up. "Don't interrupt!"

Nevertheless, Su-chan and I give a bow in greeting to the duo. I owe him for the good turn in my life. "Hey, Suzuki-kun. What's up? You and your mom came to the temple today, too?"

"Yep! And I got ten thousand yen in my New Year's envelope!" He's bouncing, unable to contain his energy. "What did you get?"

"Sojirou!" His mother scowls, joining our trio. "We don't talk about money!"

It's difficult to cover my smile at his childish excitement. "I'm too old for the red envelopes, bud."

"Really?" His disappointment on my behalf makes me wish I could have the New Year's gifts again.

"Yeah. How are your lessons with Matsuo-kun?"

"Good! I avoided a punch. And the bully's in trouble!"

"Awesome! Be stubborn about it. They'll come at you for a while, but they should buy a clue in time. Hang in there."

Pressing his palms together, he pleads. "Please, will you watch my classes?"

A glance conveys his mother's consent. "I'll check with Matsuo-kun to see when it works out."

Then the mom tugs, but he stays rooted to the spot. "Did you make up with your friend?"

Looking over at Su-chan with chagrin, I mouth the word, "Sorry."

She raises our interlaced fingers. "He did."

"Was it hard?"

The kid is relentless! "Terrifying. Apologies aren't always enough. I had to tell her everything I did in the yakuza so it wouldn't hurt our relationship again."

His brows furrow and I can see the wheels turn in his mind. "You weren't really scared, were you? I mean, you couldn't be."

Letting out a breath, I run a hand over my hat, half expecting it to glide through my hair.

"Sojirou, don't be rude," his mom chides.

The kid needs to hear I'm not some invincible, tough guy. "Oh, I was. The hardest thing I've ever done. I gripped the door handle the whole time, ready to run."

Noting his narrowed gaze, Su-chan giggles, "Tatsu-kun, I don't think he believes you. But I wondered if you would rip the handle right off."

"Hey! You're not supposed to tell on me!"

Sojirou's wide-eyed expression at our banter is worth any embarrassment.

"Your grandparents are expecting us. Time to go." Suzuki Chiyo gives another tug.

This time he follows. "Don't forget you promised!"

Finally, we head to the main hall with its massive roof and wait our turn in line to offer incense and our prayers. Then we get to the fun part, buying our charms as a couple.

"I know guys get dragged along for this. But I'm glad you're here," Su-chan says as she clasps her hands in front of her, in the pose I first realized her feelings for me. That was only a month ago.

"I'm a willing victim."

As Su-chan gives me a playful nudge, movement to the right catches my attention. A guy in a suit turns around to light a cigarette. Who does he think he is, ignoring the smoking restrictions here at the temple?

Click. So much for a simple day with Su-chan.

"What's wrong, Tatsu-kun? You just got the stoniest expression I've seen." Su-chan has the sense to ask in a whisper, and I could kiss her for her situational awareness.

"Keep walking. We're being watched by Date's goons." When I see her head turning to look, I catch the side of her face, covering with a caress and putting my forehead to hers. "He doesn't know that we're aware of him, yet. Let's keep that element of surprise for if we need it."

Taking her hand, I whisk her over to the protection charms booth. The clink of a jar in her purse reassures she brought Chou, for just in case.

"What do we do?" She whispers as she holds up a miniature pair of relationship charm bags in a set of pink and blue with little knots at the closure and loops that tie to a cellphone.

"Nothing for now. See, in the clerk's window, there's no one behind us. Are those the charms you like best? We won't let him intimidate us out of what we came for today," I ask.

At her nod I pay, and we step out of the way to attach ours to each other's phones. This relationship symbol makes Su-chan more of a target. But she'd be upset if I denied her the opportunity.

"Want to get your fortune, too?"

She shivers. "No. Being watched is creepy. Why are they spying on us?"

"Dunno. But now they know I'm the luckiest guy in town." The compliment nets me her fingers interlacing with mine again.

As we exit, my gaze sweeps the grounds to see another goon packing heat. Prickles form on the back of my neck when we find Su-chan's parking spot.

"Want a ride back?" Su-chan squeezes my hand as she unlocks her CR-V.

"Sure." I don't want her to be alone until I know the goons are gone.

Despite the initial concern, a lack of other detectable threats on the trip to Sensei's house pushes my curiosity into overdrive. How long has Date been keeping tabs on us? Does she know about all my contacts? The thought sends a shudder down my spine.

Satou's car is parked out front. We burst into the house. Su-chan has the decency to bob her greeting as I blurt, "Boss! Su-chan and I were being watched. Wanted to give you a heads up before you and Mie take your turn visiting the temple."

Satou's eyebrow raises. Su-chan excuses herself since there wasn't an opportunity to use the public restroom at the temple.

To ensure my girlfriend is out of earshot, he watches her head to the add-on room off the veranda. "That moves our timeline up on the investigation. I'll make sure there's a guard with Hiro. Though, I don't think postponing the visit with Mie is an option. She'll drag me to the temple come hell or high water. You know how competitive she is—can't be outdone by Ohno-chan in getting couples' charms. Then I'll swing by for the laptop, wi-fi box, and paperwork. Hiro or I need to be present when you work. Understand?"

"Gotcha, Boss."

"Turning over the watch to you. Time to pick up Mie-chan." Mock saluting, he heads out.

Sensei drags the vacuum to the living room as if it's a dog struggling against its leash. *Oh-oh.*

Concerned, I ask, "Didn't my friends and I pick up well enough after the party?"

"I just feel like tidying." Her feelings don't hide well under the exaggerated enthusiasm as she works.

"Aunt." I move items out of her way so she can't ignore me.

"You prodded just like Kazuo does." At my narrowed eyes, she continues. "He talked you into helping investigate Date, didn't he?"

"Yeah. But you don't want me to." As I prompt, I lift the low table so she can clean under it.

"I haven't heard news about the question of you replacing me. It's concerning. I know the messenger well. Also, this local department has been on my list of agencies to be wary of, for reasons I can't speak of."

"So the two are related? Has Satou-san asked for your help? He hasn't spoken about it."

She runs the vacuum roughshod over the tatami. "Yes, I'm involved. Today, he interrogated me about Date. Working with them will provide a chance to prove yourself."

She didn't answer my first question. Before I can repeat it, Su-chan joins us and rearranges the cushions as I replace the table.

"Now, shoo. Listen to your music or something together so I can make lunch."

Satou shows up again after we finish eating. Pulling me aside to the hall, he gives me the paperwork and notarized guarantee. Everything I'd asked for.

"Time to let you in on the department you're working with. Then you can sign the agreement and we can hunt for the evidence for a search warrant on Date's property." He flashes a badge that reads Special Agent Satou Kazuo, Public Security Intelligence Agency's Paranormal Division.

I whistle. "I knew you had to have some pull for things like helping Su-chan retrieve Chou and to be a partner to an undercover officer. But Paranormal Division?"

His eyebrow raises in his signature look. "You're living in the same house with a kitsune, and you're asking if my department exists?"

"So, you see insane stuff all the time?"

He nods. "Finding out my Aunt was a kitsune didn't fly well with my superiors. The race excels at keeping their cover, yet I'm supposed to be making inroads with the species to help protect them. If our estimates are accurate, their numbers are down forty percent over the last hundred years. Guarding Aunt Hisako is a top priority now since her nemesis is still on the loose."

"Yikes. No wonder they hide."

"Speaking of, I'll need a private chat with the resident kitsune. I think she knew my job the whole damned time. It pisses me off that she didn't say a peep."

The vacuum isn't making noise anymore. I find my girlfriend showing Sensei the charm on her phone. "Hey, Su-chan. Care to go for a walk?"

"Sure! I'd love that and it's warmer out today."

Without a word, Su-chan entwines her fingers in mine. The contact—my assurance that we're dating isn't a dream. Strolling in the sun lightens the weight of my upcoming tasks for the PSIA. After a few minutes, we climb the stairs to the shrine and walk on the side of the path, freeing the middle for any kami who might pass by.

She asks, "Tatsu-kun, do you come here often?"

My head bobs, though I can't put a finger on why I came here today. I was just here recently. "Sensei and I maintain it. I don't know how many people visit. But she's particular about keeping it spotless."

"I've often seen it as I drove out of town. But the temple is in town."

We stand side by side at the little shrine, toss coins in the box, bow twice, clap, say a silent prayer, and bow once more. Mine is requesting healing for Hiro, quick thanks for my relationship with Su-chan, and my usual—to be worthy.

Out of habit, I grab the broom from the nearby shed. Tidying up the front, Su-chan remarks, "Should we refresh the offerings tomorrow?"

"Excellent idea. When we left, I was just trying to give the Boss time to talk with Sensei." After this, preparing for a task that's all too similar to what I used to do in the mob leaves my stomach in knots. My girlfriend works with a sense of calm I envy. "Su-chan..."

"Hmm?" Her feather duster stops mid-stroke.

Upon looking at her, words escape me. Nothing matches the pictures in my mind. The jumble of images and feelings aches raw like a fresh bruise.

"Forget it." I return to sweeping and work toward the entrance.

From behind, her arms enfold me. Her embrace and the scent of sakura unwind the tightness inside. "You know I'll listen, right?"

"Yeah. I-I just can't talk now."

She squeezes me. "Mom says that Dad gets stuck every once in a while. In time, the words come out."

Who'd guess a former yakuza would have anything in common with her father? Grabbing my sleeve, she leads me from the building and to the field behind it.

We end up lying in the frosted grass with our heads together, watching the clouds float by. Pointing out particular formations, she spots an elephant, a bird, and even a ship. I only see the potential for rain.

"How can you always be so positive?"

Rolling over to her side, she rests her chin on my shoulder. "I'm not always. Though, being with you makes me happy. It's been stressful lately. But I believe if we're together, we'll be ok. Does that make sense?"

Mollified, I tuck my hands behind my head as I lie on my back. "Maybe you and Sensei are my salvation—helping me look ahead, instead of always focusing on the past."

Her head jerks up as she waves her hand in front of her face to say 'no way'. "Don't put that responsibility on us, buster. We can encourage, and Nakamura-san can point you in a direction to go. But it's your feet that have to tread the path. The difference is that you're not alone, unlike when you first came to Nonogawa."

How does she know just what to say? In answer, my hand slips to the nape of her neck, drawing her forehead to mine. The glow in my chest rivals the sun as we continue our cloud watching.

Then, a fast-moving puff gives me a possibility. "See that? Think it's a fox?"

"Yeah. Looks like the cloud's running."

A bright flash by the building resembles a falling star. So I roll to shield Su-chan. But there's no impact. Is the shrine ok?

When Su-chan clears her throat, I pull away with reluctance. Though, the excuse to cover her was legit. "Let's find out what that was."

As we pick a brisk pace, we theorize about the strange flare and a golden glow catches my eye. Rounding the corner, we spy a translucent white fox—a messenger of Inari—on the top step. Su-chan's face brightens.

We bow low and a wave of peace washes over us. Su-chan glances from it to where its gaze focuses. It seems to be intent on me. Swallowing, I lower my gaze.

Its resonant voice echoes among the trees. "Umeji-san, I have carried your petition, time and again. Inari-sama has received your prayers and offerings. Though, Nakamura-san's request for a human with a criminal past is the most unusual I've encountered in my long history. Often humans are not suitable matches for the job she fills. But your requests are compatible. Thus, Inari will test you. No matter the choice, your actions will affect those around you. Choose wisely."

"I'll do my best."

"There is no try, only results. Be aware Nakamura-san's post lasts half a century and you must find a suitable replacement for the position when you leave."

What does the kitsune mean? When I dare to look up, a mist forms causing the messenger to fade from sight. Springing to my feet, I shout toward the heavens. "How do I know what the best choice is?"

A final echo reverberates, "Choose wisely."

Tugging at my sleeve accompanies Su-chan's expectant expression. "Tatsu-kun, did the fox speak to you?"

"You didn't hear it?"

"Nope."

As we finish cleaning, I relay the message.

Su-chan queries, "May I ask what you prayed?" She must see my hesitation because her fingers slip into mine with reassuring familiarity.

"I told you yesterday."

"You said you wanted to be worthy of me as your resolution for the new year. But there's more, correct?"

"Yeah."

"Makes sense. You're becoming a positive influence here in the community. Bad news spreads faster, but good reports travel, too."

Is my purpose here what Sensei asked me to replace her for?

Su-chan and I swing by Sensei's place so I can grab a few things before I meet with Satou. She doesn't know it's with the PSIA. I wish she could come.

But working for a grocery store has its downsides. She's already scheduled to work there after the holiday, unlike me, assigned to the investigation.

Why isn't there more protection for Su-chan? I hate that I can't be in two places at once. "Do you have Chou or any other of your pets with you? Because I can accompany you to the store, then get to Satou's on my own."

"I don't mind a few extra minutes with you." She smiles, patting her purse. "Chou was easy to tuck into my bag. You're the one on Date's radar. I know you're able to defend yourself. But is it safe for you to go alone, even here in little Nonogawa?"

With a wink, I whip a portal talisman from my jacket pocket, holding it between my index and middle fingers. Even under interrogation, I'll never admit how much I practiced the gesture for such an occasion. The showmanship nets me a peck on the cheek—worth every second of rehearsal.

* * *

In Satou's living room, the blinds are closed and a device similar to what I saw Hiro use buzzes on the table. "As per the agreement, your computer is a loan. After you prove yourself and they hire you on, the department may let you keep it or provide an advance for one."

He has two laptops, his and mine, set up on the low table for a secure virtual meeting that will run via VPN and proxies.

"Not a prob." Proving my worth should be a cinch. The pay advance wasn't too shabby either.

Sensei sits between us. She passed on having her own laptop because she doesn't know how to run one. So, she'll share with me. That way Satou can concentrate on the agenda. But she insisted on plastering every wall of the room with refreshed talismans.

When it starts, Satou introduces us to his boss—PSIA Okayama Liaison Chief Arai Ryouta and Officer Takahashi Yamaki with the local police. Takahashi is mid-thirties, balding, and stocky—even from the sitting perspective of the laptop camera. He would have made a great sumo wrestler.

In contrast, Arai is slender and dressed in a conservative black suit. But his image is hazy and semi-transparent, his drooping hair stays plastered to his head, and his dead pale complexion gives me the creeps. He seems to hover with his arms held out in front of him, behind someone running the computer.

Why didn't Satou give a heads up his boss wasn't human anymore? I could have avoided stuttering in the introduction. Both Arai and Takahashi greet Sensei with warmth, remarking on how rare her people are. Me? On the cold side. Such is life.

When they share they can only trace Date for the last few decades, I resist rolling my eyes. It's essential to remain professional with these folks. They're smart enough and eager for the hunt to gain traction.

From the little I've seen, the system they work under is too rigid, hampering their efficiency. Much like the day I filled out the mountain of new employee paperwork at the grocery store. Life has been more challenging since I started following the rules like a normal person. Was that only a month and a half ago?

"Aren't most of the kitsune Luddites, even more than other yokai? If the target has some level of familiarity, we should have the advantage on that front." Officer Takahashi taps his pen on the table in the station's conference room, grating on my nerves.

Sensei's lips purse, but she doesn't refute the assumption. Even she avoided most technology until she had to use a tablet to teach me history.

"Date Sari isn't afraid to use tech in ways we haven't dreamed of." I throw a mockup of the target's iPad on the screen. "When I first encountered her, she was holding this—bound to a powerful oni. She also wears a bracelet, that I believe taps into the power she's harnessed and stored in the iPad."

"Date has been likely tying the same oni to various devices for a few centuries. How she does this or finds the power to keep the oni bent to her will must be via the darkest magic," Sensei adds, sending a shudder through me.

"She's a wily vixen. Very few records of her exist," Satou says.

"A fact to add to the notes you shared for the meeting—Nonogawa's protector, the river dragon, Shion, went missing a little over..." Sensei flips through her journal, "...a hundred years ago. I've been trying to figure out why an area's protector would just disappear. They always retire or the one who kills them brags about it."

"You're connected with the League of Guardians?" Chief Arai leans into his camera as his voice cracks. His poor computer assistant shudders as he floats through her to get closer to the screen. I don't want to know how that feels. "Nonogawa and the surrounding area have an unusual amount of paranormal activity, but we can't find the one assigned here. Any leads would help."

But Sensei waves it off. "Local lore. Easy to find if you know where to look. Though, I'm curious how you know about the reclusive organization."

A throat clearing draws attention to Satou, whose brows furrow so deep I wonder if they'll recover their original spot on his face. "Aunt, I'd appreciate it if you shared where you find said information."

She's not going to answer, is she? But I can share a new fact. "Uhm, Boss. You should probably know I recently found out I'm a distant relative to Date."

Arai's glare could melt steel. Satou pinches the bridge of his nose. Finally, he dares to ask, "Anything else you two secretive magic users care to share that might apply to the investigation?"

Sensei and I glance at each other, then shake our heads. Nothing sticks out that needs sharing at this moment.

"Here are the assignments. Aunt, will you please gather any information on Date's family and notes you have on her? Umeji, you will dig into the financial and yakuza connections that we suspect, since Hiro is out of commission. Tomorrow, he'll share what he knows. Officer Takahashi, you'll be with me. We would prefer solid proof within a few days, but the Subversive Activities Prevention Law should cover us in a pinch since she's collecting former yakuza like they're going out of style."

"How many guards are with Hiro?" I ask.

"Two. That's what the department could spare."

Sensei jumps in before I can. "You'll want more. The witch can control about two dozen men at a time with her demon-infused magic."

Takahashi whistles.

"Noted," Satou says. "Chief?"

One of Arai's floating arms moves, so his hand can stroke his chin. "Agent Otsuka was compromised. There is only so much we can do."

It doesn't likely show on the tiny view for the virtual meeting, but I see the twitch that develops above Satou's eye. "If there are no further questions, we'll wrap up the meeting." He pauses. "Thank you, Chief Arai, everyone. We'll get to the bottom of this."

When everyone disconnects, Satou's professional mask falls, and he throws a pen across the room, followed by muttering a string of profanity. "This kind of shit never used to be allowed. Something stinks. Can you two make more of those protection talismans for Hiro?"

"Yeah." So, Hiro's either bait or being written off as a liability.

* * *

Nonogawa is small enough, most places besides restaurants, TaniMart, and the drugstore are closed in the evenings. So, Sensei and I settle at the low table in her living room.

She pours tea as I start up the laptop to ferret around on the internet. I intend to use her knowledge of the area since Satou got her approved to oversee my work, and, unfortunately, Hiro was removed from the list.

Having her here is better than having the boss watching over my shoulder. "Tatsuya, I didn't say anything before. But I'd like to know, what do you make of the agency's treatment of Otsuka-san?"

"It's stupid. At least Satou-san is taking things seriously. What made you bring it up?"

She looks away. "I wish we'd have heard a definitive answer back on my request. The messenger said it's on hold."

"He visited you again?"

"Of course. I always look forward to his visits. Though, shouldn't we be investigating?"

"Aunt, back to the topic." *Ha!* She won't always get the best of me.

Pursing her lips, she concedes. "Fine. You won't be able to do both—replace me and work with the PSIA long term. Your talents will be of value to both. You must decide which path to take."

"I know what I'm dealing with in this job. Though, I have no clue what you've been hinting at for months."

A quick flick of magic surrounds my laptop. "There. That should keep prying ears out. The truth is, I'm a protector of Nonogawa. The PSIA did not help my predecessor when he asked for help to investigate a lead in the case of his missing mentor. So, I'm not comfortable letting them know. Working with Chief Arai is bad enough. The messenger permitted me to share only that much. And it irks me no end."

"My loyalty can't be to both groups. Gotcha."

The glowing shield drops, and she gestures to the computer. "The sooner we get started, the sooner we can finish."

The PSIA had a VPN installed on the machine for me to use. I'd debated if I should just follow the agency's lead. Because of Sensei's warning, I opt to install tools of my own that I downloaded onto a USB drive at the library, just in case. That ensures they can't spy on me, and I can make a backup of my work.

After removing their software, including what looks like a remote monitor, I declare the laptop clean. They won't be happy about it, but they have to let me do my job without interference and trust me enough to do it. To cover my ass, I make notes and explain each step to Sensei in easy-to-understand terms.

"Do they think I can't watch over you well enough?" Sensei asks as she grabs her journal to take notes.

"They implied concerns when they said yokai aren't tech-savvy."

She harrumphs. "That doesn't make me stupid."

"I know. And Satou-san knows, considering he convinced them to let you watch over me as I work. Think they'd blow a gasket if they knew we're related?"

Her laugh is the perfect answer.

Using one of the less questionable dark web VPN and proxy pairs, we start our digital hunt. Working until bedtime doesn't net us much.

The most interesting tidbit comes from the Kyuunan local news five years ago. Two families, the Nishikawas and Godas, received letters from wayward adult sons stating they'd gone straight and took a job with a security firm, MagiSecurity.

When they heard nothing more after promises of proof from their sons, they went to the police. Nothing came of it. Though, it wasn't for lack of the police investigating. The company seemed to have pulled out of town before the police could check it out, leaving behind an empty building. Then the next week, the paper has an obituary for the reporter who wrote the article and no further news on MagiSecurity.

An internet archive search of the company has records and reviews from quite a while back. My "Bingo!" breaks the silence as I scribble down notes. "That's the logo Date had on her business card."

The few negative reviews for TekMagi seem to disappear if you go forward in the archive's history, so we dig into those. A dozen dark web searches later, we have names and addresses for those reviewers.

"Tatsuya, you are going to have to teach me how to use the legal part of the internet. I don't understand why people put so much information out there for others to find. But I see the value in it as a research tool."

"This is just the easy part, Sensei. We do the real sleuthing tomorrow to sniff out any money leads and do a few interviews. Too bad the government still relies on paper records, or we could do more tonight."

23

CHAPTER 23: WHO'S THE PREY?

A quick call to an old contact of Sensei's gives us a connection. A friend of a friend knows the Goda family from the article we found yesterday and gave us directions to the house in Kyuunan—about 20 minutes north of Nonogawa. The couple retired eight years ago, so they should be home.

Sensei parks her Nissan in front of the small, single-story, cream-colored house with windows running along the south side and a solar panel on the tiled roof. "You should renew your driver's license."

"I can when I have a permanent address. It'll be a while yet before I have money for the deposits and fees, let alone be able to afford a car. It's still strange to not be using public transportation all the time."

Sensei's nose wrinkles. "Here I thought you were getting used to the small-town life."

Shrugging, I gather up the laptop and my folder with the investigation authorization. "Can't take the big city out of me, I guess."

The front door has a collection of well-kept bonsai trees and other plants on both sides of the door. Another pot hangs by the light. The only clue of its true intent is the glint from a lens.

"Aunt, we're being monitored." The laptop and folder get tucked behind my back, so they don't think I'm the NHK guy.

"Why? This town is even smaller than Nonogawa."

"They have a reason to fear something. It might be as simple as not wanting to deal with missionaries."

With a deep breath, Sensei knocks on the door. No answer.

So she tries again. "Hello! I'm Nakamura from Nonogawa and I have a question about a news article from several years ago. You see, my nephew here was offered a similar job, but turned it down. We're working with the PSIA to investigate the company. We believe they are a danger to our town, too. Could you help us?"

Through the front door's window, we see a gentleman in a zip-up sweater shuffle his walker to the entryway door. His blue ball cap covers most of his mop of white hair. Liver spots more than wrinkles show his age.

Several clicks signal he's undone the bottom lock. But he only cracks the door, leaving the U-shaped latch in place. We bow quickly since this doesn't look promising.

I have to strain to hear his scratchy voice. "I can't help you. Go away, before you bring me any more trouble."

My words rush out. "Then we'll just ask one question and leave."

Slam. Click.

His rudeness won't stop me—the guy is scared. "Did your son mention a woman named Date? She's the one who tried to recruit me."

Through the window, his jaw shoves forward as he meets my gaze and gives the minutest of nods, then shouts, "I said leave!"

"A pity you couldn't help us. Sorry to have bothered you." I bow a little deeper than normal. He didn't have to give this confirmation.

Sensei places her hand on the siding as she mutters a spell. Faint blue flashes on the walls of his house then disappears. His wide eyes and stiff posture suggest she should explain.

"I warded your house since you don't want visitors. If you hear a shrieking tea kettle sound, someone is trying to enter."

We don't stick around for his reaction. That would be even more suspicious. In the car, I scribble a few notes and we don't talk until we're quite a ways down the road.

"The witch got to him," Sensei mutters.

"And likely anyone else who could talk. So, I'd like to hit city hall. I used to find all sorts of interesting things to use for leverage there."

A dated, white, three-story building encased in windows displays a long banner that says the next flower festival is April twentieth. It's tiny compared to Tokyo's Metropolitan Government Building skyscraper.

Inside, we follow the signs to get our number—which seems ridiculously high for the size of the town. They must not restart the count.

Within a few moments, they call ours. We're ushered to a lithe, grey-suited man with a bowl cut and a scowl who stands at the counter. Behind him, stacks of labeled filing boxes and form drawers create pseudo walls.

Staring—that's all the man seems capable of. In return, my aunt's whole countenance changes. Her head lowers in challenge as she emits an almost inaudible growl. "Why is a curse bringer here?"

"Sensei?" I gulp, unsure what to do because she's attracting attention that we don't need.

The point his pupils dilate to slits is when I step back. His name tag reads Nabeshima. That rings a bell. A story in my mythology book was about a man with that name, whose wife had been replaced by a shapeshifting, seven-tailed feline with large fangs.

"B-bakeneko..." stammers out of my mouth. Curse bringer indeed. That yokai type is known for the misfortunes they bring to the families of their victims.

He leans all too catlike over the desk. "Do not waste my time with outdated myths. What brings a vixen and her boy toy to my domain?"

"He is my nephew. And you will address me as Nakamura. Again I ask, why are you here?" Her teeth grind, but her severity lessens to keep him talking with us.

Nabeshima inclines his head, then ticks off something with his fingers. His words may be polite, but his tone grates on my nerves. "Because I have nowhere else to be, Nakamura-san. We appear to be the same in that regard. Kyuunan has no one registered here with your name. Are you two joining our happy little community?"

Before Sensei can cause more trouble, I interject. "Nabeshima-san, we would like information on a company called MagiSecurity, which was here a few years ago. May we see the records, specifically the business registration, tax records, and any complaints made against the company?"

"Interesting choice. Let me see..." There's a trill in his voice as he runs his fingers over his chin. If we didn't need his service, I'd laugh at the cartoonish gesture.

He muses, "Most of the records for that company vanished. But you're in luck. I have a photographic memory. Before I hand out such information, I will need you to fill out a form. In triplicate."

My aunt volunteers. I can't pinpoint why because she seems to loathe the bakeneko. But I won't be stupid enough to stand in her way.

"Step closer so I can speed this up," she whispers.

I do, blocking the view of her time dilation spell. I'll have to remember that trick next time I have forms to plod through.

Meanwhile, Nabeshima files several papers. Sensei clears her throat and, in a sticky-sweet, 'bet you didn't think I'd be done this fast' kind of voice, calls for the clerk.

His mind game, in turn, is pretending to verify every detail on all three copies. Out of the corner of my eye, I see Sensei's fists clench at her sides, despite the pasted-on, pleasant face she shows.

"What I remember is that there was a complaint from some of its employees about dangerous work conditions. And a complaint from the families of those men when they went missing. Likely owed death benefits. After that, MagiSecurity—poof—disappeared."

Brrrrring! It takes a moment to dig my phone out of my pocket, step aside out of politeness, and fumble to answer it. "Hello?"

"Hiro's missing." Satou's tight voice carries through the connection. "Get back here, on the double. We've got a search warrant. And I want my aunt heavily guarded."

"Shit." Hiro needed to heal, not be dragged out of the hospital!

Nabeshima doesn't stop sharing. It's tough to parse two conversations at once. "They owed taxes. So if you find the owner, please notify the authorities of their evasion. In other news, you passed the test, Nakamura-san. We get too many pushy, self-centered yokai here in Kyuunan. I will let my superiors know you are to be treated with due respect on your next visit. But you will never convince me that delicious young man is your nephew."

"How long will it take you to get here?" Satou's curtness shows his concern.

"About twenty-five minutes, Boss. We'll hurry back," I say, doing my best not to be rude and listen at the same time.

Despite the clerk warming up, Sensei's voice returns to ice cold. "He has a girlfriend. Show some respect for your customers."

"That will be 500 yen, Nakamura-san."

Why did he make it sound like he'd be nice for a fee? *Jerk.*

I join Sensei again, so she doesn't have to deal with this low life on her own. "Let's go, Aunt. We're needed elsewhere."

As we're about to leave, Nabeshima whispers into our minds. 'Don't look back, the presence left minions after the company pulled out. Do not become the prey. Sorry, I can't give you the proper deference publicly, Nakamura-san. My tenuous position doesn't allow it. Take care, both of you.'

'You, too.' Sensei sends such a friendly response, I have to refrain from a double take.

On the road, Sensei becomes a speed demon in her Nissan. She sings an old Beach Boys tune I barely recognize through her accented English. I think it's called 'The Little Old Lady from Pasadena'.

I don't want to distract her from her race home, so I tighten my seatbelt. Today, I have trouble reconciling her old lady looks with her being a powerful kitsune.

As she downshifts for a tight turn, she says, "Tell Kazuo we'll be home in fifteen minutes. Nabeshima took a risk even giving us that much information. And the hint of something bigger than Date's presence in Kyuunan is disturbing."

The question worms its way out of me despite my resolve to keep quiet. "How much of the conversation with him was cover for the telepathic communication?"

"After I filled out the form. When I gave my name on paper, he was willing to talk. Though I still don't trust him or his kind."

Quickly sending a Line message to Su-chan, I let her know we're headed back. Her response at 3:15 PM: 'Matsuo and Mie are at work. I'll meet you at Nakamura-san's.'

Satou waits in a squad car with Officer Takahashi, as Sensei and I pull up to her house. Su-chan beat us here and leans on her CR-V with her arms crossed.

Rolling down the window, Satou shouts, "You two stay here with Ohno-san! A squad is on the way to guard Aunt Hisako. We're off to find Hiro."

I volley, "You'll need more manpower and magical protection. We're coming!"

As Takahashi shifts the squad car into gear, Sensei flicks a hand at the vehicle, lifting it so the wheels spin in place. "And you can't be sure where you're going without us." To Su-chan, she tilts her chin. "Get in."

My stomach tightens at the thought of getting her more involved again. "I was just letting you know where we were, didn't intend for you to come."

Su-chan bounds over to hop in the backseat of Nakamura's car. "Umeji Tatsuya, do you think you can leave me behind?"

Better keep my mouth shut for now, so I don't get in more trouble. She's at least my match in magic, and smart as a whip!

"Civilians should not be involved in this," Takahashi growls as Sensei gently sets down the car.

"I am not a civilian." Sensei holds up her palm for him to see.

I only get a glimpse, but it looks like a serpentine blue dragon before the mark disappears.

"It's my duty as Nonogawa's Guardian! Soujoubou himself branded me. You will never mention my position nor organization to anyone." Her hand closes as a concussion-like ripple vibrates the vehicles.

My jaw drops. *Soujoubou? The legendary king of the Tengu? And guardian? Hot damn!* That's the position she wants me to replace her for. But something keeps me from opening my mouth to ask for details.

Satou's hand wipes over his face. Too many secrets, too many layers to each one. "That's why you hid from us."

"Tatsuya, please activate the tracking spell on the talismans you gave

Hiro-san." Sensei puts her car back in drive.

As I speak the word, a glowing arrow points to the southwest.

"Follow us!" Sensei commands, tearing down the street.

Her phone rings. I answer, only to have Satou shouting in my ear. "Officer Takahashi will give you a ticket if you don't slow down!"

She hollers right back. "Tell him to put on his lights! And tell that incoming squad to follow us, too! If Date took Hiro-san, we don't know how long he has."

* * *

Our destination in the temple district is a dated, two-story office building with a brick facade butted up against the steep Tsukaji Temple hill, with its many flights of stairs and flat landings for a break in the hike. Cedar and pine intersperse along the path to the temple at the top.

"Let me give you all protection spells. Tatsuya and I can handle our own," Sensei offers before we bail out of the vehicles as a unit. She also distributes talismans.

"This is the address for TekMagi. Why isn't there at least a sign?" Satou stares up at the blank area where a company name belonged.

"There used to be." Takahashi points above the entry. Then, striding through the glass doors, he clutches the warrant in front of him like a shield.

No-one greets us despite the entrance being unlocked. But the slam of a door draws us to the hall on the right. A shiver runs through me as I point down the dark walkway. Getting a closer look, we see deep grooves and large indentations that scar the white walls.

Grimacing, Takahashi asks, "Something big with claws? Tell me we're dealing with an animal, guys."

"Oni." My voice only comes out in a whisper due to my last experience with one. Not waiting for us to follow, the tracking spell arrow floats ahead. "Hiro's that way and moving."

Clinking from Su-chan's bag startles me enough that I freeze. *Get a hold of yourself.* A glance verifies she brought Chou.

Officer Takahashi has his baton raised and his other hand hovering over his pistol. Even Satou is packing a taser. I'd feel better if everyone was armed with a pistol, but those are only legal for police.

Weapons raised, Takahashi, Satou, and I rotate clearing each door as we make our way through the hall toward the back entrance. The ladies trail behind, watching our backs—magic, creatures, and potions at the ready. Piles of ash litter our path. My stomach churns at the thought that those used to be people. *Date has much to answer for.*

Nearing the end of the hall, we turn a corner. Satou swears. "Something big tangled with that exit."

Light leaks through where the doorknob used to be, and the steel door is askew, half-off its hinges.

Takahashi's brow furrows. "How big do Oni get?"

"Up to three meters," Sensei answers as she casts a spell. "Four or five life signs beyond the door. Two are close. And a magical summons just outside the door."

Satou tries to radio the backup squad, only to be greeted by static. "Jammed. We can't abort. Hiro's with them."

My hand tightens on my sword as my emotions get shoved into the deep freeze so I can gather my warrior's calm.

Takahashi gulps before directing us. "On the count of three. One, two, ...three!"

Kicking the door open we charge, weapons raised and covered in a collective shield thanks to Sensei.

Darkness spreads over us at an alarming pace. A beast's paper wings spread to slow its descent in a cacophony of rustling. Swirls of dirt and debris cloud our vision. Giant razor talons slam into the force field before the raptor lifts away for another go at us.

"What is that thing?" Takahashi shouts.

"Shikigami." My heart tries to climb into my throat as I slap on a protection talisman and step out of the shadows into the afternoon sun that makes me squint.

Su-chan joins me with Rin, her razor plant, in hand. When I whisper kotodama for a time dilation, a blue bubble forms around the enormous eagle puppet in its dive for us. As the magic slowing it causes the air to glow, the blue phosphorescence turns purple—the friction of wills ionizing the air at the leading edge.

Ending the spell when it's close enough to sweep out of the dive, I holler, "Now!"

Su-chan hurls Rin toward the raptor. Upon contact with a wing, the vine whips around like a high-pressure hose, shredding all it contacts on the paper beast and sending it spiraling toward me. I draw my sword, which hisses in the brisk January air, and rush the shikigami.

As it careens with its beak snapping at me, my blade tears through the puppet, rending it in two, and my shield pops out of existence. Rin leaps to the safety of Su-chan's arms as the remnants of the puppet flutter past us to the ground. Sensei, Satou, and Takahashi catch up to us.

Just inside the torii, two men swagger down the stairs toward us as three others climb in the opposite direction toward the temple. My jaw clenches.

One approaching is Hiro, who's pale as the snow, and the other is the shoplifter, who's upgraded to a suit from his ratty hoodie. They both sport cursed green rings. Hiro's eyes plead with me, only to close tight in pain.

I scream, "Fight it, Hiro!" I can help him if I can detect the magic he's resisting.

"Umeji!" a boy shrieks. "It's a trap!"

Shit. It's Suzuki Sojirou. And Date's dragging him along as a goon covers her escape. The trio weaves through the temple visitors.

A fire ignites in me as my old yakuza drawl returns. "Date, let him go! Only a coward hides behind a kid!"

With a malicious grin, the shoplifter smacks his fist into his palm, drawing my attention back to the oncoming fight. Hiro's neck cords and his jaw shoves forward as he moves with unnatural stiffness.

Please, don't make me fight my aniki. Burning a bit of ki, I cast a spell to heighten my senses for the oncoming battle. It highlights the silver strands from each goon connecting back to the witch.

As Hiro's lessons from the Art of War replay, my throat tightens. '*Choose your battleground, pick the advantage.'* Date and company have the higher elevation. We're forced to have the weaker position. How can we turn it around?

Behind me, I hear Sensei asking Satou and Takahashi to go with her after the boy—now the priority. I'm assigned to Hiro. The familiar clink of glass tells me Su-chan plans to fight at my side as she pulls a large jar from her purse.

I have to try. "Su-chan, stay here to direct backup."

"Don't be an idiot. Give me a talisman for Chou."

The scolding sounds more like the teasing between an elderly couple. *She's one-in-a-million.* Only she could convince me to provide a protection ofuda for that ki-sucking ooze.

As Sensei, Satou, and Takahashi use a portal to pass the guards at the first flight of stairs, Date calls out with a sneer. "Nakamura, today you pay for your sins!"

Meanwhile, Suzuki whips around, breaking free from Date. He books it down the stairs, a silver thread affixing to his neck. *Uh-oh.*

"Sensei! Watch out for Sojirou!" I belt my words out.

Su-chan and I rush forward to stop Sojirou from doing... what? Why would Date puppeteer the boy?

My shout causes Sensei to turn, her gaze focused on me. Sojirou smacks right into her. Hearing Sensei's piercing fox shriek and seeing the boy escaping Satou's and Takahashi's grasp, I cringe.

"My tama!" Sensei screams as Sojirou books it back to Date.

"This just got more complicated," I grumble when we hit the first steps.

Gasps come from higher up the hill. "Yakuza fight!" a father shouts, herding his family in the opposite direction.

"Not yakuza!" I holler back.

Su-chan asks, "What's a tama?"

"The ball that holds Sensei's magic. She can't live without it. Date's controlling Suzuki."

The witch motions her minions forward as she backs up the stairs away from Satou, Takahashi, and Nakamura. "Your alliance with the old bat and your willingness to help others provided the perfect opportunity, Grandson."

If it weren't for me, Sensei and Suzuki wouldn't be in this mess. Sickening cracking and grunting come from the third goon. *Dammit! Date, how can you do this to your men?*

"Nakamura, watch while I destroy all you love, starting with your apprentice. As they say, 'Once in the mob, always in the mob.' I'll force him to be a gangster again. You'll regret the day he was born."

That won't happen. But... Something kicks my emotional deep freeze wide open. A sick heaviness fills the pit of my stomach as I tromp up the steps to engage Hiro and the shoplifter between flights. *When I joined the Yakuza, Hiro clapped my shoulder. He knew it scared me out of my wits.*

Holiday week visitors continue to descend the temple stairs, steering clear of the oncoming fight.

Officer Takahashi shouts from above, "Everyone, leave! We need to rescue the boy!"

The crowd scatters. At that moment, my aniki and the thief rush forward. The crashing of glass to my side means Su-chan unleashed Chou.

"I'll keep Hiro-san busy!"

With a nod I stand my ground, ready to draw my sword. The blade's chill burns through the scabbard to my skin as if it's angry, too. I will not be the first to draw, nor to strike.

When the shoplifter unsheathes his sword, his hateful eyes bore into me. So I draw the katana. It hisses to life, sending more icy cold down the hilt. Its ghostly glow shines brighter than before.

The shoplifter's first attack overreaches and isn't hard to evade, letting me zip past him to gain the height advantage. My aniki didn't train this guy—he'd never allow such sloppiness. Burning ki, I leap above the thief. His weak block of my downward strike with his katana doesn't say much for his fighting skills.

In the background, Takahashi shouts, "Halt! Let the boy go!" *Is Sojirou ok?*

The thief keys in on the distraction, herding me toward the stairs that lead down to the base of the hill. When I dodge, my opponent's slash extinguishes my protection ward.

I flail to keep from falling down those steps. A second strike slices a gash on my chest, forcing me to spend more energy on a healing spell.

At his next attack, my yakuza experience kicks in. Stepping to the side, my fist strikes his face then sweeps down to wrench the blade out of his grasp, sending him tumbling beside the stairs he tried to push me down.

He's a jerk, but I don't have to take his life. As he scrambles to stand, I smack his skull using the hilt, causing the thief to crumple. There's no consciousness resisting the ring's power and his body convulses.

I swear, tossing his sword out of the way. If I can stop the conversion, he's got a chance. So, I raise my weapon, hoping to save the wretch's life. But the change is too fast. As the oni rises and the sulfurous stench roils off, I lop off its head with a sickening crunch and swallow down bile.

Next, I zip over to help Su-chan. Hiro's close to escaping as he wrestles against the blob. Su-chan tosses a glowing potion. Raising her arms, she directs blue ice to spread over his body.

Inky clouds manifest in the sky above and the temperature drops several degrees, prickling the hair on the back of my neck. Using a time dilation spell, I leap toward Su-chan. Tucking her head into my shoulder, we roll to avoid the bolt. It drains more ki than expected, sending a chill through me.

While something wet runs down my face and my ears ring, a sharp chlorine smell cleanses the sulfur from my nostrils. I'm forced to use another spell to restore my hearing.

Chou is only a puddle now. Instead of hitting Su-chan and me, the lightning must have hit her to free Hiro from his bonds.

As he struggles to remove the band, my big brother's eyes are lucid. I rush to his side, but he shoves me. "Sever the puppet strings on the others! I just have to beat the oni's will to remove it."

Hard-learned obedience kicks in.

Su-chan's fingers twist like claws as she screams. Drawing her from the sight of her dead pet, I slap on another ward.

Then I grab her chin, forcing her to look at me. "Suzuki. Cut his thread so we can retrieve what he took from Sensei. I'll handle the other goon.

Understand?"

She nods. Sharing one more spell, I help her see the silver lines. But my knees go weak. *How did my ki get this low?*

Above us, Sensei skitters out of the way of the third goon, now converted to an oni, then lunges for an attack. Satou and Takahashi approach Date from opposite sides, weapons raised but unable to shoot because of the boy.

"Tatsu-kun!" Su-chan hollers, pointing to Hiro while running for Suzuki who's frozen in place.

Hiro's face flickers between pleading and that dead-eyed puppet expression. Date got to him again. *Damn.* No time for another protection ward. I force wobbling muscles to stumble over and rip the string.

Quivering starts, despite the end of Date's puppetry. With a desperate cry, he bites at the ring to take it off his single hand. Red races up his arm and the band's glow increases.

Then the calmness I always knew him for smooths his features. "Kill me, before it takes over."

"No!"

"Tatsuya, let me die with honor!" my big brother orders.

I promised to protect and obey him, and he can't fight it anymore. My sight blurs and hot tears trace a trail down my face as I raise my ghostly sword once again.

Time slows. Putting all my strength into the swing, the katana arcs through the air. *This is the last thing I'm able to do for you, Aniki.*

When the blade contacts, I scrunch my eyes shut, not wanting to see it cleave through. Still, the noises and feel of flesh and bone parting mixed with the rotten egg reek cause me to retch. Staggering, I wipe my mouth, glimpsing the red body turning to ash. *I didn't save him.*

"Date will sacrifice the boy to protect herself!" Sensei bellows, speeding from the oni she was fighting.

Prickling raises my hackles as something connects to the back of my neck. My muscles go rigid. When my arms move against my will, my chest tightens and I want to run like a bat out of hell. But I can't. *Do something, idiot!*

Su-chan, clutching her head, staggers over to me, almost knocking me over. "Save Suzuki!" She shoves a small burst of power that weaves its way into my internal well.

Pushing against the pressure in my brain burns tons of energy. *I won't be your puppet, witch!* With a pop, I'm free. Though, only about half the ki Su-chan shared remains. The tingle keeps niggling at me and I keep blowing through ki to stop it.

Su-chan, still struggling against the control, falls to her knees. Catching her as she goes limp, I spend a little more to re-enhance my senses. Did her fight against being made a puppet take that much out of her?

Unfortunately, the flash of my spell is only a sputter, but it momentarily reveals glimmering threads between her and Date. A quick swipe takes care of the string.

Guiding Su-chan's body to the ground, I brush the hair out of her face and apply the final two talisman papers I have. *Wish I could do more.*

Not giving a second thought to spending my ki supply, I add a few extra layers in a bubble around her and a spell of invisibility over that. *I'll be back.*

Wooziness threatens to overtake my reddening vision as I repel another attachment attempt. It doesn't matter if I completely tap my ki. The witch keeps hurting people I care about. *Gotta get Date no matter what.*

An additional source of energy appears on the edge of my consciousness, a flickering flame—ample, ready for the taking, and I welcome it. The incoming rush of power flips a switch inside, hot and staticky.

My teeth grind as I brush off another puppet string as if it's merely a cobweb. *This fight ends now. Even if I have to kill Date to do it.*

"You can use your ki to rescue the child or drain this boy's energy to save yourself, just as you did to your husband's apprentices at the Battle of Toba-Fushimi. What will you choose Nakamura?" Date challenges as her ring pulses so fast it flickers.

Reverting to fox form, she maintains a shield while maneuvering so Sojirou's frozen form remains between her and the weapons pointed in their direction. *Date's struggling against the oni.*

Suzuki raises the tama high above his head, his arms shaking. Tears streak his face. He's got to be tearing himself apart inside to fight the witch. With blood rushing in my ears, my feet pound up the stairs by twos.

The last oni disengages from protecting the vixen and points to me. "Master commanded me to stop you, then dispatch the twerp and the weak-willed coppers."

Satou and Takahashi stand frozen mid-motion with open-mouthed anguish, caught in a glowing green bubble.

Not on my watch, stink bomb. To increase my attack, I cast spells without a thought for the cost. Power boils off. The reservoir fills again. My berserker war cry echoes in the surrounding hills as my blade hacks through the upheld club and the large oni holding it. Dirt and ash fly from the explosion as my katana gouges a trench.

Bounding past the remains of my last opponent in a spell-enhanced leap pushes me above the cedars—higher than I've jumped before. The cold from the sword doesn't even bother me. *I'm a fuckin' superhero.*

Stones buckle under me in a ripple, as I land in a graceful crouch. That landing should have broken bones. *Daaaaamn, this is cool.*

When a prick hits the back of my neck, catching it is a cinch. Red fire emanates from my fingers when I yank the silver string using all my might. Paws outstretched, Date flies forward.

As I reel her in, I give a grim smile to show just who's in control. "A spoiled witch like you thinks she should manipulate everyone. How's it feel when the tide turns?"

"You follow in her footsteps down to the same sin," she rasps, flailing to shake me off.

But I hold tight. The flames travel up my arms. Date whips her tail in my direction, stopping the ki flowing through me. But I pull from the plentiful mystery source to counter her spell.

"Tatsuya!" Nakamura's eyes grow wide, and her tails bristle. "Stop it, or your ki will go negative! The stolen energy will consume you!"

Who cares? Victory is so close.

Date's foreleg quivers and the ring's pulse turns to a solid light. She barks a crazed laugh. One I know all too well—the kind from someone desperate and grasping at a straw they think will bring you down with them.

I raise my katana again, ready to strike as I advance on her. *She won't bother anyone ever again.*

The fox witch sneers, "Power went straight to your head. You can't even identify the true danger, can you? Pathetic."

Then, Suzuki's lifted hand jerks.

Date's losing the battle with the oni that takes her ki drain. *Off her to end this mess.*

But I see the strain on the face of the boy that looks up to me. His eyes lock on to mine. *What's wrong with me? No more bloodshed!*

"You had so much potential, Grandson. Too bad you became your own undoing." Her voice waivers, despite the bravado, as I continue to pull her toward me little by little with one hand.

The fox witch gives a harsh tug at the boy's puppet thread, as Sensei lunges for him. Then screaming that unearthly high-pitched shriek, Date severs the lines causing blood to spurt from her toes.

But not before Suzuki smashes the ball on the paving stones, sending a blinding light in all directions. My arms fly to shield my face. I glimpse the silhouette of a fox tumbling down the stairs, blurring within the sharp power of the sun burning itself onto my retinas. Loud rustling from above swoops toward us. Unable to see, I duck.

When my vision recovers, an immense shikigami dragon carries off the red fox. Takahashi takes shots, but it's out of range too quickly, and a portal forms. Date and her puppet soar through, the gate closing behind them. The only glimpse I have of the other side is a mountain forest. Not enough to ID it.

"Date!" I bellow, shaking my fist at the sky.

My fingers don't appear to have that ghost-ish fire on the outside. It's moved inward. Instead of warming, the chill bites—racing through my veins.

Satou and Takahashi stagger over to check on Sojirou and Sensei. My teacher sobs next to the prone boy.

Nudging him with her nose, she murmurs, "The child is weak. Can you see the glow in his chest? That's part of my spirit."

Takahashi places his fingers on Sojirou's neck. "We need to get him help."

Satou raises his radio. "Where the hell is the backup unit? We need a magic trace and ambulances immediately!" His eyes raise to the sky when there's an answer.

Sensei shouts, "Kazuo! The boy needs magical healing. He fought the witch's control with all he had. A hospital will be no help in this case. We need Ohno-chan's magic. Where is she?"

"Back there," I mumble, heading down the hill toward her.

Satou calls for a cleanup team. Takahashi shoos the remaining onlookers, instructing them to erase any data on the situation and not to speak of it—a matter of national security.

Then Satou asks, "Where's Hiro?"

I shake my head. Satou slumps. Clenching his fists, he shakes.

Glancing at me, Sensei's words come slowly, as if reasoning with a wild animal. "Tatsuya, take a deep breath. *Right now.* You used a shortcut to obtain ki. It's going to kill you if you don't stop the flow."

"That kitsune witch messed with Su-chan's mind, so Su-chan poured her energy into me before passing out." Through gritted teeth, I mutter while I drop the shield and move to join my girlfriend.

Bounding in front of me, Sensei snarls. "Don't you dare go near her in that condition! Look around you! It wasn't Su-chan's ki that you used. You killed every living thing in the perimeter back there! Stop the flow this instant, Umeji Tatsuya!" She sprints toward me. "Suzuki-kun needs you and Ohno. He has only moments left. My magic is gone."

For a ten-meter radius, the energy pull charred everything. Grass and trees lay smoldering, and the snow is melted beyond that. Pungent smoke makes my eyes water. *That's where the power came from?*

I let go of the ki inflow and the fire inside extinguishes, causing blood to drain from my face. My knees threaten to buckle, and I have to lean over to keep from falling. Then an arctic blast of cold sucks my warmth like a vacuum in space.

Sensei whispers so the onlookers don't hear. "That was forbidden. It's fueled by powerful negative emotions. Stealing ki pulls it from all living things nearby, killing everything it touches including the user if it goes on too long."

Breathing deep to steady myself, I verify, "Date said you stole ki from your apprentices. The same as I did, but worse—that's what you couldn't tell me."

She droops, dropping to a submissive posture. "Yes. Doesn't matter so much that you know anymore. But right now, we need help."

Su-chan lies outside of the dead zone. Scooping her up, I press my lips to her forehead giving her my spare ki. *That used twice as much as it should.*

Date did this to her, to Sensei, to Sojirou, to Hiro, to us all. *You will pay, vixen.*

Su-chan cringes as she startles awake. "You're so cold!"

I should be warm after all that.

"Tatsuya." Sensei nudges me. "Your anger flared again. I see it. It hungers to consume more—to live, so you'll turn into an oni and it will always control you. Don't you feel its presence?"

I hold Su-chan tight for a moment, needing that connection. *Damn, it's hard to think.* But the light scent of cherry blossoms and her hand caressing my face burn away the fog. *Su-chan's alive and well. It's gonna be ok if we're together, just like she said.*

"Can you walk?" I choke the words out, forcing down the events of the day. "Suzuki-kun needs your help."

"I can. You need help, too."

"I'll be fine." Offering a hand, my attempt to help her up causes me to stumble and my head swims.

"Not believing that for one second, buckwheat. But I'll get Suzuki-kun first." She pulls a metal flask out of her bag, then plops down by him. The poor kid sputters as he drinks. So, Su-chan soothes, "I know it tastes bad. But it will help you recover from the effects of powerful magic. Drink up."

When Sojirou finishes and sits up, Su-chan kneels to offer a piggyback ride.

Satou says, "Let's get you away from here, young man. Takahashi-san can help the incoming team scour the area for any clues."

Sensei creates a portal to her house, but she wobbles precariously. "Kazuo, carry me, please. I don't have the energy left because ki is draining from my broken tama faster than it can refresh. When we get out of sight, I'll contact a cleanup crew. I just hope it will be fast enough to counter the media."

With furrowed brows, he obeys.

Once we're safe at Sensei's, Su-chan treats Sojirou once more. The boy's energy bounds back as if nothing had been wrong with him. But the events from earlier assault me.

What happened back there? Did I kill Hiro? Why didn't Sensei tell me? I thought I could trust her. And the PSIA used Hiro as bait. Gotta get out of this damned town before they arrest me.

Su-chan pulls me aside. "You're not well."

"I need to rest. Everything is so fucked up. After I grab a couple of things, I'm getting the hell out of this town. Come with me."

"I'm calling to get you help." She dials as I make my way up the stairs.

24

CHAPTER 24: AFTERMATH

Suzuki trails me to my dim room with its closed curtains. Why'd the kid tag along? Is he scared of Sensei after witnessing what a kitsune is capable of, or because he broke her tama?

As I rummage through my few belongings, I grab Su-chan's iPod. Good memories with that. But she'll want the device if she doesn't accompany me. And why should she? We've only dated a few days.

"Umeji-san, where ya' gonna go?" Suzuki's hushed question contrasts with my internal voices.

"Not sure." My words come out shaky, despite the numbness inside.

"Will you come back?"

"Dunno." After putting the necessities in my bag, I count my cash. *Gonna need a new coat. That'll take a chunk of my savings.*

"That's what my dad said."

Ouch. Shivering, I pat the futon. "He hasn't returned?"

"Nuh-uh." He plops down, looking at me expectantly.

What sort of role model runs away? Heaving a sigh, I set the wallet aside. "So you think I should stay, even after all you saw?"

He stiffens, but his stare bores into me, clearing the clouds in my brain for a fleeting moment.

"Tell you what. I'll look at things tomorrow or the next day. I'm so damned drained that I'm probably not rational." When I offer a fist bump, his face brightens as he returns it. "How are you holding up?"

His knees tuck to his chest, and he shakes his head. *Poor kid.*

A door creaking has both our heads jerking toward the sound downstairs. "Sojirou!" his mom's panicked voice rings through the house.

He books it down the narrow stairs so fast I can't keep up. Then Suzuki Chiyo scoops him into her arms, smothering him in motherly concern.

Before they leave, I wave for her attention. "Suzuki-san, have him see a counselor. I don't care about the stigma associated with it. He's been through some insane stuff and will need help to process it."

The kid wriggles from her grip. "Mom, let go!" Then at her raised eyebrow, his tone softens. "I gotta call Umeji-san later. Can we get his number? Please!"

Is he afraid I'll leave without saying goodbye? Flipping through my phone, I lean on the wall. Why can't I think straight enough to remember my contact info? "What's your number? I'll text you."

After the Suzukis leave, Su-chan gives me a burst of ki and I take her aside. "Date had a puppet string on you. Are you ok?" At her nod, I offer again. "I'm gonna get a hotel room and crash there. Come with me, unless you're embarrassed to be with me now."

"You will not go anywhere in this condition, buster."

"I'll be fine." *Hopefully.*

"Umeji Tatsuya, you aren't well." Her wrist probes my cheek. "Holy crap, your skin is even colder now!"

Sensei sniffs my leg and shakes her head. "Ripping ki from our surroundings gave him magical shock. Take him with you. If you're unsure what to do, your mother will know."

"Not a problem. We've seen this sort of thing before."

My teeth chatter so hard they might break. The world spins and I wobble trying to regain my balance. "I c-can't stay at your house!"

"You're not able to stand on your own. Besides, we're suckers for taking in strays, so bringing you home won't faze my family one bit." Her arm wraps around me, so I use her support. When I try to rest my chin on her shoulder, she props me up. "No crashing yet, bud."

Su-chan texts her dad while my aunt says, "You need help to handle this, Tatsuya. I'm serious. If I had the strength, I'd insist you stay here. But the Ohno clan will be a better help to you."

"You st-still haven't changed t-to human form."

Her tone and ears flatten. "I have no ki to spare."

Click. "Sensei, y-you gonna be all right?"

That catches Satou's attention as he helps to prop me up.

"Ever the tender heart, Tatsuya." Enforcing her words, she nudges me with her muzzle. "I have a while. Rest and recover. We can talk later."

"That w-wasn't an answer. Wh-what will happen to you with a broken tama? It wasn't in th-the legends I read as a kid."

"Go with Ohno-chan. You and I are both worse for wear, unable to deal with anything more. You must—"

"Aunt, how long do you have?" my boss urges. "And Umeji, you will get help for this. That's an order. There'll be a crowd of reporters and concerned citizens soon, so lie low for a while. We'll speak when you return."

"Nephews, stop pestering." Sensei shakes her head as she pushes my connection with Satou to the forefront.

Waiting for an explanation, my boss raises an eyebrow and purses his lips. Another secret he has to find out the hard way. "We're never going to be able to lay everything bare, are we?"

She waves it off. "You're distant cousins. Regarding my tama. I'm unsure. Tomorrow, I'll seek advice from my family."

"You c-can't manage a portal. Is the d-den still near Kyoto?"

"Yes, the same mountain on the outskirts of the city. With modern transportation, I can make do."

"I'll buy tickets." Satou pulls out his phone.

But there's a cheaper, faster way. Growling and wiping a palm over my face, I force my fuzzy mind to work a tad more. "Wh-what if I made a portal for you?"

"Please, let's discuss this tomorrow. I'm exhausted. *After* you feel better, if you and Kazuo would help me reach my family's den, I'd be grateful."

Trudging to the entryway requires assistance. Satou says he'll stay with our aunt. Collapsing on the step, I only put one shoe on before the barrage hits.

My face falls to trembling hands. As my fried brain replays the day's events, it mashes them with past sins. Scrunching my eyes closed, I force deep breaths.

What am I doing? I'll have to meet Su-chan's family, but I'm not capable of being social. The connection to a kitsune witch who has no conscience paired with my yakuza past is enough to doom any chance of her parents ever accepting me. Rejections for simpler issues happen all the time. *Su-chan deserves better.*

"Tatsu-kun?" Su-chan pulls my palms away to look into my eyes.

"I c-can't go with."

Kneeling, she sets my shoe down. "Nonsense. Lift your foot. You're shaking violently. There's no way I'm leaving you like this."

"I c-can't handle p-people."

After answering a knock, Satou hauls me up to standing. Then Su-chan and some other guy hustle me to a car. While my head rests in her lap, her fingers run through my hair. Then the pair lug me inside an unfamiliar house. The warmth and scent of strong herbs produce visions of that terrific balm.

A woman's voice asks, "Suzu, is he—"

"No questions. My boyfriend is broken."

My teeth clatter so hard they should shatter as the woman puts her wrist to my forehead and sucks in a breath. I'm dragged somewhere. Water runs. My eyes droop closed. Glug, glug, glugging. *So cold. Need sleep.* Someone peels off my winter gear and shoes.

"Naked? Mom!"

"Suzu, clothes and all is fine. It's vital he warms up. Get in. Yasu, help us!"

Gasping at the scalding liquid heat, I fight something dragging me down. But there's no strength. *Why would Su-chan let them drown me? Or did she drop me off in hell?* My head tucks into a shoulder as arms slide under mine and around my ribs.

Chop, chop, chop. A sharp pungent smell makes me think of sushi.

Something plops into the water. There's a shhhhhh of sand pouring.

"We got you, Tatsu-kun. You're gonna be ok," Su-chan's voice soothes. Her lips press into my hair. "Mom just put salt in for its purifying properties." A hint of sakura burns through the fog in my brain.

Safe? No longer do I need to fight the water. My outside is still too hot. At least, I'm not on fire anymore. Though, my insides remain ice.

"W-where am I?"

She giggles. "The tub at my house. Not bad for a first week's date, huh?"

How did I get so lucky already? Then the view converges fuzzily on a middle-aged couple. My heart stops as I flail in the water. A wet shirt sleeve I recognize—but has an odd blue sheen to it—resolves crisply in my vision. As I stand on unsure legs, Su-chan's steadying grip supports my arms. Breaths come ragged.

The man looks away, though the woman is bolder, scolding, "Suzu."

"But you told me to crawl in with him, Mother. And you're the one who put that emotion-altering potion in here!"

"Daughter." The mother's tone pleads and warns at the same time. Then she points a hefty vegetable cleaver in my direction and barks. "Young man, you sit back down in that tub and stay there until I say to get out. Do you hear me?"

Woman with a weapon! Splash! My re-submersion sloshes water to the floor, making Su-chan laugh.

"Mom has a commanding presence, doesn't she?"

Staring down at our interlaced fingers, I fidget. "This has to be the most awkward meeting of the family ever." Inside, the ice begins to melt.

Su-chan snorts, drawing my attention again to the others. Her parents look at each other shyly as her dad shakes his head and stands from kneeling by the washing stool he used as an improvised table. Tucking a cutting board under his arm, he tosses the last batch of herbs in with us.

Su-chan stage-whispers, "Oh boy, do I have a story for you."

To avoid the others' discomfort, I study the room. White tile, halfway up on the plain wall, surrounds the dark wood tub. Matching trim leads to a shoji window on one side and a door at the far end.

Her father hisses through his teeth as her mom cuts off the story. "This is hardly the time, daughter." Focusing on me again, she cleans up as she chides. "I'm Yukiko, and this is Yasu. You did a dangerous thing, young man. Stealing ki means that amount will be extracted from you with interest. Nakamura-san must have taught you that. And I assume it was you on the special broadcast news today."

Shit. Publicity. Why don't I remember what happened?

"Suzu told us not to ask questions. So, we'll wait for when you both are ready. Be back in a bit with dry clothes."

When they leave, I look to the hall then to my girlfriend. "Are your parents real?"

Su-chan rests her head on my shoulder. "Yeah. We grew close as a family when we left Hokkaido. How are you doing?"

"In the physical sense? Better. Beyond that, I dunno. You?"

"Relieved now that you're not freaking out my mom. The potion my parents added will help in the meantime. Dad made it extra strong. I suspect the effects won't fully wear off for at least a day."

"Thank you." I have no other words, so I put an arm around her.

"I'm glad we could help. Satou-san would have carted you off to the hospital, but the doctors wouldn't have understood the magic nature of the shock. When the spell wears off, we'll hit a hard emotional and physical down. Be prepared for that. Well, it's coming. Nobody can really prepare. For now, I just wanna be by you because I'm nervous about remembering what we dealt with."

Her family sets up a wooden screen for us to change, so she heads to the far side.

"Hurry, the memory block and emotional boost effects won't be enough to counter the down for long," Yukiko says before closing the door.

Extracting myself from drenched clothes isn't as easy as it looks. When I shimmy out of the tee Su-chan gave me, a rip extends the existing gash. I only got to wear it a few times. "Sorry, the K-pop shirt got shredded."

"Shirts are replaceable. You aren't."

On the button-up, wet cuffs insist on remaining fastened. The slash across the front compounds the problem. The cuffs catch on my wrists as I attempt to wriggle out. *GRRR!* I should just pop the stinkin' buttons and hunt them down later for spares.

"Hey. You decent?" Su-chan calls out.

"Decent enough. These stupid cuffs are stuck."

Peeking past the panel, she holds out pajamas for me. My gaze flits to her shoulder, only covered by a blue strap and a hint of lace farther down.

Her bottom lip sucks in as she stares. "Mmm. Boy, I wish you'd go shirtless on a summer day. But you won't with those tattoos, will you?"

Trying to cover for where my mind went, I focus on wrestling the blasted button. Her family had just saved me from something beyond my understanding and memory. The funky potion in the bath must be affecting Su-chan, too, because she wouldn't speak that way under normal circumstances, would she?

Noticing my dilemma, she sets the stack on my side of the screen. "Hold out your hand. Let me do it."

Be worthy, idiot. Staring at the ceiling, I thrust out a wrist. My skin tingles where her fingers make contact. To slow my pulse, I concentrate on breathing.

"Next."

Instead of taking the easy direction, I turn to face away from her, force my eyes shut, and give her my other arm. *I never had to show restraint before her. This sucks.*

When she releases me, I cast off the offending button-up as if it's the reason for my predicament. Shedding the rest is quicker. Drying off, I pull on the loaned pajamas. *Wait.* "Where's the katana?"

"I just put it in my duffle."

"Thanks." Tying the kimono-style sleepwear proves easier than dealing with the sopping clothing. "I'm done."

"Me, too. Come on. Leave your clothes. They need washing anyway." Holding my hand, she tugs me along, guiding me to the kitchen. At least, her fuzzy winter pajamas aren't as alluring. She whispers, "I'll never think of Dad's PJs the same way again."

Yukiko stirs a large pot of green, cedar scented gel bubbling on the stove. "Are you two hungry?" She gestures to the table, commanding with kindness, "Poke a little food down before the spell runs out."

The bright living room is just off the kitchen. Her family made a nest at the kotatsu with a plate of snacks, along with extra blankets, pillows, drinks, and boxes of tissues. Gobsmacked, I stare. *It's not even four in the afternoon. There's no way they expect us to sleep.*

Ohno Yukiko laughs. "Suzu, you weren't kidding about how new your boyfriend is to this life. His eyes are about to pop out of his head. Shall I explain what the magic and this setup are for, so the poor guy's brain doesn't overload?"

Su-chan's grip tightens as she kicks the wooden floor with her slippered foot. "This is insane for you, isn't it?"

I nod as my insides tighten. Who knows what happened in the last few hours? *Should I worry about brainwashing?* But I'm with Su-chan. She wouldn't be a part of anything devious like that.

"It's gonna continue that way for a bit. Sorry. I only hope it won't scare you off."

Resting my forehead on hers, I squeeze her hands. "Not gonna happen." Any day with her is infinitely better than my past.

Yukiko coughs to remind us of her presence. "Nakamura-san is a mystical being—who has her own ways. Magic-using humans have to see and do things that ordinary people were never meant to process. The deferment elixir and memory suppression potion are some of the ways we deal with such things. They allow us to put off the overwhelm until later. Such as helping you through the magical shock before you have to deal with a traumatic situation. But the price is that the emotion and memories come all at once as they overflow the ability of the potions. An equal and opposite effect. Once the initial dampening is done, it will slow it again until the effect fades.

"Anyway, you were through the earlier events together. So, you'll help each other through the impending emotional storm in a safe, comfortable place. Later, we'll figure out how to handle the fallout of your adventures."

Her last statement should cause some reaction. But when pushing for a memory, it flits away.

"This can cool while you two wade through the after-effects. Holler if you need us." Yukiko turns off the stove, moves the pot, and departs.

When we finish snacking and tuck in side-by-side, I spy Su-chan's ring. It shimmers a shade between purple and blue, and a silver bead rolls in a figure-eight, swirling the liquid inside the rounded jewel. *Her arm is still. How is it moving?*

"Is that new?"

Blanching, she shrinks in on herself. "When I changed. It's Mom's mood ring. Have you ever seen the toy versions? This one's real. They come in a pair, and Dad's reads hers. My parents won't admit it, but my guess is he bought it after a fight."

Why does it matter that her family can read her moods? Unless... "They're spying on us?"

"Something like that." She lets out a heavy breath. "See, each person deals with strong emotions differently. And uhm, they don't know you well enough to predict your response."

Why is she hesitant? The jewel turns yellow. "What does that color mean?"

With clipped words, she says, "That I'm upset. It's not at you."

Uh-oh. Drawing her close, my arms wrap around her. "Did you tell them about our initial encounters?"

Her nod confirms it. "But the jewel will also inform them when the fallout starts."

They act nice, but deep down they're afraid I'll hurt her. When she slides the band on my finger, it changes to gray before she puts it back on to show yellow again.

Returning my embrace, she says, "You're upset, aren't you? Both our moods are plummeting, so it's starting. My family will intervene if it turns black because that could mean something more dangerous than anger or panic, like a breakdown or worse. Understand?"

"I think so."

The onslaught hits her first—shaking over the fear she felt, crying over the loss of Chou, mourning so many people today. My gaze fixes to the darkening gray indicator as I rub her spine. *Isn't there anything else I can do for her?*

If the emotional storm does this to my strong, sweet Su-chan, what the hell will it be like for me? Because I took my big brother's life, then stole ki—which feeds on negative emotions.

Bam! A tsunami unleashes.

The confrontation replays on fast forward. My anger at seeing Date in control of Hiro. Worry for Su-chan and Suzuki-kun. Shock from the vixen using the boy to steal Sensei's tama. Dread at watching men turn to oni I have to banish. Chou's death and Su-chan's grief.

The wave sweeps in, engulfing my legs and pulling the sand from under my feet. *I wasn't able to stop Hiro's conversion.* Submersed.

Hiro asked me to do one last thing for him. And there was no giving my life to do it, as I had promised. I had to take his. *Su-chan shouldn't have to cope with my baggage.* Can't breathe.

Cold, spicy scented water splashes my face. I gasp for breath. *Did I reach the surface again?*

"Tatsu!" Su-chan shrieks while I struggle against being held down. When she comes into focus, her expression is wild as she shouts, "Look at me!"

Sobs wrack me from the inside. Words spill out. "I killed him. Su-chan, I killed him."

"Who? Tatsu, tell me who." Her forehead meets mine.

As my throat constricts, something grasps me and ki flows in. Using the energy, I'm able to force the name out. "Hiro."

"Who's that, Suzu?" Not a familiar voice. "Nakamura-san and Satou-san just arrived."

Getting into my face, Su-chan barks, "Date murdered your big brother! Not you!"

Breaths come in rasps. "My katana went right through him!"

"Date made him leave the hospital! She forced him to wear the demon ring, causing him to turn! You did the only thing you could! Listen to me, Umeji Tatsuya! It wasn't you!"

Hands press down and warmth fills me. Then a familiar nuzzle and soft fur reach my arm.

Sensei's quiet determination halts Su-chan's shouting. "Nephew, breathe deep and slow." She waits for my compliance. "Ohno-chan's correct. The witch was out to destroy me by hurting you and taking my hoshi no tama. She knows those I care for are my strength and my weakness. Don't you ever doubt that it was Date who killed Otsuka Hiro."

I shudder. "She broke your tama." *If only I could change that.*

"Ki donations are enough until I can reach my family."

"But—"

Her intensity arrests the room. "No buts. Look at everyone who cares for you. Ohno-chan, her parents and brothers, Kazuo, and myself. I'm sure little Suzuki-kun and his mother plan to message or call in the morning. And Matsuo-kun will check on you since you made the news. Even Mie-chan will worry."

Blanking my brain, Su-chan's mouth reaches mine. My arms encircle her on instinct.

Su-chan sniffles as she says, "You had us terrified."

To calm her, my lips caress the top of her head. Then her mother mumbles to her father, "Was the second potion that strong, Yasu? Suzu and the young man have no inhibitions."

"It needed to be. The young man almost didn't make it out of that negative spiral."

Aw, shit. She kissed me in front of a crowd! Even the most brazen people don't do that. Too private.

Ducking my gaze as I cling to their daughter, I say, "Sorry."

Her dad shrugs. "I've never seen a person's mood turn that black—as if there was no light in it whatsoever. We raced in, thinking our Suzu was in danger. But she'd placed the ring on your hand when you wouldn't respond. You must've internalized everything. And what we know of the events today—that's too much for one person to carry. Lean on our family, Umeji-kun."

Words gum up, so I manage a grateful nod.

"These two should wash their faces and rest. Thank you for coming quickly. Umeji-kun needed your presence to emerge from that darkness." Ohno

Yukiko shoos the group out and sends us to refresh.

When we return, she brings a stack of mochi. *Comfort food!* Su-chan's mom rocks.

"Eat up." After we each take a few of the sweet-bean rice cakes, Yukiko's face grows serious. "Remember the mind processes trauma slowly. Grief has no time limit. Got that?"

Through a bite of the treat, I say, "I think so."

When Su-chan and I are alone again, she pulls the kotatsu cover over us, then drapes an arm over my chest.

"What do the colors mean?"

"Well, it's green for you - so you've calmed down. It ranges from black—which is extreme distress or anger to yellow—which means agitated, all the way to blue—relaxed and happy, and violet—thrilled and passionate." She clears her throat. "Speaking of, take the ring off. My big brothers said guys often wake up turned on."

So she's the baby sister. And she understands that aspect. *Wait a minute.* "Why in the world would your parents let us sleep together in their living room?"

Placing a finger on my lips, she gives the faintest smile. "One, if you say you have the energy, I won't believe it. Because I'm spent. Two, I'd fight to keep you here, after what we were through today."

"Thank you." I won't argue, but the mention of intimacy...

Well, I can at least remedy the fact that our first kiss was public. To give her a chance to refuse, I run my thumb over her lip and lean in. Her lazy, slow smile welcomes as she pulls me closer. Though, her closed mouth kiss catches me off guard.

I pull back thinking she's saying no more, but the light in her eyes says otherwise. *Everything will be new for her.*

"Tatsu-kun?"

Did she see the emotions flash across my face? Gently, I kiss her again. This time I open my mouth, drawing her along. Repetition rewards with her response.

When she rests her hand on my chest, I let up, kissing her forehead to say 'message received'. Instead of pushing me away, Su-chan rubs small soothing circles over my heart, causing warmth inside to spread.

How could I have been so dumb, thinking there were no new experiences left for me to give her? She stills.

Breathing in the trace of sakura and lingering spice on her skin lets me soak up the privilege of being here with her. *Oh yeah, I'd sell my soul for this kind of peace.*

25

CHAPTER 25: FALLOUT

According to the clock on the wall, we slept over twelve hours. *Why did Hiro have to die that way?* Then the tightness in me fizzles and that thought turns hazy. Is the potion still at work?

Su-chan has her back to me, so I scoot in closer. Tucking the covers up over our shoulders, I match the slow, steady rise and fall of her chest as we lay spooned together. My arm tightens around her and she intertwines our fingers.

Nuzzling into her shoulder, my mouth grazes her pajama collar, and she pulls my knuckles to her lips. "Good morning, Tatsu-kun." Her words muffle as she yawns.

"Morning." Pressing my cheek into hers, I whisper, "Waking up like this every day would be great. I'm gonna hate sleeping without you tomorrow."

"Same." She turns over, with a sleepy, contented expression. "What time is it? Is it raining?"

"About 5 AM. Yeah, it is."

"Drat. Dad will be up soon for work."

Chuckling, I kiss her forehead. "I won't take advantage, no matter how tempting. I owe you all my life."

"You want me, even after the insanity of yesterday?" Her voice goes quiet as she leans in, scrutinizing my expression.

She can't be serious. "I do. You're the calm in this whole mess."

Suddenly, her lips mash against mine and her fingers lock into my hair—such a fast learner. *Do we have a few moments?*

Idiot. Don't shred the remainder of rapport with her parents. To catch my breath, I disengage.

The hurt in her expression has me backpedaling. "That was so good. But we gotta stop before I'm unable to think straight."

Doe-eyed, she bites her bottom lip. I have to look away to avoid further entrancement. "Oh girl, don't do that to me. That look'll get you anything you ask for."

The compliment earns a giggle. "I'll remember that. Oh, and the potion may take a bit to wear off, FYI. How about some breakfast?"

"Should we cook for your dad?"

Their kitchen is bigger than Sensei's. With plenty of room to work, it doesn't take us long to whip up a meal. I've not cooked for this many people in years, but Su-chan's a pro.

She's started the rice and coffee before I find the ingredients for miso soup. To show off my culinary skills, I volunteer to finish the broth while she gathers the pickled veggies and eggs.

"Taste this." I hold out a spoon, cupping my palm under it.

Her eyes close. "Delicious." The reward for my work? A smooch on the cheek. "You can cook for me anytime."

Walking in on us, Ohno Yasu clears his throat causing me to jump. "In older times that would be a marriage proposal."

Shit. He saw us. Again.

"Morning, Dad." She has the grace to blush this time.

"Daughter. Umeji-kun. How are you both feeling?"

Such casualness raises my hackles. In my mob days, that kind of attitude could precede nasty surprises.

"Good morning, Sir." The formal bow matches my greeting. "Much better. Thank you for everything you've done for me."

He waves it off. "Magic users watch out for each other. Is breakfast almost ready?"

"Yep! Tatsu-kun, would you dish some soup? Bowls are in that cupboard, spoons in the top drawer."

Her father invites me to join him while he eats and reads the newspaper at the low table. So, I grab a bowl, sitting on the opposite side. Su-chan zips off to change.

"Suzu's been talking about you since you moved to Nonogawa." Her dad peers over his paper.

He's watching for my reaction. I stop mid-bite.

"She was so excited when she found out you're a magic user. It's rare these days. How did you convince Nakamura-san to teach you?"

Why is he speaking so frankly? Rubbing the nape of my neck, I try simplicity. "She offered, Sir. I was glad to have a friend in town."

"And she's a kitsune, no less. It was on the news."

Oh yeah, there's that to deal with on top of everything else. My palm covers my eyes to ward off the oncoming headache. "Now the world knows that I'm a spell caster." The pain smooths away. *Can I get some more of this potion?*

"They also witnessed you defending the Suzuki boy. People will gossip about your powers. Beyond our family and your teacher, I doubt any understand that you took ki from your surroundings. Date never was popular in town. And the report said she's on the area's most-wanted list. Humility will help to handle the repercussions."

"Your daughter has been secretive about her abilities. How would you recommend I shield her from that fallout?"

"Protect her?" He folds his newspaper. "Your intention is noble. But Suzu is a force of nature, like her mother. They each have an inner strength and power exceeding both of us combined. I'm surprised you haven't seen that."

When my stomach growls at the smell of the food left untouched, I poke at it a bit. "She knows her mind and has put me in my place a few times already."

The quirk of his lips reveals my misinterpretation. "You don't care that she'll always exceed your magic skill? Or that she keeps dangerous pets because she often feels different, like them?"

I shrug and gather my courage. "She's not the only one more powerful than me. Being new to kotodama, I have much to learn. But your daughter believed in me before anyone besides Sensei did. Su-chan's given me some of the best advice I've ever had. She's also smart as a whip. I guess it's just another thing to admire. Regarding the pets. Hopefully, she doesn't see me as one." His eyebrow raises, but he lets me continue. "She cares what people think, allowing herself to be vulnerable. Sir, I'd like her to always have that open innocence. Once gone, I'm not sure it's possible to regain it."

"You're speaking about yourself?"

I'd thought he was the quieter of her parents. "Not only me."

"She's hinted you have a past. One of those nights she came home crying and locked herself in her room. She has good judgment, so..."

What's taking her so long? To keep from fidgeting, I force my eyes to the meal that's going cold. *How much do I tell him?* "I do, Sir. Saying that I swear not to return won't do anything to ease your mind. I'll have to prove my intentions over time."

"Care to share what that past was?" He sips on his coffee, portraying a nothing's out of the ordinary vibe.

The gut reaction says no. Keeping everything close to the vest was always the best approach to avoid ostracism.

Feet pounding on the stairs announce an arrival. "Dad! Stop interrogating my boyfriend," Su-chan whines from the kitchen. "Is this for me? I was gonna dish up, but there's a bowl on the counter."

"Yeah, I prepped some for you," I stall. *But this family saved my life yesterday. I owe them the truth. What if later he says she can't date me? It'll hurt her more if I procrastinate.* I gulp, then confess. "Sir, I was yakuza."

He sputters into his mug, taking a few seconds to recover. "We saw a hint of the tattoos, but—"

"Su-chan knows my entire story, so there won't be any more hurtful surprises. I thought you should know, 'cause I'd want to in your place."

In a bold stroke, she sits beside me. "It shouldn't have surprised me. I knew what you had been. Your actions here in Nonogawa spoke of your intentions. When you shared everything despite your fears, that's when I decided."

Directing the conversation to her father, she continues, "He was convinced

I wouldn't speak with him ever again. But he took the risk."

If I eat, he might not ask any more questions. "I'll always be grateful you didn't reject our friendship."

Forcing a calm smile, I attack my soup. Her dad nods, though he remains quiet while I finish up.

To allow them a moment, I down my coffee and wash the dishes. There's no privacy in the open space that constitutes the kitchen-dining-living room space. This is the closest alternative. But silence reigns at the table.

When I return the drying towel, I ask, "Are my clothes somewhere?"

"Do you need another shirt? I think one of Ichiro's would fit you," Su-chan offers.

"Yes, please."

To watch my reaction, she walks backward as she leads me to the bath. "I'm gonna replace the band one. But that style sold out." She pouts.

So I strum her lip, causing her to laugh and swat my hand. "I'll do it. Don't worry about it."

"You'd buy one yourself?"

"Doesn't seem right to make you get another, so we match. We didn't even get to show off the shirts together. Wasn't that the point?" I reach for my clothes, but she pulls the whole drying hanger down to check my pants pockets.

"Uh-huh. These aren't quite dry."

The last thing I want is her investigating every article. In the nick of time, I snatch the clothing rack.

"I'll cope. Before the funeral..." My voice falters, and her eyes have nothing but sympathy as I try to rally, pushing the pain away. Something evens the spike out again. "Let's go shopping so I can pick up a new coat. Then I want to check on Sensei."

"Should we look for something in another color? I just wanted to see what I could get away with when you said no pink."

Snatching her fingers out of the air, I bring them to my lips. "You pick the color. Only because you called me Tatsu. No others have." *Another first for her.*

"No one else?"

While running the back of my hand down her cheek, I shake my head. "It was the piece of me they couldn't have." The kiss she gives me makes me forget where we are.

A knock on the open door startles us as Su-chan's oldest brother shoos. "Out. I need the bath."

"Ni-chan, you're jealous that, Tatsu-kun, Ken, and I don't have to work today." Su-chan puts one hand on her hip, then tugs my wrist with the other.

Yanking my clothing off the hanger, I replace the contraption before stepping aside for Ichiro. "Where should I change?"

Through the door, her brother answers, "Let him use your room. Ken's still asleep."

She rolls her eyes. "See why I don't want you to speak for me? Everyone else does."

"Gotcha."

* * *

As we head out, I message Satou, asking if they need us to pick up anything.

The response? 'Reporters surrounded Aunt's house. Shop for anything you might need before arriving.'

Su-chan grabs an umbrella. I growl and I hold my phone up for her to see. But my insides unwind again. "May I buy your gas for the drive to Shimosaki?"

"Deal. Let me zip back and tell mom to expect the media." Kissing my cheek, she adds, "Wish we could stay there."

"Me, too. By the way, the potion that's evening out my emotions. It seems kind of dangerous."

"I suppose a person could get too used to having it in their system."

"What about being numbed to the point where they don't feel anything but for a fleeting second."

"Perhaps. Though, we only use it in desperate cases." She pales.

My hands fly up. "I wasn't insinuating... What I mean is that this stays a secret, right?"

"Yes, please."

* * *

Returning from our trip to the covered shopping arcade, I'm wearing all I bought—my simple leather coat, two Ts, and a pair of cargo pants that have a pocket big enough for the sword hilt. The outside shirt matches my girlfriend's—black with a cute cat and white lettering that says 'Eat, Sleep, K-Pop, Repeat.'

"You know Tatsu-kun, that old sukajan jacket you had was cool, but this new one suits who you are now."

"I won't stick out like a sore thumb anymore."

"You said to toss it. But would you mind if I make a pillow out of it?"

"Sure." I don't want the memories associated with it, but she has better recollections. At least the rebel symbol served some good.

As we park in Satou's driveway, a chirp emanates from Su-chan's phone. "Oh, that's Mom." Squeaking, she wriggles in her seat. "Yes! She kept a few milliliters of the original batch of Chou before giving me the ooze!"

Then her seriousness returns, knowing my loss won't be regained. A little lightness replaces the heaviness inside at the news. Su-chan will have a protector again. Hopping out, I zip around the car with the umbrella to share it in the downpour.

Satou's dour face sports dark circles under his eyes. *I should have been here for the Boss and Sensei.* Though, I had little choice yesterday.

"Aunt needs you two. Hurry. Then we complete arrangements for Hiro." His monotone voice smashes into me as he holds the door open.

Instead of a wet blanket, a heavy frozen one smothers any semblance of good mood we had. The potion must have worn off.

Sensei, in fox form, lays under the kotatsu. Su-chan and I both pour ki into her. Harsh reality sits raw and festering inside as we plan Hiro's funeral. It'll be a simple affair tomorrow.

We only invited those who knew him. He doesn't have any immediate family, since he was an only child and his parents had died a few years ago. Attendees will include Satou, Sensei, a few officers and agency folks he worked with, and me.

Su-chan clings to my hand. The contact grounds me until she gets a drink. *Aniki walked through this very house's entryway into my life again. Now he's gone. Sensei may not recover, to boot.* When Su-chan returns, the voices quell.

Satou folds his hands. "Plenty of witnesses saw your fight with Date and cronies, and that you tried to save the boy. So, you might still face societal repercussions. I'll do what I can." Shifting, he shoves an envelope my way. "Hiro said I was to give this to you if anything happened to him."

My heart is heavy as I read the name with my old mentor's precise handwriting in the exact center of the square packet. All eyes light on me. I flip it over and a spark hits my finger, much like static electricity, as I unseal the flap, slide the contents onto the table, and set aside the envelope.

"Wasn't your name on the outside?" Su-chan asks.

My eyes dart to the packet. "Yeah. It was." My head shakes, then I unfold the note. I start to read it aloud but choke up on the first word.

> Tatsuya,
>
> When you meet another carrying this symbol, they'll answer your questions about the katana.
>
> Hiro

The card tucked in with the note is embossed with a sword and flame. When I look more closely, the symbol disappears.

Satou scowls. "Before you ask. I have no idea what that means."

"Quite the spell there. I'm going to have to investigate that, too," Sensei says.

"Thanks." Excusing myself for a breather from the somberness, I give Suzuki a quick call. His mom answers but hands it off. Full of questions, he chatters a million miles an hour. "Slow down. Yes, I'm gonna stay for now. How are you holdin' up?"

He speeds right up again. "Ok. But we're stuck in our apartment. The people with cameras and microphones won't let anyone through unless they talk to them. Mom's afraid to go outside."

"Hang in there. If you need out, call the police to help you through the gauntlet. I'll contact you again soon."

When I return to the table, Sensei paces. "Tatsuya, you told Ohno-chan about your past. Yet, I hesitated. It's time I tell the secret I've kept from all but those who witnessed it. Please, fetch my journals."

26

CHAPTER 26: NAKAMURA'S SIN

Nakamura, April 1863:

Our Emperor ordered the expulsion of all foreigners in March. His stance was stronger than that of the timid Shogunate. Confrontations with foreign powers made it clear that keeping the Westerners out was impossible. They forced their way into our land, demanding treaties from the government that were only to their benefit.

My Yuki said Japan can't return to isolation. If our country doesn't become a world power, then we end up a colony like India. Modernization is imperative.

The flame of revolution has placed its hooks in my spouse's heart. He joined the Isshin-Shishi, the revolutionaries who want to restore the emperor to power. While ideals are important, a united nation is essential. Now that it's not just people we know involved but our own family, I have trouble sleeping at night.

Will we pay in blood? Despite having lived over a century more than my husband, I can't keep an overarching perspective. We're hurtling into something unstoppable.

June 1865:

Yuki offered to teach magic to Kubo and Iwasaki, fellow Isshin-Shishi members we'd helped hide years ago. Starting with ofuda, they showed promise. But I was furious when I found he was about to share the deep secrets of kotodama he'd learned from my father. He didn't even consult my family or me to verify this was acceptable! Betrayal!

In his eyes, I overstepped my authority by halting the lessons. Yuki never had the nerve to yell at me. But he was so embarrassed over my interference, he wouldn't speak to me for a week. I considered moving back to my parents' den.

Reconciling before Kinya's 10th birthday, my husband agreed not to train his friends in the full measure of the word. To maintain peace, I conceded despite it not being what I asked.

News came to us that the Shogunate is commissioning battleships. Japan has a viable naval force. But western province forces also pushed to gather more weapons and warships. I pray they use neither navy against our nation's people.

The news spurred me to hire an instructor to teach Kanoko and me how to use the naginata. Yuki disliked the idea but understood we need to defend our home. Circumstances are forcing our small daughter to grow up faster than I wish.

February 1867:

Emperor Komei died in January. Thus, Emperor Meiji ascended to the throne at fourteen years of age. He's barely older than my Kinya. It's hard to accept the next generation taking the reins.

After turning forty in January, Yuki said he felt old. I laughed since I have a good century on him.

November 1867:

At the beginning of the month, the Shogun, Tokugawa Yoshinobu, put himself at the Emperor's disposal for the sake of the nation. The news spread rapidly in the capital. Our household celebrated by going out for beef hotpot—too expensive for our normal budget.

January 23, 1868:

Weren't we supposed to be heading toward peace? Why did the western provinces send trouble to the capital by demanding Shogunate members turn over their lands? Shogun Tokugawa's officers were livid over the decision. So, his army marched news of the political intrigue to the Emperor.

We sent Kanoko to stay with my parents.

I wish we'd delayed Kinya's coming of age ceremony. Yes, he's mature for thirteen, but I feel he's too young for a coming war, though I will not tell him so. When the Shogun had stepped down from rule, we thought the coast was clear, so we allowed it.

Kinya chose the personal name Yoshikage, a combination of syllables from his lord's name and Yoshida-san's. The gesture touched us.

Yoshikage was angry with me for calling him Kinya in front of his friends. He'll have to cope. A mother needs time to adjust!

Our son was with his lord's company south of Kyoto, blocking the Shogunate military's access. Spies warned that Date is among the Shogun's troops. Yuki tried to forbid me from going. Informing him of my choice to the contrary, I accepted the silent treatment.

January 26, 1868:

"Are you refusing magical assistance when the opposition outnumbers your troops more than two to one? They have a kitsune who's an expert at turning men into puppets. If you want your soldiers used against you, that is your choice. But be aware I am capable of defending your regiment from her." I prodded General Tobu, dodging attempts from his guards to drag me off in my fox form.

Only a fool would anger a yokai. Nevertheless, he turned his back. "You're only here to protect your son."

"I have a score to settle with Date. Yoshikage earned his place here. While he knows how to resist her control, you and the rest of the men do not. Your troops won't stand a chance of resisting her without me."

"Your tall tales fail to convince, Kitsune-san."

In winter, I prefer to be in fox form with my warm coat. But General Tobu would not listen to 'an animal'. After I shifted to human form, Yuki touched my arm as he left to join his Isshin-Shishi comrades. "I do not speak for you, Wife."

Tobu's laugh showed he thought that meant I was being chided. But Yuki's words were the opposite—that I'm a force to be reckoned with. We always supported each other once we reach a decision.

Lifting my hands, I concentrated my ki, forming a powerful ball. To snake an invisible string under his gorget, I pointed at General Tobu. Upon contact with his spine, the struggle for control over his body engaged. His shoulders twitched as I chanted 'submission'. He turned, with eyes afire and a hand clenching the hilt of his katana.

The guards surrounded me. Pushing more energy through the connection, I clamped his mouth, avoiding an order to dispatch me while I focused. The icy wind going up my sleeves was distracting enough. He advanced with slow forced steps, putting up an admirable resistance. Raising his blade, he narrowed his eyes. More swords rang around me.

Another rush of ki and whisper of kotodama. The blade stopped less than a hand's width from my nose, hitting a glowing shield. Submission was harder than expected. But I had to show him what the men would deal with. Bile burned my throat at this distasteful task. Commanding him to replace his sword, remove the neck plate, and draw his tanto to his exposed neck , I allowed his predicament to sink in.

Then I growled to the warriors. "Back down if you value his life. Attack me, and he'll slit his neck. I am merely demonstrating the technique. The other kitsune is a puppeteering master. My specialties are protection and time. If I can do this to General Tobu, what chaos will the vixen wreak when she makes minions from a dozen of you at once?"

Tobu's dagger pressed into the vulnerable flesh. They advanced anyway. After a flick of ki, the knife drew a trickle of blood.

"I said, back down!" Then I addressed my captive. "Once you've been a puppet, you're easier to manipulate again. I hope you understand the threat to your soldiers. Rest assured, I have no interest in a repeat performance."

After giving him control of his face and voice, his complexion turned beet red, and he gave a strangled, "Yes."

"Then I'll release you."

Running my fingers above the minor cut, I murmured the word for healing, stopping the blood but leaving the trail as a reminder. Then I backed out of sword range to drop the puppet string.

He bellowed a war cry and his feet pounded toward me and his hand raised in an attack with the tanto I'd left him holding. Using kotodama, I launched myself straight up, to float in safety from all but spears and arrows. Spotting Yuki in the crowd, I smiled to show I had the situation in hand.

In the end, the General and I came to an understanding. If I gave my word never to puppeteer him or his troops again, I could assist in the coming battle.

We noticed quite a few men tucking quotes from Yoshida-san into their clothing as if they were protection talismans.

January 27, 1868:

To be the best defense for the warriors, my husband and I stood shivering near the front line guarding the bridge. We were both clad in metal armor that transferred the cold straight through our clothes. Snow fluttered down.

Overwhelming numbers of the Bakufu contingent advanced with their request for passage to deliver a letter for the Emperor. I despaired. But my pulse quickened at seeing Date riding beside the leaders.

With a deafening boom, a cannon fired into the ranks near the vixen and her general. The officer fell. His troops were in disarray, leaving my nemesis with her hands full. Another rank charged, armed with swords and spears.

Watching the slaughter sickened me. I craved running out to end the witch, but my duty was to the ofuda-tagged troops. A magic user getting wounded would not help our warriors. My chance to end Date would rear its head soon enough.

When the first soldiers' wards extinguished, they glowed blue for identification. Yuki was ready with a stack of replacements. I sent several speeding toward the squad. The vixen possessed a soldier before I could stop her. Slashing with skill at his fellows, he was grimly efficient.

I launched a spear spell to end him since it was the most merciful thing. If I'd gone for the silk thread, it would be too easy to miss. A man was a much larger target.

The group panicked at an attack from two sides. So I sent a message to resist the fox witch with every ounce of strength they had.

Spotting us, Date retreated farther from the chaos. I lost track of the location of my son's battalion in the fray. Through the night, my husband and I took turns writing and casting. As one would tire, the other would pick up the laborious spell duties.

January 28, 1868:

General Tobu ordered us to sleep for a few hours before dawn. Yuki and I huddled together to double our blankets. Then we were allowed a visit with our son, while the reinforcements pursued the retreating forces. From our vantage point, we saw the blazing homes in the enemy's wake.

The Prince took command of the Imperial army. Anyone firing on our troops will be branded a traitor to the Emperor. This should be a decisive advantage.

January 29, 1868:

Date snuck through the lines, causing chaos among our units. Yuki sent his students to protect me today since he was accompanying the General. With Kubo and Iwasaki at my side, we cleaved our way through the throng to engage her.

I heard my son's voice over the din. Seeing my distraction, Date, in human form, made the troops around Yoshikage the object of her spell. He resisted her but couldn't hold against ten of his men.

Despite having to kill friends, he fought bravely. He'd not wanted to learn kotodama in the times he came home to visit, feeling it would make him stick out. So, he only had his martial arts for defense. In a normal situation, this would be enough, but a puppeteered squad overpowered him.

To provide a shield wall, Kubo and Iwasaki made their way to him. Stopping Date would allow me to rescue my son. With the vixen in my sights, I poured a spell into my velocity, while tightening my grip on my naginata.

Shrieking a war cry, I leaped into the air above the warriors only to come in contact with one of her paper puppets. A single swipe was enough to dispatch it. But a contingent with a phosphorescent green haze surrounded me. Yuki's glowing shield meant he was coming to help.

Expanding my force field, I could eliminate individuals from the circle of enemies. Crouching low to the ground near one let me sweep the blade upward through his center. Nine to go.

After spell-strengthened horizontal swings, five remained. My husband launched himself airborne, using the warriors' helmets as steppingstones for additional height and speed. Upon reaching me, he slapped another talisman on each of us. Then he created an opening for me to pursue my nemesis.

Prickling at the back of my neck alerted me to a lightning attack. So I lobbed an ofuda toward my son and his guards, praying the wards would arrive in time. Our soldiers' armor was lacquer dipped steel. They'd roast alive without a protection spell.

Date summoned an oni. It moved slower than my polearm, highlighting the beauty of my training. Lunges and slashes kept it on the defensive. As it raised its weapon, I flicked the tip of the blade through its ribs to its heart. The club tumbled as its owner disintegrated to ash.

The vixen held twenty puppet strings. By the gods! How did she do it? Then she tossed a shikigami creature at me, but the expanding paper bounced off my magic enhanced armor. Leaping straight at her, I shrieked kotodama to smash my polearm through the shield I knew she'd raise. Her defense failed, allowing my blade to connect with her shoulder.

With another whoosh my naginata whirled, cutting all the threads she maintained. She scrambled backward toward the rapidly growing paper figure. Not this time witch! To disperse the spirit in the shikigami, I whispered the word 'free'.

Catching up to Date, I shoved my blade with vicious efficiency under her throat. Her lip trembled, but her eyes flicked to something behind me. No way would I fall for such a simple trick.

My insides warmed at the grim pleasure within my grasp. Even a nearby thunderclap didn't deter me. Warm fluid ran down my cheek. After jabbing into her ribs with merciless repetition, I left her corpse and hunted down my loved ones.

Yuki held Yoshikage's limp body. His expression contorted as he voiced a howl I couldn't hear, and a nauseating burnt smell permeated the air. Most surrounding were dead or unconscious. My breath came in ragged rasps.

Could we do anything to save him?

To check our son's vitals, I collapsed beside my spouse. No breath. But the spirit seemed to remain. Pouring my ki into him, his pulse jumped for a few beats then faded. Yuki tried, too.

The fighting was over. Not wanting my husband here as I attempted the forbidden, I asked him to fetch help. My son's life was expiring and there wasn't time to move him to where there weren't other people.

When Yuki was a sufficient distance, I reached inside for my drained energy to find an additional source flickering on the edge of my awareness. I threw myself into the temptation and greedily grabbed at everything offered— knowing full well it was not my own. I paid no heed to where the ki came from.

A rush of power filled me that I poured into my Kinya. Tears fell unbidden as the red fire ran up my arms and legs. I didn't care what he called himself. He'd always be the baby I nursed at my breast. My little boy who stumbled taking his first steps. The child who fought like mad with his sister but brought her flowers and made toys to reconcile.

Absorbed in the energy transfer, it took Kinya's gasping breath and a set of hands shaking my shoulders to break my concentration. Only then did I see the scattered, charred corpses. No grass, no plants, or living things except for those that had significant ki sources remained. Almost drained, the remaining humans hunched over with their haunted looks directed at me.

Yuki helped Yoshikage up but would not meet my gaze nor assist me. I'd deceived him. Trembling from more than the cold, I let them herd us from camp. Tripping, I reverted to fox form to conserve energy.

Those we fought beside would offer no help to my family. My act was unnatural and too high a cost in the army's eyes for a single life. A life that meant the world to me.

My husband tended me enough to fend off the magical shock, then dumped me at my father's den. When I confessed my sin, Father was so stunned that he refused to speak.

July 1868:

After our son recovered in February, General Tobu forbade him from re-joining the army. While Yoshikage thanked me for saving him, he questioned the cost.

How many people did I sacrifice for him to live? I didn't know. Yuki believed his two students were among the living until I performed the dark magic.

I only knew I couldn't lose another child so young.

Our son headed west to find training in a new profession. He said he needed space from the stalemate between his parents. Word spread. So, I stayed in our old cabin outside the city to spare my family. I didn't want them driven out.

The toll for my sin included my relationships. It was possible to live with that if my husband would forgive me, someday.

The effects even reached Kanoko. She had hoped to continue charming the young doctor in the neighborhood, but he spurned her. To hide our daughter from my reputation, Mother fled with her to Iga. Kanoko wanted to marry even after her first love's cruelty.

Several months passed before my husband and I made peace, and we moved back in together. He informed me he'd never blindly trust me again. Wounded, I accepted this part of my penance.

We moved to Osaka so people would hire Yuki. While I was still opinionated, the circumstances had knocked the stuffing out of me.

March 1877:

The Battle of Toba-Fushimi, where Yuki, Yoshikage, and I helped the Imperial Army defeat the Shogunate forces, was only the start of the war. It lasted until June 1869, establishing the Meiji Era under our Emperor.

As a nation, we scrambled to modernize. It served Japan well since the foreign powers recognized our country last year.

Now my husband and I are only quiet citizens, unwilling to even talk politics. Yuki's twin brother, Kinya—for whom we named our son—fought in the war. Afterward, he joined a monastery stating a wish to retreat from the world.

Disturbing rumors say Date might still be alive. But how? I was sure I'd ended her.

27

CHAPTER 27: CONSEQUENCES

After the reading from Sensei's journal, no one moves nor speaks. Her canine chin drops to her chest and her fur lacks the vibrant, natural sheen it usually has.

She breaks the oppressive silence. "You three are the only ones I've shared this with since Yuki passed. The crack in my tama might be karma's backlash."

How can I trust someone who chose to take lives, to work dark magic, draining the life force of those nearby? *She acted as if I was the only danger. Sure, I took lives, too, but her hypocrisy...*

My insides churn. Clenching and unclenching my fists doesn't stop the twitchy need to move. "Be back later."

Su-chan joins me at the door, slipping her hand into mine to offer companionship. Without an intended destination, my feet plod the path I know best, stopping at the familiar torii gate to the shrine where I first got to know Nakamura.

The red varnish, starting to peel, doesn't seem so vibrant anymore as I place my hand on one of the gate's pillars. It could use some TLC and a coat of paint. Most of the fox statues' red bibs have faded and have blown into their eyes like they're hiding. One even tipped over on its side, a pathetic sight.

Patiently, Su-chan waits as I'm drawn to help them perform their guard duty again. Reaching the top leaves me still at a loss for words. Tossing coins in the box, I bow and press my hands together with a simple 'What do I do now?'

"So what do you make of Sensei's story?" Su-chan asks as we step down and I glance around like a lost puppy unable to figure out which way to go.

I shrug.

"Well…" She steps in front of me to tuck a lock of hair behind my ear that the wind had whipped into my face. "I think I understand why she did a forbidden spell. If someone I cared about were dying, my temptation would be the same. Can you imagine knowing you could have saved them? Even if it were wrong to do, I'd be haunted if I didn't try. Though, it's hard when you find out someone you look up to isn't perfect."

The consequences still haunt Sensei. Words finally flow. "A person died no matter what she chose. Either course had a negative outcome. Her choices had impacts beyond what she could see, and she accepted them."

"True." Su-chan nods.

"But why wouldn't she tell me before? Sure, she knows my past and warned me against shortcuts with ki that wasn't my own, so you'd think she'd want to ensure that particular lesson would stick. And your family knows how to treat the aftereffects."

"We're familiar with it because of our quiet healing profession. Maybe she didn't mention it directly because ki theft is too easily abused."

"So, I have no right to be mad?" In the unfairness, I scowl.

"I wouldn't say that."

Sensei asked me to wait, not that she wouldn't answer—probably from the same fear of judgment that I deal with. "No. Looking at it from her angle, I don't have that right."

When we return, Nakamura clears her throat. "Tatsuya, I owe you an apology." She crouches with tails lowered. "Where do I begin? I was such a hypocrite in my zeal to protect Nonogawa. Even after trusting you with the mysteries of kotodama, I hesitated to instruct you properly about a danger that could have cost lives, including yours. And I tried to drive you out when you sought a new start, the same as I needed in 1868. If you hadn't saved me that day—"

"Sensei, in your place I..." My words dissolve into thin air. *I'd do the same thing.*

"I see. I expected to have less of a role in your life now that you have Su-chan. Teacher is all I can be in your eyes anymore. If you trust me to be even that."

To unjumble inside, I take a stabilizing breath. "That's not it. Teacher is the role you had when you first believed in me."

Her nose nudges my arm. When I lay a hand on her furry shoulder, Satou echoes my gesture. Su-chan's hand rests on mine and contacts my aunt's fur, sharing this private moment. We're in this together, as family and friends. Ones I couldn't have guessed I'd have a few months ago.

Over lunch, we discuss how to help Aunt Hisako. She's afraid to leave with Date on the loose. But the Boss and I share a concerned look. Our aunt's reliance on ki donations is a problem, and my boss doesn't practice magic. Worse yet, Sensei isn't sure if the need will grow or remain constant. It's up to Su-chan and me, and maybe her family if they'll help.

Come to find out, my brilliant girlfriend messaged her parents. We'll discuss shifts as soon as the barricade of media hounds leaves.

Su-chan lifts an eyebrow. "Can we rescue my family from the press?"

Retrieving my supplies, I quip, "So, my everyday carry will have to include paper, ink, and a brush?"

"I knew you weren't just handsome! Welcome to the world of magical service. Once word spreads, requests pour in." She winks as I zip upstairs.

One portal talisman later, the Ohno clan arrives in the living room. Her brothers want to see the dojo, but they'll have to wait. We opt for a ki charge rotation of two per day until Sensei returns to Kyoto.

The Suzukis text to check on me. They need to go shopping, but the reporters trapped them.

"Why isn't the media here, too?" Satou asks.

Shrinking, my aunt confesses, "Because I used my ki for an illusion to misdirect them. Now I don't have the energy to be in human form."

"You wily kitsune." Su-chan giggles. "Do you suppose I could learn that trick?"

Sensei nods. "We could teach you something similar."

The duo could cause a ton of mischief.

Before we bring the others here, Satou pulls me aside. "Do you understand why I had to be so secretive about my position in the agency?"

"No, I don't, Boss."

His mouth scrunches to the side as he considers. "Date's not the only one we're watching. She's working with an entity. Agents have disappeared."

"Do you mean the oni she's bound for her magic?"

Shaking his head, he mutters, "Hiro always said you'd be two steps ahead of us. That's likely the one. I think you saw a hint in Kyuunan when the bakeneko said there were minions there. Since you've been in the public spotlight, I can't exactly recruit you for undercover work anymore. But Aunt Hisako said her plans for you may pair with my work in the Paranormal Division. But you'll have to choose the PSIA or the L—" His mouth clamps.

He mutters something under his breath about her damned spell and waves his hand. "That group I can't talk about. You, of all people, know how much it irks me she kept her identity and her job a secret. Keeping our aunt safe is the priority. Stick to her like glue or make sure she's with her kitsune clan. Not just because she's family, but the mythical foxes are the best link we have to the spirit realm with the trouble brewing."

His confiding in me goes a long way toward reconciling his deception. "Understood, Boss."

Next, Satou agrees to let the Suzukis visit, offering them a ride to the store in a neighboring town. Sojirou runs full tilt through the portal, looking like he might knock me over on impact. Instead, he skids to a stop a few centimeters in front of me.

"Here's your New Year's card." He shoves the envelope forward—both arms extended. "Open it now, please!"

Normally we wait to open gifts for when we're in private, but I melt at his pleading expression.

I should send one to him, too. "Thank you."

The rounded stick figures and the little kid scrawl of his wish for good health and happiness tugs at me. "Is this us?" He nods, pleased that I recognized the characters. "My first card of the year." How long has it been since I received a proper New Year's greeting? Ages. Placing it on the table for display, I ask. "So you're ok?"

"Yeah. But I had nightmares last night."

"You might for a while. Yesterday was intense." Hiro's death haunted my dreams.

His mom chides, "Don't bother Umeji-san too much. Come here so we're ready." Though, she's staring at Sensei.

He obeys, making a wide arc around the fox. "May I stay with Umeji-san?"

Suzuki Chiyo deflects. "I'm sure he has plans."

That's what Su-chan *means by not wanting others to speak for her.* "It won't be a problem. I'd promised to show the Ohno brothers the dojo. Sojirou-kun can tag along if it's ok with you."

Perking up, my aunt motions toward Su-chan. "Should we watch? Entertainment would be nice after the recent events."

An audience? Gulp. At least my aunt and Su-chan aren't able to plot mischief behind my back then. Though there's a bonus to the situation.

This small house I first called home is bursting at the seams. Warmth fills me as I survey the room. I don't know everyone well, but I'd like to. And not even all the folks I care about are here.

Satou presents the cards that arrived from my friends. In the bustle of the last few days, we forgot to retrieve the mail. They get tucked carefully into my coat pocket to savor later.

Hyped, the boy vibrates with energy as he waves goodbye to his mom. "Umeji-san will you spar with me?"

I chuckle. "Sure. Are you still enjoying your sessions with Matsuo-kun?"

"Uh-huh. We were supposed to have a lesson today. Mama canceled because of the reporters outside our house."

"Let's practice, so you're ready for next time."

"May I be the teacher?"

"I'm depending on you," I say with utmost seriousness, causing Su-chan to grin.

In his giddiness, he forgets to bow before entering. So, I tug at his sleeve. "Sojirou-sensei, please show me how to enter."

He blanches. After he bows in, the group follows. Our spectators sit against the wall. And the Ohno brothers join me in letting the boy lead warm-ups. I'll have to thank the guys for playing along.

Once focused, he recalls the routine. Soon, the young teacher has us rolling aikido style. The circular movement has us on our feet right away, which will be fun to use when sparring with Matsuo.

When we've run through what Sojirou has learned, we spar round-robin. Using only the moves we reviewed, I make him work for every dodge and throw. But the delight in his eyes fills my heart, as he causes a much larger opponent to hit the ground.

His mother, Satou, and Mie walk in, joining the spectators. Wrapping up, Ohno Ichiro asks our junior leader if we should repeat the drills. He gives a solemn nod, then calls out the forms, performing the exercises alongside the trio of adults.

Heading to the house, Sojirou remembers to give his respects on the way out. "Thank you for allowing me to be the teacher today."

Now he has two more role models besides Matsuo and me. Su-chan's oldest brother winks and slaps the boy's back. "They say that you understand something more if you have to teach it."

Next, we make a plan for everyone to return home without the media being aware. Intent on watching my brush, Sojirou sits beside me while I write several portal ofuda.

So, I share how I had to learn the kanji I'm writing. "I couldn't finish school. I hope you do, then you'll read better than me."

"How's it work?" He leans in as the talisman sizzles with blue light.

When Sensei asks for permission to train the boy, he whips around, pleading only with his eyes—a marked maturing. But his mother stiffens. "Uh. I'll consider it."

"Please, allow your son to do the honors." I hold out the paper, offering gently. "If he learns to do spells, you both should understand what he's getting into." Sure, I'm pushing my luck, but something niggles inside saying not to drop this.

Skeptical, she looks to Nakamura, who directs him to put the ofuda on the wall. "Speak the name of the place. It has to be a location you've visited."

A mischievous look flickers on his face before disappearing. *Is he weighing the cost of picking somewhere else?*

He chooses, "Home." Blazing with light, the door opens to his room.

We glimpse a staghorn beetle in an aquarium and a plethora of giant robot and dinosaur posters. He waves and thanks me for watching him.

When the portal is closed, my aunt pads over. "That boy doesn't just idolize you. You're becoming a substitute dad."

I freeze.

Later, we invite the Ohno family to stay for dinner. Satou relates that Suzuki-san declined, and Mie volunteered to cook.

Quickly, I zip over to the dojo again, stealing a few moments to work on my sword skills. With the enemy lurking out there, I've got to improve. Practice every day, no exceptions. Su-chan joins me, though her watching doesn't help my concentration.

To have enough spots as we set out the dishes, Su-chan and I convert the blanketed kotatsu to a regular table. Then we move it beside the main one, setting places for more people than I've heard of at a home meal. We have to punt with dishes. I'll use the smallest plate to save the larger ones for the others.

"So why is Suzuki Chiyo-san so skittish?" Mie asks as she preps curry for the crowd.

"Her husband was drunk most days. The rest of the time, he regretted what he did when he drank." Satou snatches a spoonful to taste. More roguish than I've seen him be before.

Sensei adds, "I helped her hire a lawyer. Such a—"

"So it's not just me? She's that way with everyone?" My words rush out.

Su-chan ribs me with her elbow, an action I deserve for interrupting. "She let her son stay here. I've not heard of her leaving him before."

"You should have seen her in the car. Mika-chan, that's why I begged you to come along," Satou says.

Mie's nickname? So, they're close now.

We lend Sensei enough ki for her human guise, despite her protests. Normally, it seems to recharge in a day or two, but her broken tama makes her ki well act more like a conduit. Who knows where it ends up.

Dinner for nine is chaotic but pleasant. Mie's curry rocks so much that no leftovers remain. *May our families gather like this again.*

When the topic returns to Sensei's recovery, she says, "Kazuo, I appreciate you hosting last minute. My parents' opinion is necessary for long-term recovery plans. If there's any trouble with Date, you all retreat to my family's den. Understood?"

After cleanup, the seven of us give Satou and Mie time to themselves. Using a talisman, we slip over to Sensei's residence and breathe a sigh of relief when we see the media has retreated. Su-chan's family leaves, stating they have potions to tend.

Sidling up to me, Su-chan nudges flashing an adorable grin. "Walk me home later?"

Time to ourselves? Heck yeah! Nodding and grinning like a fool, I hand a talisman to Sensei so she can get to her family's den. Until now, Nakamura was always the one with the most magic. That sobers me. The house will feel strange without her tonight.

Sensei gestures to the glowing gateway that opens to a cozy stone-walled cave room. Tatami floors have cushions arranged around the central cooking fire pit and a stand shows off a large tea set at the ready.

"Step through, Tatsuya. Then, you'll be able to return in a pinch. We'll do proper introductions later." Sensei's family surrounds her, yipping in concern.

Doing so and pulling her aside, I whisper, "See you tomorrow, Aunt. If you don't arrive before 7 PM, do you want me to fetch you for the wake?"

"Yes, please."

28

CHAPTER 28: MECHANATIONS

Su-chan is waiting for me when I return. I grab a couple of beers, delivering one to her at the table. Both of us could use a drink after the insane day. Most of mine gets chugged down. Primly sipping hers, Su-chan licks her lips before her gaze darts coyly to the floor.

"What?" I shake my head to clear my thoughts. I've not seen this side of her.

"Sleep with me."

The can drops from my grip onto the table, spilling the remnant of its contents as it rolls. *She doesn't mean that.* "Come again?"

Tipping the container right side up, her fingertip drags across the opening. She leans over, tracing my mouth then toying with the collar of my shirt. Her voice turns sultry. "Sleep with me, Tatsuya."

Swallowing as I kneel beside her, I have to ask. "Is this what you want, or do you think you have to act like the girls I dated when I was yakuza? Because you don't."

Her fingers snake their way under my tee to my stomach. When she tugs on my pants, it steals my breath. Her lips smash into mine and find no resistance. With desire coursing through me, I pull her close and let my hands roam. *When did she learn to French kiss like this? It's as if she's had experience.*

Quickly snatching her arms breaks the contact. "Su-chan—"

"I want you," she whines with insistence.

Then she mouths something. I can't discern it, but it's not 'you', nor is it my name. *And she didn't call me Tatsu.*

"Something's wrong." My grip tightens on her wrists. Why do I suddenly feel the need to protect myself?

Curling up and drawing her fists with her, she convulses and shrieks. *What the hell? Is she mad about my reluctance?*

When I release her, a rasp emerges as her face pales. "Date."

"Here?" The squeaked question lacks my usual dignity.

Click. *She was being controlled.* It wasn't Su-chan giving consent. The hurt in her gaze—*she'll never trust me again.* My fists clench and I cast an incantation for enhanced senses.

A silken line appears as it attempts reattaching to Su-chan's neck. *How did Date get past the protection wards?*

My blood boils. Snatching the puppet string, I wrap it around my palm. To pull her in hand over hand, I lean against the tension. The effort yields a yelp and the sound of claws scrabbling that is worth the thread biting into my hand.

Grunting against the pain, I resort to staccato phrases. "Ofuda. Coat pocket."

Su-chan scrambles. Snarls emerge from beyond the kitchen door, and the line jerks hard. *The vixen messed with people I care about. Again.* Dead-certain calm stills the anger, just like when I picked up Hiro's pistol and took out those shooting at us. *This ends today.*

I heave hard and, with the help of a time dilation spell, trace the string outside to the walled-in, formal garden. Date crouches behind a bush along the path to the veranda. The front leg that sports a glowing metallic band is missing a toe.

"I will not allow you to dig farther into secrets that must be kept! Your mentor wasn't strong enough to kill me, no matter how hard she tried. When I crush you, I'll turn you into the worst of the yakuza. First, you'll go on a killing spree, starting with this little hussy. Then Nakamura will have to intervene. The old bat will never trust you again."

A tic starts in my jaw. To shut the fox up I proclaim 'silence', directing extra ki into the spell. Her mouth clamps only for a second until she whisks the magic away.

Su-chan's steady grip on my arm sends warmth coursing through me, renewing my ki supply. "Date's baiting us," she says.

Su-chan isn't showing any fear, either.

"Through your betrayal and fall, everything you've worked for, everyone you and the old hag care about, I'll destroy them." Her labored breathing speeds up as she thrashes between sentences.

Then, a rippling in her flesh makes me shudder. *The witch is barely keeping control!* Holding the silk thread strains my hands. *Hiro trained you for this.*

Su-chan shouts over the vixen's hysterics. "Do you think she's done spouting her master plan yet?"

The fox's tails poof. My laughter only makes the witch growl. *Brilliant, Su-chan!*

Then, the kitsune's threats raise to a shriek. "The last thing I'll have you do is kill the bitch fox for me, sacrificing her for another few decades of giving me complete control. You'll rot in jail, with no memory of the deeds, until I retrieve you again to be the lowest of my servants."

Not on my watch. As I drag the witch toward me, Su-chan slaps an ofuda on my shirt and stuffs something into my rear pocket. The vixen gnaws at the thread as one of her tails whips to enact a spell. I'm not fast enough to catch it.

On the walls of the courtyard phosphorescent puffs of smoke roil violently, creating a small tear from some hellish dimension. An all too familiar stench wafts our direction, making me want to gag.

Using a sleeve to cover my nose doesn't quell it. With a roar, seven red oni contort and fight with each other to squeeze through. My stomach drops and the bravado falters. *It's only Su-chan and me against eight.*

"Let's take out as many as we can before they get through!" I shout.

Man, I wish I could create a projectile weapon. With my free hand, I pull my katana from my cargo pants to energize the ghostly blade. Holding on to the string will hinder me, but Date won't be able to use it on anyone if I have it in my grasp.

Su-chan bounds inside, emerging with her goodie bag. "On it!" Potions fling one after another toward the oni who are almost through.

Cackling, the vixen raises shields to cover her muscle-bound minions, eliminating the vials. "Amateurs!"

The demons' protection fizzles upon contact. *Su-chan's had excellent aim so far.*

"Now!" I leap off the veranda toward Date with my sword raised, burning extra ki to power my jump.

The vixen shields herself from my oncoming attack, then the silver line in my hand yanks her off the ground. *Boo-yah!*

Su-chan hurls a vial that smashes into the southernmost emerging opponent. She directs the acid to spread rapidly, melting the flesh off the beast as it struggles to free itself from the dimensional tear. Sudden crackling and the monster turns to ash. One down. Six plus Date to go.

As the vixen and I fall, my katana arcs. Date lands on her back, gasping as red hazes my vision and deadly calm fills me again. *I've got her!*

Between breaths she rasps, "You... would dare... kill me?"

The force from our fall adds power to my sword smashing into Date's shield. Green sparks fly before it gives way, allowing the blade to continue its deadly path. Something switches inside. My sight clears. *Shit.*

I halt the swing—which almost costs my balance—leaving the blade hovering over her throat. *There's got to be a better way.*

Date must have sensed my hesitation because she rolls to her feet. *The band! It's on the same leg as the control thread.*

A flick of my wrist slips the tip of the blade under the oni controlling bracelet and she yelps. Blood wells from the cut. I press the katana into the wound, hoping to crack the band.

Date scrambles backward, hunching over the wound. Still grasping the control thread the vixen had manipulated Su-chan with, I use bodyweight to jerk her toward me and take another swipe at her leg.

Date flies through the air, but a new shield blocks then evaporates under the strike. She lands in the rock garden on the southwest side of the enclosure.

Sensei had spent hours raking the wave designs only to have them spoiled.

Another vial crashes into a target. The beast's screams cut through the air as Su-chan works her magic. Out of the corner of my eye, I see a spray of ash that sends the oni back to its realm. Its brethren howl curses at us as three finish squeezing through, emerging in the garden area on the north and west sides.

Date's tail swishes, flinging a wadded paper that pops to human size between herself and me. Its razor-thin arm severs the thread. When the puppet's arm raises again, my strike slices through it like butter.

Date skitters behind the advancing trio of horned minions. The brutes brandish spiked clubs the size of my leg as if the weapons weigh nothing. A cold sweat runs down my back.

In its rush toward me, the first oni swings. I dodge. But its club smashes into a bonsai planter along the path, causing me to cringe. It hasn't been that long since I fixed up the house and that tree was special to Sensei.

Glowing water splashes an oni to my right, followed by crackling and Su-chan's cheer.

Trying a new incantation again, I mutter, "Can't miss".

It doesn't sound cool. But mistakes could be deadly. Efficiency is key. When I dodge using the roll I learned from Suzuki-kun, the oni's club gets stuck in the veranda step.

Date moves to the porch, releasing a rippling wave of pressure. As I raise my sword once more, the roaring blast knocks me off balance. My weapon homes in on its target anyway, dragging me with it. But the blow doesn't banish the beast. I stumble off as a meaty fist plows into my ribs, knocking the wind out of me and vaporizing my protection talisman.

A shout of kotodama halts the oni's attack, though only for a moment. *Finally, an effect I expect!* My next strike nets a bullseye. Though, my muscles protest from the rapid ki expenditure.

Su-chan joins me in the grassy area by the rock garden. Giving a weary thumbs up, she moves back-to-back with me as the remaining oni circle. Three left plus Date.

A frigid wind picks up as snow drives into our faces. My skin tingles, not only from the cold but too much static. My stomach tightens.

Pulling a couple of ofuda from my pocket, I slip one to Su-chan then slap the other on my side. "Is it possible to convert ki from lightning?"

Su-chan whispers, "I don't think it works that way."

Kotodama affects an object or action.

Date advances on us as her band pulses and her fur bristles with the electricity in the atmosphere. "Nowhere to run."

Su-chan raises her chin in defiance. I mirror the action as my stomach sinks. Still not good odds. But we won't cower.

The vixen gloats while her foreleg's skin blisters. "Grandson, after a lightning bolt knocks you both out, I'll convert your wench to an oni that you fight. Then I'll frame you for her death."

Click. *Use that old bravado to your advantage.*

"Tell me you have a plan." Su-chan's voice raises with a hope I dare not disappoint.

"You're having trouble controlling everything, pathetic vixen. That's what happened at your company here in town."

The moment allows me to adjust my grip on the sword's hilt. I may not be able to convert lightning, but that doesn't mean I can't use it. Date snarls, as green flashes from her paw's band and fleshy bubbles form on her foreleg.

Here comes the bolt. Under my breath, I utter kotodama. Sliding my arm around Su-chan's waist, I point my katana at the fox's band. "Hang on to me!" The chill of the driving snow melting on my clothes seeps into my skin.

Please protect Su-chan. Time slows. The hair on my neck raises as three hulking oni advance. Raising their clubs, the red monsters coordinate their attack.

I bark the word for power, then leap. Unprepared, poor Su-chan almost crushes the air out of my lungs as she clings to me, and we soar into the sky. Oncoming lightning barrels through us and then zig-zags along the sword to the band. A banshee screech from the vixen confirms the hit.

Su-chan floods me with the sunshine confidence of a ki boost. When I raise my sword, she uses a potion to eliminate another oni. *Date can't spare the ki to shield her minions now?*

My turn. Uttering a time dilation, I gently let go of Su-chan to allow her a safe landing near her bag of goodies.

A targeting spell will guide my upcoming strike, but the magic uses much more ki than it should. *Why am I burning through the boost this fast?*

Snow around me slows to a stop as I plummet past it. Slamming down onto the oni on the scorched path, the blade shears through, disintegrating the beast. Bam! My protection ofuda pops out of existence. *Someone's stealing ki?*

Shattering glass precedes Su-chan's shout. "Get the fox, Chou!"

While I swing at the next oni, my muscles cramp up causing the stroke to miss. *How the hell am I gonna defeat the beast if I can't hit it?* In my distraction, the oni's weapon smashes my shoulder, sending blinding pain shooting through my frame.

There's one more paper in my pocket. *Be a healing charm.* Slapping the ofuda on my bicep makes me wince. *Nope.* My knees wobble, and a wave of nausea rolls over me as I stumble out of the way. It'll be impossible to use my left arm well until it's healed. *At least it's a protection talisman.*

Where's the storm? The plants around char at an alarming pace. *Rob Date of the power source. Who cares about afterward? Gotta stop her.* Red fire ignites on my hands as power rushes in.

Sensei's warning echoes in my ears, 'Don't take the easy way. That only leads to forbidden magic and death.'

The neighbors and Su-chan! To cease the flow, I drop the connection and snuff the flames climbing my arms. The she-devil tried to trick me into hurting Su-chan.

"Date!" I roar.

Adrenaline pumps through me and should give me the needed strength to finish the fight. But my muscles protest as I charge the oncoming oni. To make a decent one-handed strike, I use half of my minuscule amount of remaining ki for targeting. This one lands true, banishing the monster.

Despite the pain, I scramble toward Su-chan's scream. A second draining wave causes me to stumble. Whipping around, I find Su-chan wrestling for the melted control band with the flame-engulfed vixen in the blackened grass.

Su-chan's muscles cord when the fox's sharp fangs tear at her fingers. While Chou pins Date in place, she noisily gulps down energy. Then I spot the reason Su-chan attacked this way—ominous bubbling continues to creep up Date's furred foreleg.

"Hold her paw!" Barreling in, my teeth chatter while I drain my usable ki for a spell. Who knows how powerful that captive oni is? *Stop the conversion!*

When my blade slices downward, the fox jerks, dragging Su-chan's wrist into range. Instead, the sword wrenches to the side, causing me to yelp as my injured arm flails to help balance. The strike cleaves clean through, causing an ear-piercing howl.

Then, the weight of the ki drain disappears, causing me to feel like a gangly teen again. Su-chan flings away the detached demonic paw. She's out of breath as she crawls to her bloodied hands and knees.

Date skitters in place on her remaining legs as Chou hangs on. Blood gushes from the fox's severed foreleg. Despite our efforts, the red skin still inches up.

This mess ends if Date dies. There's no other way. Saying a silent prayer, I plead for the strength to do this. My uninjured arm shudders with the effort to heft the blade.

What if we return her to her people for judgment? We'd have to subdue her and the oni. Only have one shot. "Ki, please!"

Su-chan slaps my leg to give me a small supply, but not the usual full-blown sun inside sensation. *She must not have much left either.*

Flipping the sword to the blunt side, a hard thwack doesn't knock Date out. She spits in my face. The katana isn't the tool for this job. So I let it go to seize a fistful of fur. Su-chan directs Chou to press down on the fox's skull, shielding me from the kitsune's razor-sharp teeth.

Then I pant, "Neutralize!"

Date tries to flail out of the hold we have on her. "Imbecile! You don't know what your meddling will unleash. I have to keep the oni under control! Otherwise, her vengeance will be beyond your worst nightmare!" The vixen utters the same command I did.

The heat drains from my limbs as ki draws away from me, and the vixen's eyes narrow. *Did I make the wrong choice?* This witch has hurt so many people I know.

We know her weakness—the shortcut of relying on an oni to take the ki drain. So, I pour more energy into my kotodama. *It's got to be enough!*

Su-chan must have spotted the panic in my face. "Chou, remove the tama from her tail!"

Then she, too, presses bloody hands on the vixen who's caused us so much trouble and pain. With eyes locked on me, she utters a word of kotodama to add power to my own. *She hasn't cast this magic type before.* I could kiss Su-chan for her dedication.

A sharp tug on my energy chills me. *Focus! Be worthy.* Putting the rest of my easy-to-spend ki into the kotodama, I make a last wager in this gamble. If this fails, I'll push my life's flame over to Su-chan so she has a chance.

Moments pass. Date doesn't flinch. *I wasn't enough.*

Catching Su-chan's attention, I search for the final drop of energy. "Let go."

"No." The resolve in her eyes bowls me over.

She can't die because of me. A lump forms in my throat as a cold vacuum expands toward my core. I prepare to shove Su-chan out of the way before sacrificing my life.

Underneath us, the fox falls limp. With a loud burp, Chou collapses, releasing the unconscious witch. Pressure builds in the room and explodes in a brilliant light, searing my vision.

A stabbing, awful stretching under my ribs bursts where my ki well resides, filling the space beyond capacity, and I gasp unable to scream.

As fast as the blaze came, it disappears. I blink, trying to catch my breath. *What the hell just happened?* With a palm going to where I felt the pain, I half expect to notice a difference. Nothing.

"Tatsu-kun, you have a glowing fox inside." Su-chan shakily reaches for my chest. A peace settles in me at the touch, despite my teeth chattering.

"What? We won? Are you ok?" My ki well exceeds anything I've experienced—an energy charge multiplied by a hundred times.

"I think so. Do I have the same thing?"

Idiot. I'd only focused on myself. Turning her shoulders to me, I watch a pulsing glow. "Different. It seems to morph, so it's hard to tell."

"Oh." Her face falls. Rallying, she asks, "Is it the magic dwelling in us?"

"Where are my tails? You filthy humans!" Date lifts her single fluffy one and squints in our direction. Her injured front leg is hideous, but there's no more bubbling. *If the spread stopped, where's the oni?*

The vixen whispers a word of kotodama that only fizzles, turning her shouting to a wail. "Magic theft carries a heavy penalty!"

Seizing the vixen by the scruff of the neck, I run an experiment. A glowing pet-carrier appears from only a simple thought. *Hot damn, I can create stuff! And it was wicked simple.*

"You'll pay with your life! My family has sway, and we'll take this to the highest of the kami!"

Shoving Date into the box, I slam the door, soundproof it, and toss it aside. Su-chan tackles me and I swing her in circles. "We did it!"

Then I inspect her torn-up fingers. Pressing them to my lips, I breathe a spell of healing. When she returns the favor for my shoulder, though, there's a distinct lack of kiss where the injury had been.

That glint in her eyes—did she consider it? Instead, she whispers a spell to warm us.

I nuzzle into her cheek, reveling in the heat. "How'd you do that?"

"I just manipulated the moisture in the air to heat it. Potions at their simplest need water and the word. That's all."

We defeated Date! "You're amazing." Smooching the top of her head, I tighten the embrace. "Thank you. For this. For everything."

"It would have been better if I'd practiced fighting the puppeteering," she whispers. "Well, what do we do with Date?"

"Take her to Sensei's family? They should know what to do with one of their kind. And Sensei said if something went wrong to go there."

When I lift the crate, Date's hackles raise. She snaps ineffectually. The copper tang of blood hits my nose and slick red pools on the bottom of the container from her shortened foreleg.

Surveying Sensei's formerly beautiful garden makes me cringe. Similar stains cover the blackened grass and mar the rock garden. The veranda will need repairs, along with the garden and portions of the path. A priest will need to purify Sensei's house before any repairs.

The adrenaline rush withdraws, and my legs turn wobbly. A quick word of healing has me bright-eyed and bushy-tailed again.

Gathering up Chou, who's now far too fat to fit into a jar, Su-chan commands, "Tama, please."

With a squelch, the slime spits it out. "Chou, you didn't crack it in two, did you?" The ooze forms an appendage that motions 'No'.

This time, creating a portal to the Nakamura den is a piece of cake. No talisman needed. My free hand sweeps grandly toward the opening. To the surprise of the family gathered around the den's fire pit, we step through the door with our prisoner and bow.

Su-chan gapes at the cave home with its tatami mats, human-style furnishings, and oil lamps. I say, "Sorry for the interruption. We have a delivery. Date attacked us at Sensei's home."

"T-tatsuya?!?" Sensei pads up as I drop our nemesis at her paws, and I glimpse the glowing fox inside my aunt.

Members of the Nakamura clan sniff the air and their brows furrow. They too have the beating kitsune heart.

"Daughter, what did you teach this nephew of yours?" The male's tone has a sour note.

"Not this!" When Su-chan presents the tama pieces, my teacher hisses. "What have you done? Why did you take her magic instead of coming for help or killing her?"

I bristle. "It was bad, Aunt! There wasn't an opportunity to open a portal! I had to try something and 'neutralize' seemed reasonable. I refuse to have more death on my conscience. Otherwise, she'd force Su-chan and everyone else to be a puppet again. It took both of us plus Chou to overpower Date!"

Su-chan says, "I had Chou snatch the tama, so we could have a chance against her. We won't keep it."

"You don't understand what happened, do you?" Sensei snaps.

"Tell us," I growl through gritted teeth. Tightness builds in my muscles, out of proportion to the situation. "I just know we removed her magic."

"Daughter, why did you not teach them this is forbidden?" A different female joins the fray.

My tension changes to twitchiness, similar to forgetting my keys, only much worse. *It's not from the argument. So what is it? And why didn't I know that was forbidden?* It was the only way to handle Date without killing her.

Sensei sighs. "Tatsuya and I didn't get that far, Mother. I taught him the general principle. Though, we couldn't dedicate every day to his training to cover the major aspects. I couldn't have dreamed he was capable yet of something only the kami are allowed to do. It must have taken the two of them together. Also, I assume Ohno-chan broke through in use of kotodama today. She isn't my student, yet."

Pausing, Sensei motions. "Ohno-chan, give Tatsuya half of the ball. You will need to keep those with you always."

Holding a piece out to me, she grimaces then gives me the other instead. Upon contact with it, the twitchiness disappears. But there's still a strange lack of wholeness.

Sensei's father circles us. "Physics teaches that energy is conserved. So, the reservoir transferred to the nearest ki vessels."

Then a fourth kitsune sniffs at Su-chan before shifting forms into a lady almost identical to my aunt's young guise. "This one, she has a powerful magic I don't recognize. Father, are the two types in conflict?"

Su-chan draws a sharp intake of breath. When I take her hand, she relaxes again.

"They should be fine. The varieties are compatible. But I'm concerned about the amount of ki her well can hold." Sensei's dad changes to human form to move closer and evaluate. His stark white hair and long, wispy beard contradict the smoothness of his skin.

"Hisako, the young couple has displayed a recklessness unbefitting of their magic. You know we won't teach those we deem unworthy and eliminate those considered too dangerous. If you can't trust those two with their new powers, end them now. Otherwise, he must stay to receive training in our customs, since you can't return long term to Nonogawa. And we must find the girl a mentor." Despite the threat, Sensei's mother exudes a calmness that sends chills down my spine.

If they want to end us, they'll have to go through me. In a flash, I maneuver between the threat and Su-chan.

"Tatsu-kun?" Su-chan's voice rises. She grips my sleeve so hard the fabric bites into my flesh as she scoots to my side. So, I block.

"Umeji Tatsuya, I know you meant well. But don't you dare shove me behind you again. Your actions were the same as speaking for me." Su-chan's words sting, but there's no way I'm gonna budge.

With a barking laugh, Sensei's mom says, "Sound familiar?" It brings an eye roll from her dad.

"His record is dubious, but his heart is in the right spot. He grew up with the myths but has only glimpsed the spirit side of the world. Being human, he could not have known only the gods remove magic for punishment. As Tatsuya said, they did not intend to steal magic, only immobilize Date. And Su-chan's an angel compared to my nephew's past. Yes, I trust them both." To prove her point, Sensei sits next to me as her tails wrap around my leg in a protective gesture.

Sensei continues. "As I told you, there's one more who needs training. But I'm unsure how his mother will handle it because her trust was broken."

"Suzuki-kun has a kitsune spirit, too?"

"Correct, Tatsuya. Therefore, I required my family's guidance. It's unknown what would happen if we try to remove it. The piece merged with his soul, like Date's magic has to Su-chan's and yours. The odds of this happening to the three of you are astronomical. So, what's the reason?"

"No idea."

"In the meantime, we'll wait. Tatsuya, you need to get your affairs in order for a long stay here. Su-chan, my family and I will be on the lookout for a proper mentor for you."

The earlier mention of Sojirou reminds me. "I felt very unsettled until I held part of the tama. The boy's been without one this whole time. Will he be ok?"

My aunt nods. "He has a small shard embedded in his wrist that matches the kitsune abilities he has. Leaving it there may be the best thing for a forgetful youth."

"Well..." Gesturing to the glowing cage with the snapping fox, I ask, "What about her?"

"Date Sari attacks our family at every opportunity. Justice will be served. Do not worry about her fate." Sensei's father waves it off.

"Sir, the police need to be informed. She's on the most wanted list."

"Messengers of the gods judge for us. Her actions and losing her tama have strong ramifications. We'll contact her family so they may attend. Know that I don't expect her to survive the encounter." The deadpan tone he relays it in sends another shudder through me.

Though, I bow my head in acceptance. *All the hells would freeze over before I'd return the power to Date, even if it wasn't attached to my soul.*

When a fifth kitsune trots into the room, her tail is a happy flag before it falls. "A new male and he's already got a female. How unfair!"

My girlfriend blushes. *That's my Su-chan.*

Before promising to meet me in the morning, Sensei gives a round of introductions. Then her father makes a return portal for Su-chan and me.

When we call Satou to share the news, he warns the media is hunting for me. Sensei's spell must have worn off. He's done everything he can to protect me from it, but I'll have to be ready.

At my aunt's place, it's past 11 PM. The house feels cold and empty, despite sitting next to Su-chan on the couch. The cleanup in the garden tomorrow will suck because the priest will probably have questions.

"We have a portion of kitsune magic now. Where do we go from here?" I ask.

"You have a fox spirit. But I have something else that they weren't able to identify." She frowns for a moment before continuing. "I can't see how it changes us other than we have more power and abilities. That comes naturally, anyway. I'm a little worried about the consequences of taking the magic, though."

"Speaking of, I couldn't have defeated Date on my own. Thank you."

"Tatsu-kun…" Turning away, she stares out the window.

Is she ok after I almost took advantage of her? My heart aches at the thought of what she must think.

"Thank you, for seeing it wasn't me."

"I should have seen sooner." Wrapping my arms around her shoulders, I crush her back to my chest. "I'm so sorry."

"How did you know?"

"The comments and actions didn't fit you, the kiss was wrong, and she used my name, not Tatsu."

"She said what any guy would love to hear."

"It wasn't you speaking."

Leaning against me, she confesses. "The most frustrating part about her puppeteering was that I want to be with you, someday."

"I'll wait until you're ready." My head buries into her shoulder. "I promise."

"May I stay for a while?"

Gulp. *Was my previous declaration only words?* She's probably feeling as raw as I do. I sure as hell don't want to be alone after what happened. Plus, Hiro's wake is tomorrow.

"Hold me for a while." She head-butts my chest. "Then I'll walk home."

"Wait right here." Booking it upstairs, I fetch my blanket and our iPod before lying down on the couch to lift the duvet for her. Sharing the headphones and playing her K-pop list, we drink in the peace of being together.

When I peek down, Su-chan's inner light brightens, beating out a rhythm that matches my own heart. *Just having her here is good.*

29

CHAPTER 29: HEART OF THE MATTER

I loathe taking Su-chan home at 2 AM via portal. When it closes, the room turns lifeless. The lack of her presence leaves me tossing and turning. I've never been this moody about not having a girlfriend around. *What's wrong with me?*

By mid-morning, I figure Su-chan should be up. So, I message that I miss her, then stare at the phone. Her sweet text saying she woke thinking of me gives me the strength to face a tough day.

My aunt returns early, handing me a package with a formal kimono. "You'll wear the Nakamura crest today."

She also gives me two leather necklaces that the tama halves fit into before sharing the news on Date. "We summoned one of the messenger kitsune after you dropped off the witch. Her family arrived within moments to be there for the judgment. They couldn't assist her, except to stop the bleeding from her leg. After the facts were laid bare, neither of Date's parents spoke on her behalf. Her father only said she was a disappointment.

"As punishment, Inari diminished her intelligence to animal-level and released her into the wild. Nothing was said regarding your magic theft. Considering the number of dogs in the area, Date's not expected to live long. The neighbor's Shikoku Inu has her scent already. Killing her outright would have been a kindness."

I disagree because some may have thought the same about me before I

271

changed. But I keep the thought to myself.

The wake and funeral the next day blur into one. I'm left wrung out and numb. Though, more people attend than I expected, including the Ohno clan, the Suzukis, Matsuo, and Mie.

Hoping Hiro's presence is here, I whisper, "We brought Date to justice. Let that bring you peace, so you can pass on to the afterlife."

* * *

The media catches up with me in the evening after the funeral. Mentally listing off a string of curses, I heave in a stabilizing breath to handle the horde. *Couldn't they have the decency to give me even a day or so to grieve?*

Microphones force their way into my personal space.

"Can you tell us what happened at the temple? Concerned citizens have a right to know."

"Witnesses say you performed magic. How is that possible?"

"Did you know Nakamura-san is a kitsune?"

"How is it you avoided arrest for disturbing the peace and wielding a weapon?

"Wasn't one of Date's men your former kyoudai in the mob?"

"Are you planting a mafia group here?"

The queries cause my temples to throb. They don't understand Hiro's role. And worse, the implication that I want to be a yakuza leader? *Hell no!*

As I growl "Silence!", my hand slashes through the air and a ripple of blue light passes over the throng. "Let me answer without interruption."

Then we have blessed quiet, though the reporters squirm—trying to work their mouths as they digest the predicament. Finally, they nod acceptance and tip their microphones farther forward.

"Understand this, I'm done with the yakuza life. I regret what I did in the mafia and won't return. I helped the authorities at the temple, that is all. The one you refer to as my kyoudai was a respected undercover officer. His name was Otsuka Hiro. Write that down. He served his country for years with no recognition, an unsung hero and a man I can only hope to emulate.

"Date Sari killed Lieutenant Otsuka by turning him into an oni with warped spells. In the end, the kami judged the witch. She won't return.

"Yes, Nakamura-san is a kitsune. One who loves her family and this town. Know that she doesn't use her powers to manipulate as Date did. She's training me for a better life, serving the community as a shrine keeper to atone for my past. That's all I have for you. Please, allow me through to buy a few things for dinner."

Instead, they crowd me when released from the spell to continue the interrogation. Pushing away the mics shoved in my face, I escape into the grocery store. But the customers and staff clear a path. *They're afraid. Gotta earn their trust, again. Damn.*

"Umeji-kun!" Matsuo's expression lights with recognition.

My friend's welcome diffuses the tightness creeping up the back of my neck.

"Hey, how are you holding up?" His concern means more than he'll ever understand as he leads me to the break room.

"Ok, I guess."

"Rumors are flying that you're not human because of how long Nakamura-san hid."

I groan and pinch the bridge of my nose.

"How about something to look forward to? I was planning a trip to Tokyo and wondered if you wanted to be my guide."

"When? I have to train out of town."

"February."

Rotten timing. I bob as I say, "Sorry. Don't know if we'll return by then. If I do, I'd love to. There's this little back-alley joint that serves out-of-this-world beef hot pot."

"See, that's what I want! The places only the locals know about."

"If not this time, then next. I promise."

"I'll keep you to that! Wanna spar with me before you go?"

"That'd be great."

"By the way, my parents aren't aware you live with Nakamura-san. How do I say this? We can't tell them. They're very superstitious about any kind of fox."

"I remember your reaction."

"Yes." He murmurs, "My dad's family is from Korea. His parents adopted a Japanese name to register our family when his dad was little. When he saw a kitsune on the news, he freaked out. Doesn't want me going near her."

"Gotcha. My lips are sealed." *Too bad Matsuo can't tag along to Kyoto.*

When I return to the house, the porch light illuminates a note hanging on the door. 'Your kind isn't welcome here. Leave if you know what's good for you.' I crumple the note. *Breathe. Change is slow in small towns. Gotta prove yourself.*

* * *

The PSIA says it doesn't have a job for me right now. So, Satou puts me on the schedule again at the store. Practice sessions with Sensei switch to early morning. Otherwise, we won't be able to fit them in with work.

Now that my ki reserve is closer to hers, she takes pleasure in showing me a new trick each session. Watching over the shrine was only the beginning of Sensei's plan—a test to verify I was a candidate to protect Nonogawa.

It's been her task for the last fifty years after a tanuki, that she refers to as 'the annoying raccoon dog', transferred the duty to her. Soon, she hopes to pass the torch to me. But I have to undergo special training and gain final approval.

This morning, Sensei invites the Suzukis for tea to bring up teaching Sojirou. My shift starts in a few minutes. Leaning on the doorway, I debate whether to join the conversation. Sojirou hides behind his mother, avoiding my aunt. Shoved up sleeves on his Spider-Man shirt allow for the bandage on his wrist, which he rubs.

Is he hesitant to go? Catching his attention, I motion for him. His eyes widen as he barrels up to me. "Umeji-san, you have a fox spirit, too!"

"Yeah kiddo, and I see yours."

With brows furrowing, he considers a moment. "Did you break a tama, too?"

"Not intentionally." My throat tightens. *He'll deal with heavy-duty stuff as he grows up. Why not cut to the chase?* "Date attacked Su-chan and me. I didn't want more blood on my hands, so we neutralized her magic. With nowhere else to go, the spirit energy went into the two of us."

His lip trembles, and anguish overshadows his features. "You didn't mean to. But... but I broke Nakamura-san's magic ball. She's hurt because of me!"

Shaking my head, I shush him. "No. Date did that. She used your body as a puppet. It wasn't you. She won't be able to do that ever again."

"I hope she dies!"

My brows furrow. An edge enters my voice. "Didn't you listen when I said I don't want to kill again? How can you wish her dead?" His mother looks up as I admonish her son. "People will miss that person—friends, family, schoolmates, coworkers. Her parents had to be there for her judgment. Imagine how they felt."

"But you killed the monsters!" he retorts, raising a fist and smashing it into his palm.

"I don't fully understand how the oni possession that Date forced on the thugs worked." Meeting my aunt's gaze, I verify, "But Sensei will correct me if I get this wrong. To my understanding, those men were dead already. I sent the oni back to where they came from and wish I'd been able to stop Hiro from turning into one."

My aunt nods.

"So I pray I'll never have to kill again. I would only do it to protect those I care about. And I hope you'll never be forced to make that choice." My hands shove into my pockets, and my eyes fall to my feet. "Be a better man than me."

Tugging on my sleeve, he rallies, asking, "So, you and Nakamura-san will go to Kyoto?"

How does he switch topics so fast? "Yeah. Sensei's family would like you and your mom to come with us. So we can learn about the spirit inside."

"What about your friends here?"

Blowing out a breath, I admit, "That's the rough part, though I'll visit. It's important to find out what's permissible and what I'm forbidden from doing.

I've already done things I shouldn't. Did you see the Spider-Man movies?"

His face lights up. Something besides the weirdness we've seen that we have in common.

"As Spider-Man's uncle said, 'With great power, comes great responsibility.' I need to understand what that means. You should, too."

Running over to his mom, he insists they come along. Sensei mouths 'thanks' and winks.

* * *

Two nights before I leave, Sensei is at her family's again, helping arrange the den for long-term guests. Su-chan works over my back as I lay on the tatami floor in the living room to record hours of practice. I sure don't mind being her guinea pig.

Picking up her bedside manner chatter, she asks. "So you're packed and ready for the new adventure?"

"Kind of." Muscles tighten again, all the way up my neck, and a heaviness settles in my chest.

When she brushes my cheek her eyes mist up, and she returns to the massage. "I'm gonna miss you, you know. But I checked and they haven't found a mentor for me yet."

"I know. I keep pestering Sensei."

She taps twice to signal the end of the massage, then draws lazy figures on my shoulders. "You're still tense. Sorry it ruined the massage's effect. Is there anything I could do to help you relax?"

"Nah. I'll be ok." *Probably.*

"What if I start you a bath before going home tonight? That would let my hands rest, and I could work on those tight spots afterward. Oh, and I got my certificate yesterday! I don't need to record hours anymore."

"Congrats! I'm so proud of you!" Rolling over on the floor, I watch as she continues the tracing on my abdomen.

I should have had a gift or something. And leaving her will suck. What can I do for her? It'd be nice if she stayed.

Fighting down a fluttering in my stomach, I say, "Tonight, it's only us. We could bathe together to celebrate."

Her hand stills. "Tatsu-kun?"

Did I just overstep my bounds? "Never mind."

As she kisses her index finger, pressing it to my lips, her voice drops. "You surprised me. That's all."

"I said I'd wait. I meant it."

"You'll stop if I ask?" Her fingers follow my collar bone down my chest, in cautious, meandering lines, causing those spots to tingle under the fabric.

"Of course."

"Remember when we made your futon at Satou-san's?" Her eyes sparkle as she recalls.

"Yeah." That was when I first wished she could be mine.

"I wondered what it would be like to be with you."

"Knowing that had been my bed, I stood arrested, keenly aware you'd been there." Taking her hand, I brush lips over her knuckles and lead her upstairs. The little lamp fills the room with a light matching the warm glow inside my chest as we kneel on the futon. "You're the first girl I dated that didn't want something from me."

"I do want something. Give me time with you," she leans in as she whispers.

When my mouth meets hers, I consume every sensation of being here with her to be as drunk as possible.

After pulling her to my lap, we explore each other through our clothing. She lifts my shirt off and traces the foxes in my tattoo, pressing her feather-soft lips to each of them—as if she likes the designs. *How could she? They scream reminders of my past.*

"Is your ink why you asked me to call you Tatsu?"

"Part of it." My chuckle echoes too loud, making my voice go quiet when I speak again. "Is that stupid?"

"No, but I like puns. I've wondered since you first asked me to call you that. And the magical change we went through made the picture different, didn't it?" She tenderly runs a finger over the muzzle of one of the kitsune.

"Yeah. The white fox reversed direction, no longer needing to chase the other."

"Or, it doesn't have its back turned from you anymore. Let me check for any other changes."

"When did you see it all? You got a gander at part of the design only twice."

She sucks in her lip and glances away.

"Oh girl, don't do that. Remember when I said you could have anything you asked for with that look?"

She rewards my confession with the boldest laugh I've seen her give. That radiance—I want to scoop up every drop. Hold all of it. Instinctively, my arms encompass her.

She whispers, "When you turned around, trying your darnedest to be chivalrous and not look, I stole another peek around the screen, 'cause I wanted to see what you hide from others. Not out of some morbid curiosity, but because it's part of you."

"Really?"

Her shy smile and nod as she leans back to meet my gaze make my heart beat faster. Playing with the hem of her top, I tug and her arms lift, letting me slip it off.

"You're beautiful." With a reverence I've only ever had for her, I slip the bra straps from her shoulders, trailing with kisses. The desire to see all of her—to touch all of her—wars with not wanting to push her too far, or have this time together spent all too quickly.

After removing the garment, her hands slide around my neck. My head buries into her shoulder and I sigh as her chest meets mine. She's trembling, but she slips her hands down my abs to work at the button of my pants. I lean back to make the job easier, watching her as she sucks in her lip in concentration. *You can have anything from me. Anything at all.*

My breath hitches when her fingers graze my stomach. She freezes. Her head pops up as her eyes meet mine, brows knitted in concern. "Did I do something wrong?"

"No." A smile flashes across my face before I reach up to caress her cheek, lingering over the constellations in her freckles. "It's just been years." *And never with a girl like her.*

The chill of the room has me grabbing my duvet and we help each other shimmy out of the barrier of our remaining clothing. Then I lay her back, ensuring she's comfortable and taking in all her graceful curves. Her arms encircle my neck, dragging me down, welcoming me.

At first, my lips gently press to her mouth. But when my body comes into contact with so much of her skin, it sends me into overdrive. My kiss turns feverish, begging her to allow me access inside her mouth. When she returns the insistence, it adds fuel to the already burning fire inside.

Better be sure. "More ok?"

"Um-hmm."

She wants me. ME and the ink of my past.

* * *

Later, we drag ourselves downstairs to clean off while the fire warms the water in the slowly filling wood tub. I'm transfixed as she sits on the wooden stool to wash, blushing—still shy despite what we just shared.

When her washcloth drapes over her shoulder and she reaches around with her other hand to scrub, it finally dawns on me that part of my privilege now is to help wash her back and rinse her hair before we soak. I'm happy to oblige.

Hissing at the temperature, we crawl into the deep bath. She scoots close. Basking in the warm water couples with the fuzzy-brained contentment. *I could get used to this. Too bad I leave in two days.*

* * *

Waking spooned with Su-chan's naked form is as peaceful as it is enticing. The glow in my chest rivals the sun itself. Morning light peeking through the curtains warms my shoulder, but her heat is so much better.

Then a piano slams into my chest. *I'll say goodbye tomorrow.* Unable to breathe, I shake.

"Dammit." The word slips out of my mouth, making me regret the instant it escapes. *Shut it, so she doesn't wake up.*

How the hell am I gonna manage? I've never been this possessive before, and we only made love once. *This isn't normal.*

When her palm covers my balled-up fist, the over-tightened muscles in my torso unwind and the tremors subside. Snuggling as close as possible, I tuck this moment into a mental treasure box for when I'm forced to sleep alone again—her scent, how it feels to have her beside me, the satisfaction of last night, the peace of her expression as her lips twitch in dreams.

"What's wrong?" She stirs, still groggy.

"Nothin'."

She tugs my arm farther over her shoulder and laces her fingers with mine. "Mmm. Let's share the same bed every night now that we're lovers."

"Don't..." *tease me.* My muscles lock up again.

Releasing, she flips over. Her gaze pierces with tenderness. "Tatsu?"

Pressing her knuckles to my lips, I vow to avoid wrecking our remaining moments together. "Not important."

"I have two introverted older brothers. Don't play the avoidance game, please."

No decent words fit the situation. "Let's not think about it. I'd rather enjoy being here with you while I can."

As her head pops up, she collides with my chin, mumbling a quick apology. Then her face falls. "Umeji Tatsuya, talk to me. Please."

Telling her how much I'm gonna miss her is more than I can deal with. We've only dated for a short while. It'll sound creepily possessive. So, I slip on my trousers to step away from the situation.

"I'll give you all the time you need, but I can't handle it if you flat-out refuse to talk." Her soft voice turns hard by the end of the declaration.

That stops me in my tracks. I just hurt her when I was trying not to. *Shit.* My head does a one-eighty, dragging the rest of my body with it.

Drawing the covers over her chest, her face softens. "It's about you leaving, isn't it?"

All I can manage is a nod as my heart plummets at having to face the topic

I'd been avoiding.

"I've been dreading it, too. At first, I worried my feelings were just puppy love, but I can't shake it. What if I come to Kyoto?"

"But your family's here. Your relationship with your parents is priority. That's how families work. I can't expect you to uproot your life after dating me for only a few weeks."

When she pats the futon, I accept. She goes quiet as she says, "Last night, while we soaked in the tub together, I decided. I just didn't know how to bring it up. Besides, I have to leave home, at some point. I didn't work my butt off to earn my certification early for nothing. And there's only so much call for massage therapy here in Nonogawa. Plus, we may have an easier time finding a mentor for me in the city."

"So, your family's ok with this? I mean, your dad knows my past."

"Yes, my parents have been encouraging me to spread my wings. The Nakamuras should be able to help me find an inexpensive place nearby, right?" A few heartbeats pass before her voice turns quieter. "Though, having a portal ofuda for an emergency will make them feel better."

Snatching her up in my arms, I bury my head in her shoulder, rasping, "Come with me."

* * *

While I'm at my last day of work, Sensei arrives to prep the property since we'll stay in Kyoto for a few months at least. She's arranged with the former guardian to watch over the town in her absence.

That night, my coworkers meet Su-chan and me for drinks to wish us luck. The folks here in little Nonogawa look for any excuse to celebrate. Su-chan and I stumble to the house through the poorly lit streets, giggling and weaving the entire way.

"Welcome home!" Sensei trots over with her tails wagging happily. Then she sniffs the air, only to bristle.

Su-chan leans on me, despite me being a tad unsteady, too. "Sssssorry Auntie, we jussst drank a little too muchhhh. Oh, did you know the ssssushi chef is a tanuki? He didn't like me noticesssing. And Ssssu-chan's coming to Kyoto!"

"Take Ohno-chan home so her family can spend this final evening with her. You and I need to talk. Use a talisman to get her home, because spoken kotodama and alcohol are a terrible mix."

My bottom lip sticks out, as I hope she'll recant.

"You'll see her tomorrow, Tatsuya." The sharpness in her words leaves no room for argument.

But I can't shake the crushing weight in my chest at the thought of Su-chan having to leave. *Why am I so reluctant to have her out of my sight?*

After depositing Su-chan in her bed, I return to find Sensei pacing. An oncoming lecture hangs in the air as my aunt directs me to join her on the couch, and her fox face sports such furrowed brows that my stomach tightens. *What the hell is wrong?*

After a boost of ki, she flushes the alcohol in my system with a spell that leaves me with a nasty headache, but I'm capable of logic.

"Tatsuya, I couldn't predict the effects of you gaining a mythical being's spirit. And lately, you're about two steps beyond my ability to teach you because my condition makes me exhausted. Though, I should have considered this before I left you both alone. I make a point to stay out of your business, but it's imperative to know if you..." She looks out the window, clearing her throat before she tries again. "I'm guessing that you took advantage of my absence to have sex before you're stuck living in a group. Am I right?"

My hands fold in my lap as my gaze locks there.

"Oh my, Nephew. I wish I could have warned you. We don't know the full effect yet because of your unusual case."

A palm wipes over my face. *Like I need any more drama.* "Warn me about what, Aunt?"

"First off, you read all the kitsune legends, correct?" At my nod, she says, "Do you think there's more than attraction?"

What a kick in the gut. Kitsune sickness affects humans who sleep with a fox if there's only lust from at least one partner. Eventually, the human becomes ill and dies if the sexual relationship continues.

"On my end, there is. I believe it's the same for Su-chan. Though, I can't say with certainty."

While my aunt's hackles relax, my guard is still up. She says, "Good. I agree her side is affection. That was the most pressing issue."

"What's the other? Pregnancy? We'll be ok on that count."

"That's not it. This only affects you." Butting her head into my shoulder, she whines in fox speak before reverting to Japanese. "My people mate for life their first time. After the spouse passes, they have freedom. You probably slept with other girls before, considering your past. But since you just received your tama, I suspect you bonded to your girlfriend last night."

When I splay my fingers in my hair, my elbows slam to my knees. It's late, and the headache throbs, so I scrunch my eyes closed. "Explain."

"If things go pear-shaped with her, I'll be here for you. It'll be difficult, extremely so."

That clarifies my obsession with Su-chan. "I get fucked over at every turn, don't I?"

"I'm not thrilled with the language, but I understand your reaction."

"Sorry. I'm just so tired of the drama. Why is there always some nasty twist?"

"Teaching you about your new nature will eliminate some of this. And Ohno-chan, she's a perfect choice. I wouldn't have encouraged you two to date otherwise. I saw the red string between you when she came to visit in the hospital."

Avoiding her gaze, I swallow. "And the last issue?"

My aunt's ears flatten. *Not a good sign.* "This one is more of a hunch. It's about Ohno-chan." I gulp and my insides tighten and cramp, but she plows on. "Her half of the tama doesn't hold the same powers. When the spirit split, it was into two beings' worth. You received the kitsune side.

"But your girlfriend has magic from something else. She had a vast reserve to begin with and you've seen how bright her aura became. I've not met another human with such an incredible pool. It seems the more power a person has, the more often temptations and troubles happen. And we both know how easy ki theft is. So…"

Tightness runs up my neck, increasing my splitting headache to an all too familiar migraine. "Are you saying she could be a danger to others or herself?"

"What will she encounter? Who knows? I'm sharing what little information I have, hoping that's enough. We'll research the legends in the hope of learning more."

"Got it. Please, tell me there aren't other surprises. I can't handle more."

"Not that I know of." Circling three times, she curls beside me. "How is Matsuo-san handling Suzuki Chiyo-san leaving? Gossip at orchid club says he's interested in her. Nothing official yet. But she's opened up thanks to you both."

"No clue." *Sorry, Matsuo.* "What about the boss and Mie-san?"

Giving a contemptuous sniff, Sensei shrugs. "They've been off and on for months. Mie-chan doesn't read him well. They're both so defensive. She's straightforward, but he's close to the vest. I'm not sure what will come of it."

Oh yeah. "Hey Aunt, I forgot to tell you about something that happened the other day. I'd like your thoughts on it."

"Hmm?"

"I mentioned when Su-chan and I were at the Shrine, a fox messenger showed up. But I never told you he said Inari heard my request, so I'd be tested. I've got to make wise choices because they'll affect me and those I care for. But have I so far? 'Cause, everything seems like a pop quiz and I'm constantly second-guessing myself. I keep doing things I'm not supposed to with my magic."

She huffs a chuckle. "That's adulthood, Nephew. Choices you make have lasting impacts, whether or not the kami put you through trials. You've seen that truth from your experiences in the yakuza and how hard you had to work to create a place in society."

"What if I fail?"

"You dust off and try again. Fall down seven times, get back up eight."

* * *

Sensei and I wake early to clean the shrine a final time. Now that a fox spirit lives in me, the cloudy white phosphorescent transition from the mundane to the sacred stands out as we pass under the torii gate. Even the center of the path has a sheen to it. Perhaps a remnant of the kami's presence as they walked through. *Will the messenger arrive to say my test is complete?*

No such luck. Still, it feels right to leave the building and grounds in good shape.

* * *

On departure day, Sensei's face beams as she shoves a bowl of rice covered with an egg in my direction. "Last night the messenger visited. We have an answer!"

"We do? When? I didn't hear anyone at the door, and I'm a light sleeper."

The morning sun coming through the window highlights her blush. "Portals, Tatsuya. After he delivered the news that I have permission to train you to be Nonogawa's next guardian, we went on a date."

"Wait, you're in a relationship with a messenger of Inari?"

"Why are you fixating on my love life instead of the fact that we've proved a former yakuza is worthy to train to join the League of Guardians. That is, if it's what you want?"

Of course, it's what I want! My open-mouthed gape gives her time for a self-satisfied head bobble. *Worthy...*

* * *

Mid-morning, I get a series of texts from Su-chan.

'Should I bring the ointment you prefer? I'm not sure they'll have high-quality organic ingredients when I need to prepare more.'

'Should I pack a spring wardrobe, too?'

'What are you bringing for hobbies?'

'Do they have extra futons?'

'Think we can find my allergy meds nearby?'

'How many bags do you have?'

Clothes, the iPod and my phone, the katana, my calligraphy supplies, a few toiletries, my small pillow, a gift for the Nakamuras, and Su-chan are all that I require. A duffel for my things leaves a hand free to help her. *Why is she worrying so much?*

'One bag for me. Kyoto's a big city. It should have anything we need. We'll have portal talismans, too.'

The Suzuki duo with Matsuo tagging along arrives first. Excitement rolls off the boy as he bounces and chatters a million miles an hour, infecting the entire room. Even his mom seems to look forward to the change. Though Matsuo's happy-puppy look isn't as bright today.

I pull my sparring partner aside. "They'll be fine. I wouldn't have made it without your friendship, so watching over the pair of them is the least I can do."

Running fingers through his hair, he says, "So my feelings for Chiyo-san are that obvious?"

After all the teasing I got from him, I wink and slug his arm.

"And you're ok with going to live among a kitsune clan? 'Cause my dad told me why he freaked out. He saw a kumiho kill a man. Though, what he described sounded differed from Nakamura-san."

"They're family. We'll be fine. Sensei and I ensured both of them have talismans to portal home in an emergency."

When the Ohno clan shows up, they all carry packs. Suddenly, Sensei's living room feels crowded. *Tell me they aren't all joining us in Kyoto. Awkward!*

Each drops luggage on the floor by the pile before stepping away, leaving only Su-chan there to clutch her bag. So, I join her as I bite my lip to keep from laughing. I should have guessed she'd bring a ton of stuff.

Mie and Satou show up last minute. He motions for me to follow to the other room, giving me strict instructions to check in every week for my parole report. "I didn't want the others to hear this. Someone disturbed the ashes from several of the Hiragi members. Thankfully, I'd had Hiro's purified before the funeral. Any ideas on why anyone would desecrate a grave?"

The news sits raw in my gut. "Nope, but I'll see what I can find out."

"Speaking of. Cousin, I'm depending on you to watch over Aunt Hisako and keep her out of trouble." Surprising me, he bows. "And for you two to be ambassadors to the kitsune race. I assume you going means you won't be working for the PSIA."

"Yeah. I want to see if I can serve Nonogawa like she does. I'll do my best to keep an eye on her. Though, you know how Sensei is. She'll drag me into whatever scheme she has."

His eyebrow raises in his trademark look. "Hardly comforting. Is there a solution for this issue with her spirit ball? Relying on others, that's not who she is."

"Kitsune society has connections. If anyone knows, they do."

After Su-chan's brother gives my aunt a ki charge, she changes to human form. With a flourish, she opens the portal to the warren.

How will five of us carry the mountain of backpacks and duffels in a single trip? To my relief, the crew from the store each picks up our extra bags.

Sensei crosses over to the brightly lit, stone-walled den to be greeted with happy yips. In his exuberance, Sojirou dashes through, followed by his mother who shrugs then shyly waves to Matsuo before following. Everyone else goes through except Su-chan and me.

I offer my arm. "Ready?"

Riveted in place, Su-chan stares at the opening. Her bottom lip sucks in, and her knuckles turn white. *Is she having second thoughts?*

"Suzu, he's waiting." Her mom motions in encouragement.

Taking a deep breath, she squares her shoulders. "This is what you wanted, girl." Striding forward, she pastes on a smile. "It's hard moving for the first time."

Just because I don't get along with my mom, doesn't mean she won't miss her parents and brothers. "What if we video chat with your family tonight after settling in?"

Her smile relaxes into the natural one I know well. "Deal." Interweaving her fingers in mine, she says, "Let's go."

* * *

My powers don't make me the chosen one. Despite recent heroics, many folks refuse to accept me because of my past. But, for the first time in over a decade, I have a hope, a future, and people who believe in me. My dream started small, inconsequential even. But now, I want to protect the people of my new home as the next Guardian of Nonogawa.

Having people willing to stand at my side—that's what made the difference.

If You Enjoyed This Book

Subscribe to my newsletter at go.amywintersvoss.com/news for the latest scoop on my books in the Liminal Chronicles series and to receive a free story in the same universe.

Thank you for reading Rise. I'd be thrilled if you left reviews on your favorite platforms. I read every review and love to hear from you all.

Ready to find out where Umeji goes from here? His adventure continues in Guardian: The Liminal Chronicles.

CAST OF CHARACTERS

I put the two major characters in the story at the top of the list. Everyone else that recurs in the story is in English alphabetical order.

Portraits, pronunciations, and many more details can be found at liminalchronicles.com under the Meet the Characters sections.

Modern Day Characters

Umeji Tatsuya
  (a.k.a. Tatsu)

Former Hiragi Clan yakuza, starting over in Nonogawa after being released from jail in Tokyo. This is his best chance, and he knows he's got a lot to make up for from his past. He tries to keep a low profile, but that's hard when his tattoos show through his shirt after it gets wet, and the town's dowager, Nakamura Hisako, has it out for him.

Nakamura Hisako
  (a.k.a. Sensei, Aunt Hisako)

Nonogawa's protective busybody. She is curious and shrewd. Nakamura has her fingers in everything and knows the entire town. Most consider her the town's sweet dowager, but she's a real spitfire if upset. She loves deeply and enjoys teasing and bantering with those she views as family.

Chou
  (Short for Chou Chou, which means Butterfly)

A semi-sapient slime. She seems to be more intelligent than research on slimes would suggest possible.

Date Sari

Charismatic owner of TekMagi, a magic-driven security company. She's willing to do whatever it takes to accomplish her goals and isn't afraid to try new things. Watching people's amazement at her use of simple spells gives her a kick.

Matsuo Eiji

Works at TaniMart as the assistant manager. He's glad when Umeji starts working there. Most of the employees are women, he needs a few more guys to hang out with.

Mie Sumika
   (a.k.a. Mika-chan)

Works at TaniMart and is friends with fellow cashier Ohno Suzu. She suspects the new guy that Ohno is curious about because he's trying very hard to blend in. Ohno won't be hurt again on Mie's watch.

Ohno Suzu
   (a.k.a. Su-chan)

Works at TaniMart and is friends with fellow cashier Mie Sumika. Wants to get to know Umeji when she notices something unusual about him but is wary when she finds out about his past.

Ohno Yasu

Ohno Suzu's father and Ohno Yukiko's husband. Shift lead at Nonogawa's sawmill.

Ohno Yukiko

Youngest daughter from a rich family of onsen proprietors, the Shibasakis. Wife to Ohno Yasu.

Otsuka Hiro

(a.k.a. Big Brother, Aniki to Umeji, Kyoudai—in the Hiragi Clan)

An active yakuza member. Fostered Umeji Tatsuya in the Hiragi Clan. Truly an expert on the money side of things: extortion, stock manipulation, protection payments, and money laundering. He taught Umeji, his 'little brother' everything he knows about surviving and thriving in the mob.

Rin

Ohno Suzu's pet, a semi-intelligent Razor Vine.

Satou Kazuo

(a.k.a. Boss)

Owner and manager of Nonogawa's grocery store, TaniMart. Volunteer Parole Officer for Umeji Tatsuya. Nephew to Nakamura Hisako. Hates secrets being kept from him, though he hides many of his own.

Suzuki Sojirou

Elementary student. Suzuki's grades have dropped, despite being smart as a whip, because he's bullied at school.

Meiji Era Characters

* Indicates the person is a historical figure.

Ii Naosuke *
(a.k.a. Chief Minister Ii)

Poet, tea master, feudal lord of Hikone and later Tairo (which some translate to Chief Minister or Regent) to the Shogunate. Signer of the Harris Treaty, instigator of the Ansei Purge, staunch Bakufu supporter, and the man who tried to stabilize the Shogunate's power.

Iwasaki Hiroshige

Samurai and member of the Isshin-Shishi. Close friends with Kubo Takeuchi.

Kubo Takeuchi

Samurai and member of the Isshin-Shishi. Close friends with Iwasaki Hiroshige.

Tsuchimikado Yukitada
(a.k.a. Yuki)

A lower-ranked samurai, but his choices made impacts far and wide.

Yoshida Shouin *
(a.k.a. Kawanouchi Manji (undercover name in letters to Commodore Perry), Shouin (pen name), Nijuu Ikkai Moushi (21 times audacious samurai – pen name))

Political activist and the father of the Meiji Restoration. One of Japan's greatest teachers.

GLOSSARY

A story set in Japan has to have the vocabulary to make it feel like the real deal. I've tried to provide context with the words. But if you need it, here is a list of words you'll come across.

A quick note on spelling: I have tried my best to represent Japanese pronunciation with Roman letters. Numerous ways exist to attempt this. One of the choices I had to make was regarding the 'long vowel' sounds, which are held for a beat longer when spoken. I chose what seemed to me to be the simplest option available—a doubled vowel in a word, such as 'torii'. Please note, in the case of the long o, it often appears in hiragana (an alphabet of the symbols for the sounds) as 'ou'. Exceptions such as the location name 'Oosaka' exist. Westerners shorten the sound to Osaka, but it's not correct.

There are also a few that I didn't keep the long vowel for, because they are pretty well entrenched in English with the shorter vowel - such as 'bento', 'dojo', 'tanto', and 'shoji'.

Please remember, these are quick and simple definitions. Each word or phrase can have many more layers than this surface glance. Feel free to explore more than I can offer in a simplified glossary.

Aniki - 'big brother', a respectful term for a superior.

Bakufu - Shogunate-run military government from the late 1100s until the Meiji era in 1868.

bento - a boxed lunch. Can be homemade or purchased (also pronounced 'obento').

bo - long wooden staff used in martial arts.

bushido - the code or way of the warrior.

chan - an endearing and cute name suffix often used for children, young women, or by a significant other.

daimyo - a feudal lord. Subordinate to the shogun.

dojo - a space for learning and training traditionally for martial arts.

Edo - Tokyo's ancient name.

futon - thin mattress put on the floor for sleeping. Not the Americanized college furniture that folds up into a couch.

geisha - an entertainer who is trained to dance, sing, converse, serve tea, etc. Dresses in beautiful traditional clothes, and does hair and makeup with traditional style.

gyuudon - beef, onion and rice bowl.

hakama - pleated skirt-like pants that are worn over the bottom half of a man's kimono. They tie at the waist.

hi/bi - fire, can be created by mythical creatures.

hime - princess or young noblewoman.

hiragana - one of the two sound-based syllabaries in Japanese. The first one taught in school. Can be used for names and to evoke emotions.

hoshi no tama - ball that legend says holds a kitsune's magic and/or soul. In this story, it's also shortened to tama.

host - a man at a club who gets paid to entertain and be attentive to a female client. Physical attention can be part of the host's duties. There are hostess clubs/bars, too.

Inari - god of rice farming, prosperity, entertainers, and various other things. White foxes are the messengers of Inari.

inarizushi - fried tofu bag cooked in a sweetened soy-based sauce filled with sushi rice. Can have other ingredients such as sesame seeds.

Isshin-Shishi - political activists in the Edo period. Most were anti-shogunate and pro-emperor.

Itadakimasu - an expression of thanks for the meal one is about to eat.

kami - a god or powerful spirit.

kanji - the most complex of the Japanese characters systems in writing. Chinese was the language of scholarship in ancient Japan. Many of the kanji symbols were imported from China in the 6th century.

katana - the larger of the two swords samurai carried.

kendo - martial art that uses bamboo swords. Protective armor is worn.

ki - the life force that flows through all things.

kiai - a quick shout made when attacking in martial arts.

kimono - a long robe with loose sleeves. The front opening is kept closed with a sash. Formal wear in Japan.

kintsugi - repairing a cup, dish, etc. with silver or gold. The repair is said to make the piece more beautiful than it was before, by showing the breaks.

kitsune - a fox. Many myths tell of them being magical tricksters and shapeshifters.

kosode - an outer layer robe.

kotatsu - a low table with a heater under it, covered by a heavy blanket and a tabletop.

kotodama - the belief that words and names have magic or mystical and divine powers. The power can be accessed by speaking them. People may be able to make something happen by speaking or writing it.

kumiho - Korean word for a 9-tailed fox that hunts human males, to feast on their liver or heart.

kun - a friendly name suffix for boys and young men.

kyoudai - sibling, brothers. In the Yakuza, they are high-ranking members of the clan.

miso - a thick fermented soybean paste. Often used as part of a soup base but can be used in many dishes. Has that distinctive umami taste.

mochi - a sweet rice cake, often filled with a sweet bean paste. They can have many kinds of fillings from fruit to jelly to ice-cream.

naginata - a pole weapon with a blade on the end. Women were often taught to use this effectively against a samurai with a sword. The long reach of the pole keeps the wielder out of the way of the sword.

ni-chan - big brother (affectionate term).

noren - the split curtain outside a store. Put out when the shop is open.

ofuda - paper talisman. For this story, it's the paper a spell is written on.

oni - a large red, blue, or green-skinned ogre-like creature that has protruding tusks. May also be translated as ogre, troll, or demon (though in English this carries a connotation I didn't want).

onigiri - a rice ball, often with a pickled plum or other fillings inside.

onmyouji - a person who practices onmyoudou.

onmyoudou - a style of magic spell casting and divination, for purposes of this story. In the real world, it's a mix of science and occultism. A combination of practices such as divination, the Five Elements, Yin and Yang, shikigami, ofuda, and alchemy.

sake - rice-based alcoholic drink and the national beverage of Japan. Can refer to alcohol in general. To differentiate, the rice-based drink is often called nihonshu.

sakura - cherry blossoms or cherry trees. A treasured symbol in Japan - reminds people to treasure the moment because life can be fleeting.

sama - respectful title put after the name of a person, with a higher rank than 'san'. Also very polite speech from store employees to call their customers. 'Customer-sama' might be translated 'honored customer'.

san - respectful title put after the name of a person. Can be translated as Mr. _, Mrs. _, or Miss _.

sensei - teacher or another authority figure.

Shichi-Go-San - a celebration of children who reach the ages of 7, 5, and 3, held on November 15.

shikigami - a summoned servant spirit. For this story, they occupy a paper puppet.

shinai - slatted bamboo practice sword.

shogun - a military commander that led or, later, ruled feudal era Japan from the late 1100s to 1868. The position was inherited.

shoji - a wooden lattice door, covered in rice paper.

soba - buckwheat noodles, often served in a hot soup or chilled with a sauce to dip them in.

sukajan - a brightly embroidered silk jacket styled after baseball jerseys. Originally made as souvenirs to sell to soldiers, they meshed American military unit symbols with Japanese tattoo style designs. Later the jackets came to be a symbol of rebellion and defiance, much like the American leather biker jacket.

tani - valley.

tanto - a dagger.

tanuki - a raccoon dog. Can be sometimes translated as a raccoon or badger. In mythology, they can transform into human and other shapes. They're often rivals with kitsune.

tatami - a reed mat used as a traditional floor covering. Their length is twice as long as the width. The size varies a little by region. But in general, a room can be described as an X tatami room - where X is the number of tatami that fit in it. Tatami are hard to clean.

tengu - mythological creature. There are two main types. The greater tengu may look like a person with a large nose and wings. The lesser tengu look more like a birdman with more crow or bird of prey characteristics.

tokonoma - alcove to display items like a picture or vase of arranged flowers.

torii - a traditional gate at the entrance of a Shinto shrine, marking the entrance to a sacred space. They're often red.

udon - thick wheat flour noodles. Or soup with this type of noodle.

VPO - *(not a Japanese word but a translation utilized in the story)* volunteer parole officer. Japan uses a system of volunteers to handle parole officer functions. The few official (paid) parole officers train the volunteers. The idea behind this is that if someone is seen to care about the wellbeing of a criminal, there will be less likelihood they'll return to prison.

wakizashi - shorter of the two main swords a samurai wore.

yakuza - the Japanese mob, a Japanese mobster.

yama - mountain or hill.

yoisho - an expression of effort or strain. Much like "Heave ho!"

yokai - a supernatural being.

yukata – causal, unlined, cotton version of the kimono. Often colorful and worn for festivals or summer garb, or at a traditional inn (where they are publicly acceptable bathrobes). Remember to wear it left side over right. (Only the dead are dressed right over left.)

About the Author

Amy is a former programmer turned author after her first trip to Japan in 2017. Now she writes Japanese myth-based urban fantasy to reconnect with the country and culture that captured her heart. She lives in South Dakota with her supportive husband, two wonderful kids, a mellow old cat who adopted the family when he was a tiny stray, and three wily and crazy ferrets.

You can read more about her, find the occasional ferret picture, and sign up to receive a free story at amywintersvoss.com.